Jinnie

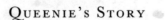

JOSEPHINE COX

Jinnie

headline

First published in Great Britain in 2002 by
HEADLINE BOOK PUBLISHING

10 9 8 7 6 5 4 3 2 1

British Library Cataloguing in Publication Data

Cox, Josephine
Jinnie
1. Domestic fiction
I. Title
823.9′14 [F]

ISBN 0 7472 7155 0 (hardback)
ISBN 0 7472 7003 1 (trade paperback)

Typeset by Palimpsest Book Production Limited,
Polmont, Stirlingshire
Printed and bound in Great Britain by
Clays Ltd, St Ives plc

HEADLINE BOOK PUBLISHING
A division of Hodder Headline
338 Euston Road
London NW1 3BH

www.headline.co.uk
www.hodderheadline.com

This is a special message for Tom – bless his heart!

I've been smiled at by boys and men who think of themselves as Jack the Lad, and I've had some interesting propositions in my time. But I have to confess I've never been propositioned by an eighty-two-year-old rogue in a wheelchair! All the same, you won me over with your cheeky grin and twinkling eyes – and that wink!

I bet you were a devil in your time, you old rascal you. I'll cherish the poem you wrote for me, and I'm glad you came to see me – you made my day. Good on yer, Tom.

CONTENTS

PART ONE

SUMMER, 1963
AFTER THE
STORM

Chapter One

Blackburn Town

Dropping her carrier bags to the floor, Louise Hunter kicked off her shoes and with a long, heartfelt sigh, leaned back and closed her eyes. It had been one of those days.

From the rear of the tram, a young woman caught sight of her and, knowing what she knew, found it hard to tear her gaze away. Her companion, a bright young thing called Helen with painted mouth and long, bare legs, was suddenly curious. 'D'you know that woman?' she asked.

Keeping her gaze on Louise, her friend nodded.

Impatient, Helen nudged her. 'So go on, Stell, who *is* she?'

'Ssh!' Shifting her gaze, the girl called Stella warned, 'Keep your voice down or she'll hear you.'

Offended, her friend slithered down in her seat. 'All right, all right – keep yer bloody hair on! I were only *asking*!' A moment or two passed, before her curiosity got the better of her once more. 'Well? Are you gonna tell me who she is, or what?'

Rolling her eyes to heaven, the dark-haired young woman cupped her hand to her mouth. '*It's Louise Hunter*,' she hissed.

'And who the devil's Louise Hunter when she's at home?'

'Ssh!' Stella said in a whisper, 'Do you remember when

3

we were kids, there was a scandal about a big murder on Craig Street?'

'Oh, my God, *'course* I remember! A man was arrested . . . he killed that woman Maggie Pringle and her boyfriend.' Excitement trembled in Helen's voice. 'But what's *she* got to do with it?' She raised a wary glance to Louise.

'Everything.' Stella leaned close again. 'The murdered man was her brother-in-law, Jacob. There were them as said it were Louise Hunter's sister Susan who'd really killed them, on account of she was already having an affair with Jacob Hunter when the bugger went and set up home with this Maggie. Had a couple o' bairns, she did – a little lass, and a boy.' She shivered. 'After the murders, they found the kids hiding in the cellar . . . poor little buggers.'

'How old were they?'

'I'm not sure.' Screwing up her eyes she made a calculation. 'From what our mam said, the lad saved his sister's life. He were about six year old then. That were ten years ago, so I expect he'll be coming up towards sixteen or seventeen by now. Adam, his name were – aye, and his little sister were Hannah. She were a couple of years younger than him.'

The other girl was both impressed and disappointed. 'You seem to remember a lot more than *I* do.'

'That's because you're three years younger than me, and you didn't listen at keyholes like I used to.' It was all coming back like yesterday. 'Besides, I used to earn money of a weekend, running errands for the women down Johnson Street. By! They never stopped gossiping about all the goings-on.' Stella chuckled. 'And I don't mean just the murder, neither. They were a randy bunch up that way! According to Mrs Newsom at number ten, she and her old man were at it every night o' the week!'

'Cor! That must be why she ended up having twelve kids!' Helen smirked.

'And not all of 'em her old man's, neither. She "couldn't get enough of it", that's what she said.'

The image of Mrs Newsom with her scary hair and bandy legs came into their minds; the idea of her cavorting naked with a man was all too much, and try as they might, they could not contain their laughter.

Wiping her eyes, the older one glanced up, relieved to see that Louise was not disturbed by their hilarity.

'Where's the sister now?' Helen said ghoulishly. The one they said might have done the killing?'

'Gawd knows. She disappeared off the face of the earth, and as far as I know, was never seen again.' Her gaze went back to Louise who, deep in thought, was oblivious to their interest in her. 'Happen *she* knows and she ain't saying.'

'She's not a bad looker, is she?' Helen remarked. 'How old d'you reckon she is?'

Another minute, another calculation. 'Hang on, there was summat else, as I recall.' The older one reached deep into her memory. 'Some time before the murders, there was a suicide.' She gestured to Louise. 'It was her husband,' she breathed.

'Bloody hell! She's had a colourful life an' no mistake!'

'According to our mam, Louise Hunter was about twenty-five when it happened, so she'd be what? In her mid-thirties by now.' Stella couldn't imagine how terrible it all must have been. 'Me and our mam were in the market last week, and we saw her then. Our mam said she'd never married again.'

'Bit of a waste though?'

They looked appraisingly at Louise, taking in the straight, proud cut of her shoulders, and the long brown hair that fell loosely down her back, and just then as she turned to check the whereabouts of the conductor, the two young women were surprised by her warm, hazel-coloured eyes and her pretty smile. 'For all her troubles, she's managed to keep her looks and figure, ain't she?' The girl called Helen was impressed, and a teeny bit envious.

'Oh, I don't know,' said her friend peevishly. 'She's not bad, but I've seen better, even at her age.'

And that said, they got onto the subject of dating, and how they were sure to pick up a fella at the Palais on Friday night.

***

UNAWARE OF THEIR interest, Louise settled back and closed her eyes. She felt incredibly weary, anxious to get home to Jinnie. After a while, her thoughts inevitably returned to Eric Forester. It had been ten years since the tragedies, and for a long time afterwards, she and Eric had kept their distance, though there had not been a day when she hadn't wanted to go to him.

These past two years had been the worst. When Eric's handyman had moved on to pastures new, Louise had left her job at the factory and returned to work at Maple Farm, where she had once lived with Ben, her late husband. The farm had been in the Hunter family for generations, until it had been auctioned to pay for an outstanding debt. Now Eric owned it; Eric, the man she had loved, in secret and in torment, for so very long.

Louise was thrilled to be back, working on the land, but there had been a price to pay; working alongside Eric was tearing her apart. He didn't know that, and she could never tell him. *She wanted him, needed him like she had never needed any other man.* But the past would not set her free.

Some years ago, Eric had vowed to love her for ever. When she turned from him then, he never spoke of his love again, but she knew he loved her still, and always would. For didn't she see it in his eyes every time he looked on her, and didn't she love him in the very same way?

Theirs was a powerful love – but not as powerful as the guilt they felt over what had taken place all those years before. Oh, the times when she had wanted to reach out and touch him, aching for his arms to enfold her! But she never did; and for the same reason, he never made a move towards her. Because, like her, Eric was imprisoned by the past, and too afraid to grasp the future.

'Montague Street next stop!' The conductor's cry carried through the tram, shattering her thoughts. 'C'mon, ladies, let's be 'aving yer!' As he passed Louise's seat, he caught her eye. 'Sorry to disturb you, luv.' He gave a cheeky wink. 'I saw you deep in thought – or were you having a crafty little kip, eh?'

Louise smiled. 'A bit of both.'

'Had a busy day, 'ave yer?'

'Busy enough.'

Still chatting with Louise and not looking where he was going, the conductor was flung forward as he tripped over a young man's legs that were stretched out in the gangway. Composing himself, he straightened his unkempt hair and gave a little embarrassed cough. 'You'd best tuck 'em in, matey,' he warned, 'afore you cause a nasty accident.'

Disgruntled, the youth did as he was asked, albeit it with a sour face and surly manner.

'Young buggers these days,' the conductor chuntered softly to Louise, 'they think the world revolves round 'em, so they do!' As he continued forward, clanking his ticket machine and chatting to the other few passengers on the tram, it was just as well he didn't see the look the young man gave him.

A murderous glare if ever there was one, Louise thought to herself.

Collecting her bags, Louise made her way to the exit, at the same time helping an old lady who was jostled and unsteadied by the lurching of the tram as it meandered along the line. 'Thank you, dear.' Small and frail, with seemingly poor eyesight, the old lady leaned heavily on Louise's arm. 'I don't usually go out on my own,' she went on, happy that somebody should take the time to listen to her. 'My sister normally comes with me to the shops, but she's not been well lately . . . fell over and sprained her ankle, she did. I'm allus telling her, "tek your time, Annie, you don't have to *run* everywhere", but will she listen, No, she won't!'

At the thought of her beloved sister, the prettiest of smiles crossed her wizened features. 'She meks me mad at times, but I don't know what I'd do without her.'

Louise helped her off the tram. 'I'll be all right now, dear,' the old woman told her. 'I'd best get home and see what *she's* up to. Knowing her, she's probably up the chimney with a long brush, filling herself and the house with soot. She's done it before when I've been out. By! I'll have a word or two to say if she's at it again!'

With that she set off at a sedate pace, across the boulevard and on towards Ainsworth Street.

When she realised that the old dear was about to try and cross the busy road on her own, Louise set off after her. 'No! Wait a minute, I'll see you across!'

Unfortunately, as Louise made for the old woman, so did the bad-mannered young man – but with a very different intent. In the split second when the old woman turned to see why Louise was calling her, the surly young fellow from the tram came at her like a bull at a gate; the impact sent her reeling backwards, and her shopping bags went crashing to the ground. Sweeping up her handbag as it fell at his feet, the young man sped off, while from somewhere behind, the cry went up, '*Thief!* Grab the bastard!'

When a policeman appeared out of nowhere across his path, the young man skidded to a halt. He turned and ran in the opposite direction, almost colliding with Louise, who was running to help the old dear. She saw her chance, swung her shopping bag at him, and caught him on the knee with it. He went down, taking her with him, and in the scuffle that followed, she managed to swing her bag and hit him again, by which time the policeman and a pair of burly passers-by had him by the scruff of the neck.

'You did well, missus,' one of them told Louise.

'Lost all me apples though,' she panted, and groaned to see her freshly picked apples rolling into the gutter. When he offered to collect them for her, she laughed out loud. 'Thanks all the same, but no,' she said graciously. 'Every dog in Blackburn must have done his dirty business in that gutter. Never mind though.' She thought of Eric and how he had helped her pick the apples that very morning. 'There's plenty more where they came from.'

When the handbag was returned intact and the ruffian had been marched off to answer for stealing it, Louise escorted the old lady safely across the road. 'Are you sure you're all right?' she enquired. After all, she thought, the ordeal must have shaken her badly.

'I'm fine, dear,' the woman answered in sprightly manner. Then, to Louise's surprise, she laughed out loud. 'Wait till I tell my sister,' she chuckled. 'Tackled to the ground by a thief, and saved by a pretty young woman.'

Louise was flattered but realistic. 'Not so young these days. Too much water under the bridge, more's the pity.' It hardly seemed possible that she was coming up to her thirty-sixth birthday.

'You might not think so, but you're young next to *me*!' The old dear leaned forward, so no one else could hear. 'I'll tell you summat else if you like?' she confided wickedly.

'Oh, and what's that?' Louise was intrigued.

'You've got nicer legs than I ever had, *and* you wear prettier drawers than I do an' all.' She giggled like a naughty child. 'All blue and frilly. I saw 'em when you were rolling about on the ground with that devil.'

'Oh, did you now?' Louise had to laugh. 'They're nothing special . . . two and sixpence on Blackburn Market, but you're right – they *are* pretty.'

'It just goes to show, doesn't it, dear?'

'What does?' Louise had taken a liking to her.

The other woman wagged her finger. 'You must never go out without your drawers on. You never know when you might be suddenly upended, showing your bare arse to all and sundry.'

Before a shocked Louise could respond, the old dear was hobbling away down the street, singing to herself and clutching her bag so tightly it would take a steam train to wrench it from her.

Gripping her own bags more tightly than usual, Louise quickened her steps towards Derwent Street. By! She couldn't wait to tell Jinnie and Sal about her exciting escapade. No more than she could wait to hear what the two of *them* had been up to!

She glanced behind her to see the old lady rounding the corner and, recalling her *cheeky* words, she laughed out loud, instantly embarrassed when a fat lady with two children glanced curiously her way. 'It's been a nice day,' Louise said lamely, and without replying, the woman quickly ushered her children on before her.

'Please yourself,' Louise shrugged, but the smile was already creeping over her pleasant features again. Amazed that such a sweet little old lady could use such ripe language, Louise chuckled all the way home.

Chapter Two

A S ON EVERY other afternoon, Jinnie waited patiently for
her mam to come home. A small-boned child, with wild
fair hair and dark, sapphire-blue eyes, she was a familiar sight
down Derwent Street.

The ritual had begun two years ago when she was eight
years old, after Louise had gone to work with Eric Forester
on Maple Farm. At four o'clock, the girl would rush home
from school and help her Granny Sally to prepare the tea,
after which she would go outside and perch on the front step
with her arms wrapped round her knees, her head laid down
against them, and her intense gaze focused on the bottom end
of Derwent Street.

Her mam would usually appear by five o'clock, when
Jinnie would give out a whoop of joy and run down the
street to meet her. There wasn't a soul thereabouts who
wasn't touched by their very special relationship. Very few
people knew how Jinnie's own mother had deserted her as a
newborn babe, and how Louise had fought tooth and nail to
adopt the child and bring her up as her own. Thankfully, those
few were trustworthy and kept the secret to themselves.

The period following her sister Susan's disappearance after
the double murders had not been easy for Louise. For a long
time, the gossip raged on, curtains twitched and every eye

was turned in her direction. Questions were muttered. Was it possible that Louise had *not* miscarried with her husband Ben's child after all? In which case, was Jinnie really her true daughter? Or on the other hand, did Jinnie belong to Louise's sister, Susan – a wild and careless girl, carrying a child out of wedlock. All along, Susan had refused to name the man who made her pregnant; not even her own family knew who the father was.

True to character, it was rumoured that one day she just ran off, and was never seen again. It was also rumoured that she had given birth to a daughter, who she then deserted. Others said that wasn't the case, and that Susan had gone away with the child still in her belly. Those who were privileged to know the truth gave support to these rumours, in order to protect the child.

The speculation continued for several years . . . who was this child, now raised as Louise's own? Where was Susan? Why did she run away? It was a mystery. So many burning questions, and as yet, no answers. However, with the passage of time, folks got on with the ups and downs of their own lives. Familiar neighbours came and went and empty houses began to fill with strangers. Gradually, the curiosity waned, especially as those who knew the family could see with each passing day how little Jinnie had the same handsome smile and winning ways as Louise's late husband, Ben Hunter.

Blissfully unaware of her complicated background, Jinnie was a happy young girl, loved by all who knew her. To this day, she had no idea that the woman she believed to be her mammy was really her Aunt Louise. And as far as she was aware, her father Ben had died in an accident soon after she was born.

The sorry truth was that her real mother, Susan – the wayward, selfish girl who had always envied her sister Louise's happy marriage – had enjoyed a brief but shameful coupling with Ben on the night of his death. Jinnie was the result of that evening.

Louise herself was not entirely innocent in all of this. The day would never come when she would entirely forgive or forget her own part in having triggered the tragedy that cost her husband his life.

⟫•0•⟪

ON THIS LATE October afternoon in the year 1963, after an unusually warm, bright day, the sun was already beginning to dip in the sky. Shivering in the rising breeze, Jinnie hunched her shoulders and drew herself into a ball, but her gaze never left the end of the street, where at any minute she expected Louise to approach.

'Cold, are you, lass?' Unbeknown to Jinnie, her granny had come to the front door. Aged now, and withered at the jowls, Sally was a kind old soul; her whole life was wrapped up in Louise and this child. 'D'yer want me to fetch you a coat?'

Turning her head to smile up at her, Jinnie answered warmly, 'No, thanks, Gran. I'm all right, honestly.' She saw how the old woman was wearing only a thin cardigan over her dress. 'You go in though,' she urged. 'We don't want you catching pneumonia.'

Grinning widely, Sally shook her head. 'By! You're more of an old woman than *I* am,' she declared. 'You'll be asking me next if I've tekken me medicine.'

'And *have* you?' Jinnie grinned, well aware of how Sally would find any excuse not to take her cough medicine.

'Not yet, but I will.'

'Promise?'

Sally nodded.

'*Say* it then!'

Her granny laughed out loud. 'Yer a little bully, so yer are!'

'*Say* it!'

'All right.' Loudly tutting, the old lady groaned, 'I promise.'

'That's all right then.' Satisfied, Jinnie turned away to watch for her mammy.

Sally returned to the front parlour, where she stopped by the window; the contented smile resting on her face. 'By! Yer a little darling, so yer are.' She thought of Louise and all the events that had overwhelmed them for so many years. When things were at their worst, it was the child who gave them hope for the future. Jinnie had been the shining light in their lives.

For a long time she stood there, her old eyes on the child, and her heart heavy. Lately, she had found it hard to sleep, forever wondering what might become of the girl. 'By, lass, what shall we do, eh?' Her eyes welled with tears. 'Yer a little innocent, allus there for yer mammy an' yer grandma. Yer never question owt that's told yer. So long as you've a mammy to love yer, an' strong arms to hold yer tight, it seems there's nowt else in the world as matters to yer.'

She gave a long, withering sigh. 'I'm glad I'll not be the one to shatter yer warm little world, lass. I only wish to God yer didn't need to be told at all, but yer do. It's only right. No matter how painful the truth might be, *nobody* should keep yer birthright from yer. Not me, and not Louise.' Hard facts, but facts all the same.

Returning to the kitchen, Sally deliberately busied herself. Opening the oven she drew out the steak pie and carefully dotted it with butter. She then returned it to brown and afterwards, set about mashing the potatoes. That done, she scooped the resulting creamy whirl into an oblong earthenware dish, and placed it on the top shelf of the oven for the peaks to crisp. She strained the carrots and left them lidded to keep them warm; swilled the teapot with hot water for the third time, and checked that the table was set properly for their meal.

And all the while, unsettled and worried, she muttered to herself, 'By! Yer a wrong 'un, Susan Holsden. You and my Ben, fornicating behind Louise's back – an' now look what you've done to that little lass out there. How d'yer think *she'll* feel when she finds out what happened? Shamed an' disgusted, that's how she'll feel, the same as me – especially when she knows how her mammy walked away from her without a second thought. All these years an' never a word. Not a letter nor a card to ask after the child.'

Her voice dropped to a whisper. 'For all that bugger cares, the child could be buried down in the churchyard alongside her daddy!'

Clapping the palms of her hands over the flat of her knees, she groaned, a low, shivering sound that seemed to come from her very soul. 'Jesus, Mary an' Joseph, what two sons did I raise, eh? A pair o' divils an' no mistake. One as cheats on his wife and then kills 'isself, an' the other who'd sell his soul to the divil if the price were right . . .' Suddenly realising what she had said, she leaned back in the chair, her eyes wide open and a look of horror on her face.

Pressing the flat of her hand to her mouth, she cried out, the words emerging in a muffled, 'May God forgive me. They were my sons, Lord rest their souls.' She sat up straight, instinctively unrepentant, a hint of defiance marbling her voice. 'No! Why should it be *me* as begs forgiveness? 'Tweren't *me* as misbehaved. 'Tweren't *me* as carried on outside me marriage. No! When it came right down to it, them two buggers were their own worst enemies!' Her voice shook with emotion. 'Why did yer do it, Ben? *Why?*'

For most of his life, she had expected the worst of Jacob, because he was one of those people who were born bad. But Ben had made her proud. He had been a good son, kind, loyal, hardworking. But now, the things he had done . . . taking his own life and everything, would haunt her for ever.

After a while, unable to rest, she went back into the front room where, like Jinnie, she began watching for Louise. 'Come on, lass,' she muttered under her breath. 'Where the devil are yer?' It wasn't like her daughter-in-law to be late.

Opening the side window, she saw how Jinnie had not moved, her head still to one side and her knees under her chin. Nor would she move until Louise turned that corner. Such devotion filled Sally's old heart. 'By, lass,' she called out, 'you'll get piles sitting on that cold step.'

'I'm all right, Gran,' Jinnie told her.

'Come in for a while. Happen yer mammy got caught up in some overtime. If that's the case she'll likely be some time yet.'

'I can wait.'

Sally shook her head. She had no doubt the lass would wait. Even if her little bottom got stuck to the step and she slept where she sat. 'Right then, I'm away inside for a brew.' But she didn't go, not yet. Instead she stood there, watching the girl and growing anxious. No one was more aware of the dangers in not telling the child the truth about her parentage. 'Mek no mistake, you'll 'ave to be told soon,' she murmured, 'afore some big-mouthed bully finds out and uses it to torment yer!'

Just then, Jinnie sensed that her grandma was still up at the window. Looking round she wanted to know, 'What's the time now, Gran?'

Sally glanced at the mantelpiece clock. 'Half-past five,' she answered. 'Happen she'll not be long now.'

Contented, the girl looked away and continued her vigil.

Closing the window, Sally leaved another long sigh. 'Poor little bugger! I don't envy yer mam having to tell you the truth of how yer came into this world.' She felt a shiver of fear. 'I only hope it won't send yer down the wrong path, lass, 'cause yer a fine young thing. It would be such a pity if we were to raise a terrible resentment in yer.'

The thought of Jinnie having to share a burden of guilt that was none of her making, was a real heartache to the old woman, and more so to Louise.

The minutes ticked away and still the girl sat watching. It was amost six o'clock when suddenly there was a shout of, *'She's here, Grandma. Me mam's here!'*

Having rounded the corner, Louise was not surprised to see Jinnie running down the street at full pelt. 'Whoa! Hang on, love!' Catching Jinnie as she tripped headlong into her arms, Louise asked, 'Where's the fire then, eh?'

'You're late!'

'I've a good reason to be late.'

'Why?'

'Come on. I'll tell you later.'

Content in each other's company, they walked back together, with Louise lost in thoughts of Eric, and Jinnie chatting incessantly. 'I were really worried when you didn't come straight home. So was Grandma.'

'Oh? Did Grandma *say* she was worried?' She had noticed how Sally seemed slower of late, quicker to sit down after doing little household tasks that she might normally have swept through in no time.

Since the devastating business of the suicide of one son and the murder of the other – apart from having the loss of her husband Ronnie and of the family farm to contend with – Sally was no longer the strong, contented woman she had once been; these days she was often deep in thought, and pacing the floor of a night-time when she should be asleep. Louise was concerned about her, but no amount of persuasion would entice Sally into seeing the doctor.

'No, she didn't say she were worried,' Jinnie answered, 'but I could tell.'

'She's all right though, isn't she? I mean, she's not ill or anything?'

'Oh, no.' Jinnie gave her a little nudge. 'Go on, Mam. Tell me why you're late.'

Louise smiled coyly. 'I've had a bit of an adventure.'

'What kind?' Jinnie persisted.

'Wait and see.'

By the time they reached the house, Sally was waiting on the pavement. 'Where've you been, lass?' She was obviously relieved to see Louise home. 'Another few minutes and the tea'd be spoiled.' She gave a cheeky wink. 'Did Eric catch yer for some overtime, is that it?' Sally chuckled. 'By! He'll mek *any* excuse to keep yer back, so he will.'

'Behave yourself, Sal.' Though Louise knew it was only too true. 'It's got nothing to do with Eric wanting to keep me back.'

'What then?'

Pushing her way between the two of them, Louise climbed the three steps to the front door. 'If you'll only let me get inside,' she pleaded, 'I'll tell you both over a cuppa tea.'

While Sally dished up the evening meal, Louise went straight to the bedroom. Here, she slipped out of her working clothes, before going to the bathroom where she had a wash and changed into a plain dark skirt and pretty lemon blouse; the blouse being a present from Sally for her last birthday.

Brushing her long brown hair into a ponytail, she then tied it with a fine white ribbon. Feeling refreshed and energetic, she ran down the stairs like a two year old. 'It's good to be home,' she said, coming into the parlour. 'I don't mind telling you, Sally, I'm starving hungry!' She sniffed the air. 'Mmm. Summat smells good.'

With everything prepared, Sally and Jinnie were already

seated at the table. 'Sit yersel' down, lass,' Sally told her. 'I've done yer favourite – steak pie, with Spotted Dick to follow.'

Louise gave her a hug. 'You spoil us,' she murmured. 'It should be *me* looking after *you*.'

Sally swiftly dismissed her comment. 'Stuff an' nonsense!' she scoffed. 'What would yer have me do, eh? . . . Sit about all day, growing corns on me arse, while you work every hour God sends? Go on. Sit yerself down and be told!'

Louise gave her another hug. She knew from experience that it was no good arguing with the old woman, because Sally always came off better. So she did as she was told and sat down, and when Jinnie was about to make a comment, she wisely gave her a little kick under the table. 'Sally knows best,' she told the girl, and Jinnie took the hint, though she had a mind to reveal how Sally had 'come all over faint' while cleaning the windows earlier.

Aware that Jinnie had been about to tell on her, and quick enough to see the kick under the table, Sally rounded on them. 'By! Would yer look at yerselves? The pair of youse would have me sat in the chair all day, a blanket round me knees and a pair o' knitting needles in me hands. Well, you'd best forget it, 'cause I mean to pull my weight in this house as long as I'm blessed with me health an' strength. I've allus worked . . . in the mills as a lass, and on the farm when I got wed. If I die with me boots on I'll not be sorry. So you'd best understand this . . . I intend working and doing till the Good Lord sees fit to tek me.'

One eye closed, the other fixed on them in a warning stare, she wagged a finger. 'I expect Jinnie wants to tell how I got dizzy when cleaning the winders, but it were only that slice of ham I had in me sandwich. Indigestion, that's all it were. Ham does it to me every time. I'm a martyr to it, so I am. So yer can stop all that kicking and how-d'yer-do under the table, cause I've got me beady eye on yer!'

'Sorry, Gran.' Jinnie felt ashamed.

'It's all right, lass. But think on, next time yer want to tell tales. I'll not be happy about it.'

Relieved that the ice had been broken, Louise took a forkful of pie; the pastry was crumbly, the meat deliciously tender and the rich, thick gravy wrapped it all together like a dream on the tastebuds. She took another forkful and sighed. 'Honest to God, Sal, I swear I've never tasted steak pie like yours.'

The old woman's smile belied the pride in her voice. 'Go on with yer! Steak pie's easy enough to mek,' she said. 'It's what yer put in it that's the secret.'

'Well, it never comes out this good for me,' Louise confessed shamefully. 'Not even when I do it exactly as you say.'

Sally grinned from ear to ear. 'Away with yer. It's not that bad!' All the same, she was delighted with the flattery. 'Jinnie made the custard,' she announced. 'The lass is getting better all the time.'

Louise laughed. 'What? You mean we won't have to throw it away this time?' she teased.

'Give over, Mam.' Jinnie blushed bright pink. 'It tastes lovely, don't it, Grandma?'

'Aye, it does,' Sally agreed. 'Nearly as good as mine.'

'Come on, Mam,' Jinnie said eagerly. 'Tell us about your adventure.'

And so, Louise told them about the old dear she had helped, and the young man who had then sent her flying so he could rob her of her handbag, and how he had been caught, and then how the little woman gave Louise a shock by coming out with a word that was not befitting of her.

'What word was that?' Jinnie needed every detail.

'Never you mind.'

'I bet it was "arse".'

Shocked, Louise reprimanded her. 'That's enough o' that, my girl!'

'Grandma says it all the time.' Jinnie had a naughty twinkle in her blue eyes. 'You don't tell *her* off.'

'That's because I've got no control over your Grandma, more's the pity. But I've still got a bit of authority over you, young lady! So let's have no more of it – all right?'

'All right.'

Having turned away to smile at Jinnie's cheeky comments, Sally composed herself. 'That young fella as knocked the woman over – d'yer reckon he'll be put away?'

'If there's any justice, he will,' Louise retorted. 'He could have done her a lot of damage, crashing into her like that.'

'Have yer thought how *you* could have been hurt, swinging at him with yer bag like that?'

'I bet you'd have done exactly the same.' Louise knew only too well how feisty old Sal could be.

'I'd have gone for his ankles,' Sally promised. '*That* would have brought the bugger down an' no mistake.'

They laughed at the idea of Sally 'going for his ankles'. 'He'd have run off all the same,' Jinnie screeched, 'only with you clinging to his boots for dear life!'

The small talk continued, with Sally itching to tell Louise her disturbing news. The offending letter had arrived soon after her daughter-in-law had left for work that very morning. All day, Sally had been plagued with her conscience, wondering whether she had done the right thing, or whether she had taken too much responsibility on herself, and wondering if, one way or another, she would surely be punished for it.

Now, fearing the consequences, she delayed the moment when she must tell Louise. But the moment was uncomfortably close, and so she mentally prepared herself. As soon as Jinnie was abed, she would impart the news to Louise, and hope for the best.

I T WAS HALF-PAST seven when the meal was finished, and another half-hour by the time they got up from the table. 'I'll do the dishes,' Louise told them. 'You two get on with whatever you want.'

'I'll help you, Mam.' Jinnie was never far behind her mother.

'What about your homework?'

'I'll do it later.'

Louise was not pleased. 'No, Jinnie. Do it now.'

'It's only maths!'

Exasperated, Louise took her to task. 'How many times have we gone through this? Homework is really important, if you want to do well.'

But Jinnie could be stubborn, too. 'If I'm coming to work on the farm with you and Eric, why do I need maths?'

Louise had to think quickly. 'That depends.'

'How do you mean?'

'Well, let's see.' Shrugging her shoulders, she gave the impression that she didn't really care, when in truth she cared a great deal. Jinnie was her pride and joy, and like any parent, she wanted the best for her. 'If all you want to do is pick apples and sweep the yard, then you won't need maths. But if you want to do the same work that Eric and I do . . . the same work your daddy did, an' your gran and grandaddy before that, I can tell you now – you'll *definitely* need to know your figures.'

Jinnie was not convinced. 'Why?'

'Look at it this way, sweetheart. Most of the time, me and Eric share all the work . . . including the books and ordering, but when he's away on business, it's me as does it all. Oh, he gets old Mike Ellis in, but it's me as does all the ordering and selling, and it's me as keeps things going.' Louise thought of Ben and how it used to be when Maple Farm was theirs, and she smiled wistfully. 'I did it for so many years, it's second nature to me now. It's a wonderful life, lass, but it can be hard, especially in winter. And there's not much money to be had, neither.'

'But why do you need to know your sums?'

'Because there's money changing hands all the time. Buying an' selling is a serious business these days. There's fruit to be weighed and priced, ordering to be done, and part-time wages to be paid through the summer, when the harvest is ready. Every penny has to be accounted for. There's the ledger to be kept, a wages book, and everything else in between.'

Hoping her words had sunk in, she turned away. 'Like I say, if all you want to do is sweep the yard and clean out the chicken-houses, it won't matter. But if you want to be serious about it, you'll need your maths, 'cause you'll not be able to do it without.'

She placed the pile of dishes on the drainer and turned to speak again, but Jinnie was gone, and in her place stood Sally, beaming from ear to ear. 'I heard what you said,' she confided, 'an' you'll be pleased to hear, she's gone upstairs to do her homework.'

A smile creeping over her pretty features, Louise gave a sigh of relief. 'That's good.'

'An' *I'm* here to give you a hand, so we'll have no arguments, if you please!' Feeling worn, and seeing how Sally was so keen, Louise gave her none. 'All right,' she said, and threw the dishcloth at her.

It didn't take long with the two of them working, and soon the kitchen and living room were spick and span. 'Now you go and sit down while I make us a brew,' Louise insisted.

'I'll not say no to that,' Sally replied, and went away without a backward glance.

When they were both seated either side of the fireplace, supping their tea and exchanging news of the day, they appeared content enough. Their bellies were full, they had each other for company, and with Jinnie upstairs, her young head lost in her homework, they were free to indulge in light-hearted matters.

They laughed about little Harry Arnold's antics when Mike Ellis the milkman came down the street with his old horse; Harry begged a ride on the cart and when the cartwheel ran over Mike's foot, the lad ran backwards and forwards, collecting the money and bringing it to Mike, who then filled out the book and sent back the change.

'Did Mike do any serious damage to his foot?' Louise asked.

'No, but when he took off his socks to show young Harry's mam, they say the stench near knocked the poor woman over. It's been said that old Mike doesn't wash from one week's end to the next.' She laughed out loud. 'If only he'd say yes to Mabel Preston, she'd mek sure he were washed an' scrubbed, I'll be bound!'

Louise chuckled. 'I can't see that happening. Mabel's been after him ten years that I know of, and she's still no nearer getting him down the aisle. The poor old devil daren't retire from his milk-round in case she gets her hands on him.'

Sally was more confident. 'You'll see, lass. She'll catch him unawares one o' these days, an' he'll wake up one morning a married man.'

'Poor old Mike. Even *he* doesn't deserve a fate like that.' She had always liked the old fella. 'I'm glad he didn't hurt his foot too badly. It's a good thing little Harry was there to fetch and carry for him.'

'His mam did all right out of it an' all,' Sally revealed. 'Old Mike were so pleased at the lad, and at her bathin' and dressin' his foot, that he let her have two pints o' milk an' a dozen eggs for nowt. An' as if *that* weren't enough, little Harry held out his hand for a tanner!' She wagged her head from side to side. 'By! He's got the makings of a real businessman, has that one.'

Laughing with her, Louise had to agree. In a way, she thought, it was a good thing that they couldn't afford a television set. One or two people had them in Derwent Street, but she preferred a good old sit-down and a natter any day.

Each aware that there were more intimate matters to be discussed, and neither of them yet willing to open their hearts for whatever reason, they lapsed into a momentary silence.

Finishing her tea, Sally discreetly eyed Louise as her daughter-in-law settled deeper into the comfort of the old armchair. Lowering her gaze, Louise became lost in thought – of Eric, and Ben, and of the future. Right now, there seemed little for her to look forward to, with the exception of Jinnie, who along with Sally, was her entire life.

The mantelpiece clock ticked quietly in the background, and for a time, all seemed well enough with their little world, though Sally was obviously on edge, and Louise was as yet unaware of the bombshell to be dropped in her lap.

Startling them both, Jinnie came bursting in. 'I'm going to bed now,' she told them.

'I shan't be long behind yer, lass.' Sally knew it was no use going away to her bed just yet. She wouldn't be able to sleep until she'd told Louise her little secret.

Louise kissed the girl goodnight. 'Done your homework, have you?'

Jinnie nodded. 'It was easy.'

'There you are, then,' Louise told her. 'It's not so bad after all, is it?'

Jinnie made a face. 'Bad enough!'

'Go on with you,' her mam chided. 'I'll be in to check on you later.'

Satisfied, Jinnie kissed her gran and bade them both goodnight.

When the door closed behind the girl, Sally struck up a conversation. 'How's Eric then, lass?'

Louise hesitated. 'Same as ever,' she answered warily. 'He never changes.'

Sally wagged a finger. 'That's not what I meant and you know it.'

With the slightest hint of a smile on her face, Louise tutted. 'If you mean, has he asked me again to marry him, the answer is no.'

'If you're not careful, he'll find some other woman and then you'll be sorry.'

'We've got an understanding.'

'Oh aye? I know all about the "understanding".'

'Then you'll know he won't raise the question of marriage again – not unless I raise it first.'

'An' when, might I ask, will *that* be?'

Louise took a moment to answer. When she did it was to say in a quiet, regretful voice, 'I can't let myself get close to Eric. It would be like a betrayal to Ben.'

'Oh, lass! Why do yer go on tormenting yerself? What happened was not your fault. Ben was never the same after he lost his Da. When the farm was tekken away from him, it was like the end of his world. Working the land was all he knew. He wasn't cut out for life in the back streets. You *know* how he hated working on the roads, driving a lorry, being cooped up for most of the day.'

'I know all that, and it's why I should have helped him through it. I should have been more understanding.' Louise was haunted by her part in it all.

'Look, Lou, yer did all yer could. By! He got so difficult to live with, there were times when he wouldn't listen to either of us. No woman could have done more than you did. Can't yer see, lass? He were a free soul. He craved the open fields and the wind in his face. He couldn't be content the way he were, not any more. In the end he just couldn't go on.' Making the sign of the cross on herself, Sally Hunter added in a broken voice, 'May the Good Lord forgive him.' Sally had been shocked to the core that a son of hers could take his own life. Like Louise, it was something she had found hard to live with. 'It was his decision,' she argued softly. 'You'll have no peace nor future neither, till yer can learn to accept that.'

Now, with the memories overwhelming her, Louise openly wept. 'I cheated on him with Eric,' she whispered. 'Oh, Sally! What if he found out? What if he took his own life because of me?' Covering her face with the palms of her hands, she took a moment to compose herself.

When she looked up again, it was to see Sally coming across the room towards her. 'Aw, come on now, lass. Yer not to upset yerself over that, not after all these years. It's all water under the bridge . . . gone an' best forgotten.' Sitting on the arm of the chair, she draped an arm round Louise's shoulders. 'Ben changed, lass. Yer saw that for yerself. When he got that strange mood on, he'd be away out, walking the wilds, and sometimes we'd not see him for hours on end. If yer went to Eric, it were only because there were nobody else you could turn to. But yer mustn't punish yerself for ever. You've a right to some kind of happiness now, lass. Nobody knows that more than me.' Looking at Louise's distraught face, she asked softly, 'Yer love him, don't yer, lass? Eric, I mean?'

Louise nodded.

'And he loves you, ain't that right?'

Again, Louise nodded.

'Then, if he ever asks yer again, lass, to wed him, yer must tell him yes.'

Louise shook her head. 'I *can't*, Sally. Eric knows I can't. We work together and we talk a lot, mostly about things that don't matter. We sit in his kitchen; I make the tea and we eat our sandwiches together. We discuss work and the market and the price of this or that, but that's as far as it goes. We neither of us ever talk about what happened between us. We keep our feelings to ourselves. It's best that way.'

'Huh! If yer think *that*, then yer a fool. Eric's a good man. They don't come many to the dozen, I can tell yer. Let him go, an' mark my words, lass, you'll live to regret it.'

'I know that, but I can't forget what we did.'

'Yer *must* forget . . . both of youse!' Lowering her voice, she reminded Louise, 'An' what about *Ben's* cheating, eh? With yer own sister, no less? An' that poor child upstairs, deserted, left on a doorstep like a pint o' milk. By! Them buggers have a lot to answer for, so they do!'

Deeply moved, Louise made no comment. Instead she reached out and took Sally's small, frail hand in her own. Sally was right, she thought, to remind her of the way Ben and Susan had deceived her. Yet, in the long run, what they had done was no worse a thing than what she and Eric had done. Thinking about it only made it worse.

'I don't want to talk about it any more, Sally.' She looked up, her eyes still moist. 'Leave it now. Please?' Talking about it would change nothing, she thought bitterly.

'All right, lass.' Sally didn't give up easily though. 'You won't forget what I said though, will yer, about you and Eric?'

Louise smiled. 'If I know you, you won't *let* me forget.'

In that quiet little parlour, with so much of the past pressing on their minds, Sally thought the moment was right for her to confess what she had done.

'Louise, lass?'

'No more now, eh?' Louise suspected Sally wanted to

talk more about Eric. 'I promise I won't forget what you've said.'

'No, lass.' Getting up off the arm of the chair, Sally ambled over to her own chair, where she sat down and, looking Louise in the eye, said, 'I've summat to confess.' Ashamed, she dropped her gaze to the rug. 'I've done summat real bad.'

Disbelieving, and with the hint of a smile on her face, Louise returned her gaze. 'Don't give me that, Sally Hunter.' She let the growing smile linger on Sally's worried face. 'I've yet to see the day when you do summat bad.' The idea was unthinkable.

Undeterred, Sally continued, thinking that if she didn't get it off her chest now, she'd never again have the courage. Then, at some time in the future, she'd be found out – and it would be a worse matter altogether. 'Yer had a letter this morning, lass,' she began.

Louise sat up. 'A letter? By! I can't recall the last time I got a letter . . . well, not one that wasn't a bill or a circular.'

'It weren't neither o' them, lass. It were a *proper* letter.'

Louise's smile fell away. 'Who was it from? Where is it now?' Her glance instinctively went to the mantelpiece.

Sally's eyes filled with tears. 'I'm sorry, lass. I threw it in the fire.'

'You did *what?*' Louise couldn't understand. 'You mean you accidentally dropped the letter into the fire – is that what you're saying?'

'No, lass.' She heaved a great sigh. 'I did it a purpose.' Now that she had started, Sally found it easier to go on. 'Y'see, I knew who sent it, 'cause I recognised the writing.'

'Who, Sally?' Louise pleaded. '*Who* sent it? And why in God's name did you think to burn it?'

'I didn't want yer to be upset, that's why. So I threw it in the flames an' I watched it burn to ashes. Aw, Lou, I'm sorry

I have to tell yer all this.' Her homely old face hardened. 'But I'm not sorry I burned it, so don't think *that*!'

Her horrified gaze fixed on this little woman who meant the world to her, and who had done something so drastic, Louise was momentarily silenced. She had never known Sally to do anything so out of character. In a gentle, forgiving voice, she asked, 'Who was the letter from? I have to know.' In her heart she had a sneaking suspicion who it would be, but she needed to be certain.

Her mother-in-law hesitated. Then: 'It were yer sister's handwriting,' she said in a low voice. 'I've seen it many a time in the past on Christmas an' birthday cards and suchlike.'

Although she had half been expecting it, the shock seemed to spring Louise out of the chair. '*Susan*? The letter you burned was from our Susan?'

'It were for yer own good, lass.' Sally's torrent of words tumbled one over the other. 'I weren't going to tell yer, but then I thought you'd find out some time or another an' you'd likely hate me to the end of me dying days, so I thought I'd best tell yer now, an' get it over with.' Before Louise could get a word in, she went on, 'I know how distraught you were when Susan ran off an' left the bairn. I saw yer face when you read that letter she left behind, saying as how she and Ben had . . . had . . .' She couldn't bring herself to say it. 'I swore then that I'd never let her hurt yer again.'

'Aw, Sally.' Louise's loyalties were torn apart. 'I know you meant well, but I wish you hadn't burned that letter.'

'I'm glad I did. *Glad*, d'yer hear me?' The tears ran down Sally's weathered cheeks, and her heart was broken. 'What she an' my son did to you was unforgivable. The pair of 'em, creating that little innocent . . . then deserting yer both, one after the other.' Through her sobs she poured out all the pain that had crippled her for so long. 'An' now she has the barefaced cheek to write to yer – as if she's been away on holiday an' now she wants yer blessing to come back.'

Louise's emotions were confused. 'Is that what she's asking? To come back here, after all that's happened?' It was an unwelcome surprise.

'Aye, and more besides! Aw, lass, I don't want yer upset all over again. An' what about little Jinnie, eh? I wouldn't put it past your Susan to tell her she's the child's mammy. An' don't say she wouldn't do that to yer, 'cause she took yer husband, didn't she? I'm sure, if it suited her purpose, she wouldn't think twice about tekking yer child an' all.'

Louise read between the lines and her heart missed a beat. 'What are you hiding, Sally? Has she said she means to take Jinnie?'

'Not in so many words, but I wouldn't trust her as far as I could throw her – an' that's no distance at all.'

'So, what *did* she say?'

'Well, she said as how she missed yer – an' that's a bloody lie an' all, if yer ask *me*.'

'What else did she say?'

'She said as how she were sorry for what she did to yer with Ben. She claims it were more his fault than hers. Then she talks about the lass . . . about how she's never forgiven herself for leaving her behind, though she knows you'll have tekken good care of her, and she thanks yer for that.' Hanging her head, Sally paused.

Sensing her reluctance, Louise urged, 'You're hiding summat, Sally. You'd best tell me. I want to know everything that was said in that letter!'

'All right, lass.' Sally continued, her love for Louise and the girl spilling over in her voice. 'Every time she spoke about the lass it were as though she were laying claim to her. It were "my daughter" this an' "my daughter" that. I'm sorry, Lou, but it seems to me that she's asking to come back an' tek over the child, as if it were her right.'

'But she can't do that!' White with fear, Louise began pacing the floor. 'Jinnie's *my* daughter, officially adopted and everything.' Swinging round she pleaded with the old woman. 'My God, Sally what makes her think she can just waltz back in an' take Jinnie from me?'

Sally shook her head. 'She can't. Like yer said, Jinnie's your daughter now, all legal and above board. You took her on when she were only days old. You fought tooth an' nail to keep her, an' now you've raised her to be a fine young lady. Yer not to worry, d'yer hear? Yer not to upset yerself.' Sally was all for action. 'Go to the courts, lass. Get the authorities on her back. By! They'll soon send her packing, and no mistake.'

Louise turned the suggestion over in her mind. It was one solution, but not one she fancied. 'No. I'll go to her myself,' she decided. 'I'll reason with her. She'll not take the lass from me, not unless it's over my dead body she won't.'

Sally smiled. 'That's the spirit,' she agreed. 'Coward that she is, she'll be no match for you when yer hackles are up!'

'All the same, I'm frightened, Sally.' Louise was not afraid for herself, but for the girl. 'Jinnie's getting on so well. She's such a lovely, happy girl. What if Susan really means to cause trouble between me and her? What if she manages to turn her against me?'

'Have a word with yer mam, lass. Happen she'll tek Susan in hand.'

'I'd rather not involve Mam if I can help it. You know she's not been all that well lately.'

'Aye, well yer might be right. Happen it's as well to leave her out of it altogether.'

'The trouble is now you've burned the letter, I can't go to her, can I, because we don't know the address. So now we'll just have to wait for her to turn up here, more's the pity.'

Sally gave one of her little smiles. 'Oh, I've not forgotten the address,' she revealed. 'It were easy enough to remember.'

'Where is she?' Louise held her breath.

'She's still in Blackpool. And according to the letter, she's doing very well there, thank you – though the Lord only knows what badness she might be up to!' Sally had no faith whatsoever in Louise's sister.

'Blackpool, still?' Louise wasn't all that surprised. 'She always had a weakness for the fun of the fair and all that.'

'Be careful what yer do, lass.' Sally grew increasingly nervous. 'It seems to me she's hardened with the years. Who knows *what* she's done – or what she's capable of?'

Louise was quiet for a time, turning it all over in her mind, and still reluctant to believe that Susan had 'done well'. Up to the day she left Derwent Street, Susan had ruined everything she touched; except Jinnie, thank God!

She voiced her thoughts to Sally. 'What's happened to my sister since leaving Blackburn, Sally? What made her write that letter, talking about Jinnie like that? And does she really think she can walk back into her daughter's life and pick up where she left off?'

After what had happened in the past, nothing would surprise Sally, 'One way or another, she's got to be stopped, that's all I know.'

Sally was right, Louise thought. If Susan intended taking Jinnie away from her, she needed stopping in her tracks and no mistake! She couldn't tell what might happen when she and Susan met face to face but one thing was certain. 'I'm going to see her,' she said out loud. 'I'm going over to Blackpool, to reason it out with her face to face.' She had never been more determined in her life. 'If she thinks to come between me and Jinnie, she'll have me to contend with!'

Seeing the determination on Louise's face, Sally knew there would be trouble.

'Write the address down for me, will you?' Louise asked, and Sally wrote it down as best she could. 'Jacob's Restaurant, The Promenade.' She spoke the address as she wrote. 'Sounds very grand, don't yer think?' There was cynicism in her voice. 'Jacob's Restaurant, indeed!'

'She must really have loved him,' Louise said quietly.

'She's got more imagination than sense, that's the trouble with Susan.' God help them all if she really had got her sights set on young Jinnie, Sally thought. By! Would Louise *ever* have any peace?

Chapter Three

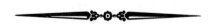

A FEW STREETS away in Blackburn Town, old Sarah Harpur listened politely to her visitor, but when he was finished she collapsed into a chair and broke down in tears. 'No, please! You *can't* turn us out.' Vigorously shaking her head, she looked up from the big, worn armchair and implored, her voice broken with emotion, 'Mr Martin, won't you please change your mind? I've been a good tenant for the past twelve years. I've always paid my rent on time, and I've kept the place neat and tidy.' Waving her arm to embrace the tiny front room of the house in Montague Street, she entreated, 'Look for yourself. You can see I've worked hard to keep it really nice.' She pointed to the walls and the ceiling. 'I painted it meself, from top to bottom, upstairs and down.' Having said her piece, she hoped to have persuaded him to change his mind. 'As a matter o' fact, Mr Martin, it wouldn't surprise me if I hadn't added to its value.'

He heard her out, but then dashed her hopes. 'I'm sorry, but there's nothing I can do.' Ralph Martin was the only son of Alan Martin, the very same man who, ten years ago, had colluded with Jacob Hunter to cheat his brother Ben out of his rightful inheritance.

'We've sold the property for development.' Like his father, Ralph could be ruthless when the occasion demanded. 'If you're not out of here in a week, I'll have you forcibly removed, you *and* them.' Without turning his head he gestured with his thumb towards the street outside, where Sarah's two teenaged grandchildren were chatting with their friends after school.

Sarah was beside herself with worry. 'But where will we go? I've no savings as such, just the Family Allowance for the young 'uns, and the money I get from cleaning, and I can tell you now, *that* doesn't stretch to much.'

'You're not my responsibility, Mrs Harpur, and neither are them two.' This time he looked out of the window; Adam and Hannah were now sitting on the kerb, deep in conversation. 'Get in touch with the authorities,' he suggested callously. 'Tell them you've been given notice and you've no money to find another place.' He shrugged. 'Happen they'll take the kids into care.'

'Over my dead body!' Sarah had scrambled out of the chair and was now staring at him with defiance. 'I'm not out on the street yet, young man. While I pay the rent on this house, I've a right to choose who I want and *don't* want in my front room. And I don't want *you*! So clear off out of it!'

He laughed at her anger. 'At your age, you should be glad to be rid of them kids. I mean, when all's said and done, they're not yours, are they?'

'What would *you* know?' she asked quietly, looking him in the eye with such dignity, he felt momentarily humbled. 'Them children are my flesh and blood, and I love them like my own.'

He sniffed. 'Have you told 'em their daddy's in prison for killing their mammy?'

Sarah paled. 'My God! How did *you* find out?'

'Oh, it's common knowledge round here. You can't keep a thing like that secret.'

Sarah bowed her head. 'They were both there when it happened,' she revealed in a whisper. 'The lass was only a bairn of four. She's never talked about it. Sometimes she has these terrible nightmares, and I have to rock her back to sleep, even though she's a big girl of fourteen now. At first the doctors tried everything to get her to talk about it all, but she never would, and now they've given up. They reckon she doesn't remember after all.' Tears filled her eyes. 'But I know better. She's pushed it down, into the dark place, where it can't hurt her. Her brother's the same: no one can get a word out of him on the subject.'

'I'm sorry.' And he was. Because hadn't Ralph Martin himself got memories to haunt him – like when his own father thought he was dying and offloaded his guilty secret onto his son . . . confessing that he and Jacob Hunter had cheated and stolen, and robbed Jacob's brother of the farm he was left by his father. It was no wonder that Ben Hunter had killed himself soon after.

That was the secret with which Alan Martin had burdened his son – how, out of greed and badness, he had caused the death of a good man.

Sarah had seen the haunted look in his face and suspected there was more to this young man than met the eye. 'Do *you* have nightmares?' she asked meaningfully.

He gave a nervous little smile. 'We *all* have our own dark places,' he told her.

Sensing a more sympathetic attitude, Sarah dared to ask, 'Can't you let me and the kids stay here? Please? You see, ever since it happened, the two of 'em have lived here, with me. They feel secure. I don't want them to be uprooted.'

The landlord seemed not to have heard. Instead he let his sorry gaze run over the children – Hannah first, such a delicate, pretty child; he could imagine what trauma she must have suffered, and what a great pity it was that she could not talk about what she had seen. And Adam, full of dreadful memories that had never been released: it was like a ticking time bomb, waiting to explode. 'Poor kids.'

Sarah cocked her ear. She imagined she had heard him speak but couldn't be certain. 'Mr Martin – did you hear me? *Is* there a way you could agree to us staying here?'

Ralph Martin heard her speak to him, but was too intent on the boy to reply. Such a handsome lad, what was he – fifteen, sixteen years old? They said he had saved his little sister's life all those years ago, but could he save her now? Could he even save himself from those awful, crippling memories?

Ralph knew all about that! He knew what it was like to have such a burden on your shoulders, and know you could never be rid of it.

'Are they good kids?' he wanted to know.

Sarah didn't even have to think. 'Wonderful!' she answered. 'They've kept me sane all these years.'

'What about their father?'

On the defensive now, she asked impatiently, 'What d'you mean?'

'I mean does he know what wonderful kids they are?'

'Not him! He doesn't know them at all. Never clapped eyes on them since the day they carted him off to prison.' Sarah's voice stiffened ominously. 'If I have my way, he'll *never* clap eyes on them, neither.'

'Do they ask about him?'

'The lad does, sometimes. He's not forgotten what happened.' She was quick to add, 'The girl never speaks of him, nor would I want her to. Thank God, neither of them have any feelings for him. Terry Harpur is a wicked, dangerous man – a bad lot through and through.' She made the sign of the cross on herself. 'Though I say it myself, and I'm his mother, God forbid.'

'You do right to keep them apart.' Ralph Martin turned to address her in serious tone. 'It wouldn't do for them to come face to face with the man who murdered their mammy, would it?'

By this time, Sarah was beginning to feel uncomfortable. 'Have a word with your father, will you, son? Ask him if he can let us stay, at least until I find somewhere suitable.'

But Ralph's thoughts were back there in the house, with his own father. 'It's a pity they have to know what their father did.' He gave a wry little laugh. 'The sins of the father are visited on the son, isn't that what they say?'

'*Please*, Mr Martin?'

Startled, he pushed aside his own dark thoughts and jerked his head back to look at her. 'What did you say?'

'I only asked if you could let me and the children stay here after all?'

'No!' Irritation sharpened his voice. 'I already told you: the house and all the others along this terrace have been sold for development, to make way for a block of flats or some such thing. You know full well, it's not *me* who owns this house, it's my father.' His voice dropped to a harsh whisper. 'I sometimes think he owns me too!'

The implication of his words went straight over Sarah's head. 'Look, do you know of any house round here that's empty? Not too much rent, mind, and not in some god-forsaken place?'

He shook his head. 'No, can't think of any.'

Sarah's heart sank. 'You will let me know if you hear of any, won't you?' Crossing to the dresser she took out the rent book and handed it to him. 'You'd best have this before I spend it on summat else,' she smiled.

When returning the signed book to her, he seemed to gather his thoughts. 'I'll tell you what though. It's a pity you *don't* want to live in some godforsaken place because there is an empty house on our books not too far from here. I dare say you know it very well.'

Sarah's eyes lit up. 'Where?'

He smiled, but not unkindly. 'It's the kids' old house –

Craig Street . . . on the corner of Derwent Street. I think you'd be the first to agree, Mrs Harpur, that it's a godforsaken house if ever there was one. And, considering what happened there, I'm quite sure *you* wouldn't want to live there.'

Realising he meant the very corner house where the double murder was committed, Sarah's face crumpled with shock. 'Oh no.' She had to sit down again. 'Oh, dear God, I couldn't. No. No!' She shook her head so hard her false teeth rattled. 'Dear Lord above, I'd have to be out of my mind to live *there*!'

He understood. 'Can't say as I blame you for that,' he remarked. 'Like I said, I will look out for somewhere for you, but there's not much about. At least, not for the rent you can afford. I'll tell you what though, murder or no murder, I'd be surprised if anybody takes that house on. It's in a terrible state, been empty for months. I had to go and take a look, and I did not enjoy the experience. The wallpaper's gone mouldy, the floorboards have started rotting – looks like there's been a leak from the tank at some time or another, and the water went right under the floorboards. All the ceilings downstairs are affected, and as for the plumbing, I can't even begin to tell you.' He wrinkled his nose. 'Talk about *smell*!' Waving his hand before his face, he groaned, 'Phew! It was as if the doors and windows hadn't been opened for years.'

'Was there anybody living there?'

'I'm told an old man was living in it up to three months ago. He popped his clogs, and it's been empty ever since. My father refuses to spend any money on it. He says it's allus been hard to let, and that for the low rent he's chargin', the tenants can muck in and clean the place up.'

Sarah could see the house in her mind's eye. 'The thought of anybody living there makes me shudder,' she told him. 'I'd rather sleep rough on the streets than lay my head down in that place.'

Ralph Martin gave a short laugh. 'It might be cleaner on the streets,' he revealed. 'The neglect is unbelievable.'

Sarah had listened and was saddened by the news. Number fourteen Craig Street had, after all, been her 'daughter-in-law' Maggie's home at one time, until the terrible night of the murders. 'Shame,' she said. 'It used to be so clean and cosy when the kids were little. Why won't yer dad spend a few quid to bring it back to scratch? I thought that was his business . . . buying houses, doing them up and renting them out. Why would he let this one go to pot?'

It took a moment for her landlord to reply, and when he did, it was in a thoughtful voice and with a look on his face she couldn't fathom. 'Oh, I think he had his reasons.' Ralph Martin glanced again at the teenagers sitting on the kerb out-side. His voice dropped as he whispered inaudibly, 'Sometimes a dark conscience can send a man out of his mind.'

'Sorry, I must be going deaf.' Sarah moved closer. 'I didn't quite hear that.'

'Talking to myself,' he said lamely, then more briskly, he told her, 'I'd best be off. I've a good deal to do yet.' Before he left he reminded Sarah, 'A week's notice, mind, Mrs Harpur. You'd best be out of here before my father comes to check the place over. He doesn't take kindly to squatters.' When she opened her mouth to speak, he pre-empted her question. 'Yes, I know, and yes, I *will* keep my ear to the ground for a place. But don't count your chickens.'

Sarah saw him out. 'Jacob once told our Maggie that your father was a good friend of his dad,' she remarked casually.

'Is that so?'

For one fleeting moment, Sarah thought he looked afraid. 'She said he lent Jacob's dad Ronnie Hunter a deal of money against his farm.'

'Folks should keep their noses out of other folks' business!' Now there was a definite edginess about the young man.

'Besides, what would *I* know about any of it? I was only about the same age as your grandson at the time.'

'Still, it seems strange your father never talked to you about it,' Sarah persisted, 'seeing as the two of you work close together, like.'

'*You* might think it strange,' he retorted impatiently, 'but I don't. My father answers to no one. He's his own master, and always has been.'

'All the same, lending the money was a grand gesture between friends, so it was. He took a loss too, so they say – your father, I mean – when Maple Farm didn't reach the sum that was owed him.'

Eager to be gone, the young man bristled. 'I don't think it's a good idea to talk behind people's backs.' It was a veiled warning. 'You should know – nothing good ever comes of listening to gossip.'

Sarah frowned. 'Sorry if I've offended you, Mr Martin, I'm sure, but I reckon you should be proud of your father. He lent the money, and when he didn't get it all back, he was gentleman enough not to press Jacob's brother Ben for the balance of the debt. That's the sign of a good man in *my* books!'

He turned away, his face contorted with disgust. 'You know nothing!' he muttered.

Sarah cupped her ear. 'What's that you say?'

He didn't turn round. Instead he put his hand up in farewell to indicate that he was in a hurry and had stayed too long already. Regretting the fact that he had allowed himself to be caught up in conversation with a tenant, Ralph Martin hurried away as fast as his legs would carry him. The sweat ran down his temples and his heart beat faster. 'Stupid cow!' he breathed, then instantly regretted the abuse. How could Mrs Harpur know what torment she had put him through in asking what she imagined to be innocent questions?

Behind him, he could hear her calling the children. 'Adam, fetch your sister in for your teas. The rent man's gone now.' She never liked discussing delicate matters in front of them, and nothing could be more delicate than the prospect of being homeless. 'Come on then, you two,' she urged. 'Let's be having you.'

Unable to resist, Ralph Martin paused to look round. He saw the children go into the house, and he envied them. 'For all you've no proper roof over your heads, you've got the love of that woman.' He smiled sadly. 'She thinks my father's a hero, but I wonder what she'd say if she knew the truth, eh? I wonder how she'd feel if she knew he and Jacob Hunter had plotted to rob Ben of the farm his father left him?'

It was a terrible thing to know and not be able to tell. 'Dad should have kept it to himself,' he fretted, hurrying away. 'He should never have confessed it to me when he thought he was on his death-bed.' He spat on the ground. 'It might have been better if he'd died and taken his guilty secret with him!'

⟢⟡⟣

'RIGHT!' IN NO time at all, Adam and Hannah were washed and seated at the table. 'It's beans on toast, or chips and egg.' Hands on hips, Sarah looked them over with a beaming face. 'What's it to be?'

They looked at each other, and the answer was unanimous. 'Chips and egg!'

'Work first, food after,' she declared, and ambled her way into the kitchen.

A few minutes later, she emerged with a large tray, piled high with plates, cutlery and condiments. 'I've already chipped the taters, so by the time you've set the table, I'll have them ready, along with the eggs.' Pointing to the loaf and butter, she advised Adam, 'Mind you don't cut yourself on the knife, son.

I sharpened it this morning and it would split hairs!' She had no real qualms about her grandson using the knife, because there was nobody more sensible. 'Two slices each, sliced thick and plastered with butter,' she suggested. 'I'm that peckish, I could eat a scabby donkey.'

'Ugh!' Hannah pulled a face, and Adam laughed out loud. 'Gran doesn't mean it,' he said, and Hannah blushed pink for being so credulous.

While the kids busied themselves, Sarah dropped a large cube of lard into the chip-pan. Soonever it was sizzling and bubbling, she slid in the chips, licking her lips as she watched them spit and dance. *'Lovely!'* She then cracked the eggs and dropped them into the adjacent frying pan; the warming plate was on, so if the eggs were done before the chips, she would just slide them over and let them sit awhile. Sometimes they were even tastier for the experience.

Hearing her grandchildren's excited chatter, she went to the kitchen door, her homely round face glowing with love as she watched them carefully set the table. 'No, Hannah, the fork goes on the *left*, remember?' Adam was saying, and Hannah listened to his every word, just like always. Adam was her hero, and always would be.

Sarah watched and listened, and loved them so much it hurt. 'Don't you worry,' she murmured. 'Whatever happens, we'll not be without a home. While I've my health and strength, I'll watch over you.' She wiped away a tear. 'Trust me. I would never let any harm come to either of you.'

Adam and Hannah had seemed to be with her for a lifetime now, Sarah thought. They had always loved and respected her, but after ten years under the same roof together, they were, all three, incredibly close. After the murder of her mother, the four-year-old Hannah had gone into shock. When she had first moved in to live with her granny, she had been distraught; frightened and trembling at the slightest thing, and waking up each night in the grip of nightmares. In the depths of night she had clung to her granny and called for Adam, but not once had she disclosed the sights she had seen on that dreadful night.

Now aged fourteen, and quite the young lady, these past two years, Hannah had learned to live with whatever haunted her; she was peaceful, seemingly more content.

Sarah worried about her though, because Hannah found it hard to stick up for herself. Youngsters as defenceless as her were often picked on, taken for granted and overlooked when good things were being given out. In spite of her worries though, Sarah was greatly relieved that the girl seemed gradually to have gotten over the bad memories.

Adam was a leader; stronger in every way than his sister. Coming up to his seventeenth birthday, he was well-built, and handsome too, with those bewitching dark eyes and mop of thick, black hair. With the other boys, he enjoyed every minute. He rode his bike in the park, and played tag on the cobbles. Sometimes he went to listen to records in his friends' houses. They were all keen on the Beatles, Elvis Presley and the Rolling Stones.

Adam could be solitary, too. He was perfectly happy in his own company, strolling along the towpath by the canal, waving to the bargees as they chugged past on their brightly painted barges, or let their horses pull the barges along. They all knew and liked Adam, for he had become a familiar figure along the Leeds and Liverpool Canal.

But he was one of the lads all the same. In the street, he would join in a game of football, or run a race from one end of the road to the other; able to run like the wind he would leave the others standing, and off they'd go to sulk, until the following weekend, when refreshed and confident, they would be back to race against him once more. Adam was a natural sprinter, and there was no one there to catch him. Losing heart, his mates dropped out of the challenge one by one, until there was no one to run against him.

Now that most of the lads had done their O-Levels, their attentions were taken up with the prospect of leaving school and looking for work. With the onset of maturity their priorities inevitably had to change. They began to compete for the local girls' affections ... worrying more about their appearance, and how they might match up to one another. Suddenly they were seeing the girls in a different light. It occurred to them that these pretty things were the same girls they had played with since childhood, yet their figures had changed and they no longer resembled the boys in any shape, way or form. It was a revelation, which the lads found exciting, but somewhat unsettling.

Not yet having seen a girl who took his fancy, Adam concentrated on his fishing technique. He spent most evenings till dark, mastering the art of fishing. With his home-made rod he caught many a fish which he proudly took home to Sarah; his grandmother cooked it for the next day's meal, along with mashed potatoes and green peas. There were often more fish than Sarah needed so, during the course of a month, the neighbours would each receive a fish in turn, and were immensely grateful. Adam was quick and easy to make friends and was a favourite with everyone; especially as he never refused to run an errand or give a hand where it was needed.

All of this and more went through Sarah's mind as she watched them now.

No one was more aware than she of how cruel life had been to Adam and his sister, but they had come through it all, and now had much to be thankful for. Sarah, their beloved granny, was the rock on which their contentment was built, and as long as she had them to love and watch out for she, too, was content.

Though they never mentioned it, Sarah was hopeful that they had learned to live with the knowledge that they would never again see their mammy; a good but misguided woman, who had degraded herself time and again in order to keep her babies fed and clothed, and in the end, paid for it horribly, with her very life.

Just then, the sound of a car backfiring made Hannah cry out, and she looked from Adam to Sarah for reassurance. 'It's all right, love, it's just a car – nothing to worry about,' Sarah told her, while Adam wisely took her mind off it by reminding his sister that she hadn't set out a fork for their granny. Her attention distracted, Hannah instantly forgot the noise and finished her task, but her hands were still shaking and Adam had to enclose her tiny fist in his. 'I'll help you,' he suggested, but she shook him off. 'I can do it!' she announced, and much to the relief of Adam and Sarah, she did.

As she made her way back into the kitchen, a cold shiver ran through Sarah's soul. 'He might be my own son, God forgive me,' she whispered harshly, 'but for what our Terry did to those kids and their mammy . . . he deserves to rot in jail till the end of his days!'

⟞⟝⟞●⟝⟞⟝

THE FOLLOWING SATURDAY, four days after the landlord's visit, Sarah received a letter postmarked *Her Majesty's Prison*. It was from her son, Terry, and its contents shook Sarah to her roots:

Hello, Mam,

I don't suppose you were expecting to hear from me. In fact, I wouldn't be surprised if you never wanted to see me again. All I can say is I never meant to hurt the kids, and I never wanted to hurt you neither.

It's been real hard in here. A visit from you would have made it more bearable, but as you chose to desert your only child ten years ago, there don't seem a lot I can do about it. I reckon it was cruel of you to have turned your back on me like that, but believe it or not, Mam, I have found it in my heart to forgive you. Unlike you, you see, I don't forget my own flesh and blood.

And how are my kids then, eh? I bet Adam's a fine young man in the making. By my reckoning, it won't be long before he's out to work and earning a wage. If I get myself a place to live, he'll be able to pay half the rent and bills, eh? I'm sure you'll agree that he'd be better off with his dad than with his old granny. I bet he won't hold the past against me. Not like you seem to have done.

But never mind, Mam, that's all water under the bridge, so we'll say no more, eh? Besides, like I said, I've forgiven you. Anyway, if you hadn't looked after my kids while I've been in the nick, God only knows what might have happened to the poor little buggers. I dare say you've done a good job, and being your age, it can't have been easy.

All that aside, I'm writing because I need a favour. You'll be glad to hear that I'll be out of this hole in a couple of months. Bet you can't believe I've been commended for good behaviour! Well, I have, and if the Board agree with the recommendations, I'm to be let out. FREE! Back on the streets and living a life. What d'you think to that, eh?

I'm told they try and find you somewhere to live, but considering what I hear from them as knows, the places you're put in ain't all that grand. So, like I say, Mam, you'll have to help me out.

I need to come and stay with you and the kids, just until I find a place of my own. I'll take Adam off your hands then, I promise. As I said, he'll soon be out to work, but what with me being an ex-con, it might not be so easy for me to get a job. So you see, his wage will come in real handy.

It's best if the girl stays with you. I can handle Adam, but I'm not sure about her. I reckon she's set herself against me, just like her no-good mother. Either way, I want nothing to do with her. She can stay with you, and good shuts, I say!

Anyway, Mam, I'll tell the authorities that you're taking me in, and that they needn't find me a place. It's best that way, I reckon. I know you won't turn me down. After all, what's a mother for, if not to help out when she's needed?

Right then. I'll sign off, and write to you nearer the time. Mind though! I'll want a room of my own, so if space is tight, the kids will have to share.

Keep well,

Your loving son, Terry.

After reading the letter, Sarah sat in her chair, the pages clutched in her hand and her face grey with shock. For what seemed an age, she did not move a single muscle. Instead, she sat bolt upright, her glazed eyes staring ahead, and her mind growing increasingly frantic.

'I can't let him near them young 'uns!' she murmured at last. 'I won't let him take advantage of Adam just as he's starting out.' Dropping the letter to her knees, she covered her face with the palms of her hands, asking herself what she must do.

After a moment she collected the letter and, folding it into four, placed it carefully on the mantelpiece.

She had a plan!

<hr/>

WHEN THE SKIES began to darken, she called her grandchildren in; Adam was giving a younger lad a piggyback ride home, after he'd fallen and cut his leg. 'Will I die?' the lad asked in wonder. Adam instantly reassured him. 'Not unless your leg falls off,' he said with a grin.

Nearby, Hannah was chalking out the numbers for hop-scotch after the recent shower had washed them away. 'Mek 'em bigger this time, Hannah!' cried Dolly Lassiter from number four. 'Molly can't read without her specs.' Molly was a seven-year-old 'know-all' from Craig Street. 'She says you never do it proper.'

Mortified, the older girl drew the numbers large and clear. 'Can you read them now, Molly?' she asked with concern.

''S' all right, I suppose.' Cherished and pampered, Molly was never satisfied.

'Kids these days don't know they're born, do they, eh?' Fat Lucy Patterson addressed Sarah; she was the street's nosy parker. 'In my day, we were lucky to be allowed out on the street, never mind playing hopscotch and defacing the pavement!' Folding her arms she watched the children file into their respective homes. 'We were seen and not heard,' she declared. 'Our dad would belt us till our arses bled if we so much as dared to backchat.'

Sarah had her own views on that. 'It's just as well times change then,' she answered shortly.

'Hmh! Discipline never did *anybody* any harm.' Lucy glared at two young lads fighting at the end of the street. 'A thick belt round *their* arses wouldn't go amiss neither.' With that she went inside and slammed the door, leaving Sarah chuckling. For just that briefest minute she had forgotten about Terry's letter.

By the time she had gone down the passage to call in the kids, Sarah was once more on edge. 'I must do right by them two,' she muttered. 'When it comes down to it, I'm all they've got.' Moreover, the children were all *she* had an' all. The idea of being without them was unthinkable.

Hardly able to keep her eyes open, Hannah yawned through her wash and while drinking her cocoa, then she yawned all the way up to bed. 'Goodnight, God bless,' she said sleepily as Sarah gave her a hug.

'Goodnight, lass,' Sarah said. 'Sleep well.' By the time she had reached the door, Hannah was already asleep. 'Aw.' Sarah lingered before closing the door. 'She's tired herself out, poor little bugger.'

Downstairs, Adam was just finishing his cocoa, and was waiting for her. 'What's wrong, Gran?' Ever observant he had seen the trouble in Sarah's face. 'There *is* something wrong, isn't there?'

'I think that's for you to decide.' Thankful that he was of an age and maturity when she could confide in him, she confessed, 'I've had some news.'

His expression darkened. 'What kind of news?'

With bowed head, Sarah went to the mantelpiece and taking down the letter, handed it to him, still folded. 'You'd best read that. It's from your dad.'

Adam put down his cup and unfolded the piece of paper. He didn't look up again until he had finished reading. When he spoke, his voice was cold and shaking. 'Do you want him living here with us, Gran?'

Sarah sat down beside him. Unsure as to what she should say, she decided to speak the truth. 'No, lad, I *don't*.' Deeply ashamed, she let her gaze fall to the table-top. 'After what he did, I don't want hin anywhere near us.' May God forgive me, she thought. Afraid to look him in the eye in case she had gone against his wishes, she kept her gaze averted. 'I'm sorry, lad, but if it's what you and Hannah want, I'll not stop him from coming here. He is your father after all's said and done.'

There followed a moment when the silence became unbearable; when the ticking of the clock echoed round the room, and even the sound of the flames licking the coal in the fire-grate seemed deafening.

In that awful, nerve-racking minute, Sarah was convinced that she had taken too much for granted. What if the boy really wanted his father? What if Hannah felt the same? Neither of them had said too much over the years, so what was she to think? And what right had she to come between the children and their father, however bad he was?

Suddenly, gently, the boy slid his arm round her shoulder. 'Me and Hannah . . . we haven't got a mother. *And we haven't got a father*,' he said softly. 'We've only got you, Gran. We don't need nobody else.'

Sarah looked up, the shivering tears breaking away to trickle down her face. 'I'm sorry, lad.' He would never know how much!

'Don't let him come here, Gran.' Adam's face hardened. 'I hate him! We don't want him. He'll only spoil things.'

Lifting her hand, Sarah stroked his face. 'Don't worry, lad, I won't let him.' Right then and there she knew she had to put her plan into action. 'Tomorrow morning, I'm going to see Jeff Sharpe, the house-clearance man. I'll ask him to come and empty this house of everything we own – all except the things we might need along the way. Oh, I daresay I'll not get much of a price, but every little bit counts as they say, and I'm certainly not leaving it here for nothing!'

Adam was puzzled. 'What are you saying, Gran?'

'I'm saying that if your father does come here, he'll not find us, 'cause we'll be long gone. Besides, we've already been given notice to quit by Mr Martin the landlord so we might as well get it over and done with. The whole terrace will be coming down eventually. They're building flats here or summat.'

'Where will we go?' Adam was amazed at this piece of news.

Sarah chuckled. 'Off on an adventure.'

He had to smile. 'But where?'

She winked. 'We'll have to see, won't we?'

Because she wasn't sure what Adam's reaction might be to his father's letter, Sarah hadn't thought her plan right through. But before morning came she would have it all straight in her mind. 'Now then, lad, you'd best get off to bed and get a good night's sleep,' she coaxed, ''cause we'll have to be up bright and early to catch Jeff. Most days, he's away on his rounds at first light, and I want this house to be his first port of call.'

Suddenly aware that someone was watching from the door, Sarah swung round, horrified to see Hannah standing there. 'What's wrong, love?' She went across to draw her into the room. 'Couldn't you sleep?' She had an awful feeling Hannah might have heard everything. But then, she would have to know soon enough.

The girl looked from one to the other. 'I heard what you said,' she told them. 'What's happening Gran? *Why* are we going away?'

While Sarah considered how much to tell her, Adam took his sister to one side. 'We would have told you in the morning,' he promised. 'The thing is, Hannah . . . Dad will be out of prison soon.' He held the letter out, but she didn't take it. 'He wants to come here and live with us, then when he finds a place of his own, he expects me to go and live with him, and you to stay here with Gran.' When he felt her stiffen in his grasp, he swiftly put her fears to rest. 'That's why we're going away,' he told her. 'Gran's taking us off to live somewhere he will never find us. Is that all right with you, Hannah?'

His sister's answer was to throw herself into Sarah's arms. 'Quick, let's go now – before he comes!'

Sarah gave a deep sigh of relief. 'First thing in the morning,' she promised. 'Soonever Jeff Sharpe's been and agreed a price.'

'Can I pack my things now?' Hannah pleaded. 'Please, Gran? I'm not tired any longer.'

Sarah looked at Adam, and he suggested, 'I don't suppose she'll sleep a wink if you don't let her.'

'You're right, lad.' Pointing Hannah in the direction of the stairs, Sarah told her, 'Go on then. There's a plastic bag in my wardrobe . . . it's the one I brought the blankets home from the market in. It should be plenty big enough to hold your belongings, so go on. Get on with it!'

As Hannah went away, Sarah called after her, 'I'll be up them stairs to my bed in an hour. I want you tucked up and fast asleep by that time. All right?'

'All right, Gran.'

With Hannah gone, Adam was unusually quiet. He sat in the chair watching the dying embers in the grate; the letter crumpled in his fist.

Sarah came to stand beside him. 'Are you all right, lad?'

'I hate him!'

'Hatred is a bad thing.'

'Are you sure he's my dad?'

'As sure as I can be.'

'I wish he wasn't!' Adam came over to her and held her tight. 'Me and Hannah . . . we love you so much, Gran.'

Sarah would have answered, but she knew if she so much as opened her mouth, she would not be able to stop the tears.

Adam stepped away. 'I'd best go and make sure Hannah's okay,' he told her. 'I might as well pack too, in case you need my help in the morning, when Mr Sharpe comes.'

Grateful, Sarah patted him on the shoulder, amazed at how tall he had become of late. 'Whatever you think best,' she murmured. 'And . . . you *do* know how much I love you and Hannah, don't you?'

He nodded. Then, opening the letter, he read it through once again, his face dark as thunder. With a deep, angry cry, he tore it into the tiniest of pieces, before dropping them one by one into the red-hot coals. 'I wish he was dead!' he cried.

'Go to bed, son.' It hurt her to see him so raked with bad feelings.

Adam continued to watch the pieces of paper curl and

blacken. 'He killed our mam, the bastard. Why didn't they hang him!'

Sarah drew him away. 'It's not for us to reason why,' she said cautiously. 'So many lies were told, and he had a quick-tongued barrister, who seemed to believe his every word.' She smiled sadly. 'I know your father better than most, and I know how he can lie and deceive his way out of anything, if he has a mind to.'

Sarah had never seen her grandson like this, so filled with rage and deeper emotions she had never suspected. The agonised expression in his dark eyes touched her deeply. 'Go to bed now,' she instructed him. 'Pack if you want to, or leave it till the morning. Either way it's all right by me.' She held him towards her, her gaze searching his face. 'Don't let him mar your life . . . promise me that?'

Adam knew what she was saying, and he loved her all the more. 'I promise,' he murmured, but it would be hard, for he had never forgotten what he'd seen that night, and he never would.

'Goodnight, lad.'

'Goodnight, Gran.'

When the echo of Adam's footsteps had died away, Sarah lay back in the old armchair and closed her eyes. 'God help them,' she prayed, 'and give me the health and strength to see them settled.' She thought of the ordeal ahead and wondered whether she would be able to fend for the children. She was worried and fearful, and yet, deep in her heart she felt as though somebody was already answering her prayers.

When she found herself almost falling asleep, she clambered out of the chair. 'You'd best get off to your own bed,' she chided herself. 'Or you'll be fit for nothing in the morning!'

Before going into her own bedroom she sneaked a peep into Hannah's room, and there she was, tucked up in bed, fast asleep, with her bag full of things beside her. 'Goodnight, lass,'

Sarah smiled. 'Sleep tight, eh?' Peering into Adam's room, she was surprised to see that he too, was spark out. Going across the room on tiptoe, she looked down on his sleeping face. 'Such a handsome lad,' she whispered. 'You get that from your grandad. He were a good man, Lord rest his soul.'

Lying beside Adam was a tatty green holdall, bought from the market with money he had earned over the last summer holidays. His clothes were neatly piled beside it: a pair of canvas shoes, three shirts and a brown pullover. At the foot of the bed was another pullover and his two pairs of trousers; the grey ones he'd worn today, and his best, school pair. Sarah smiled. 'You'll not be needing *them* for much longer.' She could see his underwear already tucked into the open holdall.

His cricket-bat and football, and other precious things were bundled together and laid on the chair. He'd have to get rid of his bike – that'd upset him. Happen Jeff would give him a few pounds for it. Other 'boyish' things, like the catapult he'd made some time back, and old clothes now too short or too small, were in a heap on the floor by the window, presumably, like his old life here, to be discarded.

Leaving the room as quietly as she had entered, Sarah closed the door and stood outside, her mind going over the past ten years since she had taken them in. She had seen them through their infancy and into school, watched them grow strong and fine, and now they had opinions, likes and dislikes, weaknesses and strengths that were already shaping their personalities.

But tonight, she had been impressed by Adam's maturity.

As she turned the corner on the landing, she looked back at his bedroom door, imagining him inside, asleep and, she hoped, having pleasant dreams. 'Goodnight, son,' she whispered. 'I know for sure now we'll be all right, the three of us.'

In her room she wearily got undressed and got heavily

into bed. Then she lay awake for a long time. Gradually the tiredness began to overwhelm her, and still her thoughts were mostly with Adam. 'I saw something wonderful tonight,' she murmured. Her eyes moistened, but her smile was filled with wonder. As she turned over to sleep, her heart swelled with pride. *This night . . . I saw a boy become a man.*

Chapter Four

E MERGING FROM THE chip-shop on King Street, Jinnie broke into a run. 'Best get home quick,' she muttered as she ran, 'or they'll be cold and horrible, then Linda Masters won't want to pay me, and I need the money. I'm still two and six short of Mam's birthday present.'

Turning the corner into Derwent Street, she paused to take a breath. 'It wouldn't be so bad if her birthday wasn't on Christmas Eve, because then I'd only have to find one present. But now I've to find two presents, *and* a Christmas present for Sally.' However, it was always worthwhile making the effort, and so far she had never failed to raise enough money to make the presents something special.

It was a real challenge. But, just like last year and all the years before, Jinnie had planned far enough in advance, doing odd jobs here and errands there, and when he could find work for her, she helped Eric on the farm – that was the best time of all! She really liked Eric. In fact, she liked him so much she sometimes wished he would ask her mammy to marry him. She knew Louise liked him a lot, because she had seen them talking together and after he'd gone, her mammy would watch him walk away and there would be a dreamy look in her eyes . . . kind of contented and sad, all at the same time.

Eric would look after them. Jinnie was sure of it. And oh, it would be so wonderful to have a dad, though that would never make her forget the 'good man' her mammy had always told her about. But sadly, he wasn't here, and Eric was. Besides, if Eric and Louise *did* get married, she was sure her own daddy in heaven would approve.

Realising she was beginning to dawdle, she put a spurt on. 'I bet Linda's got the kettle on and the bread buttered, and they're all waiting for their teas.' The thought made her groan. 'I'll cop it if the fish and chips are stone cold when I get there!'

From the downstairs front room where she and Sally were putting up some new curtains, Louise saw Jinnie run past the bottom of the street. 'Just look at that child!' Her face lifted in a smile. 'I wonder what she's up to *now*?'

Handing her the second curtain, Sally came to look, but Jinnie was long gone. 'If yer mean our Jinnie, she's doing errands to get the money for your presents – *that's* what she's up to.'

'Well, there's no need, I've told her before. I'm happy with whatever she gets me.'

Sally ambled across the room to the fireplace, where she arranged another knob of coal on the flames. 'The lass wants you to get the best that money can buy,' came the answer, 'so leave her be and hurry up with them curtains. I want to talk to you, afore our Jinnie comes in.'

'What about?' Straining her neck, Louise almost fell off the chair.

'This and that.' Sally had things on her mind that she needed to share.

'Nearly done.' It didn't take Louise long to hang the second curtain. 'What d'you think?'

'Hang on a minute, lass. Me fingers are all covered in coal.' Clapping her hands together, Sally watched the coal-dust fall into the hearth where it settled like black snow on the tiles.

Taking up the fire-brush, she flicked the dust under the grate. 'Right then, let's see!'

Groaning as she straightened up, Sally turned her head to examine the new curtains. 'Oh, yes.' Pale blue with darker blue flowers, they made a pretty sight. 'Very nice.' She nodded approvingly. 'They go well in this room, I must say.'

Kept for best, the front room of the house in Derwent Street was small and cosy, with varnished picture-rails hung with seascape prints, and a tiny Victorian fireplace, dressed with pretty floral tiles. Arranged round the hearth was a small sofa covered in cream and blue material, and two dark leather armchairs, got for a pound each from the sales room in town. 'What will you do with them?' Sally pointed to the discarded heap of curtains on the floor.

Louise clambered off the chair. 'I'll ask about,' she said, 'see if anybody could make use of them.' Holding up the old brown curtains, she grimaced. 'I don't know how we managed to put up with them for all these years. They're *awful*.'

Leading the way into the passage and on, into the kitchen, Sally had her answer ready. 'We put up with 'em 'cause we didn't have enough money to buy a new pair,' she reminded Louise. 'An' if it weren't for you working all hours up at the farm with Eric, I don't suppose we'd have been able to afford a new pair of curtains for another five years! My pension wouldn't run to it, an' that's for sure.' Looking back from the kitchen door, she asked, 'Tea or coffee, is it, lass? Though how yer can drink that Nescafé stuff, I will never know.'

Seeing how pale Sally was, and how she seemed to be breathing hard, Louise cupped her hand under the old woman's elbow and declared firmly, 'You go and sit down. I'll get the drinks.'

'I'm not too feeble to put a kettle on, lass!' Though if truth were told, Sally didn't feel all that grand. Still, it wasn't her way to worry other folk, especially Louise, so with a wag of the finger, she soundly chided her. 'The way you mollycoddle me, anybody'd think I were on me last legs.'

While the kettle was boiling, Louise stole a glance at the old dear. It made her smile to see Sally making herself busy brushing the hearth from where she sat, her face now pink from the glow of heat. 'Have you got worms or what?' she reprimanded her. 'You can't sit still for a minute, can you, eh?'

Leaning back in her chair, Sally chuckled. 'Stop spying on me! And get a move on wi' me drink, afore I die o' thirst.' When at last she got her tea, she cupped it awhile then she sipped, and now she cupped it again. 'By, lass. That were worth waiting for, an' no mistake,' she nodded in satisfaction.

Seated in the opposite armchair, Louise glanced round the room. 'We'll have to start in here as soon as we can afford it,' she declared. 'I'd like to make a clean sweep right through the house – new carpet and lino, new furniture – oh, and lovely new curtains for the bedrooms.' Leaning back in the chair, she joked, 'At this rate, I'll be drawing *my* old age pension before it gets done.'

Sally had other ideas. 'D'you know, Lou, I like this room the way it is.'

Louise smiled sympathetically. 'I know what you mean, and you're right.' Somewhat jaded with its papered walls and worn lino, this little room was always a delight to be in. The furniture had seen better days, but it was good, solid stuff. The chairs were comfortable and the atmosphere embracing – and what better company could they have than each other?

'Still, it might be nice to have all new,' Louise mused aloud. 'I've seen some really pretty three-piece suites in that shop at the top of King Street.' A mood of contentment washed over her. Sitting here chatting to Sally, with the glow from the fire warming her toes, she felt grateful, though it was strange the way fate gave with one hand and took away with the other.

Sally noticed her thoughtful expression. 'What's on yer mind, lass?'

Louise shook her head. 'Nothing.' Then she corrected herself. '*Everything.*'

'Do you want to talk about it?'

Louise sat up. 'Not really.'

'Well, *I've* got summat to say.'

Louise had seen it coming. 'It's about our Susan, isn't it?'

Sally nodded affirmatively. 'Yer haven't mentioned her lately.' She lived in hope. 'Does that mean you've changed yer mind about going to see her?'

''Fraid not, Sally.' Louise had not forgotten. How could she? 'The only reason I haven't mentioned her, is because I've been trying to decide what to do for the best.'

'Don't go, lass – that'll be for the best.'

'I *have* to go.' Louise hated disappointing the old woman but she had to make her understand. 'If I don't, she's bound to come here, and you know what that means? I don't want her coaxing her way round Jinnie. She's up to no good, I'm sure of it.'

'Write to her instead.'

'That won't do it. She'll still come after Jinnie.' One thing was certain: 'Somehow or another, I'll have to stop her in her tracks.'

'It seems whatever I say, you're still intent on going to see her.'

'I've thought long and hard, and now my mind's made up.'

'I see.' The old lady sighed.

'Look, it'll be all right. I'll reason with her.'

'What if she won't listen? Happen the best way is to see a solicitor. After all's said and done, Jinnie's legally yours, and has been these past many years.'

'Susan's never been one to worry about who's in the right

and who's in the wrong,' Louise said ruefully. 'She'll not take notice of anything "legal". Besides, where would we get the money to pay for a solicitor?'

'Happen yer right, lass. Happen you should go and have it out with her – if you're sure there's no other way.'

Louise wasn't sure, but what else could she do in the circumstances? 'I'm more concerned about Jinnie than I am about Susan,' she confessed to her mother-in-law.

'In what way, lass?'

Louise shrugged, a look of apprehension on her face. 'Do I tell her about Susan . . . that she's really her mother and not me? Would it be too cruel if she was to learn the facts, about Susan and Ben, and how Susan went away only hours after she was born?'

Sally had been thinking along the same lines. 'If your sister does intend causing trouble, happen yer should tell the lass. Besides, it might be more cruel for her not to know.' This was the day Sally had long dreaded.

'Are you saying I should tell her now?' Louise's mouth had gone dry. It was a terrifying prospect.

'I don't know. It's for you to decide. Oh lass, I know it'll be painful for her, but she's a sensible creature, contented with her lot. All she needs is her home and her family, and to know that we love her. Besides, she's allus known you as her mammy. As far as I can see, nothing will ever change that.'

Louise hoped Sally was right, but, 'The thing is, now that Susan seems to have got it into her head that she still has some kind of rights to Jinnie, how can I be sure she won't get in first and tell her the truth, and hope to swing the girl's affections in her direction?' Suddenly, Louise felt threatened, more so than at any other time in her life.

'That's why you must think about telling her', the old lady said gently, 'and because of what Susan said in that letter, it had best be sooner, rather than later.'

'I will tell her, Sally, I promise. But not yet.'

'Don't leave it too long, lass. There are other folk who know about Susan. Like me, they might be old in the tooth and a bit addled, and they could just blurt summat out one day, without meaning to – and the cat will be out of the bag afore you know it.'

'I want to do right by Jinnie, that's all.'

Sally cogitated, weighing it all up. She could see what a state her beloved daughter-in-law was in. 'Mebbe you shouldn't tell the lass anything at all for now. Go and see Susan if you must, an' keep her away if yer can. But be careful. She's a cunning little bugger, for all she's yer own flesh and blood.'

Louise turned Sally's advice over in her mind. 'Don't you worry. I'm a match for our Susan, especially where Jinnie's concerned.'

'So, when d'yer mean to go and see her?'

'This coming Saturday.' Louise had it all worked out. 'Eric's already promised Jinnie she can have a day's work on Saturday, so she'll be content enough to think I've gone shopping. If all goes well, I should be back before she gets home.'

'D'yer want me to come with yer?' Sally clenched a tiny fist. 'If the bugger starts any trouble, I'll be in there like a flash!'

Louise smiled at the offer. 'Best not, eh? But thanks all the same.' The thought of Sally being 'in there like a flash' was an image she could hardly contain.

With the talking over for now, Sally clambered out of her chair and wandered across the room to the dresser, where she took out a paper-bag. Returning to her chair, she opened the bag and offered it to Louise. 'There you go, pet, have a humbug,' she said. 'It'll help settle yer mind.'

Louise thanked her and, digging deep into the paper-bag, drew out a brown and white striped humbug of the strong sort.

She popped it in her mouth, and saw Sally do the same. For a long while the two women sat, cuddled into their armchairs, contentedly sucking at their humbugs; Sally with her arms crossed and her gaze focused on the dancing flames in the fire. Opposite her, Louise kept her affectionate gaze on Sally, thinking how cosy it all was.

Suddenly, a smile spread over her face, then she gave a little chuckle. The sound made Sally look up and ask worriedly, 'What's to do, lass?'

'I was just thinking how lucky we are, you and me,' Louise explained. 'How we've always been able to share our troubles, and now here we are . . . sharing a bag of humbugs.'

Sally widened her eyes. 'I've a box o' snuff tucked away an' all if yer fancy some?' When she saw the expected look of horror on Louise's face, she burst out laughing, and Louise soon joined in.

'Life can't be all that bad,' she giggled. 'Not when you've got a friend with humbugs and snuff to share.'

Though she could hardly talk for laughing at her own joke, Sally had to agree.

And for that precious minute, their worries were put aside.

Chapter Five

'THERE GOES A man who should never have been set free.'

The two prison wardens lingered at the main gates of the prison, each with their penetrating gaze on the swaggering man who walked away, his coat flung over his shoulder and his fist thrust deep into his pocket, for all the world as if he was out on a Sunday stroll.

The older of the prison officers shook his head. 'Terry Harpur's a bad lot, all right – but he'll be back, and for a longer stretch. His sort always are.'

From a distance, the man turned, his face twisted into an evil grin. Raising his arm he waved, sniggering out loud when the two men looked at him with disgust and went back inside. 'That's it, you bastards!' he yelled after them. 'Lock yourselves inside where you belong!' Then he quickened his footsteps, 'I'm on my way, Mam,' he said under his breath. 'Your darling son Terry is on his way home.'

At the end of the street he caught a tram. Settling himself into the seat he caught sight of his image in the window. 'Sorry, Mam, but seeing as you never came to visit, you might be shocked at the change in your little lad,' he sneered. 'My hair's receding and I've lost a couple of teeth . . . oh, an' there's a scar or two on my pretty face.'

He recalled the fierce fights he'd had inside, before he got wise and buckled down to do his stretch as quickly and painlessly as possible. Bastards!, he thought viciously. There's allus some clever sod who thinks he can get the better of you. Well, I learned how to look after myself in that place, and now I reckon I can look after myself *any* place I go.

'Fares, please!' The conductor made his way through the tram. 'Have the right change ready, if you please.'

Terry had the few pounds and a number of coins he'd been given on release. After checking the tram's destination, he asked the price of the fare.

'Return or one way?' The conductor's brusque manner irritated his passenger.

'One way,' Terry snapped. 'I certainly don't intend coming back *here*!'

'One way it is.' The conductor had picked up many a released prisoner from the stop near the prison. Some were well-mannered; others, like this one, were best left alone. Eager to be on his way down the tram, he took Terry's money, ran off the ticket and after handing it to him, was away without a backward glance; though he did sneak a crafty look on his return. There's a nasty piece of work you wouldn't want to meet down a dark alley, he thought to himself.

The conductor was relieved when Terry got off near Montague Street. 'See you around,' the man told him – in such a way that the conductor was left wondering if it was a veiled threat of some kind.

Sarah's address was only a short distance from the tram stop. Terry looked up and down the street. 'Bloody dump!' he muttered. 'What did me mam ever want to stay here for?'

'Who yer lookin' for, mister?' A snotty-nosed boy with a dog straddled Terry's path. Small-built, with fiery hair and striking green eyes, he had the look of a warrior about him.

Gesturing with his thumb, Terry snarled, 'Get out the way!'

The boy was persistent. 'If you're looking for somebody, I can help you, 'cause I know 'em all down here.' Despatching a dewdrop with the cuff of his sleeve, he went on, 'It'll cost yer though. I don't do owt for nowt.'

'What makes you think I need the help of a little toe-rag like you, eh?'

'Like I say . . . 'cause I know everybody.'

'D'you know a woman called Sarah?'

'I might.'

'She's old – fifty odd. Got a couple o' kids in her charge.'

The boy held out a grubby hand. 'Give us a shilling then.'

'You what?' Terry gave him a hard stare. 'You'd best bugger off, afore I kick your arse!'

'You do, an' my dad'll kick *your* arse!'

'You'd best fetch him then, hadn't you?'

The boy shuffled uncomfortably, a trace of sadness in his voice. 'He's gone away.' Slowly he looked up and squaring his little shoulders, announced proudly, 'I'm the man of the house now.'

Terry was not moved by his bravado. 'Right then, "man of the house" . . . clear off out of it.' Bending his neck he stared the lad in the face. '*Now* . . . if you know what's good for you!'

'What if I set me dog on yer?'

'What? That bundle o' snot?' Straightening up, Terry looked the dog over; a mangy little thing with soulful eyes and its head cocked to one side as it stared curiously back up at him. Laughing out loud, he pushed the boy aside. 'The pair of you make me shiver in me shoes.'

As he continued down the street, he could hear the boy calling after him, 'Okay, mister, 'ave it your own way! But I'll stay here just in case you need me. Tell yer what . . . I'll mek it a tanner instead of a shilling.'

Behind his back, Terry made a 'V' sign, and to his horror, the dog growled, as if he meant it. Having a fear of marauding dogs, he quickened his steps. After finding the number he was searching for, he stood outside the house, frustrated by the graffiti-covered front door and boarded-up windows. 'What the devil's all this about? It's the right street,' he muttered, 'the right house too, so now what?' Having planned his journey to the last detail, he was angry, and confused as to what he should do next.

His gaze was drawn to the neighbour's house; the door was slowly opening. After an agonising moment, an old man with white hair and a crooked back emerged. 'Can I help you, son?'

Terry took a step towards him. 'I'm looking for me mam,' he explained impatiently. 'I've been . . .' he checked himself. 'I've been away, d'you see? Look, I've got her address and everything.' Handing the piece of paper to the old man, he urged, 'According to that, I've not made a mistake, have I? It *is* this street, ain't it? And that must be the house.' He pointed to the empty property.

'Mmm. Let's see now.' Holding the piece of paper close to his face the old man, whose name was Arthur Willis, screwed his eyes into tiny pinpoints as he read it. 'Aye lad, you've got the right address, but there ain't nobody living there no more.' He handed the paper back to Sarah's son. 'Seems to me you've had a wasted journey.'

'It can't be!' Terry had recovered from the shock, and now anger was taking its place – anger against the system which had given him this old address, and against his mother for not being here where she should be. 'Her name's Sarah,' he explained. 'She's my mam. She were looking after my kids while I were away.'

'I see.' Showing a set of false teeth too large for his shrunken mouth, the old man grinned. 'So you've been away, 'ave yer?'

Terry squared himself. 'That's what I said, ain't it?'

'Aye lad, it's what yer said right enough.' Arthur Willis decided to guard his tongue. It was plain as the nose on your face that this man had been in prison; in fact one night when Sarah had sat and had a drink too many with him, she had let slip about the son she feared, and how she meant to guard the children against him.

'Well?'

'She ain't 'ere,' he answered flatly. 'She's gorn.'

Terry took another step forward, his unshaven face too close for comfort to the old man's. 'Gone where?'

Arthur shrugged. 'Can't tell you. We was all told that our terrace was goin' to be pulled down, and we all had notice to quit. I refused to go, and then the plans fell through but Sarah, she went straight off. Took the kids with her.'

Terry considered this for a minute, his instincts telling him that the neighbour had no reason to lie. 'But she never told you where she was going, eh? Never told nobody else neither, I shouldn't wonder.' He snorted. 'She always were a cunning old bag.'

'I allus found her pleasant enough.' In fact, since his missus had gone these past twelve months, Sarah had been a real godsend. 'Mind you, she had her troubles, poor soul.'

'Oh?' Terry's ears pricked up. 'And what troubles might they be?'

'Mostly money troubles. She found it hard to mek ends meet.'

'I should have thought the lad would be earning after school. There's work enough of a weekend, ain't there?'

'Now there's a fine lad!' Arthur Willis had the highest regard for Adam. 'Used to run errands all over the place for a threepence. Aye, an' he didn't mind dirtying his hands when needs must, neither. He'd spend all Sat'day collecting newspapers, then he'd tek 'em to the paper-mill for whatever he could get. He were like a dog wi' two tails, so long as he could fetch his gran a bob or two.'

'You reckon he's a hard worker then, d'you?' Terry's eyes lit up at the thought of his son fetching home a pay-packet.

'Oh, he'll never be a lazy lad, will that one. In my opinion, he'll do very well for himself. He's an intelligent lad, an' he knows how to sort a shilling from a penny.' Suddenly curious, the old fella asked, 'The lad'll be starting work full-time soon, won't he?'

'The sooner the better.' In fact, Terry wasn't sure of Adam's true age, but then it wasn't surprising, when that bitch of a mother of theirs had taken full charge of the bairns! Still and all, he had had no love for them and Maggie knew it only too well.

'Well, as far as I can see, you need have no worry about the lad.' Because he was lonely the old man was beginning to warm towards the stranger. It was a long time since he'd enjoyed a conversation with anybody. 'In fact, if it weren't for the lad earning a bob or two whenever he got the chance, I reckon they'd have been put out of the house long since.'

'And you're sure you don't know where they've gone?' Unlike the old man, Terry wasn't all that bothered whether his family were all right or not. All he was concerned about was himself.

'Nope.' Arthur shook his head. 'I've no idea at all, more's the pity.' If he *had* known, he might have taken a tram and visited. What's more, he believed he'd have been assured of a warm welcome. When his visitor began pacing up and down like a tiger in a cage, he began to feel sorry for him. 'Look, son, you'll find her, I'm sure. Meanwhile, yer welcome to come inside and join me in a cuppa tea.' He winked. 'I might even find a drop of beer if I look hard enough. What d'yer say?'

'By rights, I should get after 'em.' Though the chilly nip in the air might warrant a few minutes beside a cheery fire, and a drop of hot liquid down his throat wouldn't go amiss neither.

'Aw, come on, son. I'll find the address of yer mam's landlord, if yer like. Happen he might know where they've gone. I admit it don't seem likely, seeing as he were the one as tried to throw us out on the street, but if yer ask me, these bloody landlords are all in each other's pockets. So, it must be worth a try.'

For a long minute Terry Harpur regarded the old man, his brain ticking over with nasty thoughts – of how the fella might let slip a snippet of information – though he seriously doubted whether he knew enough to help him find his witch of a mother. But then, with a bit of luck, the senile old bugger just might have a few quid tucked away.

'Go on then.' He smiled winningly. 'You've twisted me arm.'

As Arthur led him inside, he chatted merrily away. 'It's been a long time since I had company, but I haven't forgotten how to treat a visitor. Afore she had to leave, yer mam used to pop in now an' then. In fact, she'd do the washing an' ironing when it got too much for me. She's a good sort, is your mam . . . not a bad-looking woman neither.' He chuckled. 'By! If I were younger I might have set me cap at her mesel'.'

'Hmph! It wouldn't have done you much good, old fella, 'cause she's not all that fond of men.' Sauntering through the door into the tiny living room, Terry threw himself into the armchair. 'She were wed to "the best bloke in the world" for too many years, you see, and no other fella can live up to 'im.'

'Aye, well, I'm glad to hear it.' Going to the kitchen

door, Arthur asked, 'Is it beer yer wanting, or a cuppa tea?'

'Beer.'

Terry's host chuckled. 'I can see yer a man after me own heart.'

While the old man shuffled about in the kitchen, Terry got out of the chair and sneaked across the room, where he rifled through the dresser drawers. Nothing doing there. He slid his hand under the runner, but found nothing there either. Noiselessly opening the left-hand cupboard, he spied a tobacco pouch, which he quickly opened and there, much to his wicked delight, next to a wad of tobacco, was a bundle of old pound notes secured with a rubber band. 'Crafty old sod!' Stuffing the money into his trouser pocket, he replaced the pouch exactly as he'd found it and hurried back to his chair, where he was sitting relaxed when the old man returned.

'There y'are. I ain't got no glasses, but it tastes just as good out of a mug. So, get it down yer!' Handing him a mug of beer, Arthur Willis then settled himself into the other armchair, and resumed their conversation. 'No, son, yer mam's 'ad her troubles, tek it from me. Many's the time she's 'ad to hide from the rent man.'

Sarah's son took a great gulp of the beer, smacking his lips and promising, 'Don't you worry, old fella, I'll track her down, and when I do, I'll . . .' His eyes narrowed meaningfully, but when he felt the old man's gaze on him, he winked. 'I'll take good care of her, you see if I don't.'

'Good lad.' Arthur nodded with approval. 'I'm about to light up me pipe. I've a wad o' spare baccy, an' another old pipe, if you're interested?' Without waiting for Terry's answer, he disentangled himself from his chair and began to make his way across the room, towards the dresser. 'It's not often I light up these days,' he confided, 'but it's not often I get a visitor neither, so I reckon it's a special occasion.'

Horrified that the old man would discover he'd been robbed, Terry leaped out of his chair. 'Thanks for the offer,' he said calmly, 'only I need to find me mam, afore it gets dark.'

'Aye, 'course yer do, son.' Arthur was mortified. 'I should have known better than try and keep you 'ere, only I get lonely, y'see. It's a real treat to have company.'

Putting his arm round the old chap's shoulders, Terry said fondly, 'See me to the door, eh?'

They went to the front door together, the old man in front and his visitor bringing up the rear. 'You will come an' see me again, won't yer?' Poor lonely Arthur needed reassuring.

'You just try and stop me.' Terry secretly congratulated himself on being the smoothest liar on God's earth.

On the outer step they shook hands. 'You'll not forget to give yer mam my regards, will yer? I should 'ave told yer before, me name's Arthur – Arthur Willis. She'll know who you mean, right enough.'

'I promise, Mr Willis.'

'Are yer all right, son?'

'In what way d'you mean?'

'I mean, 'ave yer got money enough for summat to eat, an' tram fares, an' all that?'

'It's kind of you to consider me, and well . . .' It was on the tip of his tongue to tap the old man for as much as he could get, until he remembered that he'd probably already stolen every penny the old git had ever saved. 'No, I'll manage well enough, but I'm grateful for the asking.'

'Look, lad, I've a bit put away for a rainy day. I can't leave meself penniless, you understand?' Arthur put a comforting hand on the young man's shoulder. 'All the same, I'd be a sorry creature if I couldn't spare a bob or two for a friend in need.'

'Nah, you've no need to wory, Arthur, 'cause I've a bob or two myself. Look 'ere.' Dipping into his pocket, Terry drew out the old man's own wad of notes. Waving it under his nose he grinned wickedly. 'I reckon you've helped me enough already, don't you, Arthur?'

Confused, the old man fixed his attention on the wad of notes. It looked uncomfortably familiar, old and worn, and secured with an elastic band top and bottom. For a long, agonising minute he refused to believe what was before his eyes. At length he uttered five desolate words and the truth gradually sank in. *'You stole it from me!'*

'That's very clever of you, Arthur, and yes, that's exactly what I did. *I stole your money.*' Enjoying the old man's discomfiture, he chucked him under the chin, and murmured, 'And there ain't a thing you can do about it, 'cause if you open your mouth to anybody . . . anybody at all . . . I'll just have to come back one dark night, and button-up that big mouth of yours, once and for all.'

Terry gave a harsh cruel laugh, his eyes bulging as they stared back at the old man. 'Don't look so shocked you, old fool. You must have guessed by now: I'm a bad lot, and I can't deny it.'

Arthur Willis stared at him a moment longer, until his tired eyes glazed over. Then he turned away and quietly closed the door.

Through the letter-box, Terry could see him walking down the passage, shoulders bent and footsteps dragging along. 'Remember what I said!' He kept his voice just low enough so as not to be overheard. 'Keep your trap shut, or I'll be back!'

He went away whistling, and even had the gall to pass the time of day with the boy and his mongrel. 'If I were looking to rent a house,' he asked, 'who'd be the best person to see?'

'Alan Martin owns most of the property round here.' The boy held out his grubby little hand. 'That'll be a tanner, if yer please.'

'Worth every penny, I reckon.' Terry handed him a sixpenny piece. 'Now bugger off afore I kick yer arse.' He watched the boy run down the street with the dog at his heels. 'Little villain,' he muttered, but he smiled all the same. 'I'm buggered if he ain't a man after my own heart.'

Inside the house, the old man knelt beside the open cupboard. The pouch was open on his knees, and the baccy lay strewn across the floor. He didn't cry, or moan. He didn't make any noise or movement. Instead, he just sat there, his face grey with shock.

And all he could think of was his poor friend, Sarah.

PART TWO

AUTUMN, 1963
THE VISIT

Chapter Six

Louise was in a hurry. 'Come on, Jinnie, move yourself.' 'All right, all right.' The girl's voice sailed down from the upper regions of the house. 'I'm being as quick as I can. It still feels like the middle of the night to me!'

From the foot of the stairs, Louise went to the peg behind the front door and took down her winter coat. She put it on, took her gloves out of the pocket then instinctively thrust them back again. They only had ten minutes to catch the six o'clock tram. She didn't want Jinnie finding her own way to Eric's, but she couldn't wait much longer.

She thought of her errand and of how vitally important it was. She *must* have enough time to talk things through properly with their Susan. Louise had it all planned right down to the last detail. She would go on the tram to Salmesbury with Jinnie, to Maple Farm, where she would leave her in Eric's capable hands, then she'd catch the early bus into Blackpool, in order to get to Susan's café by breakfast-time and be back in Derwent Street before Eric brought Jinnie home.

'*Jinnie!*' Hurrying past the stairs into the living room, she called up again. 'If you're not down in two minutes, I'll have to go without you.'

In the living room, Sally was on hand with a cup of tea. 'You've time enough to gulp that down. It's blowing a cold wind out there.' She caught sight of Louise's coat flung open to the hem. 'An' do yer coat up, afore you catch yer death.'

Supping the tea, Louise paced up and down. 'I need to catch that early tram if I'm to see her delivered safely to Eric.'

'Yer told Eric where you'd be going today, didn't yer?'

'You know I did.' Sometimes Sally forgot things; more often than not these days, bless her old heart.

'An' he offered to collect the lass from here, didn't he?'

Louise groaned. 'All right, I know what you're getting at. You're saying I should have accepted his offer, then I wouldn't be panicking now?'

'Well – didn't yer accept his offer?'

'Because he does more than enough for this family as it is, and I don't want him to think I'm taking advantage of his good nature.'

Sally rolled her eyes. 'Oh, I see.'

'*What?*'

'Yer thinking, if yer accept too many favours, he'll begin to hope the two of youse might get together after all.'

'Something like that, yes.'

'An' what would be so wrong wi' that, eh? He thinks the world of you, so he does.'

Groaning, Louise put her empty cup on the table. 'Please, Sally, don't let's get into all that again.'

But the old woman persisted. 'Oh, lass! You'll never have a life, if you don't let go of the past.'

'You know it's not that.' A look of sorrow shadowed the young woman's pretty eyes. 'It's the past won't let go of *me*.'

Stabbed to the heart, Sally regretted having raised the subject. 'Oh, I'm sorry, lass. It's this big gob o' mine. I can't seem to keep it shut.' Going to her daughter-in-law she put an arm round her shoulders. 'I'll not mention it ever again.'

'Right, Mam, I'm ready!' Rushing into the room, Jinnie

looked incredibly grown-up in her blue beret and woollen coat.

'Best get your wellies from the back door in case it rains, and for goodness sake, hurry, my girl. We've only minutes to spare.'

'Louise, yer still haven't done yer coat up.' Fetching a carrier bag for Jinnie's wellies, Sally pointed to the big bone-buttons on the younger woman's coat, looking on with satisfaction when she did as she was told.

'Honest to God.' Louise had to smile. 'You'd think I were no older than Jinnie, the way you go on at me.' But it was comforting all the same, to know that she too, had an older loved one to look after her.

'We're all here to look after each other,' Sally seemed to read her thoughts.

Another minute and they were hurrying down the passage to the front door; Jinnie in front, Louise in the middle and old Sally bringing up the rear. 'Keep away from the bull in that back field,' Sally warned the girl. 'I've heard how he can run faster than the wind when he's got his sights set on summat tasty.'

'I will.' Jinnie knew how her grandma worried.

'Bye then, lass.'

'Bye, Gran.' At the door, Jinnie gave the old womam a kiss. 'See you later.'

As Jinnie started her way down the street, Sally took Louise aside. 'Mind how you tackle that sister o' yourn,' she warned. 'She's caused you enough heartache already. If she starts laying down the law, you put her right, my girl! Make sure she knows the lass is rightfully yours, and that she's to stay away. You tell her that, an' don't take any nonsense from 'er!'

'I can't afford to,' Louise answered, her gaze drawn to Jinnie, who was waiting at the end of the street. 'There's too much at stake.'

'Come 'ere, lass.' Sally opened her arms and Louise went into her gentle embrace. 'Just mind how yer go, eh?'

Louise promised she would. 'If all goes to plan, I should be back about five.'

'I'll be watching out for yer then.'

There was no more time to linger, so Louise waved cheerio and went at the run to where Jinnie was waiting. The two of them rounded the corner at full pelt, and Sally waved until they were out of sight. 'My lovely lasses,' she whispered. 'God keep yer safe.'

⟶▸•◦•◂⟵

IT WAS SIX forty-five by the time Louise and Jinnie got off the tram at Scab Lane, and another ten minutes on foot before they reached Maple Farm. From the distance they could see Eric hard at work by the big barn.

'Aren't I the lucky man, with two lovely ladies to visit me?' Tall and smiling, his brown hair blown by the breeze, Eric was busy chopping wood. Clad only in shirt and woollen waistcoat, he seemed not to feel the cold at all.

While his arm went round Jinnie, his warm, penetrating gaze was on Louise's quiet smile. 'Have you time to stop for a brew?' He knew where she was going, and he knew Jinnie was unaware of the errand.

Her heart beating fifteen to the dozen, Louise shook her head. 'I need to get to the shops,' she lied. 'Before the crush.' She had told Jinnie she was going shopping.

Grabbing his jacket from the barn-door, Eric threw it on, his skin hard and browned by the many summers he'd worked outdoors. 'I'll walk you up to the main road.'

'There's no need.' Whenever he was near, Louise felt that she was losing control.

He gave her a lopsided smile. 'There's every need.'

84

Knowing she couldn't change his mind when he was determined, Louise allowed herself to be bullied. Giving Jinnie a hug, she told her, 'Do as Eric asks you, and no climbing the tall trees like last time!' She could remember the occasion when she herself had got stuck up an apple tree in the orchard, and Ben had had to come and rescue her. This place, Maple Farm, was full of such memories. 'And remember what your grandma told you.'

Eric chuckled at that. 'Sally been frightening her about the old bull, has she?' His smile faded when he looked now at Jinnie. 'She's right though. He's got a powerful bad temper, so don't you go anywhere near him. Is that understood, young lady?'

Jinnie nodded. 'Can I chop some of this wood while you're walking Mam back to the road?'

'Not on your life, no! That axe is sharp enough to slice your foot off in one swipe.' For good measure he took the axe and swung it up into the rafters. 'I tell you what you can do though.'

'What's that?'

Pointing to the stable he told her, 'You can put Candy out in the front field if you like. The foal Ringo will go after her, so you've no need to put a lead on him.' He knew how frisky a foal could be. 'Stay on the right side of Candy,' he warned. 'That'll keep you out of harm's way.'

'I know.' Being fond of the old mare and particularly her foal, Jinnie didn't need asking twice. 'I've done it before, don't forget.' She ran into the stable, where she could be heard chattering excitedly to the horses.

As they strolled back to the main road, Eric confided, 'Come Christmas, I intend making her a gift of the foal, if that's all right with you?'

Louise thought it was a lovely idea and said so.

'Right, that's settled then. And it goes without saying that she can keep him here. What's more, it won't cost her a penny.' Eric grinned. 'Though I might expect her to brew the tea while we're up to our neck in work.'

Louise laughed. 'You're a hard taskmaster, Eric Forester!'

Inevitably the conversation touched on Susan, and the reason for Louise's visit to Blackpool. 'You'll have to drum it into her head that she has no say in Jinnie's future now.' Eric was almost as anxious about Susan's intentions as Louise and Sally were. 'She deserted her and you took the child on as your own, as she asked you to in the letter she left with the bairn. The law is on your side. Remember that.'

'I will.'

When a few moments later the bus arrived, he took hold of her hand. 'Are you sure you don't want me to come with you?'

'Thanks, Eric, but it'll be best if I see her on my own.'

'I expect you're right. If she starts on you, I wouldn't be able to hold my tongue.'

Warmed by his concern, she climbed onto the bus and when she looked back out of the window, he was still standing there, and her heart was full.

If only things could be different, she thought. If only she could give herself to Eric, life would be so wonderful.

Chapter Seven

NORMALLY, ON AN autumn day, Blackpool would be cold and blustery. Today though, it was surprisingly pleasant. Coming off the bus at the terminal, Louise walked to the railings above the sea and raised her face to the skies, letting the wind play on her face. It was a good feeling.

Down below on the beach, it was almost deserted, yet despite it being out of season, there were always the few who were willing to brave the elements. Two middle-aged men with huge bellies could be seen splashing about in what must have been a freezing cold sea. Beyond them, a few boats were bobbing about on the waves, and on the sands, a smattering of late holidaymakers, coats on and collars up, were taking in the view.

After a moment or two, Louise walked down the promenade, her gaze drawn by the amazing display of lights hanging above her head; strung from lamp to lamp to lamp and covering the entire promenade, it was like a Wonderland. Some evening soon, the lights would be turned on and the scene would be magical, bringing visitors from all over Britain and abroad.

Passing by, a young woman with two children seemed angry and at the end of her tether. 'Come on, you two, get a move on,' she snapped. Taking them by the arms, she dragged them along. 'I've had enough o' you two buggers this morning!'

They both started crying at once, and the sound was frightening. 'It's no use you carrying on!' the mother yelled, and for good measure gave them each a smack on the ear. 'You're never bloody satisfied, that's the trouble! First, you want to come down the front and now you're down here, you want ice-cream and bloody donkey-rides. Well, you can't have them! For one thing the donkeys are away on their own holiday, and the ice-cream vans have shut down for the winter. What's more, I can't be made o' money, not when your randy sod of a father goes off with some tart from Pontins. But I'll tell you this, if he ever shows his face at our door again, he'll have a bucket o' water chucked over him. That should damp down his ardour, the filthy, no-good bastard!'

With the children crying as loudly as they could, she had to shout at the top of her voice. It was a real treat for the listening passers-by. Having arrived at the spot where she'd parked their Hillman Minx, the young woman shoved them into the back seat. 'Now bawl and cry all you like, 'cause we're going straight back to the caravan to get our things, then we're off home. I've had more than enough o' the lot of you! In fact, I've a good mind to leave you with your Auntie Tracey while I go off and have a fling of my own!'

By some unseen miracle, the children stopped crying, by which time their harassed mother had climbed into the front of the car, switched on the engine and set off down the street at breakneck speed, her voice sailing behind. 'That's shut you up, hasn't it, eh? You're not too fond of your Auntie Tracey, because she won't let you have your own way like I do. Anyway, now you've stopped your silly bloody racket, happen we'll call at the pier and see if the dodgems are still running. What d'you think to that, eh?'

The rousing cheer told all and sundry that the children thought it was a great idea.

Crossing the tramlines to get to the other side, Louise smiled to herself, but it was a quiet, reflective smile. Ahead, she could see the car turning into a side road. Poor thing, she thought, it sounds to me like she's had her share of troubles. But then, haven't we all? she mused. She thought of Ben and Susan and how they had deceived her; then she thought of herself and Eric, and it struck her that the errand she was on today was poetic justice.

And yet, out of all the intrigue and deception had come the lovely Jinnie. Whatever else happened, she would move heaven and earth to keep that darling girl out of Susan's clutches. But it was an odd thing, because when all was said and done, Jinnie *was* Susan's child. '*No!*' Startled by her own voice, she looked round to see if anyone had heard; and was greatly relieved when it became apparent that other people were too intent on their own errands to bother about her.

'You want to be careful, my girl,' she muttered to herself, 'or they'll be carting you off in a Black Maria.' Hurrying to avoid one of the handsome horse and traps that ran up and down the promenade for the transporting of holidaymakers, she kept her eyes peeled for the sign that would tell her she had found her sister's restaurant.

And suddenly there it was; a large modern building, constructed mainly of glass and timber. Straddling a busy corner, its upper facade was emblazoned in large red letters: *Jacob's Restaurant* (Proprietor: Susan Holsden)

Louise peeped inside, surprised to see that the place was already half-full with people heartily tucking into huge breakfasts, and frantic waitresses with frilly aprons flitting in and out of the tables, carrying trays piled high with food. In the background the tills were merrily ringing and there stood

Susan, hands on hips, surveying her kingdom with a satisfied smile on her face.

On seeing her sister, Louise quickly backed away. She had expected that Susan would be a changed person, older like herself, and maybe mellowed somewhat. But she still had that arrogant stance, and though it was obvious her hair had been dyed a darker colour, she was still very attractive – slimmer, more confident and, judging by the look on her face as she watched the waitresses rushing about and the tills rolling with money, she seemed still to have that feverish ambition to lord it over others.

A small thrill of fear washed through Louise; she felt incredibly nervous. How would she start the conversation? She mustn't lose her temper, that would be a foolish thing to do. Would she be able to stay calm and dispassionate? After all, she was fighting for Jinnie. 'But she's yours!' she told herself. Susan had no rights to her. Except for the initial few hours of her tiny life, the child had had no contact with her blood mother. But surely, there was a bond? All that time in the womb must have created some kind of closeness?

For a good ten minutes, Louise stood outside, out of sight, silently arguing with herself and at times, on the verge of turning away and going home. But she had never been a coward and could not become one now. 'Go in!' she murmured. 'Tell her to keep away.' Unpleasant though it might turn out, she had no choice.

But how would Susan greet her? Would she yell and scream and send her on her way without promising not to contact Jinnie? The prospect of it all going wrong was too much to contemplate.

'There's only one way to find out, my girl!' Nerves gave way to determination. Squaring her shoulders, Louise strode to the door and flung it open, her gaze reaching across the restaurant to where Susan had been. She was gone. The nervousness returned.

She crossed the room. Approaching the nearest till, she enquired of the pasty-faced girl with the pony-tail, 'Excuse me, is Susan Holsden about, please?'

'Who's asking?' The girl looked her up and down.

'Could you just tell her she has a visitor?'

'I can't see her about.' She stretched her thin bony neck to look round the restaurant then, as if everything outside of her duties was an ordeal, she casually shrugged. 'She were 'ere a minute ago, but now she's gone.'

'So, could you find her, please? It *is* important.'

Sighing, the girl shrugged again. 'Sorry, I'm serving. We're not allowed to leave the tills. Ask that woman there.' She pointed to a stout middle-aged woman wearing a pinnie and carrying a mop and bucket. 'Her name's Madge. She'll find her for you.' With that she leaned back in her chair and taking an emery board out of her pocket, began lazily filing her nails, while the woman who had come up behind Louise, stood waiting patiently to be served.

'*Margaret!*' Susan's angry voice sailed across the room. 'What on earth are you playing at? Can't you see there's a customer waiting?'

At the sound of her sister's voice, Louise swung round. 'It's my fault,' she explained. 'I was looking for you and—'

Shaken to see Louise there, Susan paused, but only for the briefest minute, before marching up to the girl. 'Go to my office,' she ordered. 'Wait for me there.' The look she gave her was lethal. While the girl sidled out of her chair, Susan squeezed past her to the till. 'Can I help you?' Addressing the customer with a smile, she took her bill and checked it, then she collected her money and gave her the necessary change, after which she bade her a cheery good day. 'I'm sorry for the delay. It won't happen again.'

When the woman seemed none too pleased, Susan offered her an enticement. 'Come straight to me the next time you're in,' she told her quietly, making sure no one overheard. 'I think we owe you a free meal.'

Content with that, the woman thanked her and departed.

Only then did Susan turn her attention to Louise. 'I half expected you to turn up,' she said. 'If you're hoping to change my mind about wanting Jinnie, I'm sorry, but you've come a long way for nothing.'

Louise was shocked that she seemed prepared to discuss it right there in front of all these people. 'Can't we talk somewhere privately?' she suggested sharply. 'You owe me that much.'

At first it seemed that Susan might not agree. She stared at her sister for what seemed an age, then beckoning the woman with the mop and bucket, she told her, 'Get your pinnie off, Madge, and take over on this till.'

The woman grinned from ear to ear. 'Ooh! Does that mean I've been promoted?'

'No, it does not.' Moving out, she let the woman in. 'But you did well enough when you stood in the last time, and anybody's better than Margaret . . . bloody daydream!'

'If I do well today, miss,' the homely-faced woman was hopeful, 'will you let me stay on the tills for good?'

Susan pointed to a young couple making their way over to the cash-desk. 'Tend to your customers, and I'll see how you go on today.' Beckoning for Louise to follow, Susan then marched across the room towards the door marked *Private*. 'I've a little matter to deal with first,' she told Louise. 'Then we'll talk if you like, but I'll tell you now, it's a waste of your time *and* mine. I want my daughter with me, where she belongs.'

Taking Louise into the office, she left her at the back of the room while she dealt with the pasty-faced girl. 'It's not the first time you've let me down,' she began, and when the girl opened her mouth to defend herself, Susan slammed her fist on the table, making her almost leap out of her skin. 'I do not want to know what you have to say,' she informed her. 'You're a lazy, bad-mannered, useless article, Margaret Hilton, and there's no place for you in my restaurant.'

By now the girl was sobbing.

Unmoved by her tears, Susan delivered another blow. 'What's more, I shall not be giving you a reference. I wouldn't want to offload you onto some other unsuspecting employer, like I was landed with you.'

'But I'll never get another job, not without a reference!' the girl blubbered.

'You should have thought of that when you were messing about in my time *and* dipping your fingers in the till. Oh, yes – don't think I don't know! I couldn't be absolutely sure, but I've kept an eye on you, and now I'm in no doubt whatsoever. By my reckoning, you've stolen at least ten pounds during this last week. By rights I should call the police, but I can't be doing with all that. Oh, but don't worry – it'll all be taken out of your wages.'

The girl was shaking. 'Please don't sack me. I won't do it again. I'm sorry, but me mam needed the money. I did it for her. It won't happen again, honest.'

'Huh! You're a liar as well as a thief, and if you ask me, I'm well shut of you.'

Opening a drawer in her desk, she took out a bag of money and counted a small sum into a brown envelope. She then filled out two forms and got the girl to sign both. 'There's your dues . . . minus what you've taken.' She pushed one of the forms, her other documents and the wage-packet towards her. 'Now get out!'

The girl walked out, her face streaming with tears. She deliberately left the office door open, and her voice could be heard all over the restaurant, and in the office as she shouted out: 'Rotten cow! I wouldn't work for her again, not if she were the last person on earth!'

Rounding the desk, Susan hurried to the door, but by then the girl had left the premises. 'No-good little bugger!' Slamming shut the door she returned her attention to Louise, who had watched the scene with a sinking heart. Susan hadn't changed one bit, and now she had her sights set on Jinnie. It was a frightening prospect.

'Right then.' Inviting Louise to sit down, she seemed hardly surprised when Louise refused. 'All right, let's have it then, sis.' Her smile was wicked. 'I expect you're here because I wrote that letter?'

'I'm surprised you need to ask.'

'And you think you can change my mind, is that it?'

'I hope to make you see sense, yes.'

'The only thing that makes sense is Jinnie coming to me. I am her mother, when all's said and done.'

Across the desk, Louise faced her defiantly. 'How did you know her name?'

When Susan stared back at her with a blank expression, she went on: 'Just now, you mentioned Jinnie. How did you know what we'd christened her?'

Her answer shocked Lousie to the core. 'That's easy. Our mam told me. Oh, I see you're surprised by that?' She was really enjoying herself. 'Oh yes, me and Mam have been keeping in touch for some time now . . . months, in fact.' Delighted by the astonishment on Louise's face, she said softly. 'So she never told you, eh?' Her features hardened. 'She knows how I feel about my daughter. She knows I'll get her back, whatever it takes. I've got money now, y' see – lots of it. I got wed to the old fella who owned this place. I worked for him and wormed my way into his affections.' She grinned. 'After he put a ring on my finger, he didn't last long, poor devil. You could say I loved him to death.'

She laughed out loud, and just as quickly her smile twisted into disgust. 'I can't say I enjoyed it as much as he did, but he died a happy man, and left me with all this.' She actually did a twirl right there on the spot. 'I've worked hard with this place,' she said proudly. 'You'll be pleased to know, I'm taking more money than he ever did.'

'Money isn't everything.' Louise was beginning to wonder if Susan was losing her mind. And as for her mam colluding with Susan, she'd be around to tackle Patsy and Steve Holsden soonever she could!

'Ah, but that's where you're wrong, sis.' Susan looked at her steadily. 'It means I can give Jinnie the best that money can buy – clothes, holidays abroad, records, make-up, a car when she's older, the best education in the country . . . What can *you* give her?'

'Love. And contentment.'

'There's no contest then is there?' Rounding the desk, Susan stood before Louise and stared her coolly in the face. 'Love only brings heartache and trouble, and contentment comes when you're dead. Whereas money can do anything! So, don't fight me, sis. Because if you push me into a corner, I'll buy the best lawyers there are, and I promise you'll wish you'd left well alone.'

'You don't frighten me, Susan, with your money and your threats.' Louise came closer, her eyes glittering bright and hard, as she regarded her sister's jubilant face. In a quiet, determined voice she told her, 'You can hire all the fancy lawyers you like, but nothing can change the fact that you deserted that baby just hours after you gave birth to her. You gave permission for me to adopt her . . . you signed the papers and you washed your hands of her. You left her on our bloody doorstep for heaven's sake!' She breathed deeply. 'Not even your expensive lawyers can explain *that* away!'

'I did what I had to.' Unnerved by Lousie's defiance, she

argued, 'I was ill. You *know* I was ill. What could I have given her then, eh? I went away from Blackburn with *nothing*! It was hard for me, coming here to Blackpool, trying to make a new life for myself. I didn't have anywhere to live or the means to look after her. I was desperate at the time . . . confused by everything that had happened. I didn't know what I was doing when I wrote that letter, and signed them papers.'

'Oh, you knew well enough what you were doing,' Louise said scornfully. 'By the time you signed the papers you'd already had time enough to settle yourself into a job, and you had a nice little flat on the promenade.'

'What the bloody hell would *you* know, eh?' The other woman's face was bright red. 'You don't know anything!'

'I know that you were looking after number one as usual. Oh, don't deny it, Susan. The police traced you and it was obvious you had feathered your nest nicely. No judge in the land would have allowed you to sign the papers if they thought you weren't of sound mind and body. No! You deliberately turned your back on that little girl, and even afterwards, when you'd had time enough to consider the implications of what you were doing, you never even hesitated once when you had the chance to sign her over to me permanently.'

'But I always wanted her. Even then, I wanted her!'

'I don't believe that. You didn't want her then, and you don't want her now. What you *want* is something to show off – your lovely, intelligent daughter, so's you can claim to have done something special in your otherwise shameful life. What you want is someone you can lord it over, and pretend to all and sundry that you're a decent, loving mother. What a sham! You just want to use her.'

'I don't know what you're talking about,' Susan said sulkily. For one fleeting minute she actually looked frightened.

'I'll tell you what I think, shall I? I think you have a plan, and that plan involves my Jinnie. I can't imagine what it is, but

I suspect it's summat nasty and underhand. You don't want her in your life because you love her, not for one minute.' Louise nodded thoughtfully, convinced that she had hit on some kind of truth. 'You're up to summat, Susan Holsden. You forget, I know you too well.'

'*Shut up*!' Susan leaned over the desk, her eyes lit with hatred. 'She's *mine*! Money talks and I've got plenty of it. You're a pathetic little nothing, Lou, and you always will be. You can't even come near to what I can do for her. I can send her to private school. She'll want for nothing.'

There was a moment of angry silence, before Louise asked quietly, 'Tell me, Susan. Do you love her?'

Her sister was visibly uncomfortable. ''Course I do.'

Louise studied her sister's face and saw the lies written there; it frightened her to think this woman might infiltrate Jinnie's young life. 'You're up to something, aren't you? I don't know what it is, but you're not getting anywhere near Jinnie. I'll see to that.'

'I *do* love her! I want to bring her up and take care of her, and do all the things with her that you've done over the years. I've really missed her.'

Louise didn't believe a word of it. 'You can dress it up any way you like,' she said, 'but the fact remains that Jinnie is *my* daughter now. Nothing you can do or say will ever change that.'

Susan smiled knowingly. 'I've got a fella now,' she lied. 'We're planning to get wed when the season finishes and I can shut down for the winter. That's why I've been biding my time, until I can be wed and then Jinnie will have a *proper* family – a mam and a dad. More than you can offer her, with your feeble old mother-in-law and a house too small to swing a cat round. I'll buy a nice, big house in Lytham. She'll have a better life with me, and it's no use you fighting me, 'cause I'll win the end. I always do.'

'Not this time, Susan.' Louise's voice was calm, when inside she was trembling. 'You gave up your right to Jinnie ten long years ago. And don't forget I have another, stronger claim on her. She's *Ben's* child, too . . . my husband's child. The man you stole for one night. You're a bad lot, Susan, and always will be. But you'll never get my daughter. I promise you that.'

'Huh! We'll have to see what Jinnie herself has to say about it, won't we, eh?' It was obvious from her trembling voice that she was less confident than before, but still adamant. 'I mean to have her Lou, so you'd best accept it. And besides, our mam knows where she belongs. I'm sure she'll help me. She'll speak up for me if needs be.'

'You don't worry me, Susan.' It was a blatant lie but Louise had to tell it. 'I came here to reason with you, but I see you're no different from before. You're cold and calculating, and you don't give a sod for Jinnie's well-being. You just want to take her away from me, like you took Ben, and like you wanted Jacob because you realised he preferred me – though you were always welcome to him. In your selfish, cruel way, you'd hurt Jinnie just to make *me* suffer.' She looked at her sister with disgust. 'Ever since we were little girls, you've always wanted everything I had – and most of the time you've managed to take it away from me.'

'And I'll do it again.'

'Oh no, you won't. Not this time.'

The thought of Jinnie put a smile on Louise's face. 'She's a wonderful girl, Susan . . . kind and thoughtful, and intelligent too.' *Everything Ben had been at one time.* 'She won't be fooled by the likes of you. Once I tell her about you, you'll be lucky if she gives you the time of day.'

'It's me that should never have given *you* the time of day!' Rushing across the room, Susan flung open the door. 'I want you out of here. But don't think you've heard the last of me,' she warned. 'I've decided I want my daughter in my life, and as far as I'm concerned, that's an end to it.'

Brushing past her at the door, Louise paused to look her in the eye. 'You'll never win her back,' she said softly. 'She'll see right through you. And like me, she won't care for what she sees.'

'Get out!'

As she went, Susan's voice followed her. 'Two can play at that game, Lou. Poison her mind against me, and I'll tell her things she should know about *you*. How, when her daddy was at his lowest ebb, you slept with his best friend. And what would she say, I wonder, if she knew you had an abortion when you found out you were carrying his child?'

Shocked and angry, Louise swung round. 'You liar! I lost that child through no fault of my own!'

Knowing she had struck a painful chord, Susan pressed on, showing no mercy. 'You know that, and I know it – but the girl won't know *what* to believe, will she, eh?'

Realising there was nothing to be gained by arguing, Louise turned away, her heart aching and her mind reeling from Susan's threats. And still her sister wasn't finished. 'Mam tells me the girl is close to Eric. If that's right, she'll be heartbroken to know how the two of you cheated on her daddy. And it won't matter what you tell her about me, it'll be the end of her little world, and that's when I'll step in to pick up the pieces.'

Louise looked up at her. So many disturbing thoughts were going through her mind just then, but she didn't speak. In that moment she had realised how her worst fears could come true. Susan meant everything she said, and there wasn't anything she could do about it.

She thought bitterly of her own naivety. She had come here, secure in the knowledge that she had the law on her side. Now though, it was past all that. Susan was doing what she was best at . . . playing with people's emotions, twisting words and events to put herself in the right, and others in the wrong. She was a master at it.

Sensing her desolation, Susan was unrelenting. 'You've lost her already, Lou. It's only a matter of time now before I take her away from you . . . just like I've always taken what was yours.'

Though Louise was not yet out the door, she roughly closed it on her sister, effectively pushing her out. Then she returned to her desk, to gloat on her cleverness. 'She were never a match for you,' she told herself proudly. 'And she never will be!'

⟫•◦•⟪

DEJECTED BUT NOT yet beaten, Louise strolled down to the promenade and leaned over the railing to view the scene below. Watching the waves rolling in and out against the shore had a soothing effect on her jangled nerves; and besides, she had a good hour or so before the next bus departed for Blackburn Town.

Intrigued by the playful antics of a family near the water's edge, she even found herself smiling. They seemed so happy, and were having so much fun, it did her heart good. For a time the two teenagers and the older woman took her mind off her problems. As they splashed and screamed in the shallows, with the woman flicking water at the two youngsters, the sound of laughter echoed across the beach. They ran and chased each other, and the woman paddled after them, her skirt hoisted above her knees, tucked into her bloomers.

It was a cheering sight; laughing heartily, she chased them across the beach, where they all fell in a heap on the sands, screeching and giggling and rolling about, though when a big black dog appeared from nowhere and joined in the fun, the woman got to her feet and the three of them ran back to the steps. For a while, the dog kept close to their heels, until its owner whistled and it shot off in the opposite direction.

Curious, Louise glanced up and down the sands, searching for the youngsters' parents, but could see no one who might fit the picture. 'Must be the grandmother,' she mused aloud. 'Or an aunt maybe.' She smiled wryly. 'Whoever she is, they enjoy her company, that's for sure.'

She couldn't resist watching the little trio for a while longer. She saw them wipe their feet and legs on a towel left by the wall, and wondered why they seemed to have only one towel between them, but it was of no consequence. Though when she saw them walk along by the wall and under the pier, she was astonished to see them disappear into what looked like a tent of sorts. A moment later, the woman emerged with a bowl. Going to the water's edge she emptied it into the sand and afterwards washed it in the sea.

'My God!' Louise was shaken by the realisation. 'They must be *living* there!' She knew, of course, that the beach gave shelter at night to tramps and other homeless people, but this was a *family*. There were youngsters involved!

'So, what d'you think you can do, Louise, my girl?' she asked herself cynically. 'Let's see now . . . you could offer them a bob or two – make them feel like beggars,' which they obviously were not, 'or you could take them home.'

She thought it through. 'All right, you might be able to put them up for a week or two, and then what? Take over their lives? Make yourself responsible for them – send the girl to secondary school and get work for the lad? And what about the woman? Do you think she'd take kindly to your charity, or would you be insulting someone who seems to have got it right? They've got a roof over their head and the sound of the sea in their ears when they wake of a morning; they've got the seagulls soaring overhead and the beach as their back yard. They're happy, and by the look of it, they're well fed.'

She felt ashamed. 'What are you thinking of?' She was angry with herself. 'What has it to do with you anyway? What makes you think you're an expert on how folks choose to live out their lives?' She gave a soft, sardonic laugh. 'I mean, you haven't done such a good job with your *own*, have you?'

She thought of all the mistakes she had made over the years, and how even now, she was caught up in a tangle of events that had been created by mistakes from the past. She thought of Eric and herself, and it broke her heart to acknowledge how lonely they both were; they loved each other yet could not be together because of what they had done and the guilt that threatened to keep them apart for ever.

Her mind went back to Susan and that awful meeting today. Her heart sank. She would need all her energy and wit to help her beat Susan and her dirty tricks. She thought of Jinnie, and wondered whether her sister really would be able to lure her away. 'I'll talk to Jinnie myself,' she decided. 'Sally was right. The lass needs to know, before Susan can fill her head with all manner of lies.' She prayed in her heart that Jinnie would understand that whatever had happened in the past – being born out of wedlock, the result of an adulterous fling between her father and her aunt – it didn't mean that she wasn't loved or wanted. In fact, it only made her all the more precious to Louise.

She would tell all this to Jinnie as gently as she could, and only in as much detail as was necessary. She must also confess how, in sleeping with Eric, she herself was guilty of the same misdemeanour as the others.

'Dear God, what will Jinnie think of me?'

Of all the intimate and worrying details she must convey to her ten-year-old daughter, the truth about her and Eric was the one she feared the most.

The sound of a woman singing made her look across the sands. Down below, beneath the pier, the two teenagers were collecting their belongings from outside the tent. Behind them, from the open doorway of the tent could be heard the woman's voice raised in song: 'Sailing down the river on a Sunday afternoon . . .' It was a strong, musical voice. Caught on the breeze, it washed over the sea and land with a strange kind of haunting beauty.

Louise thought it was magical, and was so lost in the song, that she almost leapt out of her skin when a man's voice spoke right alongside her. 'Delightful, isn't it?' Small and round, he had a kind, bright face. 'That dear lady has entertained me and my dog every morning for the past six weeks.' Tugging on the dog's lead, he smiled down at the little brown mongrel. 'It isn't often we get a free ticket to a concert, is it?' he asked the little thing, and it looked up at him with adoring eyes.

'Who is she?' Louise was curious about the woman.

The stranger shook his head. 'No idea,' he answered. 'All I know is, she turned up with the two young people some weeks ago, and they've been there ever since. They keep themselves to themselves and they're no trouble to anybody.'

He chuckled. 'She's a wily sort, though,' he confided. 'She knew where to pitch that tent so's they'd be safe enough from the water. Oh aye, it's a good spot, is that – sheltered from the wind and rain, and far enough down the beach to keep troublemakers and officials away.' His admiring gaze reached down to where the woman and the youngsters were making their way across the beach towards the steps. 'She's a good 'un for her age.' He speculated. 'She must be – what? – in her mid-fifties, maybe early sixties, and here she is, braving the elements *and* with two teenagers in tow.'

Clutching his back, he winced. 'I'm only just sixty, and I know I couldn't do what she does . . . kipping in a tent, fetching and carrying, and being responsible for them young 'uns. By!

It doesn't bear thinking about.' And just for good measure, he grimaced as he leaned heavily on the railings. 'It'd do me in, I reckon.'

'But how do they live?' In a way, Louise envied the woman.

'Oh, they do all right,' the man enlightened her. 'She's got a routine, you see.' For a brief minute, he went quiet, seeming preoccupied.

'Is something wrong?' Louise asked gently.

His smile was bittersweet. 'Sorry, lass. I were just thinking about my Edith. She was a stickler for routine.'

'Oh, I'm sorry.' It was obvious he had lost his wife and still thought deeply of her.

He thanked her, and returned to the matter of the woman on the beach. 'The lad works at a local amusement arcade. Good-looking young fella he is, and he works hard 'cause I've seen him rushing about in there, doing everybody else's share. Lazy lot o' buggers they are, especially the boss's son. By! I'd have him out the door and no mistake.'

Louise prompted him. 'You were saying about the woman having a routine?'

'What? Oh, that's right, yes.' He gestured to where Sarah Harpur and Adam and Hannah were climbing the steps to the promenade. 'You'll see now,' he urged. 'See how they've got towels tucked under their arms? Well, they'll go into the lavatories down there.' He pointed to the iron steps and the railings that led down to the public conveniences. 'That's where they wash and brush-up, every morning, regular as clockwork. I know the woman who cleans the lavvies,' he confided proudly. 'She's a cousin of my late wife's. We sometimes have a cuppa together along the front, when she's finished work.'

Louise waited patiently while he continued, 'Well, as I were saying . . . they'll wash and brush-up then the lad will go off to work at the pier, and the girl will stay with her grandma. I reckon she should be going to school, but nobody's reported them yet.'

The way the man seemed to be enjoying the conversation, Louise wondered if he was starved of company. 'Would you like to go for a cuppa somewhere . . . keep the chill out?' she offered with a knowing little smile. 'The breeze seems to be getting stronger, and I've got plenty of time before I catch the bus back home to Blackburn.'

His eyes lit up. 'Ooh! That would be lovely, thank you. Yes, and I can tell you all about Blackpool. Right, if we're going to have a cup of tea together, I'd better introduce myself. George Booker's the name, at your service!'

Louise hastily introduced herself. As they walked along in the same direction as the woman and the two children, George continued his story. 'Everywhere she goes, the woman has this bag . . . a big flowery thing it is, bulging at the seams.' he pointed to Sarah. 'See – there it is!'

Louise looked and yes, there it was, tucked securely over the woman's arm – a huge flowery holdall of the 'hippie' type.

'Inside the bag she has all these lovely little animals, all carved out of bits of wood washed up on the beach,' George imparted.

Louise was amazed. 'Good heavens! Do you mean she's carved them herself, Mr Booker?'

'Oh yes! I've seen her do it – got a little penknife, she has. There's a particular spot down the end of the promenade, where most folks have to pass. She settles herself on one of the benches there, and she whittles away. It's wonderful to see how the little animals begin to take shape. She sells them for threepence up to a couple of bob, depending on how big the thing is and how long it's taken her to carve it out.'

'And does she sell many?'

'Oh aye, she does, yes. In fact, I've got one myself – a little dog, it is. She carved it for me special, and it looks remarkably like my pal Bobby here.' He gave a tug on the lead. 'She wouldn't tell me anything about herself,' he remarked with regret. 'I did ask, mind you, but she were giving nothing away.' He took in a deep, invigorating breath, then he shivered. 'Happen it's just as well, Mrs Hunter. Telling folks your business can get you in a pack of trouble, if you ask me.'

Without any warning, he suddenly turned into a side road. Louise had to quicken her steps to keep up. 'They make the best pot o' tea in Blackpool down this street!' he cried. 'You'll see if I'm not right.'

Much to her amusement, and especially after he'd seemed so wobbly on his old legs before, Louise had a job to keep up with him as he rushed her down the street and into the little café.

'They do a nice toasted teacake,' he informed her. 'I dare say you'd like to treat me to *that* an' all, eh?'

As she followed him meekly up the three steps to the little café, Louise was trying very hard not to laugh out loud. For the time being at least, Mr George Booker and his dog Bobby had taken her mind off Susan, and the troubles that lay ahead – and for that she was very grateful indeed.

Chapter Eight

'MORNING, SARAH.' THE jolly woman in charge of the lavatories had come to know Sarah and her grandchildren very well. 'There you go, sunshine.' Handing Hannah the key to one of the washrooms, she told her jokingly, 'And don't forget to wash behind your ears.'

The girl blushed bright pink. 'I *always* wash behind my ears,' she protested, then smiled sheepishly on seeing the woman's cheeky grin.

Sarah laughed out loud. 'Go on, lass. You should know by now how Marie likes to tease.' She ushered Hannah into one of the cubicles. 'I'll not be long. Wait for me at the top of the steps if you're done before me.'

When Hannah closed the door, Sarah took the second key from Marie. 'I'm sorry,' the other woman apologised. 'I didn't mean to embarrass the lass.'

Sarah told her not to worry. 'Hannah's a bit shy. She finds it hard to make friends, that's the trouble.'

'I were like that as a child.' As she spoke, Marie followed Sarah into the cubicle. 'You don't mind if I stay and chat, do you?' she asked. 'Only there's not much going on here this morning, and I get fed up with me own company.'

Sarah nodded. ''Course I don't mind,' she assured her. 'Being as you've stood next to me every day since I've been coming here, I'm sure you'll not see anything you've not seen before.' She dug into her bag and, taking out her toiletries, laid them side by side next to the sink. 'Soap, flannel, towel, comb, toothpaste and toothbrush.' Then she draped a clean blouse over the towel rack; brown it was, with a deep collar and button cuffs.

'That's new, isn't it?' Marie was familiar by now with every article of Sarah's clothing. 'I know I haven't seen *that* before.'

'I got it on the Saturday market.' Sarah held it up with pride. 'Two bob well spent, what do you say?'

The woman looked it up and down. 'I'm beggared if I won't go next week and find one to fit me.'

'You like it then?'

'I do, yes.'

Pressing it across her breasts, Sarah admired herself in the mirror. 'Look, Marie, it's time you got a new mirror,' she joked. 'This bugger's cracked and old, just like me!'

'Give over, Sarah, you're a fine figure of a woman . . . for your age.'

As though it had burned her fingers, Sarah dropped the blouse onto the rack and stared at Marie with puzzlement. 'Oh aye – and what age is that then?'

'Well, *I* don't know, do I? You never tell me anything.'

Doing a bit of teasing of her own, Sarah wouldn't let it go. 'Well, come on then,' she prompted. 'How old do you think I am?' Placing her hands on her hips she took a deep breath, and drew in her stomach, until her face went beetroot red.

Wishing she'd kept her big mouth shut, Marie roved an eye over Sarah's ample figure. 'Forty-nine?' she guessed, praying she was on the right side of her friend's real age. 'Fifty, mebbe?'

Her ordeal ended, Sarah let out a great big whoosh of air as she deflated her chest and stomach. 'Jesus, Mary and

Joseph! If you'd have taken a minute longer, I swear I'd have passed out, right here in front of you.'

'So – was I right . . . about your age?' Behind her back, the cloakroom attendant kept her fingers crossed.

Sarah patted her on the shoulder. 'If you'd gone six year up, you'd have been smack on, but I expect you knew that anyway, you crafty little so and so!' Her hearty laughter echoed through the building. 'I bet you had your fingers crossed behind your back all the time!'

Marie chuckled. 'However did you know that?'

''Cause I've done it meself when somebody asked me to guess their age. It's a devil of a job, and you're terrified in case you guess on the wrong side. Well, anyway now you know . . . I'm fifty-six, and fighting fit.'

'You won't be though, not if you keep sleeping rough. If you don't mind me saying, it's not fair on them kids o' yourn neither.'

Sighing wearily, Sarah confessed, 'D'you think I don't know all that? But for the minute there's nothing I can do about it. I daren't go to the council, or they'll take my grandchildren away from me, and I couldn't risk that.'

While they conversed, Sarah stripped down to her under-wear, to reveal fleshy, dimpled thighs and thick table legs, which in all truth were not a pretty sight. 'I've been saving every penny I can spare,' she went on. 'Oh, I've a bit put by, but I don't reckon it's near enough. These greedy landlords want a three-month deposit up front, and then there's furniture and rent to find after that. I've tried for work all over the place, in the amusement arcades, shops and cafés – I've even asked in the factories, but they're not keen to take on a woman of my years, especially one as big and clumsy as me.'

'Away with you, Sarah!' Marie argued. 'You do yourself down, talking like that. You're big-boned, I'll admit, but you're not what I'd call fat, nor are you clumsy. I've seen you dashing about with your two on the beach, and you're as fit as a flea. To tell you the truth, you shame me with your endless energy.'

'Well, that's very kind of you, love, but the bosses want younger people, and that's the way of it.'

Marie had strong opinions on that particular subject. 'That's because they've not got enough brains to see how an older woman can be far more loyal. She's had her family and can work right through school holidays and such. She's no ties like the young ones, no, and she's not so bloody idle neither. What! You wouldn't believe the young ones I've had in and out of here . . . frightened to wash the floor in case they wet their shoes, and if you ask 'em to put a brush down the toilet, you'd think they'd been asked to put their own bloody head down it!'

'Huh!' Sarah retorted. 'No stamina at all – that's the trouble.' She thought of Hannah and Adam. 'Mind you, my two have learned to fend for themselves, and they never complain neither.'

Running the hot and cold taps together, she dropped the flannel into the bowl, rubbed it with soap and proceeded to wash herself. 'My Hannah says she wants to be an air-hostess, can you believe that? Whoo! You'd not get *me* up in one o' them things, not if you promised me a thousand pounds, you wouldn't. I like to feel the ground beneath my feet, not be cased up in a tin box, miles up there.' Her eyes rolled heavenwards. 'It turns my stomach just to think of it. Look, if the Good Lord meant us to fly, He'd have given us wings.'

Comfortable in each other's company, the two women talked about everything under the sun. They debated the state of the country under the Macmillan government and the turning weather, and inevitably their chatter turned to men. 'I can't bear to go home to my Alec,' Marie revealed. 'He's retired now, you know . . . spends all day sleeping in the chair, and keeps me awake at night with his snoring. I'd rather have a dog.'

'I know what you mean.' Sarah combed her thick brown hair and put on her new blouse. 'I had a dog for years, lovely creature he was. But he would keep peeing on my rug. The smell was awful! In the end, I gave it to the rag-a-bone man.'

'What, the rug?'

'No, the dog. I kept the rug. It were a wedding-present, you see.' She glanced up at the clock on the wall. 'I'd best go and set up, or I'll miss the lunchtime shoppers.' Leaning towards the door, she shouted at the top of her voice, 'Hannah! Hurry up, lass. It's time we were off!'

Hannah emerged, her fair hair tied back, and her face shining. 'Time to work,' Sarah told her. 'See you tomorrow, Marie,' she called out.

'Aye, that's if the old man hasn't killed me off with his bloody snoring!'

<hr />

SARAH AND HANNAH were having a good day. The creatures Sarah had carved seemed to be selling well, and at only threepence to two shillings a time, they were a good bargain.

'Look at that!' Scooping the coins out of the bag and into her hand, Sarah counted them up. 'One pound thirteen and six.' She glanced up at the promenade clock. 'And it's still only a quarter to twelve.'

'Is that the best yet?' Hannah was as thrilled as her grandma.

'It is, yes.' Sarah glanced at the dwindling supply of carved animals, spread out on a towel across the pavement. There were horses and sea-lions and any manner of dogs and cats;

there was even a bear standing on its back legs with front legs high and paws out wide. The shape of the driftwood had dictated what animal it must be, but it was a magnificent thing and a tribute to Sarah's skill with the penknife. At three shillings and sixpence, the bear was priced higher than the others, but then it was twice the size and had taken twice as long to craft, so Sarah thought it was still bargain all the same.

'Looks like I'll have to get busy carving some more,' she told Hannah. 'The only trouble is, I've used up all our bits of driftwood, so we'll need to get down the beach first thing in the morning, and hope some interesting-shaped pieces have washed up in the night.' She chuckled. 'If not, we'll have to go down the ironmonger's for some kindling wood and cheat our way out of it.'

Hannah was confident they would find enough on the beach for Sarah to carve another batch of animals. 'You'd better do some more horses,' she observed. 'There's only two left, and we had eight to start with.'

Sarah wasn't surprised. 'They're always the favourites,' she agreed, 'but you have to offer a selection, 'cause not everybody likes horses, do they?'

Hannah's brown eyes shone. '*I* do.'

Sarah gave her a hug. 'I know you do, lass,' she said kindly, 'and I know you'd love to have a horse of your own, but we ain't that kind of people. We ain't got that kind of money, and I don't suppose we ever will have.'

Hannah knew the situation and accepted it. 'It doesn't matter,' she promised. 'When I'm an air-hostess, I won't have time to be riding horses anyway.'

'That's good thinking,' Sarah agreed wholeheartedly. Taking a half-crown from her pocket, she gave it to the girl. 'I'm that parched I could drink the sea dry,' she gasped. 'Fetch us a cuppa from the stall, will you, lass, and get summat for yourself while you're at it.'

Hannah took the money and, clambering up from her cross-legged position, ran off towards the tea-stall – a covered kiosk situated opposite the beach steps. Sarah's watchful eyes followed the girl until she was at the tea-stall, then she was kept busy with a customer and sold another little dog; a Highland terrier it was, and one of her best. Just as she was putting the money away and thinking how business was booming, Hannah returned with the tea and a bottle of pop for herself.

'Keep the change,' Sarah told her as she held the money out. 'You've earned it.'

Just then an old woman with a walking stick slowed down to have a look at Sarah's wares. Hannah got talking to her, persuading her that she would never see another carving like her grandmother made, '. . . and all out of a piece of wood that gets washed up on the beach.'

Sarah watched and listened with pride. 'She'll make a good businesswoman,' she muttered with a smile. 'Pity she's set her heart on being an air-hostess.'

The woman was so impressed, she bought two carvings – a poodle and a Persian cat. 'I used to have a cat like that,' the woman told her, 'but she got run over. This little carving will remind me of her.' And she gave Sarah an extra threepence.

WHILE SARAH AND Hannah went about their business, Adam was doing the same, in the amusement arcade a mile down the promenade.

'You're a damned good worker, lad.' The boss was a big man with a kind face. 'You're always on time, and pleasant to the customers. I don't need to tell you what wants doing neither. You just come in and get on with it.'

Adam thanked him. 'It's what you pay me for, Mr Barnes, and I'm very grateful. I owe you a lot,' he acknowledged. 'You were the only one who would give me work when we came to Blackpool.'

'Aye, well, it's their loss and my gain.' The man studied Adam's handsome face and broad shoulders, and the quiet sincere look in his dark eyes and, not for the first time, he wished in his heart that his own son was more like him. 'You're a good lad,' he told Adam. 'I'd trust you with anything in this arcade, even though I don't really know much about you.'

'I've told you about my grandmother and my sister, and how we came to Blackpool because we couldn't find a house in Blackburn that was cheap enough to rent.' Adam grew instinctively wary.

'Oh, it doesn't matter to me, lad.' Mr Barnes had noticed how Adam took an involuntary step back, as though he was afraid, and he was quick to reassure him. 'It's none of my business, and I'm sorry I mentioned it. Only you never talk about your parents, that's all.'

'No, sir.'

Mr Barnes put a comforting hand on his shoulder. 'You don't have to tell me anything you don't want to. You know that, don't you, son?'

'Yes, sir. Thank you.' The last thing Adam wanted anyone to know was how his mother had been murdered, and his father was in prison for the crime. And now Terry Harpur was being released and had threatened to come looking for them. That was the real reason why they'd come to Blackpool, and why they'd been on the run ever since his Grandma got that letter from his dad. But these were private things, and not for the ears of strangers.

'Right then. I'll leave you to it.' Barnes had meant well, but sensed that Adam had been worried by his curiosity.

Adam put the last two furry toys into the glass cabinet and locked it securely. 'I've almost finished here,' he told the man.

'I'll be in the store-room if you want me . . . stacking that new delivery.'

'Right, and if you come across that son of mine, tell him he's to move his backside and help you, or he'll answer to me!'

The last thing Adam wanted was to get involved in a family dispute so, just as he had done many times before, he covered for Jason Barnes. 'I think I saw him go to the stock-room earlier on,' he fibbed. 'I expect he's already started shifting the crates over.'

'Huh!' The man laughed. 'I wouldn't put money on it, lad!' He roved his glance round the arcade. There were a few holidaymakers playing the machines, a cleaning lady wielding her mop where some child had spilled a bottle of milk, and in the farthest corner, the woman in the change-machine was filing her nails. But there was no sign of his lanky, bone-idle son.

'If you *do* happen to see Jason, tell him I'm looking for him, will you, Adam? That lazy no-good son of mine can never be found when he's wanted.' With that, Reuben Barnes strode away, angrily muttering under his breath.

'Yes, Mr Barnes, I'll tell him,' Adam called out, but he knew he would not find Jason so easily, because the other boy had a canny knack of hiding himself where he couldn't be found. Dropping the cabinet key into the office on his way to the store-room, he thought he caught a glimpse of Jason out of the corner of his eye, but when he turned round there was no sign of him. He continued on his way. Maybe he really *was* working in the store-room. Adam grinned to himself. That would be a turn-up for the books!

Adam had no idea he was being closely followed.

From behind the large pinball machines, the boss's son watched him enter the store-room. Once Adam was inside, he went stealthily forward, keeping a wary eye out in case his father spotted him and dragged him off to work; a prospect that put the fear of God in him. Unseen, he followed Adam into the store-room and, after a final look round to see if the coast was clear, softly closed the door behind him.

He found Adam at work behind the huge mound of crates and boxes. Jason waited until he had hoisted one of the boxes onto his shoulders, and then rushed forward, surprising Adam and effectively blocking his path. 'I saw you!' Prodding him in the chest, he sneered, 'Buttering up my old man ... talking about me! Making me out to be a bad bugger. I know what you're up to. You're after summat, you cunning bastard! You reckon if he gets to think more of you than he does me, he just might throw a bone or two your way.'

Adam stood his ground. 'You've got it all wrong.'

'I don't think so.' Pushing Adam hard, he sent him reeling backwards, then seemed alarmed when Adam dropped the box and stepped forward.

Calling Adam's bluff, he rolled up his sleeves, eyes wild and a twisted grin on his face. 'Come on, matey, if that's what you want!' Backing up, he spread wide his arms and beckoning with his fingers did a dance on the spot. 'What's wrong, then, eh? Turned chicken, have we?'

Aware that if he was to take this lunatic on, he would lose his job, Adam tried to cool the situation down. He had no wish to jeopardise everything his grandmother had done to keep them safe. 'Your dad was asking me where you were, that's all.'

'Yeah, and I suppose you took the opportunity to tell him that I'd gone out, is that it?'

'As a matter of fact, I said you were probably already in the store-room shifting the boxes.' Adam was determined not to be goaded into a fight.

'Liar!'

'I'm no liar!' For the first time, Adam's eyes flashed anger.

'Says you!' Leaning forward, Jason taunted him some more. 'You're a liar all right, and a thief too. I bet if I were to go through this place with a fine toothcomb, I'd find there are things gone missing.'

Adam took another step forward, his face drained white. 'I already told you, I'm no liar, and I'm no thief neither.'

'You can say what you like, but you're still rubbish! You and your sister, and that ugly old bat you call a grandmother. You're nothing but gypsies . . . selling trinkets on the promenade and living in a bloody tent on the beach . . . *rubbish*. Folk like you should be swilled out with the tide!'

Adam straightened up, his shoulders filling out and his eyes boring into the older youth's. 'I want you to take all that back.' His voice was incredibly calm, though the look on his face was one of seething rage.

'Oh? You want me to take it all back, d'you?' The other boy laughed in his face, then he was suddenly deadly serious. 'Make me!' Backing off, he continued to taunt Adam beyond endurance. 'That sister of yours knows what's what though, don't she? I've got a friend who has a liking for young girls, and he seems to have taken a fancy to her, though God knows why, 'cause *I* wouldn't touch her with a barge-pole! Still, she's easy meat, what with living in a tent and only you and that old bat to guard her.' Jason gave a meaningful wink. 'Happen we'll pay you all a visit one of these dark ni—'

He didn't get to finish his sentence because Adam had launched himself through the air to land on him with the full force of his weight. 'You might find a helpless young girl easy meat,' he cried as he tore into him, 'but you'll find I'm well able to defend myself *and* my family!'

Taken by surprise, the older youth retaliated, hitting out with fists and feet, and when they rolled over, he leaped up and, grabbing a knife used to cut the baling twine, he stood legs astride, the look of a madman on his face. 'Come on then, clever Dick, let's be having you.'

For a long, dangerous moment, Adam kept his distance, his quick eyes taking in the situation and his mind working out the best way to deal with it.

'Put it down, Jason,' he urged. 'We should be able to settle our differences without using knives.' He had his hand up, with his palm spread out as though to defend himself against a sudden, unprovoked attack.

The other boy moved forward, jabbing at the air with the blade of the knife. 'It's a different story now, ain't it, clever Dick?' he gibed. 'You might not be afaid of *me*, but you're afraid of the knife, aren't you, eh?' He sniggered. 'You will be, when I stick you through the guts with it.' As he continued to advance, it was obvious he meant what he said.

Suddenly, and without warning, his father came out of nowhere to grab him from behind. 'I never thought I'd raised a coward!' His voice trembled with disgust. 'You're lazy, and greedy, and sometimes I wonder where the hell you came from, but I swear to God, I never took you to be a *coward*!' Wrenching the knife out of his son's hand, he threw it across the room, where it fell with a clatter behind the crates. 'Now fight like a man should!' he told his son. 'Let me see how you mean to defend yourself against Adam here. Even though he's years younger than you, he's twice the man.' With a vicious push, he sent him forward, towards Adam. 'Go on!' he urged. 'Show me what you're made of.' He spat on the floor. 'You disgust me!'

It could have been because he'd been humiliated in front of Adam, or maybe he feared his father might now cut him out of his life and leave him to fend for himself, but for whatever reason, Jason Barnes was fired by a surge of blind fury. Giving out a devilish cry, he lunged forward and threw himself headlong into Adam; the impact sent Adam with Jason on top of him, hurtling into the piles of crates and boxes, which flew in all directions.

Bruised and bleeding, with a deep cut over one eye, Adam gave as good as he got. The fighting was fierce and unbridled. Several times Adam was slammed against the wall, and each time he came back for more. What Jason had said about his sister and grandma was enough to spur him on. He had to punish Jason. He had to let him know that no one was allowed to insult his family that way.

For very different reasons, Jason too, was determined to get the better of Adam. With his father looking on, he could not afford to be beaten, and certainly not by a boy some five years younger than himself. Being taller, he had a longer reach, so he went for Adam's head and face, attacking him with clenched fists again and again, until the lad was left reeling from the blows.

Tired and hurting though he was, Adam would not give in. And soon it was evident that Jason, too, was beginning to flag. The tension heightened and all the while Jason's father stood by, silently hoping Adam could give his son the hiding he deserved, the final humiliation he needed, that might knock an ounce of decency into him.

When it seemed Jason would get the better of him, Adam heard him laughing, and was incensed. Gathering his last ounce of energy, he drew back his fist and brought it crashing against Jason's jaw like a sledge-hammer. With wide eyes and open mouth, and a look of shock and disbelief on his face, Jason fell backwards, to land in a heap at his father's feet.

For a moment Reuben Barnes looked down at his son, at the state of him; groaning loudly in pain, with the blood pouring from his face and his head to one side, eyes closed.

He took a good long look, then he calmly stepped over him and took Adam firmly by the shoulders. 'I'm sorry,' he said. 'I shouldn't have let it go on, but he needed to be taught a lesson, and I knew you were the one to do it.'

Adam looked at him through a bloody mist. 'I'm sorry too,' he panted. 'But it had to happen sooner or later.'

The man regarded him a while longer, before saying in a murmur, 'I should have had a son like you.' There were tears in his eyes. 'Where did I go wrong?'

Adam looked down at Jason, who by now was sitting on his haunches, looking decidedly ill. 'He'll be all right,' he told his employer, 'though I think you've punished him enough now.'

Mr Barnes turned to look at his son, and when he returned his gaze to Adam, he was smiling ruefully. 'I think you're right,' he said. 'His mother left us long ago, and I've been too wrapped up in my work to raise him proper. Happen I should spend more time with him.'

Adam nodded in agreement.

'You do realise I can't keep you on? Not now.'

'I understand.' Adam knew it was inevitable, even though he was devastated by the news.

'Go and wash up, lad and I'll get your money ready. It goes without saying there'll be a bonus for you. And should you want references, you'll get the best from me.'

Adam thanked him, and limped off to the wash-room, where he quickly swilled off the surface blood and damped the cuts with cold tissue paper soaked in water. God, he looked a mess! How on earth would he explain it to his grandmother?

A few minutes later, he collected his wages. 'It's all there, lad,' Barnes told him. 'Three weeks' wages and a bonus on top.' He smiled. 'I've never known Jason so subdued. Between you and me, I reckon it's done him a power of good, being beaten by somebody years younger than himself.' His smile became a chuckle. 'If he ever starts to get on his high-horse again, I'll just have to remind him about today. After all, he wouldn't want his pals finding out how you thrashed the hell out of him, would he, eh?'

Adam pointed to his own bruises. 'I got as good as I gave,' he said painfully. 'Your son packs a hard punch.'

When at that moment Jason came into the room, Adam thought it might be a good time to leave. 'Goodbye, sir,' he said, and shook hands with his employer.

'Goodbye, lad. Take care of yourself, and that family of yours.' He thought it a heavy burden for a boy of that age to carry.

'Thank you. I will.' Passing Jason at the door, he dared to rest his hand on the young man's shoulder. 'No hard feelings?' he said.

He was taken aback by Jason's quiet reply. 'I was jealous. I'm sorry.' He kept his eyes downcast as though ashamed.

Adam had another question to ask before he left. 'You wouldn't have let anybody hurt Hannah, would you?'

This time Jason looked up at him, an expression of sincerity on his pimply face. 'I'd have *killed* them first.'

Satisfied, Adam went on his way; delighted and saddened when he turned back to see Jason and his father walking in the opposite direction, Jason beside his father and the man's arm affectionately about his shoulders.

'You'll be fine now,' he sighed, and wished with all his heart that he, too, had a real father. A man he could look up to, and confide in. But he had his sister Hannah, and his wonderful grandmother, and he would be eternally grateful for that.

———◆———

S ARAH COULDN'T BELIEVE her eyes when she saw Adam approaching her on the promenade. 'My God, whatever have you been up to?' she demanded. 'Have you been fighting?

Who did that to you, eh?' From the look of her, she was ready to have a go herself.

Hannah was dumbstruck. 'I've never known you to fight before,' she told her brother. 'Was it a good one? Did you thrash the other lad?'

Sitting on the wall, Adam told them what had happened – about Jason and how he'd been looking for a chance to have a go at him for some time now, and how today it had all exploded. He told them, too, about Jason's dad, and of how he took the knife away from his son and made him fight Adam 'like a real man'.

'Afterwards, just before I left, Jason and me made it up.' He thought about it and was proud. 'I'm glad we ended up friends,' he said. 'I think him and his dad will be a lot closer now, so some good did come out of it.'

Sarah had her suspicions about the start of the fight; but when she tackled Adam about it, he held back and didn't want to say any more. He didn't have to, because she could tell from the look on his face, and his reluctance to talk about it any further, that the fight had been about them. 'I knew this would happen sooner or later,' she groaned. 'People can't leave us alone. It's human nature. They'll never leave us be, while we're living the way we do. They see us as oddities. We don't live like them so they're suspicious, and when they get suspicious, they get spiteful.' She voiced her worst fear. 'The next thing will be somebody calling the authorities, and then what d'you think will happen? Well, I'll tell you . . . they'll split us up. They'll say I'm too old to look after you properly, and they'll take you away from me.'

'No, they can't!' Hannah was tearful. 'And you're *not* too old.'

Sarah wrapped an arm round her. 'Thank you for that, sweetheart,' she said gently. 'And to tell you the truth, I don't consider myself to be an "old lady" either. But there are them as do, and it worries me.' Galvanised by Adam's fight, and grateful that he wasn't injured to a greater extent Sarah made her mind up there and then. 'We'll have to leave,' she told them. 'We'll clear up here, then we'd best get back to the beach and collect our things.'

Hannah was upset. 'Where will we go?'

'Funnily enough, I've been thinking about that for some time now. What's happened to Adam has decided it for me. We'll make our way back to Blackburn.' She looked from one to the other. 'And before you say anything, I know what you're thinking, but you have to trust me.'

'I won't go!' Hannah looked terrified. 'I like it here in Blackpool, Gran.'

Adam calmed her. 'At least listen to what Gran has to say.'

And what Sarah had to say was this. 'Look, Hannah, I've heard you time and again over the past ten years having them dreadful nightmares. It took me ages settle you down after the last one. It breaks my heart and it can't go on. The only way we're ever going to help you forget what happened that night is to take you back to where it all took place.'

'NO!' Tears poured down the girl's face. 'Please don't make me go back there!'

Sarah took her into her arms. 'Oh lass, I'm not about to make you do anything you don't want to, but I need you to think about it. I want us to talk . . . all three of us, and see if we can't agree on a course of action.'

She was concerned about them all, and on top of what had gone on today, she was worried about the downturn in the weather. If it got much worse, they could be in for a really hard time. 'Before we can turn round it'll be winter, with ice and snow and bitter-cold winds. We can't live outside like we've been doing. I won't put either of you, or myself, through any more of this living rough like we've been doing. And what's more, it's high time Hannah went back to proper school. You've been off for two months now, and one day soon, the School's Inspector is going to catch up with us. It's not right, living like this.'

Adam had listened very carefully, and was as shocked as Hannah. 'You mean for us to go back to our old home, don't you – to live in *that* house again?' He shuddered. Adam could still remember his mam, Maggie, so clearly and he'd loved her oh, so much. The thought of going back to that house on the corner of Craig Street made his blood run cold.

'I just want you to think about it,' Sarah admitted. 'I'm worried that if you and Hannah aren't made to come to terms with what happened, it will haunt you for ever. But I can't make you go there if you don't want to; it has to be your choice, yours and Hannah's.'

'But there must somebody living in that house now?' Adam was being practical.

Sarah shook her head. 'No. The house has been empty for several months and it's going for a next-to-nothing rent. I've had it in the back of my mind, ever since Mr Martin told me about it. And now, what with Hannah's worsening nightmares and the fight today, we surely can't be any worse off there than we are here.'

'Why can't we find a house somewhere else?' Adam was looking for options. 'I'm working now. I can keep us all.'

'Ssh!' Aware that they were being gawped at by passers-by, Sarah got them to help her collect their wares. Afterwards, on the way back to the tent, she mapped it all out. 'You're right,' she told Adam, 'we might be able to find another house, but there's a few good reasons for thinking about the house on Craig Street, where you lived with your mam.'

When she paused, Adam asked her to go on. 'It's all right, Gran. We've calmed down now, you can tell us what's on your mind.'

Encouraged, Sarah went on, 'Firstly, as I've already said, I think it will help lay a few ghosts for you and Hannah, and happen for me as well.' She had never told the children, but there had been many a night when she'd lain awake into the small hours, thinking of her son's common-law wife Maggie, and the way she had met a violent, untimely end. And the more she thought about it, the more Sarah hated the man who had done it; her own son, now disowned by her for ever!

It had taken her many years to come to terms with what he had done, and when she finally emerged from the nightmare, it was with a cold heart and bitter feelings towards him. Terry had made an enemy of her by his own shocking actions; the deliberate taking of that young woman's life, and that of Jacob Hunter, worthless though it was, and in the process, attacking and terrifying his own helpless children almost out of their minds. Knowing it was her own son who had done such a thing was unbearable.

Even more unbearable was the danger that he might one day find them, and force his way into their lives. Terry obviously didn't realise that things had changed: Adam was now a young man, capable of taking revenge on the bully who had killed his mother. Because of that, Sarah feared the terrible consequences of Adam and her son ever coming face to face again.

She told them only so much of what she was thinking. 'We none of us want your dad in our lives,' she said, 'but he's on the loose now, and looking for us. To my way of thinking, the last place he'd come searching is in *that* house.'

Hannah was struck by this. 'Gran's right!' she cried. 'He wouldn't find us there, but . . . oh Gran, I'm still frightened.' Visions of her and Adam hiding in the cellar filled her mind with black, swirling panic.

Adam bristled. 'Don't be,' he said softly. 'He won't hurt us. *I won't let him!*'

Judging by the tone of his voice, Sarah's fears were redoubled. 'Look, besides all that,' she said, hastily, 'we could live like other people. Adam could get a job anywhere in Blackburn ... they're always crying out for good workers. Hannah could go back to her old school, and see her old friends again – that'd cheer you up, wouldn't it, love? I'm sure I'd be able to find a cleaning job or summat else in one of the factories thereabouts.'

Sarah grew excited at the prospect of having a proper little kitchen and a fireplace where she could warm her toes again. 'Adam wouldn't have to keep us all, 'cause I'd be helping fetch in some money, and we'd have a proper house.' She began to dream. 'Given half a chance, I *know* I could rid that house of its past, and make it a cosy home for us all.'

'I still don't like it.' That was Hannah again.

'Then we won't do it,' Sarah promised. 'All I'm asking is that you both think about it. In your minds, you're both still living in that house anyway. I honestly believe all the badness and the memories will go much quicker, if you can only face them head on. *Think* about it,' she urged them again. 'That's all I ask. Meanwhile, we'll get back and dismantle the tent and such.'

Hannah hugged her. 'You won't make me go there, if I don't want to, will you?'

'No, sweetheart, 'course I won't.' But she prayed that her grandchildren would find the strength and courage to trust her on this. In her heart she was certain it was the right thing. Or she would never have asked them to consider it in the first place.

───────◈───────

SOME TIME LATER, when the two of them were sitting on the sands, guarding their belongings while Sarah went to say goodbye to the lavatory-lady, Adam raised the subject with his sister. 'Hannah, what do you think? What Grandma says *does* make sense. And it will be good to have a roof over our heads, where you're safe from any passing tramp.' What Jason had implied in the heat of rage had made him realise how vulnerable Hannah and his grandmother were in that tent.

'We'd have a proper life again, like everybody else,' he said thoughtfully. 'And Gran's right, it might help us to get over what happened.' He too had suffered nightmares, though he never told anyone about them. 'I'll help you, Hannah. We both will.' Though even *he* couldn't be certain he could go through with it. The memories were still too real.

'Come on you two, let's be off.' Sarah's voice sailed down from the promenade.

As they made their way to the bus stop, Hannah asked, 'Where are we going?'

Sarah hitched her rucksack higher up her back. 'I already told you. We're going back to Blackburn.'

'Not to that house though?'

'No, not unless you want to.'

'I don't!' She swung round so smartly that one of the tin cups fell out of her bag and clattered to the ground.

'Then we'll head for the canal bank.' Sarah waited with Adam while Hannah retrieved the cup and pressed it back into her bag.

Hannah had more questions. 'Why are we heading for the canal bank?'

Adam answered her this time. 'Because we'll need to set up camp somewhere for the night.'

'Why?' She was fidgeting so much, another cup fell out. 'Why can't we find a house to rent? Not that one – another one. You said we could.'

Adam collected the cup from the ground and tied it through his belt. 'It's not that easy to find somehere, sis.'

For a long time Hannah had been more co-operative and nicer of character. Now, though, it seemed that she might be reverting to the darker side of her nature; the side that had emerged since her mother's death.

Growing peevish, Hannah was whining now. 'Gran said she didn't want to spend winter in the tent. It's what she said. You heard her!'

The questions and demands went on and on, until Sarah found she couldn't think straight.

'Right!' Bringing the entourage to a halt, she looked at Hannah for a minute, then in a kindly voice told her, 'Look, love, we have to sleep somewhere tonight. By the time we get where we're going, all the offices will be closed. We can't walk right into a house, just like that.'

'You said we could go to the other one, so why can't we go to somewhere else?'

Sarah explained. 'The other one is already empty, and our old landlord has already invited us to live there if we want to. I'm sure no one else will have taken it in the meantime. So, being as you don't want to – and that's all right, sweetheart – we'll need to look for somewhere else. We'll do that first thing in the morning. Then me and Adam will have to look for work, so's we can pay the rent, and everything else that goes with living in a house.'

'And that's another thing, sis.' Adam had the picture clear enough now. 'Our old house has got a dead cheap rent, that's what the landlord told Grandma. But if we find another place to live, the rent might be much dearer, so we have to find work, or we'll not be able to afford anything!'

Tired and weary, Hannah was close to tears. 'So, where will we sleep tonight?'

Taking her by the arm, Sarah walked her across the street to the bus stop. 'We'll set up camp on the canal bank,' she explained. 'It'll be all right for one night, sweetheart, you'll see. Tomorrow we'll find work and somewhere to live, and start all over again. Okay, lass?'

Hannah nodded, but she was not happy. In fact, she had been neither healthy nor happy, since that awful night. Which was why both Adam and her gran were uniquely patient with her.

They had a half-hour wait for the bus, during which time Adam went to the tea-shop round the corner and brought back three mugs of piping hot tea. 'I'm to take the mugs back when we're done,' he told Sarah. 'The woman told me that she loses so many in a week she'd stopped letting people take them away, but she trusted me, so I'd best not forget to take them back.'

Sarah thanked him, and thought what a lovely lad he was. 'She need have no fear of you forgetting,' she laughed. 'Like as not, you'll have them back there before we've even finished drinking from 'em.'

In fact, they had soon emptied the mugs and Adam was away with them and back again, in no time at all.

The bus arrived on time and they climbed on. 'Three one-way tickets to Blackburn Market Square.' Sarah emptied the coins into the conductor's outstretched hand. 'Two full and one half, please.'

Huffing and puffing, because she had nearly missed the bus, Louise jumped on and seated herself across the aisle from them. She handed the conductor her return ticket. 'Blackburn Market Square, please.'

Sarah looked up and smiled. 'Same as us,' she said. 'Have you been there before – to Blackburn, I mean?'

Louise welcomed someone to talk to. The journey into Blackburn could be a lonely one. 'I live in Blackburn,' she told her. 'I've lived there a good many years now.'

'You don't know of any cheap houses to rent, I don't suppose?' Sarah had taken a liking to this pleasant young woman.

Louise took a minute to think. 'No, I don't.' She turned in her seat. 'Wait a minute though.' She looked at Sarah and Hannah, and hesitated. 'There is one house. It's a sad old place, on the corner of Craig Street and Derwent Street, where I live.' She shook her head. 'The house has gone a bit derelict now. No, I don't think you'd like it at all.'

Hannah gave a little cry. 'It's *that* one, Gran. Don't listen to her!'

Astonished at the girl's outburst, Louise looked at her, noting her white face and frightened, staring eyes, and something seemed to rise up inside her, a kind of memory, something she couldn't quite put her finger on. Then suddenly, she had it! They were the family from the beach – the woman and the two kids who had been romping so happily only a few hours earlier.

Seeing the confusion on Louise's face, Sarah did her best to cover up the reason for Hannah's cry. 'We know about that one,' she said. 'We were told what happened there. And you're right. It's not what we really want.'

'Well, I don't know of any more.' Louise was unsettled by the incident, and didn't like to mention that she already knew of their circumstances. 'But there's a landlord, name of Alan Martin, a decent sort as far as landlords go. He might be able to help you. You'll find his office on Ainsworth Street.'

Sarah thanked her. 'I've heard of him,' she said. 'I rented a house from him once. And you're right, he is a decent sort. I'll look him up first thing tomorrow.' Things were getting too close to home and she, too, was beginning to feel unsettled, especially when Louise kept sneaking a curious look at them.

During this conversation, Adam had kept silent. Suddenly, Hannah leaned over to him. 'Did you hear that, Adam? This lady knows the house. She says it's derelict.'

Adam put his finger to his lips. 'Ssh. It's best we don't talk about it any more.'

When the bus arrived, Sarah and the children were the first to climb off; Louise and the other passengers were not far behind. Before they went their separate ways, Louise called out to Sarah, 'Go and see Mr Martin. I'm sure he can help you.'

Knowing the young woman was suspicious, Sarah thanked her and hurried the children away.

The past had a funny way of catching up, she thought wryly.

PART THREE

WINTER, 1963
NO PLACE LIKE
HOME

Chapter Nine

THE DAY FOLLOWING Louise's return from Blackpool, she and Sally were talking over an early breakfast about what action they should take with regard to Jinnie. 'The first thing to do this morning is to go and see a solicitor.' Sally had no doubts about their course of action.

Louise spread her toast with a generous helping of butter. 'I'm not so much concerned about the legal side, as Susan contacting Jinnie behind my back and trying to worm her way into our girl's life.'

Sally understood Louise's concern. 'Aye. If she decides to go down that route, there's nothing to stop her from making friends with the lass, and trying to take her from you in that way.' Heaping three spoonfuls of sugar into her mug of tea, she took a great, long gulp. 'She's a canny bugger, an' no mistake.'

'Why didn't you call me?' Jinnie came into the living room, yawning and stretching, her blue eyes heavy with sleep even though she was washed and dressed ready for school, with her blonde hair tied neatly at the neck with a brown ribbon. Dropping into a chair, she looked up at the mantelpiece clock. 'Oh no,' she groaned. 'It's five to eight already.'

'I did call you.' Finishing her toast, Louise made her way into the kitchen. '*And* you answered me. "I'm up" –

that's what you said.' She poked her head round the door, smiling but exasperated. 'Like a fool, I believed you. When will I learn, eh?'

Jinnie followed her into the kitchen. 'Sorry, Mam. I fell back asleep.'

Louise handed her the plate, containing one boiled egg and two slices of toast. 'You've got half an hour before we need to leave,' she reminded her. 'Now, do you want tea or milk?'

'I'm all right, Mam.' She thanked her for the breakfast and made her way back into the living room, where she planted a kiss on Sally's face. 'Morning, Gran. How are you?'

Sally held her hand for a second or two. 'I'm fine, lass, but you look tired.'

Seating herself at the table, Jinnie sliced the top off her boiled egg. 'I didn't sleep much.'

Louise returned with a glass of milk. 'You need a drink before you go to school,' she told her. 'And why didn't you sleep much last night?' Pouring herself another cup of tea, she took a closer look at the girl, and saw the dark rings around her eyes.

'I kept thinking about what you told us – about that family you met on the bus from Blackpool with nowhere to stay.' Louise had decided to tell her that she'd gone to Blackpool for the day, but without explaining why.

'Oh, I'm sure they found somewhere.' Louise had also been thinking about them. She couldn't get it out of her mind that she knew something about that family – but for the life of her, she couldn't fathom out what it was.

Sally had a theory. 'I don't know what makes you think they've nowhere to live,' she said. 'Happen they already have a house, and are just looking to move.'

Louise shook her head. 'No. They were already on the move. They'd been sleeping rough, you see. I saw their tent under the pier.'

Jinnie put her toast back on her plate and pushed it away. 'Why would they be sleeping rough?' Her heart went out to them, in particular the woman. She imagined it might be fun to sleep out if you were young, but it must be harder for a grown-up.

The same thought had crossed Sally's mind. 'How old d'you reckon the woman was?'

Louise shrugged. 'Fifty . . . fifty-five – I'm not sure. The boy was around sixteen and the girl a bit younger. But they all looked fit and healthy.'

'Gypsy types, were they?'

'No, not at all.' Louise had thought them to be a decent sort of people. 'Though the boy was covered in bruises, as though he'd been in a fight or something.' All of a sudden, she caught sight of the clock and was on her feet and panicking. 'Look at the time, lass! We'd best get going, or you'll be late for school.'

Sally saw them off. 'Mind how you go.'

'See you later, Grandma,' Jinnie called back, as Louise bundled her down the street.

They boarded the tram for Church Street, and settled into their seats. 'I wish I was coming with you to Eric's.' Jinnie loved the open fields and freedom of Maple Farm. 'I'd rather be there than in a dreary old classroom.'

Louise was having none of it. 'We all have to do our turn in the dreary old classroom,' she teased. 'Besides, the weekend will come soon enough. You'll be glad to know, Eric's already got a few jobs lined up for you.'

The tram drew up at Church Street at a quarter to nine. 'Tell Eric I'm looking forward to the weekend,' Jinnie said, 'but I'm not cleaning out the pigs again. They always chase me – and they stink!'

They both laughed at the conductor's cheeky remark: 'That's what pigs do, luv,' he chuckled. 'They chase folk, and stink to high heaven, but they mek a good sausage, I'll say that for 'em!'

'Bye, Mam.' Jinnie clambered off the tram.

'Bye, lass. See you later.'

Jinnie waved until the tram was out of sight. 'She's a bonnie lass, and friendly too.' The conductor liked to chat. 'Not like some o' the young 'uns we get on this tram . . . swear like troopers and that much lipstick and mascara on, they look more like clowns than schoolkids.'

'Aye, that's right an' all.' The woman in front with the plaid scarf and spectacles had to have her say. 'Kissing and canoodling like old sweethearts, they are, and some o' the buggers not out o' their nappies yet!' Taking a tin of snuff from her pocket she opened it up and shoved a pinchful up her nostril. 'By! If I'd'a behaved like that when I were a kid, me faither would a' kicked me from 'ere to Kingdom Come, an' no mistake!'

'She always has a lot to say for herself, that one,' the conductor leaned forward to whisper in Louise's ear. 'Bit of a cantankerous bugger, she is. In her time she's been a cleaner, a lollipop lady, a dog-handler and a barmaid. She's had ten children and four husbands.' He paused then: 'For the life of me, I can't imagine anybody kissing and canoodling *her*, but they must have done at some time or another – and often, or she wouldn't have been landed with all them kids, would she, eh?'

With her admiration of the woman growing by the minute, Louise had to agree.

When they arrived at Scab Lane, the woman started to get off in front of Louise. 'Been talking about me, has he?' she asked. 'Huh! He should mind his own business, that's what *he* should do.' To Louise's astonishment, the more the woman ranted on the more her false teeth went up and down like window-blinds. 'Well? Has he been talking about me?'

'No,' Louise lied to save the day. 'We were talking about something and nothing.'

'Yer a liar, missus!' She gave out a frightening bellow of a laugh. 'I bet he told you about my four husbands, didn't he, eh?'

Louise opened her mouth to reply, but before she could speak, the woman began to chuckle. 'I bet he never told you that *he* were me fourth, did he? The other three had the good manners to pop their clogs, but not *this* one, oh no! I had to chuck this bugger out!'

She pointed to the red-faced conductor, who by now was wisely keeping his distance. 'I'll tell yer summat else an' all,' she went on at full volume, entertaining all present. 'That randy devil won't get back between *my* sheets – not till he's got rid o' that fancy bit from the ironmongers!' With that she wagged a finger at him clambered off the tram, and waddled away, leaving a dozen passengers smiling at her antics.

'What meks you think I *want* to get back between your sheets, you ugly old bugger!' The conductor shook his fist after her. 'I'm well shut of you, and what's more, that fancy bit from the ironmongers knows how to make a man happy . . . *and* she doesn't sleep with her socks on, nor her teeth out neither!'

When suddenly she turned as if coming back, the conductor got such a fright, he backed off, promptly tripped over his own feet and had to swing round the rail to keep his balance.

Louise stifled her laughter until she was halfway down Scab Lane, when she could hold it in no longer. 'We might have our troubles,' she gasped, 'but we do see life!'

By the time Louise reached Maple Farm, however, her smile was long gone. Eric saw her coming. He knew from the look on her face that her meeting with Susan had not gone well, and his heart sank.

'Come inside,' he told her. 'We've time for a brew before old Mike Ellis gets here.' Eric had been sorting the late cabbages into their respective crates, but on seeing Louise he washed his hands at the outside tap and led her into the cottage. When Louise went to make the tea, he sat her firmly down in the red leather armchair. 'I'm quite capable of putting a kettle on,' he argued. 'So you just sit there till I come back.'

When a few minutes later he returned with a tray containing two giant mugs of piping hot tea and some teacakes he'd bought the day before, he wasn't surprised to see Louise pacing the floor.

Placing the tray on the coffee-table, he walked across the room. 'You should have let me come with you,' he said. Taking her by the shoulders, he drew her to a halt. 'I can see it didn't go too well.' He'd thought about her all the time she'd been away. In fact, he thought about Louise every minute of every day.

'It went badly.' Louise had lain awake every night thinking about her confrontation with Susan. 'One way or another, she means to have Jinnie away from me.' Saying it out loud in the cold light of day sent a shiver of terror through her.

'Come and sit down.' Curling a protective arm round her shoulders, Eric led her to the sofa where he eased her into the seat. 'Tell me what happened,' he said, and sat alongside her.

When Eric offered her the mug of tea, Louise took it with thanks. Her mind went back to Blackpool, and Susan. 'She's changed so much, Eric,' she said slowly, 'and not for the better. She's harder somehow.' A bitter little smile twisted her pleasant features. 'At first she treated me like a stranger, and when she did take me into her office, it was as if we had never been sisters at all. She didn't discuss anything. Instead she told me point blank she meant to get Jinnie back.'

Her voice stiffened. 'She's a wealthy woman now, full of herself, and bristling with authority. She owns a big restaurant straddling the corner between two busy streets. It's facing the promenade, and so busy you wouldn't believe it.'

'And even that is not enough for her, is that what you're saying?'

'She's set her sights on Jinnie. That's all I know.'

'But why?'

Louise had wondered that much herself. 'I'm not sure.'

Taking a gulp of his tea, Eric replaced the mug on the tray. Leaning back on the sofa, he scratched his chin and thought for a minute, and when he spoke it was plain he'd been turning the matter over in his mind. 'Let's see now . . . for ten long years she didn't give tuppence where the girl was, or even whether she was alive. She never contacted you, and she never made enquiries about Jinnie. Is that right?'

'Every word, yes.' The two of them had often discussed the events that had led up to Louise adopting Jinnie.

'So – why does she want Jinnie now? Why *now*?'

'What d'you mean?'

'I mean there has to be a particular reason. From what I know of your sister, she's not the kind of woman who would want to take on a ten-year-old girl, with all the expense and aggravation that might incur. She can't know how Jinnie is the sweetest, most untroublesome kid there ever was. She's never met her. She knows absolutely nothing about the girl! So, my guess is, she's up to something.'

All this speculation had already crossed Louise's mind, but: 'She could just be lonely, I suppose.'

Eric shook his head. 'Not from what you tell me. She's carved herself a good life; she's wealthy, you say, and if a woman is wealthy, there's always hangers-on. It's my bet, there's a man in the background, and friends.' He smiled wryly. 'Even a woman such as Susan must have friends of sorts.'

'Maybe that's it? Maybe she wants to show Jinnie off to her new-found friends. That's about Susan's style. She would think nothing of displaying Jinnie, the way other folk might display their trophies.'

'It's a possibility, but I'm not convinced.'

Growing suspicious, Louise began to read his mind. 'My God!' She sat bolt upright as the realisation rushed through her. 'You don't think she's into . . .' she hardly dared say it '. . . *bad* things, d'you?'

He hesitated, anxious not to upset her. 'No, sunshine, I don't think that.' In truth it had crossed his mind, but it didn't bear thinking about. 'As hard and selfish as she seems to be, I'm sure she would never harm the girl.' His eyes darkened with rage. 'If she ever tried anything like that, she'd have *me* to reckon with!'

'So what is it then? Why *is* she so intent on taking Jinnie away from me?'

'Because *you've* got her? Maybe it's as simple as that.'

Louise knew what he was getting at. 'Like when we were kids, you mean?'

He smiled fondly. 'I've heard the story often enough from your mam . . . about how, when you were children, Susan could never rest until she took everything you had.'

'But this is different!'

'Maybe not in Susan's mind it isn't.'

Louise thought about it and could see a semblance of truth in what he said. 'But that would make her unbalanced!'

Rubbing his two hands over his eyes, Eric then opened them and looked at her, longing to hold her but not daring to. '*You* would know that better than me.'

Louise remembered how it was when she and Susan were children, and afterwards, as they were growing up, and she had to admit, 'There was a time when I used to think she might be a little bit mad, but she's not – I know she's

not! She's cunning and grabbing, but not mad. No, she's
perfectly sane.'

'All right, so she's not mad, and she's not lonely, so let's
look at it another way. If, as you say, she's a wealthy woman,
then one day she'll have to leave all that to somebody. And
who better than her own daughter – her *blood* daughter, I
hasten to say. Sorry, Lou. I'm just trying to see it from her
point of view.' The last thing he wanted to do was rub salt in
the wounds.

Louise understood. 'I know,' she replied softly, 'but none
of this matters, because she's not getting anywhere near Jinnie,
not if I can help it, she isn't!' A rush of anger coloured her
words. 'For God's sake, Eric, she must know she can't have
her. She's *my* daughter now, all legal and above board, and
has been for these past ten years and more. I told her all that
and still she insists she'll have her, and that's what worries
me, because she's always managed to get anything she's ever
wanted.'

Agitated now, she leaped up and began pacing the floor
again. 'Me being Jinnie's legal mother won't stop her. She's
devious, you see. She'll try other ways, like going to see her
when she comes out of school, or approaching her while I'm
here working. She could be up to all manner of stuff, and I
wouldn't know, until it was too late.'

'And do you really think Jinnie would let her come
into her life? Especially when she knows how she was con-
ceived. What do you think she'll have to say about that,
eh? Do you honestly think she would give Susan the time
of day?'

When Louise remained ominously silent, he got off the
sofa and came across to her. 'You will tell her, won't you . . .
about Susan and Ben – about everything that happened? How
Susan deserted her, only hours after she was born?'

'She said she was ill and confused, and she didn't know

what she was doing. It's true that the doctor's report said her mind was unbalanced at the time.'

'Do *you* believe that?'

Though she'd have liked to say that Susan was lying, Louise quietly admitted, 'Oh Eric, I don't know for sure. All I do know is, so many terrible things had happened, and maybe she just couldn't cope with it all.'

'You were under the same terrible strain as well, but you didn't go running off.'

'Susan was never very strong of character, and it all seemed to happen at once, didn't it? I mean, first Jacob led her a merry dance . . . beat her up even! Then he was viciously murdered just hours before she gave birth. She did love him, you know. So hearing about his killing must have shaken her to the core.' She paused, her voice showing a deeper emotion. 'Before that, she had cheated on me with Ben. She found out she was pregnant and kept it to herself for ages, and when she did have Jinnie, it wasn't the easiest of births. It was a lot for her to deal with all at once.'

'Good God! It sounds to me like you're defending her.'

'No, I'm not defending her, I'm just trying to make sense of it all.'

'Look at me, Lou.' Taking her by the shoulders, he turned her round to face him, his grip and his voice firm as he warned her, 'I know it's in your nature to be forgiving, and I respect that, but this time you are very wrong! You seem to be looking for every excuse, but it won't work. Susan has no thoughts for anyone but herself, and you know in your heart she'll take Jinnie away from you if she can, not because she loves her, but because she wants to make you, and the girl, unhappy.'

He had to drive it home that Susan was the enemy, and not the victim she would like Louise to believe. 'Your sister wants to destroy any happiness you might have found in loving Jinnie. You have to believe that, Lou. And, more importantly, you have to tell Jinnie the truth, before somebody else tells her and breaks her heart. Is that what you want? Do you want her to come home one day and face you with what she's been told by some evil-minded devil . . . filling her head with some garbled version of what happened? The truth, all twisted and cheapened by some gossip-monger? Is that what you want? I don't think so.'

Louise looked up at him, her brown eyes soft with tears. 'I don't know if I'm brave enough to tell her,' she whispered. 'I don't know if I can hurt her like that.'

To see her this way tore him apart. His voice softened, as he reaffirmed what she already knew deep down. 'You'll be hurting her a lot more if you don't tell her.'

Louise voiced what was on both their minds. 'Should I tell her everything?' The tears spilled over. 'About you and me, and how Ben took his own life? Do I tell her that?'

The love they felt for each other was never stronger than it was at that moment. 'Oh sweetheart, when will you stop torturing yourself?' Eric drew her to him, astonished when she did not resist. 'It was all a long time ago, and besides, it wasn't what we did that drove Ben to commit suicide.' He tilted her face up to his, his eyes deep with love. 'Do you really regret that night so much?'

She couldn't bring herself to say that she regretted it, because the truth was very different. She held that night and what happened between them, close to her heart, and would for all time. 'I do love you,' she whispered. 'But I feel . . . so guilty.' The guilt was like a cloud smothering everything she felt for him.

He buried his face in her hair, his voice like a caress. 'It's time to think about yourself, and us, and the rest of our lives.'

Now, when she looked up, he bent his head to kiss her, and still she did not resist. In his hard embrace she gave herself up to that wonderful kiss, long and trembling and so charged with his love for her and hers for him, it was breathtaking.

Suddenly she broke away, and running to the window, bent her head into her hands. For a moment, the silence in that room was like a dark night descending after a sunny day. 'I'm sorry.' Her voice shook with passion. 'It's not your fault.' She turned to regard him. 'I'm so sorry.'

He gazed on her a moment longer, and knowing she would not come back to him, he nodded and smiled, and hid his feelngs well. 'It's all right,' he murmured. 'I understand.'

'I do love you, Eric.' More than she could say. More than he would ever know.

He didn't acknowledge her words. Instead, he turned away. 'I'd best go and finish crating them cabbages for Mike. He'll be here any minute.' For one incredible moment he wondered if even now, she would come to him and they might start planning a future together. But the moment had passed, and his heart grew cold.

Disillusioned, and not for the first time, he strode across the room. 'I'd best be off.'

'Eric!' Pausing, he turned. 'There was something else.'

'About Susan?'

'She said she'd been keeping in touch with our mam. She said our mam was on her side in all this.'

For a brief second he was visibly shocked then, as always, he dealt with it briskly and firmly. 'If that's the case, then you have to tackle your mam about it. You need to know your enemies, Lou. And if Susan really has got your mam on her side, then it's even more important that you tell Jinnie. If I was you, I wouldn't waste another minute.'

She knew he was right, and told him so. 'I'll tell her tonight,' she vowed. After he'd gone she thought about how she would tell Jinnie, and the prospect was like a nightmare to her.

The loud tapping on the window startled her out of her

reverie. Swinging round, she couldn't help but smile at the curious sight that greeted her. With his face squashed against the window, old Mike Ellis was grinning his usual, toothless grin. His flat cap sat askew on his balding head and his weathered, leathered face was blue with cold. 'Put the kettle on, lass,' he shouted, cupping his hands round his mouth. 'Eric says there's a fruit-cake in the cupboard. I'll 'ave a slice o' that an' all, so I will.'

'I'll fetch it out,' she called back. 'Tell Eric I'll not be a minute.'

'Good lass.' He backed away, his fixed grin melting into a terrified scream when Eric's dog ran up behind him and legged him over. 'Yer silly old bugger! Fancy creeping up on a fella like that. Get out me way, afore I kick you a good 'un up the arse!' He began cursing and swearing, and flailing his arms about: the dog thought he was playing, and leaped on top of him. 'Get off, yer mangy cur! Gerroff, I tell you!'

From a distance Eric's voice could be heard teasing. 'Come on now, Mike, stop playing with the dog when there's work to be done.'

'Get 'im off! I think he means to kill me! Help, he's tearing me pants. Phew . . . he stinks an' all!'

'Aye well, that's because he gets excited when he's playing. It gives him the wind . . . if you know what I mean?'

'Aw, come on, Eric. The joke's over. Gerrim off, afore I do him a bloody mischief!'

Laughing fit to bust, Eric made his way over. 'Serves you right,' he chuckled, helping the old chap up. 'You shouldn't step back without looking to see what's behind you. Anyway, he only came to see what you were up to, that's all. It's his job to keep Peeping Toms like you off the premises.'

'Get him off me! Gerroff, you dopey bloody mutt!' As old Mike brushed the bracken and mud from his clothes,

Eric's hearty laughter could be heard all over the yard. 'Enough!' He wagged a finger at the dog and it was instantly obedient.

First making sure the old man was all right, Louise went into the kitchen, smiling to herself. 'Men and dogs, eh?' One thing was for sure. There was never a dull moment at Maple Farm.

⟶⟶●⟵

W HEN THE MORNING was over and the many crates of cabbages were washed, packed and carted away on Michael's cart, Louise and Eric took half an hour off, for a bite to eat. Having worked up an appetite, they drank two cups of coffee each, ate a pile of cheese and tomato sandwiches made by Louise, and finished up the remainder of the fruit-cake, to which Michael had been so partial.

'Mabel baked it for me,' Eric told Louise. 'She brought it up last night. If you ask me, I think Mike Ellis could do a lot worse than marry her. She's clean and tidy, and keeps her house shining like a new pin. More to the point, and judging by that cake *and* the apple pie she brought me last week, she must be one of the best cooks in Blackburn.' He gave her a mischievous glance. 'Barring yourself, o' course.' When she made a face at him, he winked cheekily. 'But then I've got to say that, haven't I? Especially when I live in hope that we'll be man and wife one day.'

'Mmm.' Answering automatically, Louise had her mind on something else just then.

'Lou? Are you listening to me?'

She looked up. 'Sorry, I was just thinking.'

'I could see that.'

'Did I tell you about the woman I met on the bus coming home from Blackpool?'

Taking a bite of his cake, he brushed the crumbs off his shirt. 'I don't think you did. No.'

Louise described Sarah and the two children, and how she had learned from the old fella called George Brooker that the trio camped under the pier. 'You could see they were a very close family,' she said. 'Then, after I got off the bus and got to thinking, something else kept nagging at me. I was sure I knew them . . . or I'd seen them before, not just from Blackpool. I couldn't quite put my finger on what it was.'

'Strange.' He took another bite of his cake; this time holding his hand underneath to catch the crumbs. 'Got two children in tow, you say?'

'That's right, teenagers – a boy and a girl.'

'And the woman was too old to be their mother?'

'I got the impression she was their grandmother. That was what set me thinking. Something about them kept gnawing at me, and then I heard the girl call the boy by his name. It was Adam.'

Eric had been drinking his coffee, but at her words he put his cup down. 'Go on,' he urged.

'I think they're *Maggie's* children,' Louise said in a low voice.

'Maggie who?'

'Maggie Pringle – the woman who got murdered with Jacob. I think they're her children . . . the ones who hid in the cellar while their poor mam was being attacked by their own father.' She clenched her fists on the table. 'That swine, Terry Harpur, he's in the right place in jail. Let's hope he rots there till he's old and grey. Or dead!'

'So, if you're right, the woman must have been Maggie's mother . . . or Terry Harpur's?'

Louise considered that. 'Maybe. Anyway, you could tell they'd been sleeping rough. Oh Eric! What's to become of them, eh? Two kids without a mother, wandering about like that with their grandmother, who's too old to be tramping the streets.'

Eric didn't like the picture any more than Louise did. 'It's a bad business.'

'I didn't realise. I wish now I'd been more helpful.'

'Did the kids look starved?'

'No. They looked well fed.'

'Scruffy, were they?'

'No.'

'And did they look upset, or ill-treated?'

''Course not!'

'Well, there you are.' He leaned his long, easy frame forward, across the table, 'Listen to me, love. You can't carry the weight of the world on your shoulders. They've managed so far ... what is it, ten years and more? And from what you say, they seem to be in good hands with their grandmother. I'm sure they can cope without your help, so stop your worrying – or don't you think you've got enough problems of your own?'

Louise grinned in acceptance, then she had another thought. 'Isn't it strange though, how they were on the same bus as me, and leaving the place where Susan decided to settle?' She shook her head. 'It's a small world.'

Eric laid his hand over hers. 'You're a big softie who wants to mother everybody.' He smiled, his voice falling to a whisper. 'It's part of the reason I love you so much.'

For that precious while, they held hands across the table, and on this occasion, that was as far as it went.

'Right then, my beauty.' He squeezed her hand. 'I'd better go and make a start on chopping that wood, or I'll be without kindling for the fire, and here we are, coming up fast to winter.'

Louise agreed. 'I'll come and help you pile up the kindling when I've finished here.'

'No need,' he told her. 'It's blowing up chilly out there.'

'It's what you pay me for,' she gently reminded him. 'And besides, I'd like a pound for every time I've chopped up the kindling in that very yard, *and* in the middle of winter.' And he knew there was no arguing with her.

While Eric returned to his work, Louise cleared away the plates. At the sink she stood by the window looking out across the fields. For many reasons, she always felt nostalgic when standing in this particular room, by this particular window. She remembered with a heart's tug, that it was also where she and Sally often stood to watch the early-morning foxes scurrying across the fields. However, she wasn't thinking about foxes now. Instead, she was thinking about Jinnie, and Susan, and wondering where Sarah and Maggie Pringle's kids had gone.

'I hope they found somewhere to live,' she murmured aloud. 'I do hope they're safe.'

Then she recalled what Eric had said. She *did* tend to think she could put the world to rights. All the same, deep down, she wished she had tried harder to help that unfortunate family.

Chapter Ten

A LAN MARTIN HAD not aged well over the years. His treachery to Louise's husband Ben Hunter had weighed heavy on his soul. It showed in the sleepless nights and haunted eyes. It showed in his long, iron-grey hair bereft of life or colour, and the incessant nervous twitch of his fingers. It betrayed itself in his all too frequent bouts of uncontrollable rage that left him speechless and exhausted for hours afterwards.

Even now as he spoke to his son, Ralph, his fingers were alive, entwining themselves, then drumming the table, and now stretching in and out, as though doing some weird kind of dance.

Ralph noticed it and was on his guard. 'There's no need to get agitated about the house in Montague Street,' he said quietly. 'I've found a tenant now so all we lost was that few weeks' rent. It were a pity that deal fell through, to sell the terrace.' He had seen his father working himself into a state of anxiety many times and, in one form or another, it usually signalled trouble.

Alan Martin continued drumming his fingers on the desk, before, all of a sudden, swinging his chair round to face the window. His back to his son and his voice low and trembling, he said, 'You say the woman Sarah Harpur was related to Jacob Hunter?'

Ralph groaned inwardly. *Jacob Hunter! Always Jacob Hunter!*

'I asked you a question!'

Ralph slunk down in his seat, 'Not directly, no, but the woman who was murdered with him, Maggie Pringle, was her son's common-law wife and the mother of her grand-children.

'Why didn't you tell me this years ago!'

'I don't see as that matters. We don't know *any* of our tenants, not really, do we, Dad? Even though we take up references, we can't be sure where they've been or who they are – and anyway, as long as they pay their rent on time, does it matter?'

Ignoring the comment, the older man sat silent for a minute before asking, 'What was she like, this woman?'

'As I've already explained, she was regular with her rent before we had to give her notice to quit, and pleasant enough . . . middle-aged and hard-working. She often did odd jobs around the town, so I'm told – cleaning, baby-minding, that kind of thing. She's devoted to the grandchildren. They think the world of her.'

'You said there was a boy. How old is he?'

'About to start work as I believe.'

'What kind of boy is he?'

'In what way?' Ralph was beginning to think this was a curious set of questions. His father had never shown this level of interest in any of their other tenants. But it was to be expected, now he realised Jacob Hunter was known to them.

Slowly, deliberately, his father swung his chair back again and regarded his son with staring eyes. 'It's a simple enough question.' He began rubbing his fingers together, as though removing some kind of irritating substance. 'What *kind* of boy?'

Ralph Martin called up a picture of Adam in his mind. 'Tall, well-built, with black hair and dark eyes.'

'Is he a *bad* boy?' Alan's eyes narrowed until they were almost sunk in his head. 'Does he steal and fight?'

'Of course I can't be certain, but he seemed sensible enough the few times I've met him.' Ralph smiled with pleasure at the way that family looked after each other. 'He's very protective of his grandmother. I remember one time when she was late with the rent. I had to take her to task, and the boy stood beside her the whole time.'

'I see. Bad-tempered, is he?'

'Not as far as I could tell.'

'Not . . . *violent* then?'

'Not a violent boy, no.'

His father took a deep, invigorating breath, leaned back in his chair and visibly relaxed. 'Why did they leave?'

'Because you said you wanted the house vacated. That part of Montague Street was to be pulled down.'

'You should have checked with me again. I might have changed my mind in between!'

'I wasn't to know that.'

'Where did they go?'

'I've no idea. She left a note with the neighbour, but it wasn't addressed to us, so she didn't confide in me, and quite right too.'

'Who was it addressed to?' Alan Martin sat up, his arms stretched out across the desk, and a look of fear in his eyes. 'What did the note say? Did it mention Jacob Hunter? Did it say anything about his relationship with *me*?'

'I didn't get a sight of the note. The neighbour told me when I collected his rent. He said, "Sarah's gone away, and she'll not be back. She's left me a note, but it's not addressed to you."'

'And that's all?'

'Yes.'

His father gave a great sigh of relief. 'If she comes back I want to know, d'you hear?'

Ralph nodded. 'But from what the neighbour said, she won't be back.'

'What about the house on Craig Street?'

'What about it?'

'Is it rented out yet?'

'Not yet. People have long memories, that's the trouble. They know its history and so I can't seem to get a tenant at any price, especially as you won't let me furnish it. It's a damned sight easier to get tenants for a house that's already furnished. Most people haven't got the money to spend on furniture and such. They'd rather find the extra money on the rent.'

Alan Martin became suspicious. 'I hope you did what I told you. I hope you had it all cleared out . . . all the furniture that belonged to Hunter. You had it burned, didn't you?'

'It's gone, just like you instructed. After the last tenant left, I had it all cleared out. Every last item was scraped up and sent to the council tip. It fell apart as it was being lifted. Ten years is a long time, what with wear and tear of tenants in and out, some of them destructive – and anyway, the stuff was probably second-hand to begin with.'

Ralph wondered about the questions. 'Why? Are you thinking of having it refurnished? Perhaps I could get a decorator in. We could put up the rent and fit a small bathroom in one of the bedrooms. It's probably the only one in the street that still has an outside lavvy. If you intend spending that sort of money, it might help to find a tenant.'

'No! I'm not spending one single penny on that god-forsaken place!' His staring gaze pinned Ralph to the chair.

Ralph was growing nervous. He could see the signs of his father losing control. 'I'll do as you say,' he promised. 'We'll keep it empty.' In a sharper tone he reminded him, 'It doesn't make sense though. We're losing precious money. It isn't the house's fault if the man who lived there for a while was rotten to the core. The badness is in the *man* himself!'

'It's *my* property and it can rot into the ground for all I care . . . like the monster who lived there.' Alan peered up through hang-dog eyes, his face wretched and his hands crawling into each other across the desk. 'Get about your work. Off with you. Go on!'

Ralph got out of the chair and looking on his father, saw a sad, tortured man who was going out of his mind. It was painful to see. In a rush of sympathy, Ralph pleaded with him. 'It was a long time ago, Father,' he said softly. 'If you go on like this, you'll haunt yourself into an early grave.'

The man looked up, and in a rare moment of peace, his hands were still and his voice heavy with regret. 'You don't know how it was,' he murmured. 'It was a deliberate act of pure greed. Jacob Hunter was bad, but I was worse. I had the upper hand and I could have stopped the badness, but I didn't.' He closed his eyes and when he opened them again they swam with tears. 'Because of him . . . and *me*, a good man was driven to take his own life. How am I supposed to live with that, please tell me?'

'Look, Dad, there's nothing you can do to bring Ben Hunter back. All you're doing is killing yourself now!'

His father considered his remark, before answering with a nervous little smile. 'Do you know what I think?'

The son shook his head.

'I think the man who killed Jacob and that woman, is bound to come after me soon. He knows what we did, you see.'

Ralph was horrified that he should even entertain such an idea. 'Dear God, is that what you've been thinking? You're wrong, Dad. The man who killed them was the woman's ex-common-law husband. He was jealous, that's all. It had nothing whatsoever to do with you!'

'Oh, but don't you see? It doesn't alter the fact that we killed that poor innocent man. We took his home and his livelihood, and made a widow of his good wife. Jacob Hunter deserved to die. *I* deserve to die!' Thumping the table with his clenched fist, he screamed like a banshee, 'WHY ARE YOU STILL HERE? I thought I told you to get about your work!' Folding his arms across the desk, Alan Martin laid his head into them, and cried like a baby.

When he looked up, his son was gone.

———◈———

After a fruitless morning, Adam made his way back to the canal bank, to find Sarah and Hannah on a bench near the tent, feeding the ducks. 'Ah! So *this* is what you do when I'm out looking for work.' Dropping to the ground, he sat cross-legged before them.

He sounded light-hearted, but Sarah saw the disappointment in his face. 'Aw, lad. No luck, eh?'

'Not this time,' he answered despondently. 'It's not because the work isn't out there. It's the same old story everywhere I've been . . .' He shook his head and lowered his voice to mimic the men who had interviewed him.' "Sorry, son. Can't take you on if you've got no permanent abode".' He stretched out his long legs and, leaning backwards on his hands, gave a weary groan. 'I get as far as thinking I've got the job, then they ask me for an address. When they find out we're living on the canal bank in a tent, that's it: the interview's over. I tell them it's only until we find a house, but it makes no difference.'

'But that's ridiculous!' Sarah could make head nor tail of the system. 'So if you had a proper address, they'd give you work, and if you *had* work, you'd be able to afford a place to rent. Can't they see what nonsense that makes?'

'No, happen they can't.' Adam then told them where he'd been. 'I've been up to Cicely Bridge Mill, and the manager there wouldn't even see me . . . said to write in. I went to two other places where they took me in and asked me questions, then sent me away.'

Hannah grinned wickedly. 'I expect they thought you were a bad lot, with them black eyes,' she teased. 'It'll be the same wherever you go.'

'Now then, my girl, that's not nice, is it?' Sarah chided. 'Your brother's been tramping all over the place and you seem to think it's a joke.' Lately, Sarah had begun to worry about Hannah. There were times when she could be downright spiteful.

When he saw how Hannah was about to burst into tears, Adam did the right thing. 'It's a good job I didn't take *you* with me then,' he teased back, 'or they'd have thrown us both in jail.'

At which she playfully leaped on him, and they rolled over and over on the bank, until Sarah screamed out, 'Be careful, you two!' She could see them heading for the water.

When peace was restored, and Hannah in a better frame of mind, they came back to Sarah. 'Well anyway,' Adam concluded, 'after a while, I made my way back to the railway because somebody told me there was a job for a young lad going there, but this business of an address came up, and I was sent on my way *again*. Then, to top it all, I went to the metal factory, and they did the same . . . no address, no work!'

'Oh lad, I am sorry but we'll have to keep trying, there's nothing else for it.' Sarah was at the end of her tether, but she dared not show it to the children, so now, when Adam came back without work for the sixth time in the two days they'd been back in Blackburn, she put a reassuring arm round him.

'Don't be down-hearted,' she said brightly. 'It's only a matter of time before you find work of a kind.'

She took Hannah into her embrace too and gave them both a cuddle. 'It's early days yet. We've only been here two nights and it's taken us time to settle in.' She glanced up at the stormy skies. 'The weather's been good to us so far, but it looks to me like it's on the change. I reckon we'd best put our best foot forward and find us a house, with a proper roof over, so's Adam here's got an address and can get work.'

Hannah was impatient. 'I thought we were going to find me a place at school today?'

'And so we are, child! So we are! I know you've missed a bit and want to catch up. But first things first, eh?'

Adam wanted to know, 'Do I need to come with you to find a house?'

'No, not if you don't want to. Why? Got summat planned, have you?'

'There was a bloke outside the metal factory. He reckons they might be looking for a lad at the furniture place, helping with deliveries and all that.' He grinned. 'He said I were the right build to lift a sofa all by myself.'

Sarah was mortified. 'You'd better not! You don't lift *nothing* like that on your own. There should be two fellas to a job like that, and don't you be put on, not by anybody!'

'All the same, I'll go and see. I had intended going straight there, only I thought I should come back and tell you how it all went earlier on.'

'And I'm glad you did, son. Me and Hannah were wondering if you might turn up before we set off. It must be about, what . . . eleven o'clock. If we're to catch anybody of any importance we should be away now. Only, we've been tidying up and clearing away.' She glanced at Hannah, who appeared to be sulking. 'Me and your sister have been having a little chat . . . about school and all that.'

'Where are you going?'

'We're going to Ralph Martin's office on Ainsworth Street, to see if he's got any new properties to rent that we can afford. You never know your luck, do you?'

Before he left on another quest for work, Adam helped them to secure the tent. He tied the door-flap in, and fastened the straps across, and when they were ready, he went one way while Hannah and their grandmother went another. 'We'll meet back here at five o'clock,' Sarah told him.

Hannah was thinking of her stomach. 'Can we have fish and chips for tea?' she asked. 'I'm fed up with rotten old sandwiches.'

Sarah, too, had had enough of sandwiches. 'Oh, I reckon we can stretch to fish and chips for tea, just for this once, lass.' And Hannah was satisfied.

As they walked towards the road, Sarah sighed dreamily. 'Oh pet, won't it be grand when we get a proper house and a proper little kitchen, where I can cook for the two of you again to my heart's content? I can make my own jam like I used to, and bake fresh bread the way my old mammy taught me.'

Hannah licked her lips; she remembered how it used to be. 'Will you bake them lovely scones you used to make – stuffed with raisins and swimming with butter and strawberry jam? I remember eating those when Mam brought us round to your house when we were little.'

Sarah was deeply moved. 'You remember that, d'you lass?'

Without warning, Hannah's mood changed, her face stiffening with anger, and her eyes scouring her grandmother's face. 'I remember *everything*!'

There was such venom in the girl's voice that Sarah was momentarily taken aback. She had seen flashes of Hannah's rage before, and it caused her great anguish. So the girl remembered everything, did she? Did she remember the way her father would make her stand in a corner, and when Sarah intervened, how he would slap his own mother across the mouth, and afterwards be mortified – until the next time!

And what about the way he would play the children off against their mother, doing his best to turn their love for Maggie into hate? And once, when Maggie called to collect them he dragged her in and beat her in front of the children. Sarah, too, had been hurt when she tried to protect Maggie. And did Hannah recall how Terry once spanked her so hard for breaking a vase, that the deep weals bled through her underwear?

When Sarah found out, she turned him out of house and home and warned him never to come back. But he did, and the outcome had been terrible. He had murdered a good woman, a woman whose only wrong had been to sell her body to feed her children, to give them some of the things other children enjoyed – like presents at Christmas, and clothes that wouldn't make them a laughing-stock.

Sarah knew now that Hannah had seen or heard everything that had happened on that terrible night, and remembered it in detail. She wouldn't speak of it, but it was there, fixed in her mind and eating away at her. It had been there just now, in those hard, unforgiving features.

Drawing herself and Hannah to a halt, Sarah took the girl by the arms and spoke to her in loving tones. 'Listen to me, sweetheart,' she said softly. 'Sometimes we know things . . . things we don't like to talk about. Things we're afraid to acknowledge.'

'What things?' Hannah knew what her grandmother was getting at, but she put up the same barrier she had hidden behind all these years.

Sarah sighed and for a moment she regarded this slip of a girl, whose nightmare was still vividly alive in her young mind, and her heart was sore. 'That night,' she persevered, 'when your daddy came to the house, there was a terrible, *terrible* fight. You saw things, didn't you, Hannah? *Heard* things that frightened you?'

'I want to go now.' Hannah was like a bairn again, talking in that soft, babyish voice and smiling at Sarah as if she had not heard a single word.

Still, Sarah persevered. 'You can tell me, Hannah. It's all right to talk about it now. I *want* you to. Please, my love, talk to me?'

But the girl began walking away. 'We'd best get a move on,' she retorted, 'or we won't find a place to live.'

Downhearted, Sarah followed. She knew her chance had passed. At least for today.

'All right, lass,' she said heavily, 'but remember, I'm always here if you need me.'

'Come on, hurry up, Gran, or that Martin man will be closed by the time we get there.'

Sarah didn't press the issue. She knew better than that so, like Hannah, she changed the conversation, as though the matter of that night had never arisen. 'I thought you were more keen on getting back to your old school?'

'After what Adam said, I've changed my mind. If they wouldn't give him a job because he hadn't got a proper address, they might not let me start school.'

'That's very true, lass.' Sarah quickened her steps. 'If we get a move on, and secure a roof over our heads, we might still have time to register you today before the school office closes.'

With that in mind, the two directed themselves towards Ainsworth Street, and Alan Martin's office.

Much to her grandmother's dismay, Hannah had fallen into a sulk. As always, Sarah let her stew in it, until the mood passed. As it surely would.

O N HIS WAY back from business, Ralph Martin entered Ainsworth Street at the boulevard end, while Sarah and Hannah came in from the market end. Sarah saw him before he saw them. 'Oh, look!' Tugging at Hannah's sleeve, she cried, 'It's our old landlord!'

Hannah recognised him at once, and called out, 'Mr Martin!'

Astonished to see them there, Ralph rushed forward, spurred on by thoughts of his father suddenly coming out and realising that here was the woman they'd spoken of this very morning. Recalling the way his father had seemed obsessed with her, who knew what he might do?

Excited to see him, Sarah quickened her step. 'See, Hannah? I reckon we might be in luck. He knows I'm a good payer, nice an' regular. Happen we might be in line for a house after all, eh?'

Unfortunately she was to be disappointed. After skilfully turning them from the vicinity of his father's office, Ralph told her, 'There's absolutely nothing doing. I'm sorry, Mrs Harpur. There are no new houses come on the market to rent . . . at least, not in the price range you want.' He regarded her curiously. 'Unless you've suddenly come into a pot of money?'

Sarah laughed out loud. 'Huh! I only wish I had. No. We need an ordinary house, so's my grandson Adam can get work, and Hannah here can go back to school.'

'I really am sorry, but neither I nor my father have anything to offer.' He clicked his fingers. 'I tell you what, though . . .' Taking her by the shoulder, he steered her further away from the office. Intrigued, Hannah followed.

'The house on Craig Street is still available to you. It's there if you want it, and more to the point, I think I can let you have it at a nominal rent for a time. There! You'll never get another offer like that, and it's only because I don't like to see a woman of your age with two children, out on the streets with nowhere to lay your heads.' There was another reason: if that house got broken into and squatters took over like they did on Bent Street only last week, it would be on *his* back to get them out, and sometimes, the law was tricky where squatters were concerned. He didn't relish the idea of that kind of fight and legal expense.

Suddenly he gave a yelp as Hannah lashed out at him, punching him hard an the arm. '*We've told you before, we don't want the house on Craig Street.*' In a fit of rage, she threw herself at him. 'You're a liar! You *must* have another house for us somewhere.'

'HANNAH!' Sarah's voice cut through her outburst. 'Take a hold of yourself!' Shocked by the girl's behaviour, she dragged her away, and not too gently neither. 'The young man is only trying to help.'

Being chided by her grandmother was too much. Hannah took to her heels and fell sobbing in the doorway of the corner shop.

'I'd best go to her.' Sarah was beside herself. 'She has these nightmares, you see?'

Still shaken, Ralph apologised. 'I understand, and I'm sorry, but it really is all we've got. My father doesn't want the house rented out, but there are squatters on the move in these parts, and I'm far too busy to handle that kind of trouble. Besides, to be honest, I think it's a crying shame to leave it empty when it could be home to somebody. And I meant what I said . . . there'd be only a low rent.'

Sarah thanked him, but drawing his attention to Hannah, who was hunched up on the step, her face white and tear-stained, she murmured sadly, 'You see how it is?'

And of course, he did. Because that poor child was suffering similar sorts of nightmares as his own father was.

A few minutes later, Ralph Martin watched Sarah and the girl make their way out of Ainsworth Street.

'What the devil d'you think you're doing, hanging about outside when there's work to be done!' His father's voice startled him.

'I was just on my way in,' Ralph answered, and walked quickly towards the office, where his father waited in the doorway.

'Who were you looking at?'

Ralph's heart sank. 'What do you mean?'

'Just now, you were staring at someone down the end of the street.'

'Oh, it was just some woman,' he replied casually, 'wondering if we'd got a house to rent.'

'And what did you tell her?'

'I told her we didn't have any, not in the low price-range she was looking for.'

Curious, his father observed him for a while, then, going inside, he bent his head to his work and shut him out of his mind.

———⟫•◦•⟪———

LATER THAT EVENING, for the third time in a row, Sarah and the children ate their tea in the tent, but this time, as promised, Sarah had treated them all to fish and chips. 'Well, we've had no luck today.' Slapping her mouth round a juicy piece of fish, Sarah then wiped away the fatty residue with her hankie. 'Happen we'll have more luck tomorrow, eh?'

Like Sarah, Adam was ever optimistic. 'There are bound to be other landlords in Blackburn who can find us a house.'

Merrily munching, Sarah nodded. 'We'll see.'

Hannah had hardly touched her food. 'What about the authorities? Can't we try them? Other people seem to get council houses, so why can't we?'

Adam didn't like it when Hannah was in this kind of a mood, but he knew why and so was patient with her. 'You know why,' he reminded her. 'Because if we go to the authorities, they'll say Grandma isn't capable of looking after us, and they'll take us away.'

Folding her arms defiantly, she muttered, 'I don't care.'

Both Sarah and Adam were shocked, but it was Adam who spoke. 'You don't mean that, do you?'

Hannah glanced up at Sarah, who was visibly shaken. 'No, all right, I don't,' she admitted. 'But if I can't go to school, I'll be a dunce. And I'll never have any friends, because we keep moving all the time.'

'Aw, lass.' Her voice shaking, Sarah opened her arms. 'Come 'ere to your grandma, love.' Remarkably, Hannah went to her, and they clung together for what seemed an age. Presently, Sarah whispered through her tears, 'I'll find us a place, I swear to God. You'll have your old friends soon enough, you see if I'm not right.'

Seeing them like that, Adam, too, was moved to tears. In his young heart he prayed it would all come right, and soon.

A short time later, after they'd cleared away and secured the tent for the night, they went to their respective sleeping-bags and settled down for a night's sleep.

Having made peace with Hannah and with a full belly of fish and chips, Sarah felt a little more content. But she knew things could not go on as they were. In the dark, she vowed to herself that she would tramp the whole of Blackburn to find a house if needs be. With that thought in mind, she fell hard and fast asleep.

About two hours later she woke to the pattering of rain on the canvas. She was unsettled and cold, and there was something playing on her mind, but for the life of her, she couldn't think what it was. For a while she lay there, unable to sleep. She glanced across at her grandchildren. Adam was cocooned in his blanket, safe and warm, while Hannah had thrown hers off, exposing her upper arms and neck.

Ever so gently, Sarah crept out of her sleeping-bag and went across the tent. On touching Hannah's arm, she wasn't surprised to find that it was all goose-bumps. Pulling up the bag, she made certain every bit of flesh was covered, save for the girl's face. 'That's better,' she whispered, tiptoeing back to her own bed. 'I'll sleep more content now.'

For a while she kept a wary eye on the two youngsters, at the same time enjoying the pitter-patter of the rain dancing on the sides of the tent. There was something very soothing, she thought, in listening to the rain when you were warm and cosy inside. She wondered lazily whether it would ease soon. It didn't, so she turned over and let the sleep wash over her once more.

When a short time later she woke again, it was to Hannah's terrified screams. With the sleep still on her, Sarah sat bolt upright in her sleeping-bag, unsure what was happening until she felt the wet on her feet, and saw the blanket swimming in the water. 'Oh my God! Quick, Adam, we're flooded out!' she shouted urgently.

Scrambling out of bed, Sarah paddled across the tent, towards where Hannah was huddled up the corner of her sleeping-bag, her eyes big as saucers. 'RATS!' she cried out. 'There's rats everywhere!'

Woken by the pandemonium, Adam leaped out of his bag and, seeing the rats swarming all over Hannah's bedding, he took up his blanket and began thrashing out at them, sending them in all directions. 'Take her out!' he yelled at Sarah, while at the same time grabbing Hannah and swinging her aside, to where Sarah was desperately struggling to clear a way out of the tent.

'The knots have tightened in the water,' she cried. 'I can't open it. Adam, I can't open it!' Behind her, clinging to Sarah's nightgown, Hannah was hysterical as the rats swam round her legs.

Fighting his way through, Adam finally managed to rip the tent open and thrust the two women out. When he followed, it was to see Hannah running headlong towards the canal's edge, with no thought but to escape the rats. 'NO, HANNAH!' With Sarah safely out of harm's way he took after his sister. When he caught hold of her, she fought like a demon, until suddenly the two of them were off the swollen banks and in the deep water, struggling for their very lives.

In the dark and half-blinded by the driving rain, Sarah couldn't see them, but she heard Hannah screaming. Slowly, carefully, so as not to lose her footing, she felt her way along the wall, to where she could hear Adam trying to calm his sister; by now Hannah was like a wild thing, kicking out, oblivious to the danger she was putting them both in.

Nearer now, Sarah caught a glimpse of them, not too far from the edge, but in trouble all the same.

'Hannah!' Sarah called out firmly. 'Be quiet, and do as Adam tells you. It's all right now. You're safe with him. But you *must* do as he says.'

Whatever Sarah said made no difference. Hannah simply fought all the more, in the process taking herself and her brother deeper into the water. For a few desperate minutes which seemed to last a lifetime, Adam struggled to control her. In the background, rising above the heightening wind, Sarah continued to call on her granddaughter, pleading with her to calm herself.

Suddenly, everything went silent and Sarah feared the worst. With her heart in her mouth, she called Adam's name. 'Where are you, son? For God's sake Adam! Where are you?'

'We're all right! I need your help, Gran!' Adam's voice came faintly through the darkness, and on hearing it, Sarah almost collapsed with relief. Summoning all her strength, she got down on her knees and stretching out her two arms, managed to help Adam get his sister out of the water. 'I had to punch her,' he said, coughing and spluttering as he climbed out. 'I had to, or she would have drowned us both.'

Sarah was only too grateful. 'It's all right, son. You did what you had to.'

Between them, they carried Hannah back to the top of the bank; the tent had been swept into the canal by the wind, and was now drifting about in the water and being washed to the edge. 'It's all gone, lad.' Sarah hugged Hannah's limp body to her breast and, for a while, she and Adam watched as their every possession was taken by the water.

When Hannah came round, she hung onto her gran, cold and wet, and sobbing like a baby. 'I want to go home,' she cried and, knowing only too well they had no home, Sarah's heart broke.

'Come on, lass,' she said softly. 'We can't stay here.' A quiet sob marbled her voice. 'There's nothing here for us now.'

Making their way up towards the street and the cobbles, Sarah and the children stayed there for some long time. 'Where do we go now?' Adam asked. It was three o'clock in the morning, without a single soul out on the street.

'I'm concerned about the pair of you,' Sarah said. 'If we don't get Hannah inside somewhere, she'll die of pneumonia.' In her arms, Hannah shivered uncontrollably, too weak now even to speak.

'We'd best get her to the Infirmary.' Adam was frantic. 'She swallowed a lot of water.' He took the weight of his sister from Sarah. 'She was wild . . . fighting me all the time. She wouldn't let me get her out.'

Sarah was in a quandary. 'If we go to the Infirmary they'll want our names and addresses. They'll find out we've no home, and then we'll be in trouble.' She shook her head. 'I can't risk it, lad. I *won't* have us split up now, not after what we've been through.' Then, like a light switching on in her mind came the words of Ralph Martin: *'The house on Craig Street . . . minimal rent . . . it's all we've got.'*

'What can we do, Gran? We've *got* to get her in the warm!' Adam was shivering, his face white from the cold, and Hannah safe in his strong arms.

'There's only one thing we *can* do.' Threading her arm round Hannah's waist, Sarah knew what must be done. 'Come on, lad,' she whispered. 'She wanted to go home, and that's where we'll take her. She'll be safe there, with us.'

Adam stared at her with disbelieving eyes. 'You mean Craig Street?'

Sarah nodded. 'We've no choice.' She knew what must be done, and now she would not flinch from it. 'Not if we want this lass to be safe.'

In his heart, Adam knew she was right so, with the weight of Hannah between them, they made their way across the Market Square, and on towards Craig Street.

'It'll be all right,' Sarah kept saying. 'You'll see. It will be all right, lad.'

Adam said nothing. For his sake and Hannah's, too, he had to trust this woman whom he loved with heart and soul, and who had given up so much to keep them together.

Chapter Eleven

T HE NEWS SPREAD like wildfire. 'Someone broke into the house where the murders took place,' they said. 'Tommy Penrose from next door heard the sound of breaking glass, and when he looked out, he saw a huddle of figures by the door.'

It was nine o'clock in the morning when Louise heard Tommy tell his story in the local shop. 'They went inside,' he told Maisie, 'and I ain't seen hide nor hair of 'em since.'

A round, bouncy woman, Maisie worked in the shop from nine to twelve; as a rule she was a bright, jolly soul, but never in that first hour. It always took her that much time to catch up with herself. Until ten o'clock, she didn't have a smile or a word for anybody. However, this morning, even she was interested to hear Tommy's story. 'Who could they be, I wonder?' She shivered. 'By! You wouldn't catch *me* breaking in there, I can tell you. What! They'd have to pay me a fortune, just to look in the window.'

'From what I could see, there were three of 'em,' Tommy recounted. 'They looked to be a woman and two others . . . youngsters mebbe.' He shrugged. 'It were raining heaven's hardest, and the wind was blowing my curtains inside out, so I couldn't see all that clear.'

Louise listened to what he had to say, and it jogged her

memory. It was a strange thing, that for days now, she hadn't been able to get the woman on the bus out of her mind, nor the two youngsters with her. 'And you say you've not heard anything from them since?'

'Not a dicky-bird. Whoever they are, it's nowt to do with me. I keep meself to meself, allus have. That way you don't get in bother.' Having said that, he collected his loaf and ambled to the door. 'Happen they've gone anyway,' he suggested. 'Happen they were just trying to get in out of the rain.'

Before old Tommy left, he set Louise to thinking with his next remark: 'What puzzles me, though, is how they knew that particular house were empty?' With that he shut the door and left the others to ponder on what he had said.

Maisie was excited. 'He's right.' Leaning her ample bosom over the counter, she regarded Louise with beady eyes. 'If you ask me, it's very strange that somebody should come straight up and break into a house . . . *unless* they know the house, and unless they also know there's nobody living there right now.' Stretching her short fat body upright, she made an eerie, ghost-like noise. 'Or perhaps it were Jacob and his woman, come back to haunt us.'

Louise gave her a playful shove. 'Give over, Maisie, it's no such thing.'

'Well, what's going on then? You tell me that.'

'It's probably like Tommy said. They had to get in somewhere out of the rain, and they just happened to be down Craig Street.'

'All right, but why *that* house? And how did they know it were empty?' She gave an audible shiver. 'It all sounds very spooky to me.' She peered at Louise again. 'You look a bit the worse for wear,' she remarked bluntly. 'Are you not working today?'

'Not this morning. I've rung Eric and he's all right about it.'

Maisie gave her a sly little grin. 'Hmh! It's a wonder he hasn't come running round wi' a bunch o' flowers in his hand.'

'Why do you say that?' Louise had gone pink.

'Come off it, Lou. Everybody knows he's in love with you – and don't deny it, because you know it's true. If you ask me, it's only a matter of time before he proposes. You'd be mad not to say yes, especially when he's well breached . . . good-looking, wi' a farm, land, and money in the bank. That's the sort of man to go for.'

'Is that right?' Louise was being polite. Maisie was incredibly tactless at times; Louise's connection with Jacob Hunter, one of the murder victims, had been ignored, as had her former ownership of Maple Farm with her husband Ben, long before Eric bought it and farmed there.

'Oh yeah. I bet it'll not be long before the two of you get wed.' Rolling her eyes, the plump woman sighed dreamily. 'Ooh, I'd love to walk down the aisle in a flowing white gown.' The sigh gave way to a groan. 'I never will though, 'cause however much I try, I can't keep a boyfriend for more than a week.'

'That's the trouble,' Louise told her good-humouredly. 'You live in a dreamworld. If you go out with a lad and start talking about wedding bells straight off, he'll run a mile. Take it easy, Maisie, and it'll all come right in the end.'

'What? Like you and Eric, you mean?' She was a persistent devil.

Louise wisely ignored her remark. 'I'll be in to work later on,' she said, 'only I really don't feel too wonderful this morning. I had a bad night.'

'You've picked up a bug.' Maisie considered herself to be an expert in matters medical. 'Got a stomach-ache, have you?'

'Not really, no.'

'Headache?'

'Pounding.'

'And do you feel sick?'

'I *do* a bit, yes.'

Maisie had the answer. 'What you want is a dose o' castor-oil.'

Louise laughed. 'I do *not*! I can't stomach the stuff.' Pointing to the shelf behind Maisie she asked, 'Give us a bottle of Milk of Magnesia. That'll do the trick.'

Maisie handed her the bottle. 'It'll be summat you ate,' she said authoritatively. 'Fish and chips, was it? By! That does it to me every time . . . it's the fat they cook it in. I reckon they don't change it for years on end.' To make a point she gave a loud, rattling burp. ''S'cuse *me*! D' you know, it's a wonder they don't poison the lot of us.'

Louise stifled a chuckle. 'I don't think I've been poisoned.' She paid her dues and bade Maisie cheerio. 'And don't be frightening yourself with ideas of ghosts and hauntings,' she warned. 'If the truth be told, it were probably poor old Tommy having a nightmare.'

'Huh! More like hallucinations. He downs enough booze to give anybody nightmares.' With that, the plump little body began singing. She'd got through that first crucial hour and now she was wide awake.

Louise went back down Derwent Street smiling to herself. 'They broke the mould when they made you, Maisie,' she chuckled. 'A bit mad, a bit of a gossip, but you're a tonic all the same.' Pausing, she cast her gaze down Craig Street and there, not too far away, was Tommy's lanky figure, shoulders slightly stooped and his wispy hair blowing in the breeze. Unaware that she was watching, he continued to shuffle along at a steady pace. 'Hey, Tommy – wait a minute!' Louise went after him.

When he heard the call, the old chap turned to see her

running towards him. 'What's to do, lass?' he wanted to know. 'I haven't forgot summat, have I?'

'Not as far as I know.' Louise glanced towards the house in question. 'You say you couldn't tell who it was that broke in?'

He shook his head. 'It were too dark, and like I say, the wind and rain were treacherous.'

'And you didn't hear anything else afterwards?'

'Not a thing, no. All the same, it's very odd if you ask me. The windows have curtains up and it don't *look* empty. But they just went straight in, as if they knew there was nobody living there.'

On instinct, Louise glanced up at the windows of the corner house, and just as she looked up, the curtains twitched and the face was gone. But she had already recognised the woman who had been peeping out at them. It was the same one who had been on the bus.

'I'll be off then, lass, if yer don't mind,' Tommy said apologetically. 'Me limbs tend to seize up if I stand about for too long.'

Louise nodded, her gaze transfixed on the upper window of the house. 'All right, Tommy. Take care now.'

She waited until he'd gone in and closed the door, before going to the neighbouring house. She gently tapped on the door. This time, the curtains hung limp, and there was no sign of any movement. And no sign at all that anyone was inside. Louise knocked harder. Nothing. Stooping, she looked in through the letter-box. At the bottom of the passage she thought she saw a fleeting figure. 'It's all right,' she called out. 'I want to help, if you'll let me.'

Silence greeted her.

She tried again. 'I met you on the bus coming back from Blackpool,' she shouted. *'I know who you are.'*

Again, only silence.

'I won't tell. I just want to help. Trust me. Please, I don't mean you any harm.'

Suddenly, the door opened and there she was, and for a heart-stopping moment, she and Sarah quietly regarded each other, Louise with a nervous smile, and Sarah with a hint of suspicion in her eye.

'Please, let me help,' Louise said softly. 'I've an idea you might be in some kind of trouble.'

Sarah visibly relaxed. 'You're the woman from the bus,' she affirmed. 'You're the one as lives on Derwent Street.' As she spoke, her anxious gaze flitted up and down the street.

'That's right. And I really do want to help.'

Sarah was ever wary of strangers. 'What makes you think I *need* your help?'

'Because I've needed it often enough myself to recognise the signs.' She thought the older woman looked far worse than she had when they met on the bus. Grey of face and her kindly features etched with a deeply troubled look, she had obviously been through some kind of trauma. 'Are you ill?' Louise asked kindly. 'Is that it?'

Agitated, Sarah looked up and down the street again. 'How can I be sure you're to be trusted? After all, I don't really know you, do I?'

'No, you don't,' Louise agreed. 'But you *can* trust me. I've nothing to gain from deceiving you.'

'Come in then. Be quick now!' Opening the door wider she took hold of Louise's arm and pulled her inside. Almost immediately the smell of damp and neglect invaded her nostrils.

'I know it stinks,' Sarah said defensively. 'It took me a time to get used to it. I might tell you, I very nearly threw up when I first came through that door. But I daren't open any windows, you see . . . not with Hannah being so poorly.'

Her hunch now confirmed, Louise no longer had any

doubts about Sarah's identity. 'Adam, and Hannah?' She could see it all as if it was only yesterday. 'The two children who lived in this house with their mother Maggie Pringle and Jacob Hunter. You're their grandmother, Mrs Harpur, aren't you?'

Sarah looked forlorn. 'I know what you're thinking,' she said in a low voice. 'You're thinking how it were my son as killed the two of them, and frightened the children half out of their wits. Oh yes, and you'd be right – and God only knows how I wish I'd never given birth to such a vile creature. As it is, he's shut out of our lives, and good riddance to him, that's what I say.'

Realising there was a lot of pain there, Louise chose not to comment. Instead she concentrated on the immediate issue. 'You said Hannah was poorly?'

'Oh, lass! I've been at my wits' end. She's badly, and I can't take her to the Infirmary, or we'll be split up for sure. If they were to take her away from me and her brother, she'd fall apart.' Sarah dropped her gaze to the floor. 'She's never got over what happened, d'you see? That's why I were so reluctant to fetch her back here, to where it all happened. Only I had to get her in the warm. Adam's found a pile of kindling and a heap o' coal in the cellar. He's got a lovely fire going, bless him. Honest to God, I don't know what I'd have done without that lad.'

Louise drew her aside, and in a low voice asked, 'What exactly happened?'

'Me and the young 'uns have lived in my house since that terrible time, until two things happened. My son Terry wrote to say he were comin' out o' prison and wanted to settle down wi' us – well, I couldn't have that, could I? And me landlord, Ralph Martin, told us to quit the house 'cause it were being pulled down. I took the kids to Blackpool, to get away from our Terry, but we ran into a bit o' bad luck there. Since leaving

Blackpool, we've been living in a tent by the canal . . .' She could say no more, as the tears flowed down her troubled face.

Louise laid a gentle hand on Sarah's arm. 'Then summat happened, did it? Hannah got sick and you had to bring her inside?'

Sarah put her right. 'Oh no! She didn't just get sick. We were flooded out, see, and the rats came in our tent. Hannah were dead scared and she ran off and fell into the canal. Adam had to knock her out before he could get her to the bank. If it hadn't been for him, she'd have been dead for sure. In fact, she was fighting him so hard, they were *both* lucky to get out!'

'Is Adam ill too?'

'He had the shivers for a long time, then he got the fire going and he's all right now. But Hannah keeps drifting in and out of her senses, and I've done all I can. I don't want to take her to the Infirmary, but I might have to if she doesn't soon take a turn for the better.'

While she explained more about how they'd been living, Sarah led Louise into the back room. 'There y'are.' She stepped aside. 'Take a look at the lass, and tell me what you think.'

Louise peered into the room, and straight away the sight of that cheery fire put a whole different complexion on the house.

Adam had heard them talking outside in the passage so he was not unduly alarmed. When Louise came into the room, he was sitting on one of two upturned orange crates, but now, he stood up and moved aside, while Louise knelt to examine Hannah. The girl was lying on the floorboards beside the fire, her small figure covered in the three coats that had been dried by the fire before being put round her.

'Will she be all right?' Adam stood gazing down on his sister, one arm round Sarah and the other up to his head, where he ran his hands through his hair in a nervous fashion. 'She's so cold. I've been warming my hands and holding her tight, but she's cold and sweating all at the same time.'

Louise smiled up at him. 'Don't worry, son,' she said. 'You've come among friends here.' Her kinds words made Sarah and the boy smile for the first time in many long, anxious hours.

Louise took a few minutes to satisfy herself that Hannah was not beyond ordinary help. 'You're right,' she told Sarah quietly. 'She *is* poorly, but if we keep the fire going and take good care of her, I'm sure she'll come through. I think we can manage without calling the doctor out.'

Stroking the girl's forehead, Louise was surprised to see Hannah staring up at her, a little afraid and shrinking from her touch. 'Who are you?' she croaked feverishly.

'I'm Louise . . . a friend. I've come to help you.'

Hannah's eyes beseeched her. 'Will I die?'

Louise shook her head. 'No, lass. We won't allow that to happen.' Seemingly content, Hannah closed her eyes and drifted into a deep sleep.

Louise outlined her plan to Sarah. 'She needs a proper bed. You all do. You need food and more coal and plenty for Hannah to drink. She has to be kept warm, like you're already doing, and she'll need some clean blankets; the coats are still a wee bit damp, but they've been better than nothing at all.'

Sarah was stung. 'I *know* all that!' she retorted. 'You don't have to tell me what the lass needs. What I want to know is where am I to get it from? I've nowt to sell; we lost everything in the water. Adam can't work because he hasn't got a proper address, and we can't stay here, because of what happened.'

Her eyes filling, she looked down at the girl. 'Dear Lord above! If she knew where she was, she'd never pull through this.'

Astonishing Sarah by taking hold of her hand, Louise asked, 'Didn't I say I wanted to help?'

'Aye, you did, but I don't see how you can.' Worn and anxious, Sarah began crying, her voice breaking as she went on, 'You see how it is. You see how destitute we are.'

Seeing his grandma like that, when all along she had been so strong and unselfish, Adam loved her all the more. He threw his arms round her. 'We're not destitute,' he protested. 'We'll get Hannah well, and I'll explain how we have to be brave and stay here awhile. I'll be able to get a job, and Hannah will go back to school and see her old friends. Oh look, Grandma, I'm sure she'll understand. I'll talk to her, don't worry.'

Louise was touched by the affection between these two. 'Are you hungry?' Her question was addressed to Adam.

'We *all* are.'

'And I expect you could do with a proper hot drink, eh?'

'We've been heating water in an old pan we found in the cellar.'

'Right, then.' Louise knew what she had to do. 'Stay here and look after your Gran. Do exactly what you've been doing for Hannah,' she said. 'Keep her warm, and give her drinks of water, but make sure it's boiled first and allowed to cool, but I expect you know all that, eh?' She gave them each a hug. 'I'll be back before you know it.'

As she brushed by, Sarah caught hold of her hand. 'You won't bring the authorities, will you?'

'No, I wouldn't do that.'

Sarah squeezed her hand. 'God bless you,' she whispered. 'It's good to know I'm not on my own any more.' She wiped **away** a tear. 'These young 'uns mean more to me than my own life.'

Louise nodded. 'I can see that.' Quickly now, she went

down the passage and out the door. There were things to be done; people to see, and no time to lose.

Jinnie was waiting on the doorstep of their home in Derwent Street. 'I was worried, Mam.' She had been sitting there these past twenty minutes. 'Sally said you went to the shop nearly an hour since. She sent me to see where you were and Maisie said you'd been gone ages.' Her blue eyes frowned. 'I thought you were never coming back.'

Louise chided her. 'You shouldn't be sitting out here on the step. It's too cold and damp.' She wagged a finger. 'That's how you get piles.'

Jinnie followed her inside. 'Where did you go?'

Once back indoors, Louise found herself faced with a barrage of questions. 'I thought you'd fell down a manhole or summat!' Sally was relieved to see her back. 'One minute you're popping out to the shop, and the next you've disappeared off the face of the earth.'

'I've been no further than Craig Street.' Louise took off her coat and, going to the kitchen, was pleased to see that there was some still warm in the pot. 'I'll have a quick brew then I'm off again,' she said.

'What's going on, Mam?'

Turning to the door, she saw the pair of them standing there. 'That tea's stone cold!' Sally offered to make a new pot, but Louise declined. Instead she gulped down the lukewarm drink and explained what had happened; about Sarah and the children, and how they'd broken into *that* house, and the way they were living. She told how Hannah had fallen into the canal and how Adam had almost drowned with her when he tried to get her out, and now Hannah was so cold she couldn't get warm, and something had to be done about it.

Sally could hardly believe it. 'My God! Fancy their grandma taking them back to *that* place. By! It doesn't bear thinking about.'

'It seems she had very little choice.' Louise described how they'd been living in a tent and the tent had been washed away. 'It was either that house, or the streets, and what with Hannah the way she is, Sarah did what she thought was for the best.'

Sally understood. 'Caught between the devil and the deep blue sea, eh?'

Jinnie wanted to help. 'We have to do something,' she said. 'What if Hannah dies?'

'She's not about to do that,' Louise assured her, 'but you're right, lass. We *have* to do something, and that's why I'm in a rush. After being in that house, I needed to come and get warmed up.' She shivered. 'It's damp as hell in there.'

'So, what can I do?' the girl asked eagerly.

'You can run down to Maisie's and get some candles, and a couple of torches. Tell her I'll be in to pay later on. When you've got the stuff from Maisie's take it to the house on Craig Street, and tell Sarah I'll not be long.'

'Where are *you* going Mam?'

'To see Peggy Trimble. She knows everybody who's anybody, does Peggy, and I need her help.'

Sally wanted to do her own bit. 'What d'you want me to do, lass?'

Louise looked at the old woman and saw how frail and unsteady she was, and without making her feel inadequate, she suggested, 'You could make some of your delicious scones, and a bacon dumpling. I'm sure they'd appreciate that.'

Before Sally could make the offer of delivering them to Craig Street, Louise told her, 'Don't go out in the cold, pet. I'll be back later to see if there's anything ready to take down.'

Sally was thrilled. 'I'd best get started!' she said importantly, and she was reaching for the ingredients before Louise could say another word.

A few minutes later, Louise was on her way to Peggy Trimble's, while Jinnie ran down to the shop. 'Don't forget matches for the candles,' Louise reminded her.

Maisie asked a lot of questions. 'Did you find your mam? Where was she? What does she want candles and torches for . . . has the electric gone, or what?'

Knowing what a gossip Maisie was, Jinnie gave her as much information as she thought her mam would approve of. 'She went to see somebody,' she answered. 'And I'm to take these back right away.'

Disgruntled, Maisie handed them over. 'That'll be six bob,' she said, and wrote it in her book. Before she'd put down her pencil, Jinnie was out of the door and going at a fair lick down Craig Street; matches, candles and torches safe in her arms.

A little nervous, she knocked on the door and waited. First the curtains twitched and then the door opened and there stood this tall, dark-haired young man, so strikingly handsome and with such intense dark eyes, he took her breath away. 'My mam sent me,' Jinnie said breathlessly. She held out the items got from Maisie's. 'She said I was to bring these, and that she'd be along later.'

Grateful, Adam took the items from her. He couldn't take his eyes off her; he had never seen such a pretty young girl in his life before. 'Is your mam called Louise?'

'Yes.' She smiled and his heart took off.

'What's your name?'

'I'm Jinnie. And you must be Adam?'

Like Sarah before him, he glanced nervously up and down the street. 'Do you want to come in?'

'Can I see Hannah?'

'If you like.' And he took her to Sarah.

Sarah was of the same mind as her grandson. 'My, but you're a lovely-looking lass,' she said, making Jinnie blush.

'What's more, it seems to me you're as kind and thoughtful as your mam.'

Jinnie knelt to speak to Hannah. 'Hello, Hannah.'

Hannah opened her eyes, but she didn't speak, nor did she acknowledge Jinnie's friendly greeting.

'She's very tired, lass,' Sarah said. 'Happen we'd best leave her be for now, eh? She'll be fine once she's slept a while.'

Jinnie understood. 'Mam told us what happened,' she revealed. 'I'm sorry. We want to help if you'll let us.' Her blue eyes were drawn to Adam now.

Adam had seen Jinnie kneel at his sister's side and listened to her soft voice as she spoke to Hannah. He had heard her offer of help and looked into those soft, searching blue eyes and something had happened to him. Something beyond his experience. Something that made his heart soar, yet told him that he was only sixteen and Jinnie was only about ten, still a child, and he was being silly.

But somehow it didn't seem to matter. 'You've helped already,' he said in a quiet, intimate voice. 'You and your mam . . . you're very kind.'

Unsettled and excited, Jinnie couldn't understand what was happening to her. 'I'd best be going now,' she said.

'Will you be coming back, lass?' That was Sarah.

'I think so.' *She hoped so!*

'Tell your mam thanks for the candles and such.'

''Bye.'

''Bye, lass.'

Adam saw her out. 'I'm glad your mam sent you,' he said awkwardly.

Jinnie smiled. 'So am I.'

'See you later then?'

'Yes. Bye, then . . . Adam.' She felt herself blush bright pink.

He saw the blush and it made him smile. 'Thanks again.'

Neither of them wanted to part, but Jinnie made the move and daren't look back. If she had done so, she would have seen him gazing up the street after her.

———— ❖ ————

IT WAS ALMOST two hours later when Louise returned, and with her came a small army. Loaded up with blankets, food and clothing, and even mattresses, they filed into the house, laughing and smiling and filling the place with sunshine.

Behind them came old Tommy and several other retired men, carrying three single beds between them. 'We're the cavalry!' Tommy chuckled as he passed Sarah, who was sobbing uncontrollably, with Adam beside her, his eyes wide open and moist with tears. 'You've no need to worry now,' Louise told them. 'Remember what I said? You've come among friends here.'

It was all too much for Sarah, who sat on the stairs, watching this wonderful horde of people who had come to help. She laughed and cried, and by some unseen miracle, felt all the tension and worry fall away from her.

'See, Grandma? It's all right.' Adam came to sit beside her. 'The house is different now. It wants us to stay.'

To the onlookers as they went about their chores, they made a delightful sight, the woman and the boy, huddled together on the stairs, arms round each other, and so much love between them, it stirred every man and woman there.

In no time at all, the atmosphere in that place was completely changed. Saying little but working hard, Louise's mother Patsy Holsden lit a fire in the small back bedroom, until soon the room was warm and cosy. On Patsy's nod, Hannah was gently lifted into the arms of one of the men, an ex-miner from Wigan, who ever so carefully carried her upstairs.

Following behind him, Sarah waited until he'd left the room before dressing Hannah in the warm pyjamas one of the women had brought. She was then fed as much lentil soup as she could take, and afterwards tucked up in bed, warm as toast and looking better by the minute.

Downstairs, the activity was ongoing. More neighbours arrived, carrying buckets and mops and armfuls of curtains they'd cast aside and never managed to get rid of. They ferried their wares backwards and forwards, raiding their attics and sheds and even robbing their own front parlours. 'You need it more than we do,' they told Sarah, when she expressed concern that they were being too generous. Between them, they'd produced enough spare bedlinen, towels, crockery and cutlery to set the little family up, and a whipround among the men had raised more than five pounds for Sarah's housekeeping needs.

In every room, the women scrubbed and cleaned, until the house began to come alive. 'I've polished the outside lavvy, until it's fit for the town Mayor to sit his arse on!' This was Maisie. When she had heard how everybody was rallying round to help, she had downed tools and shut up shop without a second thought.

'Some things are more important than money,' she told Tommy Penrose, and he agreed wholeheartedly, though he did not approve of her colourful language and told her so in no uncertain terms.

Some of the women had lugged down a sofa and a chair; though they'd seen better days they were like heaven to Sarah. 'My old man bought me a new one last March,' Peggy Trimble said. 'This one's been stuffed in the shed ever since.' The cushions were warmed through and soon they were fit to sit on. Older neighbours brought in a bag of flour, a few apples or a tin of beans – something to put in the store cupboard.

Forbidden to help, Sarah and Adam were brought soup and tea, Sally's scones and the bacon dumpling, and they ravenously scoffed the lot. 'By! I didn't know how hungry I were,' Sarah declared, and got another helping.

When all was finished and the visitors were about to leave, each and every one of them gave Adam and his grandma a hug. 'You know where we are if you need us,' they said, and marched out the same way they'd marched in, full of excitement and chattering among themselves.

All but Patsy and Louise.

Seeming nervous, Patsy lingered by the door, while Louise went upstairs to check on Hannah. When it took an age for her to come down, Patsy eventually bade Sarah cheerio. 'You'll be fine now,' she said, and Sarah believed her.

Louise was the last to leave. 'Maisie left these.' She held out two old, flowered jeremiahs. 'In case it's too cold to visit the outside lavvy in the middle of the night. They were Maisie's mother's,' she explained, 'but they're clean and usable, so slide them under your bed and keep them handy.'

Sarah laughed. 'I haven't seen one o' them in twenty years and more.' She took them all the same, and walked with Louise to the door.

'Who was that kindly woman?' she asked Louise. 'She seemed to be waiting for you. Small person, with a pleasant face. She stood at the foot of the stairs for a while then said goodnight and left, not ten minutes since.'

Louise knew full well who Sarah meant. 'That was my mam.'

From the downcast expression and the flat tone of her voice, Sarah realised all was not well between these two. 'Had a falling-out, have you . . . you and your mam?' Sarah was never one to mince words.

Louise was taken aback. 'Why do you say that?'

'Because it were plain to me that you went upstairs to avoid her, and she was fidgeting like a nervous schoolgirl, waiting for you to come down.' Sarah smiled understandingly. 'Just now, when I asked if you'd had a falling-out, you looked angry. I might be wrong, but I've a feeling it weren't *me* you were angry with.'

Louise reassured her. 'It's a family thing,' she confided. 'I thought my mother was my best friend, and now I find out different.' She smiled. 'Look, Sarah, I do appreciate your concern, but you don't want to hear *my* troubles. You've got enough of your own.'

'Can I say just one thing, lass?'

''Course you can.' Louise had a great respect for Mrs Harpur.

'I've learned one lesson in life, and it's this: friends come and go, and sometimes when you think they'll always be there, they let you down. But families are different. Oh, sure they make you angry and there are times when they do anything but what you need 'em to do. But when it comes right down to it, and when there's nobody else around, the *family* is always there.' She sighed heavily. 'If only I could include our Terry in that.' She leaned forward and squeezed the younger woman's hand. 'Don't get me wrong, lass – I found a whole host of friends here tonight, and I thank the Good Lord for leading me to this place. But without my Hannah and Adam, my *family* . . . I would be a very sad, lonely woman indeed.'

Louise smiled at her. 'I know what you're saying,' she acknowledged. 'And I will think about what you said.'

Sarah thanked her. 'Your mam look worried, I reckon.'

Louise nodded. 'I'll be back after work tomorrow, if I may,' she said. 'Take care of yourselves now.'

They said their goodnights and parted company. As she walked away, Louise realised how lonely she too had been since returning from Blackpool, because not once had she been to see her mother. Twice in the street she had chatted with her father, Steve, but after what Susan had said, she simply could not face her mother. It struck her that Susan could have been lying, but she dismissed that idea. She had no need to lie, she told herself. 'If she says Mam's on her side, there must be some truth in it, if only because she knows I'd go and ask her.'

Overwhelmed by her own thoughts, she came to an abrupt stop. 'But that's just it – I *haven't* asked her. Maybe our mam knows nothing about it.' But if that was the case, why hadn't her mother popped in to see her as she normally would? Unfortunately, the doubt had already eaten its way into her soul.

And it would not go away.

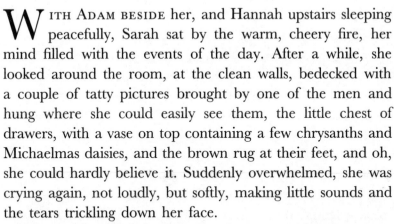

WITH ADAM BESIDE her, and Hannah upstairs sleeping peacefully, Sarah sat by the warm, cheery fire, her mind filled with the events of the day. After a while, she looked around the room, at the clean walls, bedecked with a couple of tatty pictures brought by one of the men and hung where she could easily see them, the little chest of drawers, with a vase on top containing a few chrysanths and Michaelmas daisies, and the brown rug at their feet, and oh, she could hardly believe it. Suddenly overwhelmed, she was crying again, not loudly, but softly, making little sounds and the tears trickling down her face.

'Don't cry.' Filled with compassion, Adam held her for a while. Seeing his grandmother cry had brought home to him just how much she had endured on their behalf. It made him all the more determined to take care of this family, and the sooner the better.

'Sorry, lad.' Sniffling, Sarah wiped her nose on the edge of her sleeve. Smiling through her tears, she looked up at him. 'It's just that – well, I'd forgotten there were such good folks about.'

With the tiredness creeping up on them, they went upstairs to check on Hannah, relieved to find her fast asleep, not breathing brokenly like before, nor shivering, but sleeping soundly, in a proper bed, in that warm room, with the window opened just a wedge to keep the air flowing.

One of the women had left a fire-guard and Adam secured it round the hearth. When Sarah left the room, he was sitting on the bed beside his sister, holding her hand and talking to her. 'The house isn't frightening any more,' he murmured. 'The badness is gone now.' He hesitated, as though afraid to tell her, but then deciding she had to know everything, he confided, 'I went down to the cellar, Hannah. It was a bit scary at first, but then it was all right, because there was only me down there. There were no ghosts or things to hurt me, and I wasn't afraid. Not any more.'

He knew it would not be so easy for Hannah. 'I won't let you go down there just yet,' he said. 'There's no hurry. We'll take our time, eh, and you'll get stronger. I'll help you, sis, I promise.' He kissed her on the forehead. 'If you wake in the night, we'll hear you,' he said. 'We're only across the landing.'

Having come back to see if they were all right, Sarah stood by the door, a smile of contentment on her face and a surge of love in her heart. 'Come on, lad,' she urged. 'You'd best get some sleep now.' She walked with him to his room, and suddenly laughed out loud. 'By! Look at that, eh?' She pointed to his newly made-up bed. 'It's been a while since you slept in a proper bed, lad. Happen you'll not like it,' she teased. 'It might be too comfortable.'

Adam chuckled, assuring her that he would just about be able to bear it. 'Goodnight, Gran.'

'Goodnight, lad. See you tomorrow.' Sarah ambled off to her own bed, with a smile on her face and a song in her heart. 'Tomorrow's a new day,' she whispered. 'And I'm really looking forward to it.'

It seemed a lifetime since she had thought like that.

Chapter Twelve

I T WAS NEARLY midnight. After all the excitement earlier today, Sally could not get off to sleep. She tossed and turned, threw the bedclothes off then covered herself again. Several times she got out of bed, stared out of the window and then climbed back into bed again, lying awake and feeling decidedly fidgety. 'Must have been them two scones I ate,' she muttered. 'Serves me right for being a pig.'

Giving up the whole idea of sleep, she got out of bed and putting on her dressing-gown, went softly down the stairs, taking care not to wake anyone who, unlike her, might be hard and fast asleep. Coming into the living room, she was surprised to see Louise already there. 'So you couldn't sleep either, eh, lass?' In a way she was relieved to see somebody else in the same predicament as herself, though after one look at Louise's face, she knew there was something troubling her daughter-in-law.

'I've too much on my mind to sleep.' Louise got out of the chair. 'You sit down,' she said. 'The kettle's on the boil, I'll not be a minute.'

Without waiting for Sally to answer she hurried into the kitchen, where she switched off the kettle. Getting two mugs, the milk, the bowl of sugar and the cocoa tin, she switched the kettle back on again to bring it to the boil. When it began to sing and flicked itself off, she made them each a strong mug of cocoa.

Taking a sip of hers Sal licked her lips. 'By! There's nowt like a hot drink to soothe your spirits.' Leaning back in the armchair, she looked across at Louise, who was now hunched up, cup in hand, in the opposite chair. 'Come on, lass, out with it,' Sally prodded. 'What's playing on your mind?'

Louise glanced at the old woman, her pretty eyes betraying her anxiety. 'It's our mam,' she answered. 'You already know I've avoided her ever since I came back from Blackpool.'

'I do, lass, and I've told you what I think. Have it out with her. Ask her why she's sided with your sister against you. I think she owes you an explanation.'

After her little chat with Sarah, Louise was beginning to have doubts. 'What if Susan was lying?'

'Do you think she is?' Sally hadn't thought of that, but knowing Susan, it was certainly possible.

Groaning, Louise put down her mug and falling back in the chair, threw her arms open wide. 'To tell you the truth, I don't know *what* to think any more.'

'Well, for what it's worth, my advice is still the same. Confront her with what Susan told you.'

Louise nodded. 'I'll have to,' she answered, 'but I've a feeling what Susan said is true.'

'Oh, and how's that?'

'Because tonight at the house on Craig Street, she didn't come anywhere near me. Yet Sarah told me that when I went upstairs, she waited at the foot of the stairs, fidgeting and nervous. To me, that sounds like she's guilty of something or another.'

Exasperated, Sally blew hard, her sagging cheeks temporarily blown out like two round, shiny balloons. 'Happen you're right, lass.' The cheeks sagged again, the loose folds of skin hanging to her jowls. 'And happen yer not. Whichever way, it sounds like she needs to talk to you.' Leaning forward, she advised softly, 'You and yer mam have allus got on. Don't let things get beyond repair. Go an' see her. Tell her what Susan said, and see what she has to say about it.'

Louise had already made up her mind. 'I'll go and see her in the morning.' She cast her sorry gaze down to the dying embers. 'But I'm not looking forward to it.'

'You're doing right, lass. You need to know one way or the other. You can't go on tormenting yourself.' In a knowing voice she asked gently, 'And what about the other matter, if yer know what I mean? When do you intend dealing with *that*?'

Louise knew what she was getting at. 'I've decided to tell Jinnie tomorrow as well. While I'm clearing the air with our mam, I might as well deal with all of it. I don't know if Susan really would come after Jinnie, or whether she's getting some kind of fun out of being cruel.'

'I know she can be bad, but would she really do such a terrible thing as that?'

Louise gave a wry little laugh. 'God knows she's capable of it. She was never one for caring about other folk's suffering; in fact, she gets a real buzz out of it, I reckon. That's why I'm so frightened of her approaching Jinnie.'

'I've seen how you watch her every minute you can. But you can't always be two steps behind.'

'I know that, Sally. It's why I want her to be armed with all the facts, so's she knows how to deal with it.' Suddenly she was slumped forward in the chair, hands over her face. 'I'm frightened, Sal. What if Susan manages to turn her against me?' It was that thought alone which had robbed her of sleep for so many nights, and now she daren't leave it any longer. Jinnie had to know. 'You were right all along, Sally. Keeping it from her is like playing with fire.'

'Aw, come here, lass.' Clambering out of her chair, the old woman went to Louise, and put her arms round her. 'You're doing the right thing,' she murmured. 'Yer can't do no more than that.'

When Louise looked up, her brown eyes were still deeply troubled. 'I can't lose Jinnie,' she groaned. 'I *can't*!'

'You won't lose her,' Sally promised. 'You're too much a part of each other.'

Louise had to believe that. 'Thanks, Sally.' As always the old woman had reassured her. 'Go back to bed now. You look tired.'

Sally didn't argue. The hot cocoa had made her drowsy. 'Will you be all right?'

'I'll be fine.'

'How long do you mean to stay down here?'

'Not long.'

'Promise?'

Smiling, Louise crossed her heart. 'Scout's honour.'

'And no putting the Beatles' songs on the record-player, or you'll have the street awake!'

'I'm not in the mood for playing songs.'

Sally patted her shoulder. 'I know that, lass.'

Louise gave the old woman a kiss on the cheek. 'What would I do without you, eh? You're always there when I need you most.'

For a fleeting minute, Sally looked sombre. 'I'll not always be here,' she said, before the smile returned and she addressed Louise in an authoritative voice. 'Don't you stay down here all night, mind.'

Louise assured her, 'I won't.'

With that, Sally took herself back to bed, where she promptly fell into a deep, restful sleep. Not long afterwards, Louise, too, went back to bed, but there was no sleep in her. Plagued with all manner of worries, she got dressed and on soft, silent footsteps, went downstairs and taking the key with her, she departed the house.

As she closed the front door she heard the mantelpiece clock strike two. She was so wide awake, it could have struck eight. Standing by the door, she looked up the street then down again; not sure which way to go. It wasn't too cold, she thought, not as cold as the day had been. With the street-lamps out, it was dark, save for the sliver of moonlight peeping through the clouds, and a thin shaft of light emanating from one of the houses further down. 'It seems I'm not the only one who can't sleep,' she noted.

A dog almost frightened her out of her life, when it suddenly shot past her, to disappear round the corner. 'Chasing cats, I shouldn't wonder.' As if to prove her right, from somewhere along the street, the sound of marauding cats broke the eerie silence.

Louise shivered; she had never been out this time of a morning before, and it felt spooky. 'Come on, you coward,' she chided herself. 'You wanted a walk in the fresh air, so get on with it.'

Her instincts took her in the direction of her parents' house. On drawing nearer, she was amazed to see that the shaft of light was coming from there. Carefully, so as not to be seen, she crept up to the window and peeped inside. At first she could see no one, and backed off. 'It's a good job there's no police about,' she chuckled, 'or he'd have me up for a Peeping Tom!'

Softly, she moved away, but just then a shadow fell across the shaft of light. Curious, she looked in the window again, and there was Patsy, her mother, clad in dressing-gown and pacing the floor, eyes downcast, a cigarette in her mouth and the smoke billowing up like a chimney on fire. She was obviously very agitated.

Undecided as to what she should do next, Louise watched for a minute. Then, with her heart in her mouth, she tapped on the window. Patsy looked up, worried when she realised she had not drawn the curtains; something she was always very particular about. She stood there, looking at the window yet not making a move, nor seeing Louise; because the window was positioned higher than the cellar-railings, Louise would be visible only when she stood on her tiptoes.

With more important things on her mind than closing the curtains, Patsy continued to pace the floor, sucking on her cigarette until, in a compulsive action, she threw the stub into the empty fire-grate.

Louise tapped again, this time standing on tiptoes, so her mother could see her. The last thing she wanted to do was frighten her. When Patsy glanced up and saw her there, she looked both relieved and astonished, her mouth forming the name, *'Louise!'*

Pointing to the front door, Louise let her know that she needed to talk. Patsy understood at once. Hurrying to the door, she opened it. Putting a finger to her mouth she indicated that Louise's father was still asleep upstairs.

While Patsy closed the front door, Louise made for the sitting room. Patsy followed. 'What in God's name are you doing out on the streets at this hour?' she asked.

Louise made no attempt to sit down. 'We need to talk,' she said. 'I think you know what about.'

Patsy nodded guiltily. 'It's about Susan, isn't it? She told you, didn't she?'

Louise had been ready to believe that it was all a lie, but now she knew that her sister had been telling the truth after all. Deeply disappointed, she dropped into a chair. 'So it's true then?'

Patsy didn't answer straight away. Instead she began pacing the floor, arms folded, trying to find the right words.

'Mam!' Louise had to know. 'Why did you do it? What made you side with her against me? Have you *any* idea what she's capable of? And what about Jinnie? Had you no thought for her? She's your grand-daughter, for heaven's sake!'

Still Patsy gave no answer. She paused, looking at Louise, her eyes moist with tears and a desolate expression on her face. And still she didn't try to defend herself. Puzzled by her mother's reaction, Louise didn't know what to do. She wanted to bang her fist on the table and demand to know why Patsy had done this to her. But anger would solve nothing, and besides, she knew her father was in bed and she didn't want to wake him and involve him in this. 'Dad doesn't know, does he?' She could not imagine that her gentle, quiet father would want any part of it.

Patsy shook her head. 'You mustn't tell him.'

'I've a damned good mind to!' But she would never hurt him like that, and Patsy knew it. 'Why did you do it, Mam?' Crossing the room she faced her mother. 'I was so sure Susan had lied to me. I didn't want to believe you might be part of a plan that could take Jinnie from us. Have you gone mad, or what?'

Sitting herself down as though the weight of the world was on her shoulders, Patsy wiped a stray tear from her face. 'I had no choice.'

Incredulous, Louise knelt beside her, her two hands on her mother's knees and her face uplifted in puzzlement. 'What d'you mean, you had no choice?'

'It's your dad, d'you see, lass.'

Louise was taken aback. 'I don't understand. Are you telling me it was *Dad's* idea to side with Susan?'

'No, of course not! He would never do that. If he knew how I'd betrayed you and Jinnie, I dread to think what he'd do.' The thought of Steve finding out was too much. 'You mustn't tell him, our Louise. Promise me you won't tell him.' She began to panic; her voice so shot with emotion, she was barely coherent.

'Hey! Come on, Mam. There's no need to get yourself in such a state.' Anxious, Louise quietened her. 'Just tell me what you've done, and what it has to do with Dad.' Taking a hankie from her coat-pocket she gave it to Patsy, who wiped her nose and face and composed herself enough to explain.

'About three months back, your dad lost his job. He was so ashamed, but it wasn't his fault. The owner sold the factory and they had to shed ten men. Because he was older than the others, your dad was the first to go.'

Louise was devastated. She knew what a proud, hard-working man her father was, and had been all his working life. 'I never knew. Why didn't you tell me?'

'Steve made me promise not to.'

'But ... he went to work every day. I *saw* him most mornings, catching the tram ... going to work as usual.' She recalled how little he had had to say on the recent occasions when she stopped him for a chat. 'He never said a word to me about it.'

Patsy gave a sad little smile. 'Every day he'd go out and pretend to be working. He'd come home at the same time as always, and I'd make his tea, and we'd pretend everything was the same as before.' Her voice shook. 'Only it wasn't, because without his wages it was only a matter of time before I couldn't pay the rent, or put food on the table. And there are other things too, like the coal and normal bills. It all started going wrong, and I didn't know what to do.'

She momentarily closed her eyes and it seemed she would say no more, but then she opened them and gave a big sigh, and went on, 'I didn't tell him how bad it was getting, because he was so upset at having lost his job, I hadn't the heart to worry him.'

'Was there no work about?'

'Oh, the work is there all right, but not for him, it seems.

He tried heaven's hardest ... up and down the streets, following every avenue to get himself a new job, but they don't want men past fifty, do they? So, every night he'd come home and he'd sit there, staring into the fire, getting more and more depressed.' She gave a shaky little smile. 'We had a bit put by, lass, but it all went.'

Suddenly Louise thought she saw the whole picture. 'So you went to Susan for money, is that it?'

'Never!' Patsy's face darkened with anger. 'I'd have to be on my last legs before I'd ask *her* for a penny. Even then I'd rather do away with myself first.'

Frowning, Louise wanted to know, 'So how did she get involved in all this?'

'Her dubious friends.' Patsy snorted with disgust. 'She allus had a talent for picking up with the wrong 'uns.' In a rush of words she told Louise what had happened. 'Like the fool I am, I went to a moneylender. After a while I couldn't even pay him the weekly dues. They kept going up and up, y'see, and he was making all kinds of threats. I was almost out of my mind with worry, and then suddenly, *she* was on my doorstep.'

'What?' Louise was astounded. 'Susan came *here*?'

Patsy nodded. 'Late one night, after your dad was abed, I was down here wondering what to do next, when she opened the front door with her own key and gave me the fright of my life. She told me she'd got a friend who liked a drink, and when he got drunk his tongue got loose. He told her he had a woman in Derwent Street, Blackburn, who'd come to him for money. He said it wouldn't be long before she was in over her head and he'd soon have a whole household of decent furniture and stuff to sell. He asked her if she knew anybody who might be interested ... he said whatever he got would be pocket-money, because he'd already had his money back from me and more besides.'

'What a bastard!' Louise had heard about the money-lenders and their filthy tricks, but she had never been this close to one before. It made her want to kill!

'Susan managed to put two and two together and soon found out he was talking about me.' Patsy grimaced. 'I wasn't to know I'd played right into her grubby little hands. It was exactly what she'd been waiting for. She came here that same night . . . arrived in a taxi, she did – must have cost her a small fortune.'

Louise only wished she'd caught her. Threatening her was one thing, frightening their mam half out of her wits was another. 'Pity I didn't see her. I'd have sent her on her way and no mistake!'

'She said if I was to help her, she'd pay off the moneylender and set your father up in a job, with a friend in Darwen.'

'Oh, Mam.' Feeling as if all her energy had drained away, Louise fell back on her haunches. 'Why in God's name didn't you come to *me*? Somehow or another we'd have got Dad back to work. Eric has contacts. I'm sure he'd have helped.'

Slowly, Patsy's face crumpled, and the tears spilled over. 'I'm sorry, lass,' she muttered. 'I've been such a fool.'

From behind them, Steve's voice cut the air with shocking quietness. 'You're not a fool, my love. And if anybody should be sorry, it's me.'

Realising he must have been listening the whole time, Patsy was horrified. Flattening her hand over her mouth to stifle the cry, she looked at him, and his heart went out to her. Going to her, he took his wife into his arms, a smile on his face for Louise, and hope for them all. 'Stop your crying, lass,' he told Patsy. '*I'll* take over from here on in. You've no need to worry.' To Louise he said, 'I think she could do with a cuppa tea, lass. Matter o' fact, I think we could *all* do wi' one.'

While the two of them sat together, Louise made the tea and brought it back and they all sat and talked. 'So, she paid the moneylender off, did she?' Steve asked Patsy, who nodded affirmatively.

'Do you know that for certain?' He scowled. 'We all know what a devious devil she can be.'

'The moneylender hasn't been here since that night.'

Steve was worried. 'That's good, but it's a pity we couldn't be certain.'

Going to the dresser, Patsy took a slip of paper from under the dog ornament. 'Susan sent me this. There was a letter with it. She said she'd done her part and she expected me to do mine when the time was right.'

Steve perused the slip of paper. 'It's a receipt all right,' he said triumphantly. 'Typed on his letterhead, all signed, stamped and written off.' In a heavy voice, he then read the scrawled letter that came with it:

Don't forget our arrangement. I'm sure I don't need to spell it out, but I'll be calling on you to do your part, just as I've done mine. I'll let you know when I've got need of you.

Meanwhile, if Lou asks your opinion of me having Jinnie, you'd best tell her what a wonderful idea it is, and how I'm able to give the girl more than she ever could. Work on the pair of them, then when the time comes for me to make my move, you'll have them both convinced it's for the best.

Stay ready, Mam. I've things to do in the next week or so. After that, I'll be shutting up shop and boarding a plane for sunny climates, and I mean to take my daughter with me.

I'm counting on you when the time comes. Don't even think about letting me down, unless you want the bogey-man back on your doorstep. Next time, it won't be you he comes to see. It'll be Dad. Then you'll be for it, and serves you right.

So think on, Mam. I'm sure you wouldn't want to explain to Dad what a shameful thing you've done! Like as not, he'll pack his bags and be out the door for good and all.

When he'd finished reading it, Steve Holsden tore the letter to shreds. 'Threatening you now, is it?' He flung the pieces into the grate. 'Nice of her to send a receipt though,' he laughed. 'She never was very clever.' He folded the receipt and thrust it into his trouser-pocket. 'I'll take charge of this,' he told his wife. And so relieved was Patsy, that she made no protest.

'She said summat about "shutting up shop",' he remarked. 'Where might that be?'

Louise described it. 'It's a restaurant straddling a corner on the promenade. She's called it after Jacob. She's done well though. It's taking money hand over fist.'

Steve considered that for a minute, before asking Patsy, 'You didn't do what she said, did you, love? I mean . . . you haven't been upsetting Louise here, have you? Or mentioning anything to young Jinnie?'

'No, I couldn't bring myself to do it,' Patsy confessed. 'I knew after Louise came back from Blackpool that she'd found out somehow . . . about Susan having been to see me. Only I didn't dare ask, and so I kept my distance.' She glanced shame-faced at her daughter. 'I can't tell you how sorry I am, lass.'

Louise didn't blame her. 'What I can't understand is, why did Susan tell me that you were backing her? She would have been best placed to keep that to herself.'

Steve intervened. 'Because it would give her pleasure to put you and your mam at each other's throats. She's allus been jealous of the way you two are able to talk to each other. Besides, like I said, she was never very clever. Too busy causing mischief one way or another.' He frowned. 'For the life o' me, I'll never understand why she turned out the way she did. Right from the start, you and your sister have allus been treated the same . . . we've loved you the same, and one never got more than the other. Yet she were never satisfied, no matter how much love or attention we poured on her.' He sighed, a deep, lonely sigh. 'No, I'll never understand it.'

One thing he *did* understand, and now he discussed it with Louise in tender tones. 'So that were the reason you didn't come to the house so often, eh? Because you thought your mam had ganged up with Susan against you?'

Louise was ashamed. 'I should have known better.'

'No, lass.' Patsy wouldn't let her take the blame. 'You weren't to know the truth. It's *me* that should have had the courage to tell you, weeks back.'

Louise had a question for her father. 'What will you do?'

He looked at her and winked. 'That's for me to worry about,' he answered. 'But there's summat you can do for me. If you've a mind, that is?'

'What's that?' It was wonderfully comforting and strange too, how her father could calm a frantic situation with only a few heartfelt words and a warm smile.

'Have a word with that fella o' yourn, young Eric. If he gets me work, I'll be eternally grateful.'

Louise returned his smile. 'I'll talk to him in the morning.'

'Thank you, lass. Now then, come on, let's get you home. It's late. Afore you know it, the cock'll be crowing and you'll be that tired you'll not know how to get through the day.'

She made her peace with Patsy and went with him. At her door she gave him a kiss. 'I love you, Dad.'

'I love you too, lass. But I am worried about you.'

'What do you mean?'

He chuckled. 'You know very well what I mean. You and that fella o' yourn should be together. It's as plain as the nose on your face that the pair of youse think the world of each other.' He thrust out his chest. 'Besides, it's time I had another grandchild.'

Louise blushed so hard her face burned. 'Behave yourself.'

'You just think on what I said. Made for each other, you

are. What's more, you've made that poor bugger suffer long enough. It's time you let him put that ring on your finger, and make an honest woman of you.'

Lowering her head she peered up with a kindly warning. '*Goodnight*, Dad.'

But Steve Holsden had more to say, and he said it with feeling. 'I know I shouldn't poke my nose in, but it grieves me to see you on your own, when there's a good man waiting to share his life with you. Oh, lass! I so much want you to have the happiness you deserve.'

'I know you do, Dad, and don't think I'm not grateful for your concern but there are things that I still have to come to terms with.'

He thought he knew it all, but he suspected there was something here that she had never told anyone. 'I know how hard it is for you to forget Ben and what he did. But that was years ago, lass.'

She smiled at him, a quiet, telling smile that touched his heart. 'It might as well have been yesterday,' she murmured.

'Get rid of it all, lass,' he pleaded. 'Whatever it is that keeps you and Eric apart, *get rid of it*! You and Ben were one story, lass; you and Eric are another. There'll come a day when you learn that life won't wait for any of us. You make plans and keep putting 'em off, and one day you blink an eye and it's all gone.'

He was obviously thinking of his own life too, and the job he'd held for so many years he couldn't remember. Taking her two hands in his he squeezed them so hard, she winced. 'Grab it all while you can, pet,' he urged harshly. 'Don't wait till it's too late.'

Choked by his words, Louise stood on tiptoe and gave him a long, strong hug. 'You understand me better than most,' she whispered. 'That's why I love you so much.'

'Aye.' He breathed hard and long through his nose,

appearing to calm himself. 'I'd best be off. Your mam'll be wondering where I've got to.'

'And I'll speak to Eric about work for you.' She gave him a playful push. 'All right?' Just now, she had seen the strength of emotion that had rushed through him and sensed that it was not all to do with her. There was Patsy involved, and Susan, and his anger at what she had done. And at the bottom of it all was his own shame, because he had been too wrapped up in himself to see what was going on.

'Aye, goodnight, lass. Now go on – get off to your bed!'

As he walked back to the house, Steve thought of Susan and the way she had ruthlessly blackmailed her own mother. Fired with rage, he muttered under his breath, 'You're a crafty devil, you are, but you'll not get the better of me.' He gave a hearty chuckle. 'By! I can't wait to see the look on your face when I walk in that door!'

He thought about how Louise had promised to ask Eric if he had work for him. Oh, and wouldn't that be wonderful! If he got a job at Maple Farm, he could catch up on the bills, and in time, happen he might even manage to put back the little nest egg they'd used up. He'd be able to hold his head up high, because he'd have his pride. He'd be a working man again.

By the time he got to his own front door, Steve Holsden was merrily whistling like a blackbird. All of a sudden, life was looking up.

PART FOUR

THE SEASON OF LIGHTS

Chapter Thirteen

THERE ARE TWO seasons in Blackpool when people flock to the resort; one is summer at its height, and the other is when visitors come to see the Blackpool Illuminations which, according to many, are second to none on this earth.

At the end of November 1963, Susan Holsden stood by the tills in Jacob's Restaurant watching the money pour in. 'Seems to me there's more people here this year than there's ever been,' she commented smugly to one of her more loyal employees, the small, robust woman in her fifties called Madge who cleaned the restaurant from top to bottom twice a week. With more energy than all the others put together, and at half the rate of pay, Susan considered Madge to be a valuable employee.

'We get busier by the minute,' Susan confided while smiling at a good-looking young man in the till queue. 'I reckon we acquire more loyal customers with every passing day.'

The other woman had the answer straight off. 'That's because you serve a good breakfast and plenty of it.'

Susan sighed with satisfaction, while still making eyes at the young man; in fact, she was even bold enough to offer a wink. 'We aim to please,' she replied, though right at that minute she had in mind to find a way of 'pleasing' this gorgeous young man. So explicit and vivid were the images in her mind, she licked her lips in anticipation.

'Fancy him, do you?' Leaning on her broom, Madge had noticed her employer's preoccupation with the young man in question.

'He's a bit of all right, don't you think?' Susan whispered in an aside. 'The best-looking bloke we've seen in here for a long time.'

Madge looked at the man, then nudging Susan with the edge of her broom-handle, she advised quietly, 'I wouldn't get too hung up on that one, if I were you.' She gave a cheeky roll of her dark eyes. 'I reckon he might be too much for even *you* to handle.'

'Why's that?' Susan prided herself on being able to see off any woman whose man she'd set her sights on. 'If you're saying he's already got a woman at home, you should know it won't worry *me*.'

'Mebbe not.' The woman's smile lifted to a mischievous grin. 'But it might worry you if he's got a *man*, who wears red stripy trousers and goes by the name o' Clarence.'

When Susan turned with a look of horror on her face, Madge nodded knowingly, then went away at a hasty pace, before she broke into fits of helpless laughter.

Behind her, Susan now gave the young man a lingering, hostile stare. Not knowing what he'd done to deserve such animosity, especially when she had been so friendly, smiling and winking at him just now, he began to feel dreadfully unnerved. Retaliating, he nervously batted his long, frilly eyelashes and gave her a haughty look. 'Strange creature!' he remarked to the frail old woman in front, who was so unnerved by his fluttering dark lashes that she dropped sixpence from her change.

It took fifteen minutes, and ten people on bended knees, to find it. By which time, Susan had emptied the tills into her leather pouch and made off to the privacy of her office, where she could lick her wounds and sulk to her heart's content.

———◆—◆———

ABOUT A MILE or so away, Steve got off the train and into a taxi. 'Jacob's Restaurant,' he said.

The taxi-driver knew it straight away. 'It's a woman as runs that,' he imparted confidingly. 'She does all right an' all. Serves a good plate o' food, an' the prices aren't too bad neither.'

'Really?' Steve wasn't in the mood for conversation. He had things on his mind that needed thinking through.

'Been there afore, have you?'

Steve glanced at the man in the mirror. 'No, can't say I have.'

'There are plenty of other places where they serve good food,' the driver told him. 'There's a little café on the front where they serve a blinding plate o' fish an' chips. Talk about "fish" . . . like a bloody *whale* it is – hangs off both ends o' the plate, I'm not kidding! Look, it's nobbut a stone's throw away if you've a mind to try it out?'

Steve graciously declined. 'There's someone I have to see,' he explained. 'Business, you understand?'

'Oh, that's all right.' The taxi-driver shared his little secret. 'As a matter o' fact, it's a new place. They pay me two bob for every customer I drum up.' He grinned through the mirror. 'Sorry, matey. No harm meant.'

'None taken.'

A few minutes later they drew up outside Susan's place. 'Do you want to book me for coming back?' Ever the optimist, the taxi-driver knew how to make a bob or two.

Steve chuckled. 'You might want to ride up the promenade in an hour's time,' he suggested. 'If you see me first, just give us a toot.'

'You're on!' The man reverently touched the neb of his flat cap, took the fare offered and drew back into the stream of traffic.

When Steve glanced after him, he was amused to see that the taxi-driver had pulled over to flirt with a pretty woman in a short skirt, and heels so high she tottered like a clown on stilts. 'Can't blame a bloke for trying, I suppose,' he muttered with a smile. But it wouldn't do for him, he thought. Not when he had the best woman in the world waiting at home.

Standing outside the restaurant, he kept himself hidden behind an advertising board, so Susan would not see him before he saw her. He needed a moment or two to gather his thoughts. He was amazed at the volume of people going in and coming out, and only then did he realise just how successful his youngest daughter had become. 'It's allus the most ruthless as makes the most money,' he muttered.

Yet underneath his disgust of her, there lingered a vestige of admiration. 'She's done well though,' he admitted graciously. 'It teks hard work and dedication to build up a business like this.' He mused on the reason for his visit here today. 'It's a pity she can't enjoy what she's achieved and leave other folk alone.'

But then he reminded himself of how she could never be satisfied with whatever she had or did. 'The trouble is, she's never content unless she's making somebody miserable; eying their husbands or wanting the house they live in. She *wants* all the time. Wanting and getting, then allus wanting *more*.' Unfortunately, for some reason he could never fathom, it was in her nature to be spiteful.

When the number of diners had diminished, he went inside. His first contact was Madge, the cleaner. She was busy wheeling a trolley round the tables and collecting dirty crockery, 'Can I help you, sir?'

'You can, if you happen to know where I could find my

daughter, Susan.' He liked the woman straight off. 'Your boss?'

'Well, I never.' Instinctively she patted her hair, straightened her pinnie and made cow eyes at him. 'She never told me she had such a handsome father.'

'Don't go flirting with me,' he warned light-heartedly. 'I'm a happily married man.'

Seeing how beneath his bravado, she was embarrassing him, she pointed to the office door. 'You'll find the Queen in her counting house,' she said with a little curtsey. 'Counting out her money.'

He couldn't help but smile. 'You're a cheeky one an' no mistake.'

'Just trying to make the day go with a smile,' she retorted, and pushing her trolley away, she moved down the line of tables, clearing and wiping as she went. She scraped the leftovers into her black bin bag and piled the plates into a neat, jiggling pile, her soft, musical voice uplifted in the latest Gerry and the Pacemakers song.

Steve laughed. 'Singing at work? By! I'm surprised she hasn't been hung, drawn and quartered by now.' The possibility crossed his mind that maybe this jolly, hard-working woman was such an asset to Susan that she was allowed to sing to her heart's content without being silenced.

Glancing about to satisfy himself that Susan was nowhere in the restaurant, he made his way to the office. By the time he reached the door his face was set hard and his eyes lit with the anger that had brought him here. Normally a quiet, gentle man, Steve Holsden would not enjoy the confrontation with his youngest daughter. But in view of what had happened and Patsy's distress over these past weeks, it had to be done, and he was the one to do it.

He placed his hand on the brass door knob and, taking a deep breath, softly urged himself: 'Try and reason with her first, lad. Happen there's still a scrap o' decency behind her scheming.'

Madge was right. On turning the handle, he pushed open the door, and there was Susan, 'counting out her money'. Seated at an enormous desk, head bent and oblivious to his presence, she continued her work.

Steve had never seen so much money in the raw. There must have been eight or nine piles of coins and notes around her, all divided into different units. Directly in front she had a leather pouch half open, with money spilling out across the desk. In one hand she clutched a bunch of notes and in the other, a pen, with which she was scribbling into a thick ledger.

Amazed that she had not yet sensed his presence, he spoke to her. 'I should have thought you'd have that door locked and bolted. Anybody could burst in here. What would you do then, eh? All your hard-earned money, gone to some thieving rogue off the streets.'

Wide-eyed and stunned, Susan stared at him. It was a full half minute before it registered that right here in her office was her father, the man who never strayed from Blackburn, the kind-natured fella who never interfered or had a bad word to say about anybody.

He looked her straight in the eye, his voice harsh. 'Have you nowt to say? Cat got your tongue, has it?'

She stood up, her hands clenched on the desk and her face showing a semblance of fear. 'What are *you* doing here, Dad?'

'I've come to see you. Why else would I be here?' Turning away for a second he clicked the key in the lock.

'What the hell are you doing?' Her voice was shrill, trembling as she ordered, 'Unlock that door!'

'Why?' He tutted. 'You're surely not frightened of your own dad, are you?'

'What do you want?'

When he took a step forward she visibly shrank from him. 'I'm here to see if my daughter has the smallest shred of decency left in that cold heart of hers.' His sorry eyes scoured her face. 'I expect you already know how I lost my job, and how things haven't been too good for me and your mam?'

Knowing why he was here, she swallowed hard, her Adam's apple making a plopping noise as she gulped. 'It's not *my* fault if you've lost your job.' She held out the wad of notes. 'Here, take it. If it's money you've come for, take this and get out!' As she thrust it towards him, her hand trembled uncontrollably. 'There's more if you want.'

'And how am I to pay it back?' For a while, he played her at her own game.

'You can pay it back when you get a job.' Again, she urged, 'Take it.'

Disillusioned and ashamed to his roots, he shook his head. 'What kind of person are you, Susan?' There was such terrible sadness in his voice that she was made to look away.

'If you don't want money, what *do* you want?'

'I think you already know that.'

'Oh, I see.' Her eyes dancing fire, she stared at him. 'It's *Louise*, isn't it?' She spat out her sister's name with venom, her mouth twisted in a downward shape, as though the hatred inside left a terrible taste in her mouth. 'That little cow's been telling lies about me, hasn't she? Trying to make trouble for me. It's *her* you want to go and see. Sort her out! Tell her to stay out of my business!'

'What exactly *is* your business, Susan?' Steve took another step forward, until now he was almost eyeball to eyeball with his daughter. 'You can't mean this place, because Louise already has a life and besides, I'm not sure she could run it as well as you do. I mean, it takes a special sort of person to make the staff toe the line . . .' He regarded the money lying across the desk like so much confetti. 'I'm not even sure she would put the same value on money as you do . . . sitting in here, bent to your counting, like a regular little Fagin.'

'It's *my* money. *I've* earned it!'

'I'm not denying that. I can see how well you've done, and in a strange way I'm proud of you.' He shook his head. 'But there are other things, Susan . . . hard, cruel things that make me turn from you.'

'I don't know what you're talking about.'

'Liar!' Taking a swipe at the money, he sent it clattering all over the floor. 'You know well enough what I'm talking about. I'm here to reason with you about young Jinnie; the bairn you walked away from over ten year ago; the bairn your sister took on at your request after you said you never wanted to see her again as long as you lived. The same bairn that she was able, thank God, to adopt as her own. And now, when the lass is growing up, all settled and happy, and knows nowt whatsoever of you and your evil doings, you want to uproot her, and turn her whole world upside down.'

He paused. Breathing hard and shaking inside he stood back from her. '*That's* why I'm here. To stop you from breaking up a family and ruining a young girl's life. What's more, I need you to tell me why you want that lovely girl after all this time. God Almighty, I don't suppose you even know what she *looks* like! Why are you doing this?'

But Steve did not allow her to answer. Enraged, he hadn't finished with her yet. 'And what about your mother? What possessed you to put her through such agonies? By! With the money you've got, you might have helped her. Instead, you used her to get back at Louise. You haven't changed, Susan. You didn't want Jinnie when she was born, and you don't want her now. You're using your mother and that lovely girl, just to get back at Louise. You don't place any value on family;

you never did. All you want is to tear apart what you don't understand.'

For a long moment he stood his ground, watching his daughter's face as she took in his every word. Now, when the room seemed to echo with his angry tirade, he was shaken to his roots when she suddenly began crying; big, struggling tears dripping down her cheeks, and her face so crumpled he could hardly see her eyes. 'I'm sorry.' She leaned over the desk, her whole body shaking. 'I didn't realise.'

Momentarily speechless, he didn't know quite what to do. In all his life he had never seen Susan like this.

Feeling inadequate, he rounded the desk and took her in his arms. 'Oh lass, what are we to do with you, eh? Look, I'm sorry I had to go on at you like that,' he admitted, 'but I had to make you see what damage you've done. I had to make you see sense.' He groaned. 'Sometimes I don't think you even know *yourself* what you're doing.'

In his arms she continued to sob, over and over, telling him how sorry she was, and how it was only now that she realised how much she was missing everybody.

'Wash your face, lass,' he told her. 'Happen you can show me how good you are at mekking a cuppa.'

She nodded, wiping away the tears. 'I didn't know,' she murmured one last time. 'I'm sorry, Dad.'

While he waited, she went into the adjoining room and came out washed and refreshed. 'Do you want summat to eat?' She smiled. 'We make the best fish and chips in Blackpool.'

Relieved that she had come to her senses and that his mission was accomplished, he nodded. 'Aye, why not?' Together, they went into the restaurant, where she ordered two plates of fish and chips and two mugs of tea.

Not realising how hungry he was, Steve soon downed the lot. 'By! You were right an' all,' he confessed. 'That were as good a meal as I've ever had.'

Calling Madge over to take away the plates and empty cups, Susan asked her father, 'What else can I do to make amends?'

'You've done everything I could have hoped for.' He smiled at her affectionately. 'What you can do though is to come and see your sister. I reckon it's time you two made peace.'

Susan agreed. 'Maybe I've lost all sense of reality here,' she said, and looked around her. 'I've done nothing but work and save, and there's never any time for socialising. I've no friends to speak of, and to tell you the truth, I miss you all so much.' Overcome with emotion, she covered her face with her hands for a while, and when she glanced up again, it was to say with all her heart, 'In a way you were right in what you said . . . about me wanting to destroy things I don't understand. So, maybe it's time I got to understand it, and be a closer part of it. And I won't tell Jinnie, I promise.'

'Oh, lass!' He clutched her small hand in his. 'You don't know how glad I am to hear you say that.'

She offered him money and he graciously refused, explaining, 'I'm hoping to get work soon. Louise is going to have a word with Eric. He's got a few contacts. He's a good man. I'm sure he'll find me summat.'

A short time later, when they parted company, Susan hung on to him. 'Tell Mam I'll come and see her, soonever I shut down for the winter,' she said. 'I'll be able to spend a bit of time with all of you then.' She waved him off, and once he was out of sight she made a hasty path to her office. Closing the door, she picked up the receiver and dialled a number.

When someone at the other end answered, she said in lowered tones, 'It's Susan. Yes, I'm fine, but it's time I called in that favour you owe me.'

There was a slight pause, while she listened, then, 'My

daughter is being kept from me. I need her to be picked up . . . if you know what I mean?'

Another pause, before she responded: 'That sounds okay, but it must be someone who knows how to keep their mouth shut. And I don't want her harmed in any way whatsoever, or I swear to God, you'll be sorry.' She listened again. 'Right! I want to see him first. I need to satisfy myself he's the man for the job. Ring me the minute you've got it organised.'

With that she slammed down the receiver. 'Fool! They're all fools, and my dad is the biggest one of all.'

Outside, Madge heard her chuckling. 'Huh!' She hooked a cloud of dust from beneath the fridge. 'I swear, there are times when I reckon that one's not right in the 'ead!'

Chapter Fourteen

T HE EVENING FOLLOWING Steve Holsden's visit to Susan, Louise came home from work to find him waiting for her. Thrilled and delighted, he told her of Susan's change of heart. 'She knows she went too far,' he said. 'We had a good long talk. She's changed her ways for good an' all.'

'Oh Dad, that's wonderful news!' At first, Louise could hardly believe it, but her father was so convinced of Susan's regret at having caused so much heartache, she gave herself up to the idea. 'So I've no need to worry about Jinnie?'

'None whatsoever, lass. In fact, as soon as she shuts up shop for the winter, Susan's coming to stay with her mam and me. It'll be grand to welcome her back into the family again. We can all mek a fresh start, and young Jinnie won't know anything about what's gone on. Our Susan is just her aunt, and that's an end to it.'

Louise would have liked to have given him good news about work, but it would have to wait. 'Eric had to rush out the minute I got there this morning,' she explained. 'There's a sale of farm machinery in Birmingham, and it's one he's been waiting for. He had hoped to be back before I finished; I hung on for another half-hour, but he still wasn't there. I'll ask him tomorrow,' she promised.

Just then, Jinnie and Sally arrived home with the pie and

chips. 'By! Haven't you got that kettle boiling yet, lass?' Sally took off her coat while Jinnie went into the kitchen with the food. 'You haven't even done the bread and butter either, have you, eh?' She winked at Steve. 'Been too busy nattering with your dad here, I suppose?'

While Jinnie busied herself in the kitchen, Steve quietly gave Sally the good news. 'So now we can all rest easy,' he finished.

Sally was not so forgiving. 'What she wants is an old-fashioned smack o' the arse!'

'Aye, well, happen that's what she should have had long ago,' Steve agreed. 'But all's well that ends well, and we have to be grateful for that, I suppose.'

Sally breathed a sigh of relief. 'You did well,' she told him admiringly. 'I don't expect for one minute it was easy.'

'I'd be lying if I said it *was*,' he confessed. 'She's a hard madam and allus has been, but she saw a side of me today she's never seen afore. I reckon I frightened the life out of her.'

'Not before time neither, eh?'

'I never thought I'd see the day when I might talk to my own daughter the way I had to talk to her.'

Louise saw how the ordeal had taken it out of him. 'Well, it's done now,' she said. 'And I for one am very grateful.'

Jinnie's voice cut short the conversation. 'How many bread and butters should I do?'

'I'll have one,' Sally replied.

'Me too, sweetheart.' Louise liked a slice of bread and butter with her pie and chips. Addressing Steve, she asked, 'Do you fancy a pie and chips, Dad? There's more than enough to go round. I'll share with Jinnie. That chippie at the end of Montague Street allus serves more than one person can manage to eat.'

'No thanks, love.' He stood up to leave. 'Your mam's got me a steak and kidney pudding on the boil . . . Brussels sprouts

and boiled potatoes and thick brown gravy to go with it an all.'
He licked his lips.

And so did Sally. 'Go on, be off with you,' she laughed.
'Afore I get there first and polish it all off.'

Before he left, Jinnie gave him a big kiss. 'See you later,
Grandad.'

'Aye, lass.' Cupping his hands round her pretty, heart-
shaped face with its serious blue eyes and uplifted smile, he
loved her more than he could ever say. 'You're a bonny lass.'
He shook his head with wonder. 'You'll never know how
precious you are to me.' He thought of Susan and how she
had planned to take this delightful girl out of his life, and he
thanked the Good Lord for giving him the strength to put a
stop to it.

Later that night, after Jinnie had gone to bed, Sally and
Louise sat downstairs, discussing what Steve had told them.
'I can't imagine your dad losing his temper,' Sally remarked.
'He's allus been such a quiet person.'

Louise hated the idea of him being driven to such meas-
ures. 'For our Susan to break down in tears, he must have
given her the shock of her life.'

'Well, at least now we can rest easy about Jinnie.'

But Louise had lingering doubts. 'How much can we trust
her, though? In my experience, she can say one thing and mean
another.'

Sally chuckled. 'I've known your dad a good many years,'
she said. 'He's a gentle-speaking man, even-tempered and
kind. The last thing he would ever do is raise his voice or
use violent language. By! If he were to lose his temper with
me, the way it seems he did with Susan . . . reducing me to
tears an' all, I wouldn't be thinking about going back on my
word, I can tell yer. No, lass, it were a long while coming, but
I reckon your Susan's learned a tough lesson this time.'

'So you don't think she'll ever bother us again . . . about

Jinnie, I mean?' Those doubts wouldn't go away, but Louise put great store by what Sally had to say.

Her mother-in-law was most emphatic. 'Not to my reckoning, no, lass. I don't think she'd have the nerve to stir up trouble again. Not after what your dad told us tonight.'

Louise tried to picture the confrontation between Susan and her father; it made an odd image in her mind. 'I'm astonished he even *went* to Blackpool, let alone confronted her like that.'

'Well, he did. And it seems things have worked out all right. So stop your worrying, lass.'

Louise knew it wasn't a long-term solution to the problem. 'There will come a time when Jinnie will have to be told. She's eleven soon, and already mature for her age.' Exasperated, she blew out her cheeks. 'Before I can turn round, she'll be a young woman.'

'Aye, that's true enough,' Sally remarked thoughtfully. 'And when all's said an' done, it's Jinnie's right to know the circumstances of her birth. You can't side-step it for much longer.'

Louise knew all that, but whenever she contemplated telling Jinnie that she was not her real mother, her heart shrank. 'Thanks to Dad, we've at least got a breathing space.' Like Sally she knew how, sooner or later, the truth would out.

'I'll tell her everything,' she mused aloud. 'One fine day not too far off, I'll have to take the bull by the horns.' A shadow flitted across her heart. 'I hope to God she loves me enough to forgive me for all the years of deceit.'

Sally reassured her. 'Nobody loves you more than that child does,' she said fondly. 'What! She'd cut off her right arm for you. All the same, lass . . . Susan or no Susan, don't mek the mistake o' leaving it too long.'

Louise was well aware of the dangers. 'This business with Susan has taught me a lot,' she answered softly. 'It's made me realise how vulnerable Jinnie is, and how cruel people can be.'

Before they called it a day, they talked some more, about Sarah and the children and how Hannah and Jinnie had become good friends.

'It's good to see Jinnie with a close friend, despite the age gap,' Louise commented. 'She's become very protective towards the lass.'

'Hannah can be a surly little thing at times.' Sally had caught a glimpse of her peevish nature once when the girl had come to their house for her tea. 'D'yer recall how she persuaded Jinnie to look in the cellar, when she swore she'd seen a stray kitten down there?' Sally was not amused. 'Soonever Jinnie was outside the house she locked the back door and wouldn't open it again until I gave her a ticking-off. Nasty little bugger!'

'I wouldn't be too hard on her, Sal,' Louise said. 'Not when you think what she's been through.'

'Aye, o' course yer right, lass. But I didn't like the idea of her sending Jinnie down that cellar for no reason. It seems to me she needs some kind o' help.'

'Me and Sarah were taking about it the other morning,' Louise imparted. 'She said Hannah was getting better by the day. She appears to have accepted the house now, though of course she'll not go anywhere near that cellar – and who can blame her, eh? But she's stopped having the nightmares, thank God.'

Sally smiled proudly. 'I reckon our Jinnie's had a lot to do with that,' she said. 'The lass has really tekken Hannah under her wing.'

'Adam deserves credit too,' Louise answered. 'Sarah said he spends hours on end talking with his sister; sometimes they're downstairs until midnight. Sarah sits on the stairs and listens, but she never interferes. She reckons it's ridding Hannah of her demons.'

'Not many brothers would be so thoughtful.' On the few occasions when he'd popped in with Hannah and Jinnie, Sally had thought Adam a remarkable young man. 'He seems a grand lad,' she admitted. 'Especially when you think *he* were down that cellar, too, protecting his sister while upstairs unbeknown to them, their mam and my son were being murdered. Like Hannah, he has to cope with the memories of all that.'

Louise reached for Sally's hand and both women fell silent for a minute, recalling poor, bad Jacob and his twisted, wasted life. 'Some folks can cope with bad things. Others can't,' she whispered.

Echoes of the past crept into their minds.

'It'll all come right in the end.' This was a favourite saying of Sally's. 'Let the past be, and it'll let *you* be.'

Louise made no comment. She knew Sally was referring to her and Ben, and Eric, and just now, she was in no mood to talk about it.

'I hope Eric can find work for Dad,' she said, changing the subject.

'Oh, I'm sure he will, lass.' Sally was confident. 'If I know Eric, he'll talk to everybody he knows, until he finds summat suitable.' On that lighter note, she said her goodnight, and ambled off to bed.

Louise stayed down a while longer. Her mind was still too full for sleep just yet.

<hr />

DOWN THE STREET, Sarah was feeling much the same. Unable to sleep, she had come downstairs to find Adam sitting in front of an empty fire-grate.

They sat and talked a while before Sarah said, 'You'd best get to bed, son. You look done in.'

'I am tired.' Yawning, he ruffled his dark hair. 'Only I just can't get off to sleep.'

Sarah fondly regarded him, and her heart swelled with pride. 'I'm surprised you can't,' she said. 'You should be fair worn out. Every day, from eight in the morning till six at night, you're traipsing the streets looking for work.'

'I don't mind.'

'Mebbe not, but it wouldn't hurt you to take a few hours off. Why don't you go down to the canal and watch the barges? You like that, don't you, son?'

His smile was radiant. 'One day, I fancy having my own barge,' he said. 'A green one, with a brass tiller and a big, round clock in the cabin. I'll carry the cargo up and down the canals, and at night-time, when the day's over, I'll sit outside and watch the stars.' His dark eyes twinkled. 'Charlie said that's when you can see the *real* world, when day fades and night comes alive.'

Sarah laughed. 'Sounds to me like your friend Charlie is a real dreamer.'

'He's really wise, Gran. On his barge he's got shelves filled with all kinds of interesting books, and photographs he's taken of every place he's ever been.' Pride shone in his eyes. 'He was a merchant captain, did you know that?'

'No, you never told me that.'

'He's funny too. He makes me laugh.'

Sarah was pleased. 'You've made real friends with him, haven't you, son?'

Adam nodded. 'Charlie's different from anybody I've ever met. He spent most of his life on the water on big ships, then he retired and had a little boat, and now he's got his own barge.'

'What does his wife have to say about all this travelling?'

Adam shook his head. 'He never got married . . . said he

never had time to meet the ladies long enough to get to know them proper.'

Sarah chuckled. 'He sounds like Jack the Lad to me.'

'You'll have to meet him,' Adam said. 'I've told him all about you.'

Sarah was horrified. 'Have you now?'

'He said *you* sound like the sort of woman he should have settled down with years ago. You're the one who got away, that's what he said.'

'Hmh! You wouldn't catch me on a barge, I can tell you. I prefer four walls round me, and the feel of solid earth beneath my feet.'

'Charlie's never lived in a house, and he never wants to. He says he'd shrivel up and die if he was shut up like that. He needs to be on the move. He needs to feel the sway of the barge as it slices through the water.'

'It's just as well me and him never got together then,' she laughed. 'You make me feel seasick just talking about it.'

Adam was deep in thought. 'Charlie says everything is beautiful from his side of the water. He sees things others can't, like the wildlife in the early hours, and the mist that creeps over the world like a mantle. And the quietness. He says it's the nearest thing to heaven.'

'There you go then, son. The two of you have obviously got something in common. Take time off tomorrow to go and see this Charlie the bargee. You deserve a few hours' relaxation.' Lately Sarah had grown concerned about her grandson. 'You drive yourself too hard.'

She peeked at him from under her eyebrows. 'I know how it is with you,' she revealed. 'Many a time, you and Hannah are down here till gone midnight, with her bending your ear, and you never complaining. You're a good brother, and I've a feeling Hannah takes advantage of that. But we mustn't become a burden to you. I wouldn't want that.'

'You're not a burden. I don't think *that*!' He sounded hurt. 'If Hannah needs to talk, I want to listen . . . just like you listen to me when I need to talk.'

'I know that, son, but sometimes you need to keep a little corner just for yourself.' She wasn't too sure how to put this without sounding peevish, but it had to be said. 'Hannah can be very demanding sometimes, and thoughtless too. Thanks to you, she's coming along fine, but listening to somebody's innermost thoughts night after night, when you're tired and need to sleep – well, it can be draining.'

'I need to be there for her, and you.'

'I know you do, son, and we'll always be grateful for that, but I want you to think about *yourself* now and then. I want you to promise me that you'll keep tomorrow for yourself. Just for one day, I want you to forget about Hannah and me, and do what pleases *you*. Will you promise me that?'

'Why?'

'Because I *want* you to! It'll do you good to be with this friend of yours. He makes you laugh, that's what you said, and I'm glad about that. It's what you need.'

'But I have to find myself a job, Gran,' he said. 'It's not right for a man to be out of work.'

Sarah was made to smile at his remark. 'You're too hard on yourself.' Yet she saw the man in him, and her heart was full. 'My mother had a saying, and it was this: "A watched kettle never boils".'

He loved her funny little sayings. 'What's that supposed to mean?'

'It means the more you tramp the streets looking for work, the less likely you are to find it.'

'That doesn't make sense.'

'Please, Adam. Promise me that just for once, you'll forget the job-hunting. Who knows, just as you turn your back, some wise employer will snap you up and that'll be it.'

Adam appreciated what she was saying, but, 'I'm worried we won't have enough money to pay our way.'

'Hey! Have you been listening to me or what? I don't want you taking the world on your shoulders, young man,' Sarah warned him with a wag of her finger. 'I know you want to help, and you *do*, and when you get fixed up, I know you'll pay your way. But we're not destitute yet. I've managed to get a few hours' cleaning at the pub twice a week, and I'm helping in the shop of a morning. It's not a fortune, I know, but it'll keep the wolf from the door.' She chuckled. 'Besides, Maisie lets me fetch all the leftover cakes and pies home for us tea. That saves us a bob or two.'

Adam knew she was trying to make him feel better, but it only made him all the more determined. 'All right, I'll go and see Charlie tomorrow. But after that I'll not rest till I find a job.'

Sarah offered her open hand. 'A deal then?'

They shook hands. 'A deal,' he promised.

Her faith in him moved Adam deeply. 'I thought I'd got work today at Cicely Bridge Mill,' he imparted. 'The manager said one of his lads had gone off in a temper, and if he wasn't back by ten o'clock when the lorry arrived to be offloaded, he was out the door.'

'Oh, aye? And what happened?'

Adam shrugged his shoulders. 'I waited until five minutes past ten, and just as the manager was about to clock me in, the lad turned up and got his job back.'

'Hmh! I'd have kicked him out, that's what *I'd* have done. If he's walked out once, he can walk out again.'

Adam's face lit up. 'I never thought of that! I *will* go and see Charlie, but first I might call in at the mill and see if the lad's walked out again. If he has, I bet you the manager won't be so keen to take him back a *second* time.' He suddenly remembered something else. 'Oh, and I want to call in at the bike-shop. There's a note in the Post Office window, saying *Bikes bought and sold*. It's a new shop on King Street. *Opening today*, it said.' Looking thoughtful, he gave a nod. 'After that, I'll go and see Charlie, like I promised.'

With that he took himself off upstairs, leaving Sarah shaking her head and chuckling to herself. 'What would I do without him, eh?' Another cup of tea, and a few more minutes to contemplate things, then she, too, went away to her bed, yawning and groaning as she mounted the stairs. 'It's been a funny old day,' she muttered, climbing into bed. 'I wonder what tomorrow will bring?'

———◦———

TOMORROW BROUGHT FINE weather and even a hint of wintry sunshine.

By seven o'clock Sarah and her grandchildren were out of bed and seated at the little table given them by Mrs Peters from the end house. Breakfast was a pleasant affair these days. On this particular morning, Adam was enjoying a thick bacon buttie, and Hannah had her usual scrambled egg on toast. As a rule, Sarah could never face food first thing of a morning, but today she had a piece of thick-sliced toast laden with best butter and strawberry jam.

By half-past seven, Adam was washed, dressed and out of the door. 'See you later,' he told them, and Sarah wished him well.

'Mind you keep to what you promised!' she called after him.

Overhearing the conversation, Hannah wanted to know, 'What was all that about?'

'He promised not to spend all day round the mills and factories.' Sarah tore off a slice of her toast, licking the strawberry jam as it trickled down her chin. 'I've told him he's trying too hard. It'll do him good to go and spend a couple of hours with that friend of his.'

'His name's Charlie.'

'Oh? So he's told you about him, has he?'

'He tells me everything.' Hannah looked meaningfully at her gran. 'He tells me things he doesn't tell *you*.'

Sarah smiled. 'Oh, I see.'

'It's a secret.' Her brown eyes narrowed. 'I can't tell you either.'

'Well, o' course you can't lass. Secrets is secrets, *I* know that.' It'll be something and nothing, Sarah thought, so was not unduly concerned.

'I'll tell you something else though.' It was obvious that Hannah was aching to impart at least a snippet of what she knew.

Sarah popped the remaining pice of toast in her mouth. 'Another secret, is it?'

'No. It's about Adam finding work. Maisie says it weren't so long ago when there was plenty of work about.'

'Did she now?'

'She said that employers were so desperate they even used to put cards in her window. Only now, it's the other way round. People looking for work put the cards in, and the work's getting harder to find by the minute. That's what Maisie says.'

Sarah believed it. 'It's always the way, lass,' she remarked wisely. 'One minute there's work to be had for them as wants it, money to be got, new suits and flash cars everywhere. Spend! Spend! They think it'll last for ever, and they get lulled into a false sense of security, then suddenly things start drying up and times aren't so good.'

Frowning, she remembered how it was with them, and not too long ago neither. 'You've to watch the pennies in your pocket, that's the thing. Good times are like a bubble; it gets bigger and bigger, and the bigger it gets, the sooner it'll burst and the louder a bang it'll make when it does.'

It was all above Hannah's young head. 'Do you think Adam will get a job?'

Sarah had no doubts on that score. 'Oh, I'm sure he will.'

Hannah gave a sly little smile. 'Do you think he's handsome?'

Sarah laughed out loud. 'That's a funny question, lass. But yes, he *is* handsome.' She wondered what had brought that on. 'Well, I think he is, anyroad.'

Hannah gave the same, sly little grin. 'Somebody else thinks so, too.'

'Oh, aye?' Clambering out of her chair, Sarah began gathering the crockery. 'And who might that be?'

'Can't tell.'

Sarah glanced at her grand-daughter, thinking how much better she was looking these days – sleeping better too, thank God. 'That'll be your little secret, will it?' she asked in a whisper.

'Do you want me to tell?'

'If you like. But I wouldn't want you to betray a confidence, lass.'

'It's *Jinnie!*' Hannah smiled triumphantly. '*She* thinks he's handsome.'

'And she's right.'

'And he likes *her*. He told me.'

'Well, I can't say as I'm surprised. Jinnie's a lovely lass.'

'*I* think they're in love.'

Sarah was so surprised, she almost dropped the crockery. Jinnie was only a child! But she played along. 'Well, I never.'

'Adam will be seventeen next birthday.'

Sarah paused, her mind going back to when these two children first came into her care. 'Time flies,' she sighed. 'But he's made a fine young man.' She stroked Hannah's hair. 'You an' all. You've come along in leaps and bounds, lass,' she said. 'I'm proud of you both.'

'Did you know Jinnie will be *eleven* next birthday?'

'So I understand.'

'I'm older than Jinnie, but sometimes she seems a lot older than me. Why is that?'

Realising the question was given with a hint of anger, Sarah was careful how she replied. 'I had a friend much the same,' she fibbed. 'She was eighteen and I was twenty-three, but people always thought it was the other way round. You see, lass, everybody's different. For whatever reason, some people mature quicker than others. They grow faster, or they learn more quickly, or they simply have that kind of a nature where they're naturally calm and wise – and because they're helpful, they sort of take charge, and people just assume they must be older.'

There was a span of silence while Hannah digested the information, during which Sarah took the pile of crockery into the kitchen and returned for the teapot and cups.

Much to Sarah's relief, Hannah had taken her explanation very well. 'Jinnie's like that,' she answered thoughtfully, '. . . what you said.'

'Well, there you are then.'

'She's like my big sister. She looks after me. If I'm worried about anything, she gives me good advice.'

'She thinks a lot of you, lass, that's why. You've found a good friend there.'

Suddenly there came a knock on the door. 'Talk of the devil!' Hannah leaped up and ran down the passageway, returning a moment later with Jinnie.

'Morning, Sarah.' Having been told by Sarah to call her by her first name, Jinnie always greeted her with a smile. 'How are you today?'

'I'm fine, lass, thank you. And you look lovely.' She had always thought Jinnie was unusually pretty; tall and slim, with her long fair hair hanging loose and her blue eyes shining, she made a striking figure. But she was neither vain nor above herself. Instead she was a quiet, likable girl, who made everyone feel at ease the minute she entered a room.

Before Sarah and Jinnie could get into a longer conversation, Hannah had run up the stairs and down again, and now she was eager to be off. 'Got to go or we'll be late for school!' Jinnie and she attended the same school, which was split into junior and senior sections.

Sarah opened her arms. 'Come here and give us a kiss then.'

As always, she stood at the door and watched the two girls make their way down the street, chatting and laughing, seemingly without a care in the world. It was good to see Hannah well again, and despite Sarah's fears, she seemed to have accepted the house back into her life without too much trauma. Sarah put that down to Adam and Jinnie. Adam listened to her fears at night, and Jinnie dealt with them during the day, while Sarah herself had nursed her through the nightmares.

Nor had it escaped Sarah's notice how, since knowing Jinnie, Hannah had blossomed; her brown hair seemed richer, and her hazel eyes were filled with curiosity. There was a spring to her step and laughter in her voice. And her affection for Jinnie was plain to see.

For a time after they'd gone out of sight, Sarah stood on the step, chatting to neighbours as they passed by, and thinking how kind people had been. Looking up at the shifting skies, mottled grey with eyes of blue peeping through, she murmured under her breath, 'Thank You, Lord. We've a lot to be grateful for.'

She often said a little prayer; it didn't matter where she

was . . . in her bed of a night, or in the Market Square when it was teeming with people. When the mood came over her, she would look to the skies and give thanks for what they had. It always brought a sense of peace to her.

———✦———

THE GIRLS WERE surprised to see Adam waiting at the tram stop. 'I thought you'd gone to see a man about a bike?' Hannah teased. They had talked about it this morning over breakfast.

Adam shrugged his shoulders. 'It seems he's had some sort of set-back. There's a note pinned to the door, saying that due to unforeseen circumstances, he won't be able to open until next week.'

While they chatted, the tram drew up. 'We're full to bursting,' the grinning, boss-eyed conductor told them, hanging out of the doorway. 'But we can squeeze you lot in, I'm sure.'

Boarding the tram, they sat three abreast up front; first Hannah by the window, then Jinnie, with Adam sitting beside her. 'This is cosy.' Hannah never lost an opportunity to tease.

Jinnie felt uncomfortable. She could feel Adam's eyes on her, as he pretended to look out the window. She so much wanted to speak to him, yet didn't know what to say. And with Hannah sniggering beside her, she began to worry that Adam would think they were just two silly kids, and wish he'd never sat anywhere near them.

Adam too, felt uncomfortable. He could feel Jinnie's warm thigh burning through his trouser leg, and he had to keep reminding himself that she was not yet eleven, and he was making mountains out of molehills. But he felt drawn to her, yet not in a way that grown-ups might be drawn. Instead he felt passionately protective of her, and deeply content in her company.

'Are you comfortable, Jinnie?' Looking down into those sapphire-blue eyes he felt oddly elated.

Jinnie assured him she was all right. 'Thank you.'

All the same, he could hear Hannah giggling, and sensing Jinnie's embarrassment, he eased himself towards the edge of the seat, allowing her more room. 'Is that better?'

Jinnie nodded. 'Where are you going?'

Relieved that she had started a conversation, he answered with a smile. 'I'm off to see if there's anything going at Cicely Bridge Mill.'

'My mam used to work there.' Jinnie recalled how her mother had worked from six in the morning until six at night, before she went to work for Eric and life got easier for her.

Adam related the story of the absconding lad, and how he had only just got back in time before the boss gave his job to Adam.

Jinnie was of the same opinion as Sarah. 'He deserved to lose his job, walking out like that. He's not reliable.'

'That's what Gran said, and that's why I'm going back there. To see if he's absconded again.'

With that short conversation ended, they sat together, acutely aware of each other, yet too shy to utter another word.

When they got to the school, Hannah and Jinnie got out of their seats, and brushed past him. 'Bye, Adam.' Jinnie blushed deep pink when he smiled at her with those quiet, dark eyes.

Hannah saw her blush, and embarrassed her even more by telling Adam, 'You shouldn't smile at her like that. Look! You've made her blush!'

With her face burning, Jinnie looked away.

Hannah was intrigued. 'Where are you going after you've been to Cicely Bridge Mill?' she asked her brother.

Adam shrugged his shoulders. For the life of him, he couldn't take his eyes off Jinnie.

Holding onto the back of the next seat, Hannah waited for the tram to stop. 'I thought Gran said you were going to see that friend of yours down the canal . . . Charlie, isn't it? Him with the barge?'

'I am, yes. Later.'

The tram pulled up with a jerk, sending everyone backwards and Jinnie off-balance. But Adam was there to catch her, and he did; holding onto her a minute longer than he needed. When she uprighted herself, their hands touched and she daren't look at him. In a peculiar hurry she went forward and, pushing her way through, got off the tram, only to see how he'd sat back in Hannah's seat and was looking at her out of the window.

Hannah was in her element. 'See?' As the tram pulled away, she would not be shut up. 'I *said* he fancied you, and I was right.' She nudged Jinnie in the ribs. 'You fancy him too, don't you?' When Jinnie didn't answer, she nudged her a second time. 'You *love* him! Don't deny it! I saw how you two looked at each other.'

'Stop it, Hannah!' Now, because of her friend's persistence, she couldn't get Adam out of her mind.

Hannah's voice assailed her ears. 'Adam's going on seventeen now, and you'll soon be old enough to have a sweetheart. Did I tell you, my gran got married when she was only fifteen?'

Jinnie seemed not to have heard. Instead she was still thinking about an earlier remark Hannah had made. 'How do you know Adam likes me?' The question was out before she realised.

'Because he *told* me! Look, Jinnie, why don't you go and meet up with him after school? You heard him say he's going to see Charlie. He lives on a barge by the canal.'

She grew excited. 'Go on, Jinnie. Adam will be that pleased to see you.'

Jinnie shook her head. 'I can't.'

'Why not?'

Digging into her pocket, Jinnie brought out two half-crowns. 'I'm going into town after school. I want to buy a present for Sally. She's been feeling under the weather lately, and she never complains, but I've seen her holding her back when she's in pain. I thought she might be catching a chill, so I might get her a new jumper, or something. Besides, Mam's working late at the farm. I should be there with Sally.'

But Hannah would not be dissuaded. 'Half an hour won't make any difference, will it? I'm off to get my hair cut after school, so it's all right by me, if you want to meet Adam.' She absentmindedly patted her shoulder-length mane. 'I persuaded Gran to give me two bob to get my hair trimmed. I mean, I'm leaving school next year, and I think it'll make me look more grown-up. What do you reckon?'

Jinnie instinctively ran her fingers through Hannah's long brown hair. 'I like it the way it is,' she said honestly. 'But it's up to you.'

Considering Jinnie's comment, Hannah messed about with her hair, then, in a decisive tone she informed her, 'You're right, it *is* up to me. I might even have it cut really short, like Twiggy's.' Having succeeded in startling her friend, she laughed. 'Just kidding. Gran would never forgive me.' She gave a sulky pout. 'Though I'm not really all that bothered what *she* thinks!'

Shocked by the sudden animosity in Hannah's off-handed remark, Jinnie was extremely relieved when two other girls ran up and started chatting. 'We've got old Sergeant Major for PE,' said the red-headed girl.

'I hope she doesn't get us doing the shot-putt,' the lanky friend groaned. 'I ached all over for a week after the last time.'

'She doesn't worry *me!*' Hannah retorted, and marched onwards, as if embarking on a mission to meet the enemy.

Behind the other three, Jinnie took her time. Adam was still strong in her mind. Hannah was right though, she admitted secretly. She *did* like him. But to tell the truth, she didn't know where 'like' ended', and 'love' began.

Chapter Fifteen

———⟢·◉·⟣———

C HARLIE LIKED A nap in the afternoon. Today was no different except, as he stretched himself awake, he peeped through the window, delighted and surprised to see Adam striding down Penny Street towards the barge.

'Well, look at that!' Addressing a bright pink and yellow parrot in its cage, he pointed to the approaching figure. 'We've got a visitor.' Wagging a finger at the parrot he ordered it, in mock-severe tones, 'Straighten yourself up, you lazy article! Look smart now. We don't want the young man to think we run a sloppy ship.'

Still half-asleep and stretching its feathers, the parrot cocked its head to one side. Closing one eye and peering through the other, it replied in a high, squeaky voice, 'Where's me whisky? Want it *now*!' Having itself been woken from a comfortable nap, it ran up and down its perch, demanding attention, until Charlie had to threaten it with being cooked for dinner, if it wasn't quiet.

As always, that did the trick.

Adam called from outside, 'Charlie, are you in there?'

In a minute Charlie had pulled his slippers on and was at the door. 'Come in, lad! Come in. I've told you before, if me flag's flying, I'm at home,' he chuckled, a loud, hearty sound that sent the pigeons soaring into the air. 'I might not be the Queen of England, but this is my castle and that's my flag.'

He pointed to the flag at the forward-mast, and seeing it tightly wrapped round the pole, he slapped his hand across his forehead and groaned. 'Oh, will you look at *that*! I did go out a while ago and then I had a nap, and completely forgot to set it loose.' Emerging from the barge, he fumbled his way to the front and painstakingly unravelled the flag, letting it ripple free. 'There! So now I'm home, and everybody knows it.'

Adam waited at the door. He loved the barge and everything about it, and Charlie was the most colourful, likable, most eccentric man he'd ever know. 'Come inside, lad.' Charlie slapped a long, heavy arm round Adam's shoulders. 'There's no reason why the two of us should stand out here in the cold. It's nipping my arse, so it is.' His wide, podgy nose was blue at the end, though whether that was with cold or drink was another thing, and his bright green eyes were as sharp and all-seeing as the parrot's. One thing was for sure: once you'd seen Charlie, you would never forget him.

'Come on then, lad!' He propelled Adam through the door so roughly that the pair of them fell headlong into the sofa; which caused the parrot to squawk and panic, and knock its water trough over. Disentangling himself, Charlie gave another hearty laugh, sending the parrot scurrying for cover. 'It's gonna be one o' them days,' he told Adam, who was thoroughly enjoying himself. 'I can see it a mile away.'

Charlie had a set routine. When visitors arrived, he would first make them comfortable, then break open a bottle of whisky. They would sit opposite one another – the visitor on the small, narrow sofa, and himself in the big armchair, and the two of them would talk about politics and women, and enjoy a drink or two, and after a while, the visitor would roll home, and Charlie would fall asleep.

Today was different. Adam might not be too young for

women and politics, but whisky was out. 'I've no tea nor coffee to offer you,' Charlie told him, 'but I've lemonade, or shandy . . . with not too much beer, 'cause I made it meself and it's a shameful waste o' good beer if you ask me. I've got a friend who's partial to it though, so I always keep a bottle at hand.' He grimaced. 'I never touch the stuff meself. Give me a good measure o' whisky any day.'

Going to the tiny fridge in the corner, he flung open the door. 'Look at that!' He drew out a string of fish, complete with tails and heads, and staring eyes. 'Caught 'em meself last week.' Pausing, he bent his head forward and sniffed the fish. 'Phew! There's a fair old stink an' no mistake!' Much to Adam's amusement, he flung open the window and slung the fish out. They dropped into the water below with a resounding splash.

Forlorn, Charlie shook his head, but chuckled all the same. 'There goes me supper, lad.' He eyed the parrot mischievously, warning in a loud voice, 'I can always cook the parrot. I'm told they make a right tasty stew.'

When the parrot began shouting, 'Where's me bloody whisky?' he threw a shirt over its cage, and there wasn't another peep. He laughed so much he rocked the barge. 'Somebody's taught that bird to swear.' He wagged a long, chubby finger at Adam. 'It wasn't *you*, was it?'

Adam shook his head. He couldn't talk, because he was laughing so much.

Charlie returned to the fridge. 'Right then, as I were saying, I've no coffee nor tea to offer you. There's homemade shandy, or lemonade . . . and by the way, I left the lemonade out all night and forgot to put the top on, so . . .' He scratched his ear and made a suitably guilty face. 'I might as well tell you now, it's as flat as a pancake.' He held the bottle of lemonade in one hand and another bottle in the other, labelled *Malt Vinegar* which, according to Charlie, contained the shandy. 'So, which is it to be?'

It seemed Adam had no choice. 'It sounds like I'd best have a drop of your homemade shandy.'

'Wise lad.' Replacing the lemonade in the cupboard, Charlie poured himself a glass of whisky, and gave Adam a tumbler of shandy. 'There you go, matey. It's good stuff, but it's not potent, if you know what I mean.'

Not sure what to expect, Adam took a sip and found it invigorating. 'It's good,' he said, smacking his lips.

Charlie was proud as punch. 'Though I say it meself, I'm a dab hand at making shandy. My old dad taught me the way.'

They drank up and had another one, only this time, Charlie warned Adam, 'If you start feeling a bit merry you'd best tell me, 'cause I'm not sure how much beer I put in it. Usually I measure it out, only I can't find my measure. So, you be wary, lad. I don't want to send you home feeling woozy, or like as not, I'll have that grandmother of yours down on my head.' He gave a wink. 'From what you tell me, she sounds just the woman I've been looking for all my life.'

He took a swig of his whisky. 'Tell me some more about her,' he urged. 'Does she wear 'jamas or a nightie, 'cause in my experience, a woman as wears 'jamas can be a cold fish. I prefer a woman as wears a *nightie* – preferably silk, mind. None of your cotton or Winceyette.'

Adam wasn't about to get drawn into that particular conversation. Instead, he asked, 'Why don't you come and meet her?'

'I just might do that.' Charlie had thought about it for a while now, ever since Adam had sung his grandmother's praises. 'You've got me curious, and it's an age since I enjoyed some female company.' He took stock of Adam's good looks and his strong build, and he wondered, 'And what about *you*? Have *you* got a sweetheart?'

Taken unawares, Adam considered his answer carefully. 'No, not yet,' he answered warily.

'Ah!' Charlie had seen how his question had made Adam think. 'But you've got somebody in mind, is that it?'

'Not really.' Adam was always happy to confide in Charlie. 'There *is* a girl, but she's too young. Just now, we're good friends, but . . . she's really nice. Very pretty.' He blushed. 'She's not silly or flirty, like some of the girls. She's sensible and we get on really well. If she was older, I'd ask her to be my girl, but . . .' He shrugged. 'Like I said, she's much too young.'

Sitting up in the chair, Charlie observed Adam for a moment, then in a fatherly tone he advised, 'If she's all those things you said, I reckon she might well be worth waiting for.'

'*I* think so too.'

'How old is she?'

'Just a girl.'

'How old?'

Adam took a deep breath. 'She'll be eleven next birthday.'

'Whoo!' Charlie rolled his eyes. 'So she's got nearly six years before she catches up with you, eh?'

'I said she was too young.'

'What does she think of you?'

'I've never asked her, but I think she likes me.'

'As a friend?'

'Yes.'

'Do you want some advice from an old sea-dog who's had more women than holes in his socks?' Lifting the sole of his foot for Adam to see, Charlie displayed at least six holes from toe to heel.

Adam smiled. 'What advice would you give?'

'Only that nice girls are harder to find than beans in a

pea-pod. You're obviously in love with the lass. So, if she's as sensible and lovely as you say she is, and if you get on really well with her, then you'd best wait for her to catch up with you. By the time she's sixteen, you'll still only be twenty-one or two. To my mind, that's a good age for a couple to get wed.'

He made a face. 'Mind you, I got wed at seventeen. Six months later we'd gone our separate ways. So you'd best not take me as a prime example.'

Adam had stopped listening. He'd already worked the ages out for Jinnie and himself, and had come to the same conclusion as Charlie, but, 'I don't even know if she'd want me,' he said. 'She might prefer somebody else.'

'Does she like being with you?'

'I think so.'

'Does her face light up when she sees you?'

Adam had to think about that. 'I never really noticed, but yes, I'm sure of it.'

'Well then, I reckon you're meant for each other.'

Adam had a vision of Jinnie in his mind. 'She looks older than she really is,' he revealed. 'She takes an interest in everything and everybody, and she's never afraid. When we moved into the house on Craig Street, my sister Hannah was in a terrible state.'

Charlie nodded gently. 'I remember you saying.' The bargee had shared almost all of Adam's fears. But not the big one, when he and Hannah hid in the cellar. Not that one. Not yet.

Adam went on, 'We had a terrible time with her . . . nightmares and everything. But Jinnie came to see her every day; they talked and talked, and Jinnie never got tired. She started coming in the morning to walk Hannah to school, and now they're the best of friends. Hannah's the oldest, but you'd never think it.' Then he realised Charlie wasn't listening.

Preoccupied with something he'd seen through the window, he was sitting bolt upright, his gaze stretched beyond Adam as he stared out. 'She looks lost, poor thing.'

Curious, Adam got off the sofa to take a look, but 'she', whoever she was, was already gone.

'You frightened her away,' Charlie said. And Adam thought no more about it.

'I'd best be going now, Charlie,' he told him. 'I've places to go yet.'

'Still looking for work, are you, lad?'

Adam nodded. 'It would be nice to go home and tell Gran that I'll soon be bringing in a wage. It's not easy for her.'

'Aw, lad, you worry too much. There's work to be had, but not for the old 'uns like me. A young lad like you, though – well, you'll soon be fixed up.'

———✦———

F ROM HER VANTAGE point, Jinnie peeped round the corner; the sight of Charlie and then Adam looking out of the window had panicked her. Now, with the two of them emerging from the barge, she took to her heels and ran all the way to the tram-stop. 'I shouldn't have come here,' she muttered as she ran. 'It was a bad idea.' Luckily there was a tram waiting. She hopped on board, giving a sigh of relief when it pulled away.

Behind her, Charlie was giving Adam more advice. 'Bring that lass of yours for me to see,' he said with a wicked smile. 'I'll not have you getting wed before I give my approval.'

Adam said he would like that.

'And tell your grandmother I'll be popping in to see her one of these fine days – though you'd best warn her what a big ugly lug I am. I don't want her fainting at my feet.' He laughed again, that loud, hearty laugh that sent cats and dogs running for shelter. 'Mind you, it's been a long time since a woman swooned at the sight of me. Happen you shouldn't warn her at all. Happen I'll let her have the surprise of her life. What d'you say, lad?'

The parrot's shrill squawk sailed through the air. 'What woman in her right mind would want *you*?'

Charlie groaned. 'That bugger's getting too clever for his boots. It sounds like he's managed to pull the jumper off his cage.' Cursing and chuntering, he went back inside to give it a telling-off.

As he walked away, Adam could hear the two of them, arguing and back-chatting. 'One more word out of you, and I'll wring your scrawny neck!' Charlie threatened.

'Bugger off, Charlie. You're a pain in the arse!' There was a screech and a flurry, and Charlie fell over the sofa.

'You *bit* me!' The old sea-dog couldn't believe it. 'I nearly broke me bloody neck into the bargain! Oh, you just wait till Sat'day. I'll have you down that market so fast your feathers'll fall out in the rush. I don't care how much I get for you either, 'cause if nobody wants to pay money for you, I'll damned well *give* you away! D'you hear me? I've had enough of you. Maniac bird! You've gone too damned far this time!'

There was another squawking and what sounded like a full-scale battle going on, then Charlie was yelling and shouting, and the bird was screaming at the top of its voice, and all hell seemed to be let loose.

Secure in the knowledge that Charlie would never harm a feather on the parrot's body, Adam chuckled all the way to the tram-stop.

Coming to the bottom of Penny Street, he passed the time of day with old Mike Ellis, who was on his way back from delivering potatoes to the local greengrocers. 'Where are you off to then, son?' the little fella asked.

'Up Mill Hill way.' Adam had a mind to cover that same ground again.

'Climb on. I'll give you a lift.'

Michael pulled the horse and cart over to the kerb while Adam climbed on; behind him cars tooted and drivers yelled, and Michael took not the blindest bit of notice. Just like his father before him, and himself since a lad of twelve, he had travelled these same streets, hawking his trade without interference. That was over fifty years ago, long before the roads were choked with cars and buses. Ignoring them all, he pulled out, much to the abuse and astonishment of more drivers, who angrily hung out of their car windows to give him a piece of their mind. 'Impatient devils!' But he never acknowledged them nor did he give them any abuse in return. These were *his* streets, and they could damned well wait!

'Finished for the day, have you, Michael?' Adam had learned to respect the old man.

'One more delivery to make,' came the reply. 'I promised Mabel Preston I'd take her a sack of potatoes, but it won't hurt to keep her waiting. It's like this, lad – the more time I spend on the road, the less time I need to spend with her.'

'I thought you liked her.' Because Michael delivered milk and vegetables throughout Blackburn, Adam, like everybody else, was aware of the love-hate relationship between Mabel and Michael; both in their seventies, and each as fiery as the other.

He gave a toothless grin. 'Well, o' course I do.' The grin gave way to a scowl. 'The trouble is, she can't leave it at that. Every time I get anywhere near her, she goes on about wedding bells and setting up home together.' He shook his head. 'I can't be doing with that . . . not at my age.'

He urged the horse on. 'Besides, if we got wed, I'd have to see her first thing of a morning, without her teeth and her hair in curlers and God only knows what else.' He winked at

Adam. 'This way, I go and see her when she's got her teeth in and her make-up on, and all her other secrets hid away.'

Adam could not get a word in while Michael chatted on, and ambled along, and the drivers swore at him in vain. His ears burning from the verbal abuse, Adam wisely kept his gaze averted from them.

Amazingly, Michael was oblivious to it all. 'Mind you, I haven't got all my own teeth, but I'm not about to tell her that, am I? Oh no. If a man can't have his little secrets, then what's the world coming to, eh? She keeps quizzing me, you see . . . "How much is your cottage worth now? How much money have you got in the bank? You must be worth a bob or two after all these years. And how many women have you been with?"'

He looked just the slightest bit embarrassed on divulging, 'If you ask me, she's got too many o' them "carnal" instincts.'

'Has she?' Adam had an idea what he was getting at, but didn't like to say.

His weathered old face breaking into a grin, Michael declared, 'She'll not have her wicked way with me so easy, I can tell yer.' Leaning over, he confided in a whisper, 'I'm not the man I was twenty year ago, y'see, lad. Me bits and pieces won't do what me brain tells 'em to, that's the trouble.'

When there came the sound of angry motorists trailing behind them, the volley of car-horns drowning out his voice, Michael put his hand behind his back and made a rude gesture. 'Wait on, yer miserable buggers!' he yelled. 'Can't you see we're having a conversation!'

When the din increased to an unbearable pitch, he straightened up and gave the horse a tap with the reins, making gestures as the motorists overtook him one after the other. 'Yes! You an' all!' he replied as they gave him an earful.

'Have you ever thought about getting a car?' Adam asked, wincing.

'What!' Michael was flabbergasted. 'You'll never see the day when I ride about in one o' *them* things. Oh no! This cart has seen three horses out, and my dad with 'em. It served him well, and it's served me better, an' I'll slice the 'ead off anybody as tries to separate me from it.'

Wisely, Adam said no more on the subject.

'Well? What d'you reckon, lad?' Mike asked, returning to the matter in hand. 'Do you think I'm doing wrong in not telling Mabel the truth – about me bits and pieces, I mean?'

Adam shook his head. 'It's not for me to say.'

The old man sucked in a deep breath, then winked knowingly. 'We'll keep 'er guessing then, eh? Aye, that's the thing to do. We'll keep 'er guessing a while longer.'

By the time they'd reached Mill Hill, Adam knew more about old Michael than Mabel would *ever* know.

Chapter Sixteen

A LONE IN HER flat above the restaurant, Susan looked out across the landscape. Varied and interesting, it often drew her attention, though when the restaurant was open she hardly had time to stand still, let alone linger at the window, watching the world go by.

This evening, though, with the business finally closed for winter, and with no friends or others to make calls on her, she found herself with time to lose.

Next spring, she would open the doors and the customers would flow in, and her tills would ring once again with the happy sound of money earned. She would count her takings and watch her bank-balance grow with pride; always congratulating herself on having done well in spite of everything and *everyone*. Amongst the latter, she counted her own family.

When a quiet rage began to take hold of her, she deliberately switched her thoughts from her enemies, and returned her attention to the view laid out before her. Not so busy as in the height of the season, the streets were still fairly active with youngsters and families come to see the legendary lights. Her gaze was drawn beyond them, to where the heaving sea thrashed and moaned, its shifting horizon merging with a troubled sky. After an unsettled day, the skies were darkened with the onset of evening. Low down, pregnant with rain, the clouds were already gathering.

Susan had come to appreciate this time of year, its moody, shifting nature merging with her own dark, selfish soul. 'Here's to you.' Raising her third glass of wine, she laughed out loud. 'And here's to *me*!'

Lowering the glass, she refilled it from the half-empty bottle. Swilling that down, she filled it once more and holding it by the tips of her fingers, she continued to look out the window, her face very still and oddly expressionless. Only her eyes moved, following the waves as they violently threw themselves against the shore.

Suddenly the rain was coming down in earnest, pitter-pattering on her window, making music and lulling her senses. Lost in her own thoughts, she did not hear the determined knock at the main front door. But she saw the flickering movement through the rain as the man stood back from the restaurant, looking upwards, looking at *her*!

Leaning forward, she placed her two hands on the window-sill and stared down at the street. Through the rain she saw that her caller was reasonably presentable; about her age, maybe a little older. He was bare-headed, his dark hair splattered against his face by the wind and rain. 'What do you want?' she called out, but he couldn't hear. Instead he pointed to the door, urging her to let him in.

Curious, she made her way downstairs. 'Who the devil is he?' she muttered. 'I wasn't expecting anybody.' Then she gave a sardonic little laugh. 'Huh! I *never* expect anybody! There's just me.' In a strange manner, she preferred it that way, though there were times like this evening, when she craved company.

Tonight, for some inexplicable reason, she felt incredibly lonely.

Hurrying to the private door at the side of the restaurant

entrance, she bent to the letter-box, her voice raised above the wind outside. 'Who are you?'

Pressing his mouth to the letter-box, he called back, 'Dick sent me.'

A smile crossed her features. 'Wait a minute!' Inching open the door far enough for him to sidle inside, she then closed the door against the wild weather, while he shook the rain from his hair.

In the light from the table-lamp, she observed him, definitely liking what she saw. He was taller than her, and well-built. His hair was damp, dripping about his face and bringing out the high cheekbones and smiling eyes. And he had that lean, easy way with him. Suddenly, she was made to remember that it was a long time since she had lain with a man.

There was something else about him, too – a certain hardness that excited her. When he stared at her as he did now, it was with a quizzical look, almost threatening in its nature; it was then that her excitement turned to anger. 'You say Dick sent you?'

'That's right.' His voice was quiet, but commanding.

'He never told me he was sending somebody else.'

'I'm sorry, but you'll have to take that up with Dick. All I know is, he rang me two days ago to say he'd got a job for me. He said so far you hadn't liked any of the men he'd sent you.'

'What's your name?'

'The name's Terry.' He held out his hand, humiliated when she ignored his greeting. His eyes flashed dangerously. 'I understood he'd already told you about me?'

Susan shook her head. 'NO! He said he would phone and let me know the next time he was sending somebody, but he didn't. Well, let's take a look at you, see if you are able to do the job.' She eyed him curiously. '*Are* you?'

He smiled meaningfully. 'Depends in what way you mean, lady.' Casually leaning back against the wall, he offered: 'Reliable and discreet, that's me. I get the job done and I know how to keep my mouth shut. I take half-payment up front and the rest as soon as the "problem" is out the way.'

Susan continued to look him over. He *looked* right, she thought, and he said all the right things – but what she wanted done was such a delicate matter that he would have to be much better than the crude types Tom had sent her so far.

She straightened herself to her full height. 'I need to know more,' she told him. 'Leave your coat here and follow me.' Pointing to the hall peg, she left him to hang his coat there and went ahead of him, up the stairs and back to the flat.

Behind her she could hear him following.

Once inside the flat she closed the door. 'Sit!' Her voice was curt, almost hostile. She had to be sure he knew who was boss right from the start. Going across to the sideboard she offered him a drink. 'Wine, whisky or brandy – I've got all three.'

Draping one arm across the red, leather-bound sofa, he looked at her through smiling eyes for a long minute, then in soft, knowing tones he said, 'Drinking on the job? No, I don't think so. I like to keep a clear head.'

She nodded, her face wreathed in a smile. 'Very good. You've passed the first test,' she told him. 'I've spent weeks giving Tom's men the once-over. A waste of time, every one.' As if to torment him, she poured herself more wine. 'I told him straight . . . whoever he sent next was his last chance.'

'He should have sent *me* first.'

She took a great gulp of the booze. 'Full of yourself, aren't you?'

'I've a right to be.' He winked in a way that stirred her insides. 'I'm good at what I do, that's why.'

'We'll see.' Feeling the rush of wine to her head she

placed her glass on the tray. 'You don't look like a villain.'

'Looks can be very deceptive.'

'Have you ever been in prison?'

'That's for me to know and you to find out.'

Regarding him more closely, she began to realise that here was a slippery customer and, like he said, she too, needed to keep a clear head.

'You didn't seem to like me asking you that,' she remarked. 'I might take that as meaning that you *have* been inside.'

'You can take it any way you like,' he answered with a charming smile. 'I'm here to do a job. I don't ask you whether *you've* done a stretch. Why should you ask *me?*'

Impressed, she returned his smile. 'Fair enough. I won't ask again.'

He nodded in appreciation. 'Nice place you've got here.' He roved his eyes over the red leather three-piece, and the expensive walnut dresser beside the wall. He noted the thick lush rugs and the handsome paintings on the wall. Tom had been right when he described Susan Holsden as 'a woman of means'. She also had taste, he thought. 'I see you like to surround yourself with beautiful things,' he said. 'Seems we're two of a kind, you and me.'

Spurning the comparison, she retorted sharply, 'I earn it!'

'Oh, and you think I don't?'

'If you do, it's dirty money.' Her pride trembled in her voice. 'I run a *clean* establishment.'

He nodded. 'So I'm told.'

'What else have you been told?'

Detecting the sharp, business edge to her voice, he sat up, his eyes intent on her. 'I'm told you have a daughter who's being kept from you.'

'*And?*' She slowly walked the floor, listening, taking mental notes.

'You want her back. That's why *I'm* here.' He went on, 'There's to be no harm done to the girl. I'm to take her to a place arranged by you. You'll pay me on handover, and I'll be gone.'

She came across the room to sit in the chair opposite. For a long minute she stared at him, her quick mind going over everything he had said. 'What's your name again? Terry, isn't it? Terry who?'

He laughed. 'Sorry, lady. The name's Terry, and as far as I'm concerned, that's all you need to know.'

Beginning to relax, she leaned back in the chair. 'Did Dick tell you what I'm willing to pay?'

'He did.' *His greedy eyes were drawn to the way her robe fell away, to reveal a bare, shapely leg.*

'And did he tell you what would happen if you played tricks with me?'

He smiled inwardly. *Right now, he wouldn't mind playing all sorts of tricks with her.*

'You've no need to worry,' he assured her. 'I'm not about to jeopardise my own livelihood. I do the job and I'm on to the next one. I've no time for games.'

Satisfied with his answers so far, she got out of the chair and refilled her glass; then she sat before him, sipping the wine and licking her lips with a long, wet tongue, deliberately seeming to torment him. 'I think we might have a deal,' she said. 'Just a few more questions.'

He quietly watched her sipping her wine and looking at him, like a fish might look at the bait; and he was overwhelmed by the urge to take hold of her and help himself to her obvious 'charms'.

Sensing his interest in her, she continued to taunt him. Slowly, she moved her legs, crossing them one over the other, discreetly allowing the hem of the short robe to fall away from her thighs. 'I don't want her hurt,' she said directly. 'I just want her taken away from them who stole her from *me*!'

He shrugged. 'Whatever you want is all right by me,' he murmured. 'You're the one paying the money.'

'I don't want her frightened neither. I need you to be gentle.'

He made her wait for his answer, then, in a seductive voice, he whispered, 'I can be as gentle as you like.'

Disturbed by his intimate manner, she gulped down the drink, and filled the glass again. 'Enough chit-chat!' Beginning to feel light-headed, she dropped herself into the chair. 'It's time we got down to business. The place and time. The smallest details. It has to be done quickly and painlessly.'

'I'm ready when you are.' Sitting up to the edge of the sofa, he waited for her instructions.

'Do you know Blackburn?'

Without showing his surprise, he nodded. 'I expect I can find my way around, yes.'

'Are you familiar with Derwent Street?'

This time he could not hide his astonishment. 'Hmh! I might tell you I walked down Montague Street, not too long ago.'

'Really?' She was curious. 'Who do *you* know down that way?'

'I don't know anybody, as it happens. I was looking for someone.' He narrowed his eyes. 'It has no bearing on *our* business.'

His surly manner told her that was all the personal information he was prepared to divulge. So she didn't ask. Nor did she press ahead with the business at hand.

Instead, because he seemed to have grown distant and hostile, and because she was affected by the many glasses of wine she had consumed since early evening, she decided they had probably covered enough ground for the moment. 'I've seen you and I'm happy with your answers,' she told him. 'I'll give Dick a ring in the morning, and tell him to stop looking. You'll do for me.'

He quickly rid himself of the dark thoughts that had risen at the mention of Derwent Street. 'You like me, but I'm being dismissed? Is that any way to treat a man just in from the rain?' Leaning forward, he peered into her eyes. 'You *do* like me, don't you?'

'I think you'll do the job, yes. I also think it might be a good idea if we continue this conversation tomorrow.' Looking up at the mantelpiece-clock, she called his attention to the time. 'It's almost midnight, I can't believe it!' Her voice was calm and quiet, while inside her stomach was turning somersaults.

He made no move. 'I suppose a busy woman like yourself must have a million things to do tomorrow?'

Her senses whirling, she looked away. 'I have some things to do, yes.'

'You're not lonely, then . . . like me?' He held her gaze. 'Dick said you were a widow, that you didn't go out much. Too busy making money, that's what he said.'

A flash of anger. 'Dick's got a big mouth!' Clambering out of the chair, she stumbled clumsily, lurching forward, out of control.

Before she knew it, he was by her side, one arm round her waist, the other reaching underneath her robe, touching her bare flesh. 'Dick forgot to tell me how beautiful you are.' His voice, soft and husky in her ear, mingled with the effects of the wine. It seemed to touch her every nerve-end.

Struggling to keep her composure she told him brokenly, 'You'd best go.'

His fingers travelled inward, to the curve of her thigh. 'D'you really mean that?' When she turned to speak, he closed his mouth over hers, holding her in a long, passionate kiss that left her spent and trembling.

'We're two of a kind, you and me.' He stroked her hair and kissed her again, and she didn't have the courage or desire to turn him away.

As he laid her down on the rug, she thought of Jacob. He was much like this man – rough and demanding. Since Jacob, she had been so lonely and now, here was someone who understood her. Someone who might learn to love her the way he had.

Engrossed in the undressing of her, he didn't realise she was softly crying, until she enclosed his face with her two hands. 'I lied,' she said. 'I *am* lonely.'

He chuckled. 'You're *drunk*, that's what you are.'

She laughed with him. 'You're right,' she said. 'And do you know what?'

'No, but I'm sure you'll tell me.'

'I don't care.' She threw out her arms. 'I'm drunk, and I don't give a sod who knows it!'

Another kiss, then he laid her bare before him. His breath caught in his chest at the sight of her body; he saw the delicate curves, the rounded breasts with the hard, pink nipples, and the dark area below that peeped at him invitingly.

Like a man starved of love, he ran his hands all over her, making her moan, making her want him. When he could wait no longer, he took her, like a mad beast, devoid of feeling or tenderness, and she for her part, revelled in it.

'Jac . . . !' At the height of passion she started to call him by another name. He stopped the name with a wild, wanting kiss. What did he care if she had someone else in mind? This 'Jake' wasn't here. *He* was the one making love to her. *He* was the one being offered wine, and being trusted enough to do a job that involved risk and excitement. *Him* – not this bloody Jake, whoever he was.

If he had his way, Terry thought, this is where he would stay . . . in her flat, a part of her business, living the life of luxury on her hard work. Ever since he had walked through that front door, that had been his plan. And for some reason he couldn't quite fathom, Susan Holsden seemed to have taken to him. Maybe it was because like him, she was lonely. Or maybe she wanted a man who knew how to treat a woman.

Whatever it was that had drawn her to him, he would not complain. He was grateful for the power it gave him over her. But he knew he would have to take it slowly. Drunk or sober, this was no ordinary woman. In order to be as successful in the crowded catering world as she apparently was, she was no easy pushover. Tonight, she was vulnerable. Tomorrow might be another, very different story.

All that aside, he weighed the situation as he saw it. Here was a lonely, wealthy woman, starved of a man, and partial to a drink. It was a good combination.

One which he could exploit to his own ends.

Half an hour later, exhausted and exhilarated, he carried her to her bed. 'Don't go,' she whispered. 'Not yet.'

He laid her down and covered her over and waited until she was fast asleep. Then, boldly and without the slightest compunction, he went through every room; into the second bedroom, where he threw himself onto the bed, luxuriating in the soft, silken eiderdown, spreading his arms about and burying his face in the pillows, shamelessly enjoying every minute, like a cat marking its territory. Then he returned to the sitting room, where he strolled about, examining every artefact and mentally assessing its value. Sauntering into the kitchen, he raided her fridge, before carrying his plate of food back to the lounge. He helped himself to her whisky and, gloating at his good fortune, he sprawled on the sofa and wolfed down the food, wiping the residue from his chin with the cuff of his shirt-sleeve. 'This is the life,' he muttered, his eyes gleaming with anticipation. '*This* is where I belong.'

A few minutes later, exhausted by events, he fell asleep

where he sat. It was three o'clock when he woke, confused and unsure as to his surroundings. When he realised where he was, he smiled sleepily and shivered. He was frozen to the core. Still shivering uncontrollably, he switched on the lamp, put on his jacket and, going out of the room on tiptoe, checked in the bedroom. Susan was still fast asleep, snoring noisily.

With enormous care, Terry trod softly down the stairs to the restaurant, soon finding a sign which, to his delight, pointed the way to her office. Cursing to find its door locked, he felt in his trouser pockets for a penknife. Nothing! His jacket pockets were the same.

Back in the restaurant, he quickly found what he was looking for . . . a knife and fork. With the blade of the knife, he bent and twisted the fork, until only two prongs were prominent. It didn't take him long to open the office door with that. He examined the lock. She would never know it had been tampered with, he thought, and let himself inside.

He immediately located the safe. It was locked and coded. 'Damn the woman!' To his surprise though, the desk-drawers were *not* locked. Careful not to disturb the many papers there, he took out a thick, blue ledger and quickly scanned it. In this ledger was recorded the takings for the past year. 'Jesus Christ!' Terry's eyes almost popped out of his head. 'Eight thousand pounds!' He clapped his hands. 'And that's only what she's *recorded*,' he chuckled. 'What about the money she's syphoned off, eh?' He had learned that while some people could not hide a single penny from the taxman, caterers had every opportunity.

This was more than he could ever have hoped for. It hardened his resolve to get his feet under the table here and, if he played his cards right, to take over completely one day.

Quickly now, he returned everything to its proper place and departed the room, leaving the door locked and secure, just as he had found it. The knife and fork he dropped into his jacket-pocket; he would discard them later.

Thrilled and excited by what he'd found, he went straight to her bedroom, where she was still sleeping like a bairn. Stripping off his clothes, he slid in beside her. His cool body fusing with hers caused her to cry out in alarm. 'It's all right,' he kissed and consoled her. 'It's me . . . Terry. I'll take care of you.'

Like a lost kitten she curled up to him, and he, like the predator he was, took her yet again. By the time he had finished, she was wide awake and wanting more. 'Not yet,' he murmured. 'You've worn me out.'

She fell asleep and, for a long time, he lay there beside her, counting his good fortune. Turning over to look into her sleeping face, he had the nerve to speak softly, confident that she could not hear him. 'The girl can wait a while longer,' he whispered. 'I mean . . . we don't want anyone to come between us now, do we, eh? *Not until I'm sure of my place.*'

He rolled away, lying on his back and dreaming of all he could do with the money. 'We deserve a bit of fun, you and me. In fact, I wouldn't mind jetting off to the sunshine somewhere.'

The idea made him smile.

He truly believed this was the start of a whole new life for him.

Chapter Seventeen

C HARLIE THE BARGEE was done up to the nines in a new shirt and tie and his hair combed through. He'd trimmed his whiskers and polished his shoes and was now ready for anything. 'It's Sunday afternoon, and we've got visitors,' he told the parrot. 'Mind you behave yourself!'

For once the parrot didn't have anything to say; he was so astonished to see Charlie sparkling like that, he thought he'd got a new master.

Anxious, Charlie paced the floor, looking out of the window then straightening his tie, and looking out again. 'I'll be a nervous wreck by the time they get here.' He glanced in the mirror and gave himself a fright. 'It's like looking at a bloody stranger,' he told the parrot. He groaned and sighed and groaned some more, blew out his face and sucked it in again, muttering and fidgeting and frantically pacing up and down.

The only time he wasn't looking they turned the corner; Adam in his blue corduroy trousers, and a smart new brown jumper, bought from the market out of his first week's wages at the bike-shop. Beside him and feeling all grown-up was Jinnie, her long blonde hair blowing in the light breeze, and looking lovely in a straight blue skirt and short dark jacket.

'It's lovely, Adam.' She observed the sleek lines of the

barge, with its bright yellow stripes painted down the hull, and the many colourful jugs and churns out on the deck. 'I'm not surprised you want one for yourself.'

Adam smiled down on her and thought how he would gladly forfeit all the barges in the world, if only he could be sure Jinnie would be his one day.

Hannah and Sarah brought up the rear. Hannah was sulking as usual, but looked very pretty in jeans and long black jumper, her fair hair tied back. Hurrying alongside, all got up in her best Sunday hat and winter coat, Sarah looked decidedly uncomfortable.

From the barge window, the parrot caught sight of them first; seeming only now to have realised what was happening. *'They're here!'* he shrieked. *'They're here!'* He would have gone on shrieking if Charlie hadn't threatened him with the stewpot. As it was, he scampered to the corner of his cage and kept his beak well and truly shut – for the time being.

Charlie invited them all on board. 'It's a bit cramped,' he told them, 'but we'll manage, I'm sure.' He spoke to Adam and Hannah, and smiled at Jinnie, thinking what a lovely creature she was, and when it came time to shake hands with Sarah he blushed like a young man in love. 'It's grand to meet you,' he spluttered. 'After what Adam told me, I was expecting a pretty woman with the smile of an angel.' He winked at Adam. 'I'm not disappointed, lad. Not at all.'

Sarah was her usual self. 'Away with you, you old charmer!' All the same she was pleased and flattered and took to him straight off. 'Adam tells me you're taking us up the canal . . . for a Sunday meal at the Navigation?'

'That's exactly right. What's more, we'll take a stroll afterwards, while the young 'uns do their own thing.' He smiled cheekily. 'That's if you can trust an old sailor to behave himself?'

This time she blushed vivid scarlet. 'Oh, you devil, you!' She gave him a playful push, and everybody laughed.

A few minutes later they were chugging their way along the canal. 'It's not a bad day for a jaunt,' Charlie called back from the tiller. 'The sun's trying its damnedest to come out from behind the clouds.'

When Sarah came out to chat, she noticed how his neck was red from the rub of his shirt-collar, and how he kept tweaking his toes, as if his shoes were crippling him, and on top of that, she saw how he constantly tugged at his tie. 'I hope you don't mind me saying so, but you don't look at all comfortable in them new clothes,' she commented.

'I'm not used to being trussed up,' he grinned. 'I feel like a right berk!'

Sarah laughed out loud. 'You and me both,' she confessed. 'I'd give anything to tek my coat off.' She wiped her brow. 'It's not as chilly as I thought.'

'I'll tell you what, love,' he suggested, 'I'll get Adam to take over the tiller while I change into my old togs, and you get that coat off before you cook.'

They heard the parrot squawking from below. 'Charlie will put you in the bloody stewpot!'

'Well, I never.' Sarah couldn't believe her ears, and Charlie apologised for the bird's language. Then suddenly they looked at each other, and their laughter echoed across the water.

Later, Sarah and Charlie lost no time in making themselves more comfortable; Sarah in her frock and cardigan and Charlie wearing his old boots and sloppy jumper.

Down in the galley, Adam and Jinnie made the tea, while Hannah clung to the window and complained of feeling seasick. When at last they were moored at the Navigation public house, she was the first off the boat. 'Quick!' she moaned. 'I feel ill.' No sooner was she down on solid ground than she threw up all over the flower-bed.

Having cleaned Hannah up, Sarah led her grand-daughter into the Navigation, where the girl turned down all offers of food, choosing instead to sit on the grass-bank outside; though she did accept a drink of sarsaparilla from the concerned landlady.

With the meal of pork pie and chips polished off to the last mouthful, Adam suggested taking Hannah and Jinnie along the canal bank, to show them where the best fishing was.

Hannah refused. 'I'll stay here,' she said. She had found a comfortable place and there she meant to stay; happily feeding the ducks with the pie which Sarah had bought out from the Navigation, in the hope that Hannah might at least try a peck of it.

Knowing she was safe enough there, Charlie suggested she should go aboard if she wanted. 'Talk to the parrot,' he said kindly. 'And if he swears, threaten him with the stewpot. That usually shuts him up.'

Hannah said she might just do that, and the landlady of the pub promised Sarah she would keep an eye on the lass for them.

Having put on their coats and scarves, Sarah and Charlie followed Jinnie and Adam along the towpath. 'It's a lovely walk,' Sarah observed, and slid her arm through his.

Charlie said it was the first time he'd been along this particular towpath on foot. 'And it's all the more enjoyable because *you're* here,' he told Sarah, who blushed vividly for only the second time in her life.

Further along the canal, Jinnie and Adam chatted about this and that, though mostly about Hannah. 'She seems a lot better,' Jinnie commented. 'She's not so nervous any more.'

'That's thanks to you,' Adam told her. 'You let her talk and talk, and now she seems to have got over the worst of it.'

Jinnie hardly dare broach the subject. 'She starts to tell me about the time you and her were down the cellar, and then she stops and won't go any further.' Tugging at his sleeve, she drew him to a halt. 'Was it really terrible . . . down there, while all that was going on?' She felt she could talk to Adam.

Nodding, he sank down onto the grass. Jinnie sat beside him, not talking, but waiting for him to speak first.

He said nothing for a long time. He had never spoken of this with anyone. His throat was tight, constricted. He broke off a blade of grass and began chewing on it. For a second, he saw his lovely mam smiling at him, and the vision gave him the strength to speak. Suddenly he had hold of Jinnie's hand, entwining her fingers with his own, his voice softer than a whisper as he related, 'My father killed our mam . . . and Jacob Hunter. It was awful. My dad turned up and started throwing punches and shouting. Jacob were too drunk to do much. Mam told us to get down in the cellar. I didn't want to go, but Hannah was screaming – he'd hit her, you see – and I was afraid. I wanted to help my mam but I was too small – I was only a kid. It was dark in the cellar . . . and cold.'

He shivered involuntarily, and grasped her hand tighter. 'I remember, it was really cold, and damp – it seemed to cling to us. We were on the steps, and Hannah couldn't stop shaking. We could hear all the noise, you see, Mam shouting for us to stay where we were, and *him* . . .' A look of hatred twisted Adam's handsome features. 'Our dad . . . screaming like a madman. "I'll kill the pair of you!" And warning Jacob that if he didn't get out, he'd do for him an' all.'

Jinnie saw how all this was affecting her friend. 'Please, Adam,' she whispered. 'You don't have to tell me, not if you don't want to.'

When he turned to look at her, she was shocked to see the tears swimming in his dark eyes. 'I *do* want to,' he said quietly.

'I've *always* wanted to tell you. You see, Jinnie, I need you to know everything about me.'

She felt privileged. 'Why?'

'Because one day, when you're old enough, I want us to be married.'

FROM THE HIGH ground, Sarah saw them talking. 'Look at them.' She called Charlie's attention to the young couple. 'Lovely, they are,' she murmured. 'And my, they do get on so well.'

Charlie focused on the pair and suddenly, while they looked on, Jinnie astonished them by reaching up and cupping Adam's upturned face in her hands; then she kissed him on the mouth. It wasn't a long kiss, nor was it passionate. It was the kiss of a child, a friend, a promise of loyalty come whatever.

It touched the older ones' hearts. 'By! That was a tender scene,' Sarah said, brushing the tears from her eyes. 'I never would have thought it.'

Charlie smiled. 'That was just a kiss of friendship,' he said knowingly. 'But there'll be more to come as they grow older.'

Contented, the pair walked back to the barge, arm in arm.

SALLY AND LOUISE had a quiet Sunday lunch. Content in each other's company, they sat at the table and put the world to rights. 'Jinnie is growing up fast,' Louise commented. 'Before I can turn round, she'll be a young woman, married with children of her own.'

Sally, too, had been thinking along those same lines. 'You've still not told her, have you?'

Louise looked away. 'I thought, being as Dad seems to have made our Susan see sense, I might not need to tell her after all.'

Sally gave her a severe look. 'I've told you afore, the lass will *have* to be told. There are still folks living round these parts who know enough to raise her curiosity.'

'I know. That's what worries me.'

'Then *tell* her!'

'I *will!*'

'When?'

Louise turned the matter over in her mind. 'I might tell her tomorrow.' How many times had she promised herself to tackle the matter, and then avoided the issue? Too many to count.

'Why not tonight?' Sally was nothing if not persistent.

'Because she's out having fun and I don't want to spoil her day.'

Sally doubted whether Louise would ever find the courage. 'D'you want *me* to do it, lass?'

Louise was shocked that Sally should even ask such a thing. 'No, Sally, I'll be the one to do it!'

'As you will. I'll say no more on the subject.'

Louise smiled. 'I seem to have heard that before.'

'Aye, well, it's playing on my mind, that's why. But I mean it this time, lass. I'll keep my mouth shut, and let you get on with it. All I'm concerned about is whether she might find out from somebody else, and if she does, it could turn her against you. Have you thought of *that?*'

Louise nodded. She had thought of nothing else.

'I'll not be here for ever,' Sally reminded her. 'I wouldn't like to think of you being on your own. Trust the girl. Tell her, and be done with it. If you're honest with her, she'll take it well. Oh, I know it will come as a terrible shock, but if she has you to fall back on, she'll be sound. The lass adores you. I reckon, whatever happens, she'll always be there for you.'

She puckered her mouth as she did whenever she was about to say something very personal. 'All that aside, there'll come a day when the lass will be up and off, building her own nest with the man of her choice. Aw, lass, I don't like to think of you being lonely. You're still a young woman yourself. You need a life of your own.'

Louise knew what she was getting at. 'I know you'd love to see me and Eric together,' she said, 'and to tell you the truth, so would I, but there are things to be settled in my mind before that can happen.'

Sally thought it best to leave well alone. 'Ee, look at the time. If you're to catch that tram, you'd best get a move on.'

Louise glanced up at the clock. 'I'm all right yet,' she observed. 'I'll give you a hand with these dishes before I go.'

'What time is Eric due back?' He had gone to another Sunday sale.

Louise shrugged. 'Could be anytime. You know how these sales go. All I know is, he and Dad have gone to sell a wagon-load of hay and some machinery. He'll not leave the sale-yard until he's got shut of it, and for a good price.' She chuckled. 'Honest to God, Dad's like a dog with two tails since Eric set him on. He's gone to the sales today, just for the fun of it, though if I know Eric he's bound to pay him for the hours he's away.'

Sally was off on another tack. 'I think it's shocking, having sales on a Sunday. There was a time when Sunday was sacred, for going to church and making your peace with the Almighty. Nowadays, it all seems to be changing, more's the pity.' She tutted. 'I blame it on these pop stars and their loud music, screaming and shouting and calling it singing ... strutting about in tight trousers and quiffed hair, with girls swooning all over the place at the sight of 'em. It's no wonder the values are going out the window, and now we have sales on the Sabbath. Shame, that's what I call it!'

'It's not so much a sale as a few men getting together and bargaining. For most of them, Sunday is the only time they get to trade.'

'Aye, well, we'd best get cleared away.' Impatient for her afternoon nap, Sally wanted no more on the subject.

Half an hour later the table was cleared with the crockery washed and put away. Louise went up to get ready and was back down in plenty of time to catch her tram. 'I'll go and feed the animals,' she promised, 'then I'll be straight back.'

Sally looked up from her chair. 'You tek as long as you need, lass. I'll have a doze in the armchair. Like as not, I'll still be asleep when you get back.'

Louise had been worried about her mother-in-law these past few days; she seemed to have been getting slower, not so mobile as she once was. 'I can leave it till later,' she suggested. 'So long as the animals are fed before six o' clock, I'm sure there'll be no harm done.'

'No.' The old lady was adamant. 'You go and do what's needed, pet. You know how the animals look for their food at a particular time of day.'

'All right then, if you're sure,'

'I am! Now go on – be off with you.' She offered her face for a kiss and Louise obliged. 'And wrap up warm, the wind's a bit sharp just now.'

Before she left, Louise got a blanket and draped it over Sally's knees; she also put a few more cobs of coal on the fire and replaced the fireguard. 'I'll not be above a couple of hours,' she promised as she went.

Sally didn't hear. She was already peacefully snoozing.

ON THE JOURNEY to Maple Farm, Louise let herself dream of how it might be if she and Eric got together as man and wife. She would be living at the farm again, and that would be a welcome thing. Sally too, she thought. There was no doubt in Louise's heart that the old woman would dearly love that. But then again, she had made a home in Derwent Street, so she might not want to come back to the farm at all.

The thought of being Eric's wife was wonderful, and in her heart Louise knew it would happen one day. But when that might be, she couldn't tell. There was some deep unsettled thing inside of herself that prevented it from happening. It was to do with Eric, and Ben, and a sadness that had never really left her.

'Salmesbury!' The conductor's voice shook her out of her reverie.

Making her way to the doors, she clung hold of the chrome rail, being jolted here and there as the tram slowly clattered along the lines.

In a minute it was stopped and she was off, hurrying down the lane and thinking how winter had begun to settle in with a vengeance. Already the leaves had fallen from the trees and the hedgerows thinned out. There was a kind of serenity about the fields. Every season was different. Every one a delight to the eye, even when the fields were all covered in snow. And from the nip in the air, snow wasn't all that far away, she thought, shivering.

By the time she had got the feed ready, the pigs and chickens were scrabbling at their feed-pens, as if to say, 'Where've you been? You're late!' She soon had them fed though. The old dog Boris first, then when she went from pen to pen dishing out the feed, he followed her. 'He'll be back soon,' she told Boris, as they returned to the warmth of the sitting room. 'See?' Taking off her coat she pointed to the cheery fire, now beginning to die down. 'Your master said he'd light a fire before he went and now we're all nice and cosy in here.'

She put more coal on the fire and made herself a cup of tea. When she sat in Eric's armchair, the dog laid at her feet. She dropped one hand to stroke its head, and as always, she felt as if she belonged here, in this pretty place. 'It hasn't changed,' she murmured. 'Every time I come back, it's as if I never went away.'

With the hot tea inside her and the warmth of the fire on her face, she must have dozed off, because suddenly she felt his hand on her shoulder. 'Louise?' His voice seemed far off, yet close. It was wonderfully comforting. She opened her eyes and he was on his knees before her, his eyes filled with longing as he gazed into her sleepy face. Suddenly she was in his arms and he was kissing her, with such passion that she was shaken to her roots.

Her senses were stirred, her love for him flooding her heart. Instinctively, she put her arms round him and wouldn't let go.

They kissed and caressed, and when he began removing her blouse, she wanted him. It was so right. So natural.

But then the crippling sadness took hold of her, and she drew away. 'I can't,' she said brokenly. 'I just can't.'

When she left, he stood at the window, a look of devastation in his face, but love too. *So much love.*

Heartbroken, she ran up the lane, away from him. 'How can he go on wanting me,' she sobbed, 'when I don't give anything in return?'

She wanted to run back to the cottage, into his arms. She needed him more than he would ever know. She paused, glancing back at the window where just a moment ago he'd been standing. But he was gone. And her heart sank like a lead weight inside her.

—————◆———————

WITH CAUTION THROWN to the wind, Susan got out of the taxi, laughing and singing, full of her favourite wine, and unsteady on her feet. 'Ssh!' Terry put his finger to his lips. 'Cut it out! You'll have us arrested.' The last thing he needed was the law coming to see what all the noise was about.

'Spoilsport!' She liked teasing him. She enjoyed his company and let him get away with bossing her about now and then. But she was always in charge, even though he didn't realise it.

He paid the taxi and took charge of her. 'Inside with you, woman!' Taking her by the arm, he propelled her to the side door of the restaurant. 'Key, please.' He held out his hand. 'You'd best let *me* open the door.'

'I'm not drunk,' she giggled. 'I'm quite capable of opening a door.'

He thrust his hand under her nose. 'Key!'

Fumbling in her coat-pocket, she found it and handed it over. 'I want it back,' she said, stumbling forwards. 'You're not man of the house yet, you know.'

Ignoring her, he opened the front door and was about to put the key in his pocket when she snatched it away. 'Oh no, you don't!' He didn't say anything. Instead he gave a soft laugh, while inside he was fuming. As yet he hadn't persuaded her to let him move in permanently, but he was almost there, he thought greedily. Almost there!

Once inside, he helped her up the stairs to her flat. 'You should have a house,' he told her coaxingly. 'With the money you earn, and the hard work you put in, you deserve the very best.'

She chuckled. 'I know.'

'Maybe we'll talk about it tomorrow, eh?' he suggested, 'You and me . . . moving to a big, posh house?'

She shoved him away and almost fell down the stairs. 'This is *my* place!' she retorted. 'And it's big enough for me.'

When he tried to get her into bed, she laughed and giggled and fought with him, until in the end he wanted to strangle her. 'Keep still, woman!' And she did, while he undressed her and covered her over. 'You're as drunk as I've ever seen you,' he told her. 'You'd best sleep it off it an' I'll tell you what . . .'

'What?' She peered through one eye at him.

'I won't envy you your thick head in the morning.'

Throwing off the covers she flung open her arms and legs, inviting him to, 'Give us a cuddle.'

Still smarting because she'd taken the key from him, he peevishly declined. 'We've had a heavy night,' he said curtly. 'I'm shattered.' Flicking the covers back over her, he ordered, 'Shift over and let's get some sleep.' He stripped off his clothes and put them aside. By the time he climbed into bed, she was snoring like a pig.

In a matter of minutes he, too, was deep in sleep.

He was still asleep when, some time later, Susan woke up, her throat parched for the want of a drink. Going to the lounge, she poured herself a small tot of brandy. Knocking it back, she smacked her lips. 'That's done the trick.' Oddly enough, she felt almost sober, with no sign of the thick head Terry had promised.

Needing a breath of air, she inched open the front window and peered out. The streets were silent. Even the sea seemed to be snoozing. It was half-past three in the morning. The few revellers and day-trippers were long gone and now, at this early hour, Blackpool was like any other seaside town.

With the tiredness creeping up on her, she made her way back to the bedroom. Finding that Terry had not moved and was still sound asleep, she slithered into bed with hardly a ripple.

Half-awake, with all manner of thoughts swimming in her mind, she lay there for some considerable time, wanting to sleep but unable to. After a while her eyelids felt heavier and her whole body began to give itself over to slumber. Through her dimming senses she felt him move out of bed. She heard him fumbling about then, because she grew suspicious, she pretended to be fast asleep. Even when she felt his warm breath on her face as he bent down to make sure she was asleep, she made no move.

Instead, she wondered about him. Why was he creeping about? It wasn't in his nature to worry about waking her up. It was more likely that he would want her awake and ready to make love. So, did he intend running out on her? Certainly he had been peeved about her asking for the key back.

Now, as he went out of the door, she kept her eyes closed, her breathing regular and easy. He was up to something, she knew. When, after a minute or two he didn't return, nor did she hear the toilet flushing, she got out of bed and drawing a robe about her, went after him – softly though, so he would not suspect.

After a quick search of the upper rooms, she went to the top of the stairs, where she saw a light emanating from the region of her office. Being the suspicious soul she was, she hurried noiselessly down the stairs, along the passage and, pressing herself against the wall, she waited and listened.

She could hear him rustling papers and seemingly opening and shutting drawers. There was an anger about his movements but, imagining her to be asleep, he was careful not to let the anger spill over. At one point she heard him swearing and cursing. 'Damn her! Damn the woman!' She dared to peep round the door, and what she saw raised such a rage in her that she wanted to burst in at once and confront him. But she had learned to be cleverer than that.

He had the desk-drawers out and strewn over the floor, while he feverishly checked the many cubby-holes where the drawers would normally sit. Unsuccessful, he began replacing them, all the while muttering to himself. 'Taking the bloody key back off me, the bitch! It's plain she's not about to let me worm my way into a small fortune, damn and bugger her!'

Having put back all the drawers and tidied the desk, he punched his fist one into the other. 'The safe key! Where in God's name does she keep it? I've searched every corner of this bloody place, and still I can't find it.'

Instinctively, Susan's eyes shifted to the corner of the room. The door to the alcove was open. But the safe remained well and truly locked. She smiled. *Nobody* knew where she kept that key, and nobody ever would!

When she realised that he was about to leave, she darted silently up the stairs and into bed; where to all intents and purposes she was still sleeping when he came into the room. She felt him sidle in beside her, but he made no attempt to hold her. She was glad of that, because she, too, was chilled by the cold. If he were to put his arms round her, he might well have suspected that she had been out of bed. So she laid still, and even after he was asleep, she stayed awake, thinking how she would not tell him what she'd seen. Instead she would turn the whole thing to her advantage.

In the morning, she awoke and straight away the events of the night came into her mind, and there he was, pacing the floor beside the window, and drawing on a cigarette as if his very life depended on it. Pretending everything was the same as before, she went to him. Sliding her arms round his waist, she asked softly, 'Are you coming back to bed?' From her voice and manner he could not guess what was really on her mind.

He shook her off. 'Not now. I've things to do.'

She looked suitably puzzled. 'What things?'

He stared down at her. 'Get dressed,' he ordered. 'We need to talk.'

Shrugging, she told him, 'Okay.' She could tell the anger was still on him, and she was glad. It made her feel slightly compensated for his treachery.

When a short time later they were seated at the breakfast table, him with his bacon and eggs, her with toast and marmalade, she asked him why he was so moody. 'You've been like a bear with a sore head ever since we got up.'

He wolfed down a forkful of bacon, leaving a piece trailing for a minute at the edge of his mouth. 'It's your fault!' Licking his tongue round the bacon he curled it into his mouth.

'What d'you mean? Why is it my fault?'

'Because I don't know where I am with you. One minute we're talking about getting married, and the next, you won't even let me have a front-door key. What kind of commitment is that?'

She didn't answer, so he changed tack. Coming round the table he kissed her on the mouth. 'You know how much I love you,' he whined. 'I thought you loved me the same.'

Sickened by the taste of bacon on her lips, she gave nothing away. 'I *do* feel the same.'

He tightened his arms about her waist. 'So when d'you intend getting wed?'

Now, she turned on the tears. 'I can't think of you and me, not yet,' she cried. 'Not until I've got my daughter back where she belongs.'

'I thought we'd planned some time to ourselves before we bothered about her?'

'That's what I thought,' she said. 'Only I can't leave it any longer. She's my flesh and blood, Terry. They took her from me, and now I have to get her back. *You* have to get her back, because I know you're the only one who can do it.'

Stunned by her insistence, he stood off. 'And if I get her back, what then? We'll never have any privacy, not with a kid hanging about.'

'Yes, we will.' She had anticipated his response, and she had her answer ready. 'I'll send her to boarding-school. It won't make any difference to us.'

Something here didn't seem right, he thought. Why was she all of a sudden so insistent on getting the kid back? Needing to turn it all over in his devious mind, he left her there and went to stand by the window. Taking out a cigarette he drew hard on it, his mind in a muddle.

There was definitely something going on, and it worried him. She wasn't the same. It struck him that she might have seen him last night, rifling through the drawers for that damned key. But no, because when he got back, she was still fast asleep.

Suddenly he couldn't trust her any more. And just at that moment it was fortunate for him that she couldn't see his face, because a nasty thought was running through his mind. It was obvious she was leading him along. She had no intention of getting wed. What's more, he sensed that she was tiring of him. *So, what if he kidnapped the girl, and held her to ransom?*

He smiled wickedly. She'd have to open that damned safe then, wouldn't she, eh? If she wanted her precious daughter safe, she'd have to hand over enough to set him up for life.

Suddenly she was there, arms round him, eyes looking into his. 'All right!' He slid his hand up her skirt. 'You'd best give me all the details – name, address . . . school . . . all that.' He fumbled with her underclothes, and when her skirt fell to the floor, he grabbed her to him, laughing in her face. 'First things first though, eh?' He pushed her down and laid himself on top of her.

It was not an enjoyable coupling, not like usual. Because this time he took her with a kind of hatred. If she thought she'd got the better of him, she'd better think again. He hadn't come this far without knowing a trick or two!

Chapter Eighteen

———⟫⟩•◦•⟨⟪———

L IKE A CAT on hot bricks, Louise waited for Jinnie to come home from school.

Already anxious, Sally was made even more so by Louise's constant pacing. 'For goodness sakes, lass, will you sit yourself down!'

Louise sat down then immediately got up again. 'Oh Sally, am I doing right in telling her?'

'You know how I feel about that,' the old woman retorted. 'You should have told her long since, but you kept putting it off and putting it off, and now you've got yourself in such a state, I doubt if you'll be able to keep yourself together long enough to tell her the whole story.' Coming across the room she put a comforting hand on her daughter-in-law's shoulder. 'At least she'll not have to go straight off to school the morrow,' she consoled. 'You did right to leave it till the schools break up for Christmas.'

Louise gave a long, withering sigh. 'I wonder what sort of Christmas we'll have after today?'

'Look, lass, just keep in mind that she thinks the world of yer. She's sensible . . . more mature than most girls her age. So, come on. Sit down and I'll make a pot o' tea.'

Louise had to smile. A pot of tea was Sally's answer to everything. She shook her head. 'I can't face anything just now,' she admitted. 'Not until I know she's taken it well, and doesn't hate me for the rest of my life.' She tried to imagine how it would all sound to that lovely girl. 'She'll be devastated, Sally.' Her voice broke. 'I *know* she will!'

Sally had been thinking the very same thing, but she wasn't about to tell that to Louise. 'Aye, mebbe she will, and mebbe she won't. But one thing's for sure. When she hears how you took her in and brought her up and loved her from that very first day, she'll only love you all the more.'

'But what about the shock? All these years she's been my daughter, and suddenly I'm telling her it's all been a lie . . . that I'm not her mother, but her aunt. And that her real mother didn't want to know her for the past ten years.' Anger rose above the fear. 'And as if that isn't enough, can you imagine how she'll feel when she learns that her father *killed* himself.'

All old Sally could do was shake her head. She still felt the shock, and sorrow, of her son Ben's suicide. Only now, with the moment of revelation closing in, did the enormity of Louise's task begin to take hold.

Emotionally exhausted, Louise dropped onto the sofa, her face a picture of anguish. 'It won't matter how much love has grown between us, will it? She'll be shaken to the core. She'll not know who she is or where she belongs and, God forgive me, *I'll* be the one shattering her peace of mind and there's nothing I can do about it. If she has to be told, and you're right about that, Sally, then it's *me* that has to do the telling.'

Holding her tight, Sally comforted her the best she could. 'I know, lass,' she whispered. 'I know. And all you can do is tell her in the gentlest way possible. After that, we must trust in the Good Lord, and hope she can cope with it all.'

While they were quietly talking, Louise in the chair, with Sally's arms round her shoulders, Jinnie could be heard closing the front door. 'It's raining cats and dogs out there!' she called out breathlessly, as she took off her coat. 'We managed to dodge it . . . we ran all the way from the tram-stop. I'm *so* glad it's the holidays now!'

On hearing Jinnie, Louise sat bolt upright in the chair, while Sally seated herself nearby. 'Compose yourself, love,' the old lady muttered urgently. 'It'll be all right.'

Hurrying down the passage, Jinnie kept on talking. 'Me and Hannah saw it coming. If we'd been a minute later, we'd have been soaked to the skin. Jimmy Leatherhead kept us talki . . .' Rushing into the sitting room, she paused, the words stuck in her throat. Her troubled blue eyes looked from one woman's face to the other; she could sense the tension but couldn't understand its cause. 'What's wrong, Mam?' She saw the pain on her mother's face, and the smile she gave to hide it. 'Are you and Gran upset about something?'

'We're fine, lass. Only I've summat to tell you.' She patted the place beside her. 'Come and sit down. Please.'

Confused, Jinnie came across the room, and as she did so, she noticed the discreet nod between Louise and Sally. As quietly as she could, Sally hobbled out of the door. 'What's going on, Mam?' All kinds of terrible things came home to Jinnie. 'Grandma's not ill again, is she?'

Louise quickly put her mind at rest. 'No, lass. She's not ill. She's leaving us to talk.'

Jinnie didn't like the feel of what was happening. 'What about?'

Almost as if to protect her, Louise took hold of her hand. 'It's about you,' she answered. 'And me.' Suddenly, in the face of what she must do, and recalling Sally's words, she found her courage returning.

'I've been meaning to tell you for a long time,' she began. 'Only I've never had the proper opportunity, until now.'

She started by telling Jinnie, 'Whatever I have to say now, I want you to know that I love you with all my heart. I always have.'

Aware that something beyond her comprehension was happening, and that it had to do with her and her mam, Jinnie was more afraid than she had ever been. Her dark blue eyes shone with tears. 'I know that, Mam,' she murmured. 'I love you too.' The tears began to fall. 'You're frightening me.'

'That's the last thing I want to do, sweetheart.' From then on, Louise lost no time in relating the events of Jinnie's birth. She explained how she had been born in her Grandma Patsy's house. 'You arrived in such a rush you gave us all a fright,' she chuckled, and the remark brought a nervous smile to Jinnie's pretty face.

The smile slid away as Louise went on.

She explained how she was not Jinnie's real mother, and how her own sister, Susan, had given birth to her. She told how Susan was not ready to take on the responsibility of having a child; that she had been ill, and needed to get away before she had a nervous breakdown. She described how Susan had wanted her to have the baby to bring up as her own daughter; how, later on, she had applied to officially adopt her, because she loved her and wanted to raise her as her own child. She said that no one was more delighted than her when at last she was given the go-ahead.

She then told Jinnie about Ben, and what a good man he had been, and she assured her that she was Ben's child, and as such, she belonged with this family. With *her*. She did not tell her about Ben and the suicide, nor that Eric's farm had once been theirs and how, when Ben lost it through no fault of his own, he went from being a quiet, hard-working man to a desperate wreck of his old self.

She saved all that for another day. Because it was too much for the child to take in. *All too much.*

Throughout those awful, timeless minutes when Louise told her the truth of her birth, Jinnie grew increasingly pale. She didn't speak, nor did she move, until Louise was through.

Then, scrambling off her seat, she stared down at Louise with a mixture of shock and disbelief. *'I don't believe you!'* Her body was trembling from head to toe.

Her face haggard and sorry, Louise appealed to her. 'In every other sense but your birthright, I *am* your mother. But it's Susan who's your real mother . . . my sister.'

'NO!' As the words began to sink in, Jinnie backed away. 'You're lying! She can't be my mother!' Suddenly she was sobbing, screaming. *'You're lying! I hate you, I hate you!'*

Her own face stained with tears, Louise tried to take hold of her. 'No, lass. Listen to me . . .' At the door, Sally leaned against the wall, her old eyes red and her heart breaking.

'Leave me alone!' Jinnie's scream seemed to echo from the walls. Pushing Louise away she fled to the safety of her grandma's arms. 'Keep her away from me, Gran! I hate her!'

'No, child. You mustn't hate her. She's done no wrong.'

To Sally's surprise, Jinnie clung to her, her face uplifted, and in harsh whispers she pleaded with the old woman: 'She said Susan was my mother – her own sister, that's what she said!'

'Aye, that's the truth, lass.'

Jinnie's eyes opened wide. 'Her husband!' Her voice broke and she was sobbing again. *'And her own sister!'*

Suddenly she broke away from Sally and headed for the door; where she turned just once to look into Lousie's distraught face. For a moment the atmosphere was electric, before in shocked tones, she told Louise, 'How could you even bear to be near me? Every time you looked at me, you saw what they'd done to you! Oh, you must have really hated me!'

Openly crying at the memories that tore her apart and now were tearing this child apart, Louise held out her arms. 'No, lass. Of course I didn't hate you. Don't ever say that.'

But Jinnie was already running down the passage. She flung open the front door and before anyone could stop her, she was fleeing down the street, her young life seemingly in tatters.

Louise ran to the door. 'Jinnie! Come back!' She would have gone after her, but Sally held her back. 'No, love, let her go. Let her think about what you've told her. She'll be going to Sarah's, that's it. She'll quiet down there, and then you must go and bring her home.'

Unsure, Louise turned to speak; then was horrified when Sally stared at her with frightened eyes as she sank to the floor before her. 'Sally!' Panic-stricken, Louise fell to her knees, her soul flooded with relief when, after a few minutes of Louise gently slapping her face and talking to her, Sally slowly opened her eyes. 'I'm sorry, lass,' she muttered. 'Silly old fool that I am.'

Louise rocked her in her arms. 'No, you're not,' she whispered. 'You're the best friend in the world, and I've been so blind. I should have dealt with it all myself. I expect you've been worried out of your mind, and I never even noticed. Oh Sally, I'm so sorry.'

She helped her mother-in-law to stand. 'I don't want no doctor, mind,' Sally told her firmly. 'It's just a passing thing,' she lied. 'It were the upset that did it. I couldn't bear to see you both hurting like that.' She visibly trembled. 'God forgive me, it were me as med you tell her.'

Settling the old dear into the chair, Louise chided, 'You were right. She had to know, and I should have told her years ago. Happen if I had, she wouldn't have taken it so badly.' Pleased to see the colour come back to Sally's face, she made her warm and comfortable, and rustled up a brew. 'I want you to see a doctor.'

Sally was adamant. 'No doctors and no hospitals. I'm old but I'm not out yet. So leave me be. And leave that lass be, until she's had time to think about what you've told her. Sarah will see to her. She's a good sort, is Sarah.'

All the same, Louise knew she wouldn't rest until Jinnie was back home. 'I need to know if she really has gone to Sarah's.'

'It's not a good idea to go chasin' after her, lass. Not till she's had time to calm down.'

'I'll be discreet,' Louise promised. 'I just need to know she's indoors somewhere, safe.'

As Louise was about to make her way down the street, Adam came running through the rain. 'She's with us. Gran said to leave her awhile.'

Louise brought him inside out of the rain. 'Is she all right?'

He nodded. 'We'll look after her,' he promised. 'I'll bring her back soonever she's ready.'

***

Having waited in the cold and rain, out of sight, watching the house where Susan's daughter lived, Terry congratulated himself on witnessing how Jinnie had come home from school. On an instinct, he had hung around for a while, and was rewarded when, shortly afterwards, he had seen her run out of the house and had her name confirmed when Louise called after her.

Discreetly following to see where the girl went, he was astonished to see her taken into the house on Craig Street, *the very house where he had murdered that cheating bitch Maggie and her fancy boyfriend.*

Terry was completely amazed when a tall teenaged boy emerged from the house. It took him no more than a second or two to recognise his son Adam as the youth. Even though he hadn't seen his kids for ten long years, Terry would know that face anywhere. Going after him, he saw him go into Jinnie's house, and then hurry out again, back to Craig Street.

'My luck's in today an' no mistake.' Rubbing his hands, Terry laughed out loud. 'So, *this* is where Mam was hiding! No wonder I couldn't find her, the crafty old cow. She knew it would be the last place on earth I'd think to look.'

The laughter died in his throat, as he weighed up the situation. 'You have use for the boy,' he muttered, 'and you stand to make a lot of money by snatching the girl. Whoever would have thought it, eh? Two birds with one stone.'

The idea appealed to his warped sense of humour.

S ARAH HAD BEEN comforting Jinnie, when the knock came on the door. 'I'll answer that. It'll be Louise. Look after Jinnie,' she told her grand-daughter. 'And Adam, love – fetch some more coal from the cellar, will you?' She shivered. 'It's gone a bit chilly in here.'

While Adam went down the yard-steps to the cellar, Sarah answered the front door. No sooner had she opened it than *he* was inside, one hand round her throat, the other pressed hard against her mouth. 'Thought you'd got rid of me, didn't you, eh?' he hissed. 'First of all, you left me to rot in that bloody prison, and then you deserted me when I needed somewhere to lay my head. You ran off, like a thief in the night. Cunning old bag. Well, I'm here now, and you'll not get shot of me so easily this time, I can tell you!'

Her eyes beginning to bulge, Sarah could not cry out. Instead she kicked at the wall, trying desperately to warn the children. But he was onto her. 'I could snap your neck with one twist of my wrist,' he warned: sneering in her face as he told her the reason for his visit. 'I want my son, and the girl called Jinnie. You can have the other brat. She's no use to me.'

When her frightened eyes stared up at him, he laughed at the hatred written on her face. 'You'd like to finish me off, wouldn't you, Mammy dear? Well, I'm sorry to disappoint you, but I'm walking out of here the same way I walked in, and when I go, I'll take two others with me. Don't try any funny business neither, else I'll do for you. I mean it! I'll slice you down, just like I'd slice down anybody else who got in my way.'

He gave her another warning. 'You and your precious grand-daughter had best keep your mouths shut after I've gone, because don't forget I found you this time, and I'll find you again. So think on!' Satisfied that she was too afraid to do anything but obey him, he let go of her throat, but kept his hand over her mouth, until he was sure of her. 'If you cry out, or try and warn them, I swear I'll take all three, and you'll never see any of them again. You know I mean it, don't you, Mam?'

When she nodded, he let her go.

Though she was shaking from head to toe with fright, knowing what her son Terry was capable of, she had little choice but to walk ahead of him to the sitting room; her heart in her mouth and a prayer in her soul.

As Sarah came through the door, Hannah caught sight of the man behind her. At first, she couldn't be certain it was him, then when she saw it really was her father, she started screaming and wouldn't stop.

In two strides, Terry was on her, slapping her about and telling her to, 'Shut it!' When she stopped, it was to stiffen in his arms, her eyes rolling, as if in some kind of fit.

'Let go of her!' Sarah scrambled out of the chair where he had thrown her. But Jinnie was quicker.

Taking her life in her hands, she made a rush across the room. Grabbing hold of Hannah, she drew her away. 'Ssh, it's all right,' she soothed. 'We won't let him harm you.'

No sooner had Jinnie delivered Hannah to Sarah than she found herself in his grip; he dragged her by the hair across to the fireplace, where he stood her close to the hot flames. 'Oh, don't worry, I won't let you burn to death.' He laughed when the sweat poured down her temples. 'Your *mother* wouldn't like that. And if she isn't pleased with the state of you when she takes delivery, then she won't pay me, will she?'

'Who are you?' Jinnie had gone through every emotion there was to experience that day, and now she was filled with a bold curiosity.

'I'm Santa Claus,' he sniggered, 'and you're my Christmas present to myself. You and that son of mine.' He glanced across the room to make certain Sarah was watching. 'You'd best tell me where he is. I've got all the time in the world, so I can wait. And don't tell me he's not here, because I saw him come into this house not five minutes since, and he certainly never went out again.' With a twist of his wrist he threw Jinnie across the room with such force that she knocked her face on the wooden arm of the sofa, and when the blood ran down her face, he took up the poker and prodded her in the stomach. 'You! Where's the boy?'

Jinnie shook her head.

When he now slapped Jinnie round the face, threatening her with all manner of things if she didn't tell him where Adam was, Hannah yelled at him, 'Murderer! You killed our mam. Go away. Leave us alone!'

Downstairs, gathering coal, Adam heard the screams and his instincts warned him to be cautious. Carefully he went up the outside steps and peered through the window; the same window he had peered through to witness the carnage before.

Shocked to see his father there, he seemed to grow in stature. 'Not again!' he murmured. 'I won't let you hurt any of us again!' Throwing caution to the winds he slammed open the scullery door and launched himself at Terry; fighting like a tiger, his mind going back to that night, his whole being filled with loathing, and a terrible need for revenge.

'Quick, lass!' Sarah thrust Hannah into Jinnie's arms. 'Get yourselves to safety! And get help, for God's sake!' And, though afraid for Adam, Jinnie did as she was told.

Outside, the neighbours had begun to gather as the noise filtered into the street. 'Help them!' Jinnie pleaded with one burly fellow. 'He's trying to kill him!'

When they got into the house and saw the fiercenes of the fight, one told the other, 'The lad's gone off his head.'

A kindly woman tried to lead Sarah away. 'Come on, lass. Let the men sort it out.' But Sarah wouldn't go. 'It's my son!' she cried. 'Stop it! For God's sake, help him!' she kept saying. 'Help him!' They misunderstood; thinking she meant for them to help the man and not the boy.

They tried to separate the two, but it was of no use. There was too much hatred; too much had happened for them to stop now.

'Come away, lad.' The burly fellow made a grab for Adam, but he wouldn't be taken. Covered in blood, with his shirt ripped off, all he could see was Jacob dead – felled by one blow to the skull – and his mother being beaten, cowering before this man . . . this creature who didn't deserve to live.

In the face of Adam's blind onslaught, Terry gave as good as he got. He brought a clenched fist down on his son's head and it thudded like a hammer against the boy's temple. Undaunted, Adam went for him with everything he'd got. And all the while the men tried to separate them, even though they themselves were hurt in the battle.

Suddenly the cry went up, 'He's killed him! The lad's killed him!' When they fell away, there lay Terry, still and silent, his head smashed in. Adam sat beside him gasping and bleeding. He had the blood-spattered poker in his hand, and the look of a wild man on his face. There was a moment of absolute quiet – and then the police were at the door.

They got the story from the neighbours. 'Sarah said her son was being killed,' reported one. 'We were too late to save him. The lad were like a wild thing . . . there was no stopping him.'

Convinced that here was a murder pure and simple, the police cautioned Adam and took him away leaving Sarah sobbing her heart out in the arms of that kindly neighbour.

THE COURT WAS packed on the day of Adam's appearance.

His family was there, with Louise and Jinnie; these two had been to see Susan, and settled the past between them once and for all. Now they were closer than ever.

When the judgement was given, it was said to have been made in the light of Adam's age, and the unhappy circumstances surrounding the case. Adam had been attacked first and victimised, they said, but it was no excuse for him to take the law into his own hands. However much he had been provoked by what had happened to his mother and by the more recent events, the fact remained that he had taken a life, and shown no remorse for his actions.

Throughout the investigation, Adam had claimed that while there had been many times when he had wished his father dead, he did *not* take his father's life.

His protests fell on deaf ears. There had been witnesses, they said. Even his own grandmother at one stage had called for her son to be helped. The evidence was overwhelming.

When Adam was given five years' detention, a gasp of disbelief went up, though there were those who claimed the boy got what he deserved. Sarah cried into her hankie, and Hannah, made older and wiser by the events, gave her comfort.

As they took him away, Adam's dark eyes searched for Jinnie. She was there – her heart breaking and her sad blue eyes reaching out to him. 'I'll be here for you, Adam,' she mouthed the words across the room. 'I'll always be here.'

That night she sobbed her heart out, but it would be the last time she cried with such distress. 'I need to be strong for Adam,' she told Louise. 'Five years isn't such a long time.' But it felt like it to her.

That same night, Louise saw in her daughter the promise of a wonderful young woman, already mature in heart and wisdom. She had witnessed the tenderness and love growing between her and Adam, and she knew the day would come when they would be together.

Jinnie knew the same.

It was her destiny.

———❖———

SUSAN OPENED THE door and pulled him inside. 'What the hell are you doing here? Haven't I told you never to show your face anywhere near me?' She was livid. 'We had an arrangement. You were to wait until I called!'

'I want me money, don't I?' the burly fellow growled. 'I did what you said and nobody were any the wiser. I'd have done it in some back alley, but the fight between him and the lad was a golden opportunity. The lad took the blame and I got clear away. There's nobody knows anything! But I ain't got a month o' Sundays to wait and see if the coast is clear.' Holding out a grubby hand, he wiggled his fingers. 'I want paying. *Now*, if you please.'

Susan wanted him gone. 'Wait here,' she said and hurried

into the office. Closing the door, she climbed onto a chair and removed the key, which was securely taped on the top lip of the door. There was a gap, just wide enough for the key to slide through when the door was opened and closed, so there was no way it could ever be knocked to the ground, or seen from any height – unless, like now, someone actually stood on a chair. Oddly enough, no one ever did.

She paid the man. 'I know everything about you,' she warned him. 'If you ever again ask me for money, I'll find witnesses who will swear you had long been planning to kill that poor man. I've been very careful. I don't make mistakes. So be warned – if you breathe a word to anyone . . . anyone at all . . . I'll make sure you're put away for a very, *very* long time.'

Realising that here was a bad enemy he could well do without, the man made a hasty exit, with Susan sending him round the back so he would not be seen.

On returning to the bedroom, *he* was waiting for her. 'Don't worry, Dick,' she said, climbing into bed. 'He won't say anything.'

Dick thought she was the most exciting woman he had ever met. 'I didn't know what I was doing, getting tangled up with you,' he chuckled. 'I hope you're not about to have *me* knocked off an' all?'

She tore off her robe and showed him her nakedness. When she could see that he was ready for her, she climbed onto him, and answered his question. 'I wouldn't harm a hair on your head,' she said. 'Unless you wanted my business, or tried to rob me . . . *or if you've got blackmail in mind!*' She smiled. 'Besides, when I think about it, I never really wanted the kid back anyway.'

He laughed. 'You've a cool head, I'll say that for you.'

'Cool head, cool heart,' she smiled. 'That's why I'm so

rich.' She licked the hollow in his neck. 'It's why I don't suffer fools gladly.'

'I'll have to remember that,' he murmured, and turned his mind to the business in hand.

PART FIVE

SUMMER, 1968
WEDDING BELLS

Chapter Nineteen

T HE SAME PEOPLE who were there when Adam was put away were waiting at the prison gates when he walked free; all but Sally, who was too old and feeble to make the trip.

In the five years he had been away, Adam had grown into a strong, handsome man. The harsh experience had matured him, and the values he carried before were only strengthened by what he had endured inside that sobering establishment.

On first sight of him, Jinnie walked away from the others, her blonde hair blowing in the summer breeze, and her blue eyes filled with tears of joy. She, too, had changed. She had grown stronger, and more tolerant of things she could never understand. Life was a jungle, with beasts and terror all around. But more than that, there was love, and happiness, and the comfort of knowing you were surrounded by friends and family.

She thought herself especially lucky in that way.

Adam took her by the hand, this lovely young woman who had been to see him every week for the past five years. He had watched her grow and blossom, and his love for her had only deepened over the years.

She raised her face for a kiss. 'I told you I'd be here for you,' she reminded him. 'And here I am. I always will be.'

He held her tight. 'Will you be my wife?'

The answer was written in her face for all to see. 'You know I will,' she murmured. It was all he needed to hear.

━━━━➤●◄━━━━

T HE DAY AFTER Jinnie's seventeenth birthday, she walked down the aisle to meet him. Dressed in a simple gown of ivory silk with tiny roses of gold, she looked exquisite. On her head she wore a small coronet, holding a fine, figured veil in place.

When the service was over and she turned the veil down, he looked at her and thought he was the luckiest man on God's earth. 'I love you,' he said, and right there in front of everybody they kissed and embraced, until from somewhere in the back of the church, a high-pitched voice called out, 'Where's me bloody whisky?'

Everyone laughed, even the vicar, when Charlie ran outside with the parrot clinging to his shoulder. 'I said you had to behave,' he groaned. 'And here you are, showing me up as usual. By! I'm surprised you didn't come out with a load of abuse while you were at it. Shame on you!'

'Oh, bugger off, Charlie . . . miserable git!'

From behind them came a burst of laughter. 'You'll never change it,' Sarah told him. Charlie said he wouldn't want to.

In the evening, the wedding guests enjoyed a wonderful supper in the local hotel, and afterwards they danced to the music of the Beatles. Sally sat in a comfy chair and tapped her feet to the music, while Charlie danced with Sarah, though he tripped her up and almost fell over when trying to do an adventurous bee-bop.

Outside in the summer breeze, Eric proposed again to Louise. 'Let's *all* make a new start,' he pleaded. 'It's time we put the past where it belongs, and got on with our lives, before it's too late.'

This time, after all the doubts and anxieties, Louise did not hesitate. 'I'd love to marry you, Eric Forester,' she replied, and he swung her round, whooping for joy.

The news spread quickly and everyone congratulated them. 'It's about time, our Mam,' Jinnie said, and the sound of that word 'Mam' sent Louise's heart soaring.

'I'm proud of you, lass,' she said. And they all danced to the hit song, 'All You Need Is Love'. The words made them think. They made them smile.

Later in the evening, Ralph Martin called with a message for Louise. It was common news that his father had recently passed away, and now he was here to bring Louise a letter left by Alan Martin and addressed to her.

'I know what it says,' Ralph told her. 'I'm glad he wrote to you, in the end.' He touched the brim of his hat. 'I'm sorry.' Then he hurried away.

In the privacy of the hotel garden, by its picturesque stream, Louise opened the letter. It read:

Dear Mrs Hunter,

I have to confess something before I go to my Maker.

Some years ago, myself and Jacob Hunter, your brother-in-law, cheated your husband out of his inheritance. The debt your father-in-law was said to still owe, was in fact paid in full. We stole the receipts and tampered with the accounts ledger, to make it seem the debt was still outstanding.

I beg your forgiveness, and trust that somehow, you will recover the farm from Mr Eric Forester, the man who bought it in complete innocence.

It was a shameful and unforgivable thing I did. I have rightfully suffered many sleepless nights because of my part in it.

I hope I can now go to my Maker with a clean slate.
Respects to you, and your family,

The letter was signed *Alan Martin*.

For a long time Louise held the letter in her hand. 'What goes around comes around,' she muttered. Life was a strange animal, she thought.

The memories grew stronger, but this time, she felt no guilt or sadness. Instead, she knew that life must go on, for it was cruelly short.

She looked inside the room, with its bright lights and laughing people; she saw Sarah and Charlie, and her own mam and dad, happy and enjoying the occasion.

And Jinnie, so beautiful in her wedding gown. 'Oh, that lovely girl.' A burst of pride filled her heart. 'My daughter,' she whispered. 'My pride and joy.'

She glanced down at the letter again. It meant the farm was hers for the taking. Eric had unwittingly bought it, and he could lose everything.

'Are you all right, sweetheart?' Eric's voice invaded her thoughts.

Quickly she tore the letter into tiny shreds and threw it into the fast-moving stream. 'I'm all the better for seeing you,' she teased, and together they walked back to the room arm-in-arm. Behind them the fragments of Alan Martin's letter floated away.

On that very special evening, the sound of laughter mingled with the music and echoed over the empty summer garden. The wedding guests danced till dawn.

Tomorrow was a new day. A new beginning.